A CRITICAL BOUQUET

"Anyone who loves the fairy tale 'Beauty and the Beast' will want to read Mercedes Lackey's *The Fire Rose*. . . . a beautiful and moving tribute to the redemptive powers of love. The tale is a poignant yet exciting story. . . . Kudos to Mercedes Lackey for once again giving her audience a magnificent enjoyable novel."

—Harriet Klausner, *Affair de Coeur*

"Gothic romance mixes with 'Beauty and the Beast' in this charming new fantasy. . . . the date (1905 in San Francisco) contributes a certain tension of its own, leading to a dramatic final confrontation, and adding some thrills to a delightful romantic romp." —Carolyn Cushman, *Locus*

"Once again Lackey's strength in storytelling is apparent, and the result is a fast-paced romp of a romantic fantasy. This 'Beauty' has a mind of her own and shows it in the way she takes charge of her own destiny." —*VOYA*

"*The Fire Rose* is a joy to read, another Mercedes Lackey keeper to treasure." —*The Paperback Forum*

". . . a completely free-standing twist on the 'Beauty and the Beast' idea. . . . The charm here is in heroine Rosalind Hawkins." —John C. Bunnell, *Dragon*

The Fire Rose

MERCEDES LACKEY

THE FIRE ROSE

Copyright © 1995 by Mercedes Lackey

A Baen Books Original

Baen Publishing Enterprises
P.O. Box 1403
Riverdale, NY 10471

ISBN: 0-671-87750-X

Cover art by Darrell K. Sweet

First mass market printing, November 1996
Second printing, March 1998

Distributed by Simon & Schuster
1230 Avenue of the Americas
New York, NY 10020

Printed in the United States of America

Prologue

Golden as sunlight, white-hot, the Salamander danced and twisted sinuously above a plate sculpted of Mexican obsidian, ebony glass born in the heart of a volcano and shaped into a form created exactly to receive the magic of a creature who bathed in the fires of the volcano with delight. It swayed and postured to a music only it could hear, the only source of light in the otherwise stygian darkness of the room. At times a manikin of light, at times in the shape of the mundane salamander that bore the same name, this was the eyes and ears of the mage who had conjured it. He was a Firemaster, and all creatures of the element of flame answered to him. They brought him the news of the world now closed to him; what better source of information could he have? Where fire was, there they lurked; candle-flame, or gaslight, coal-fire or stoked box of a steam-boiler, burning hearth or burning forest — all held his informants, any of which could impart their observations to him. What one saw, all saw; speak to one and you spoke to all of them, for such was their nature.

Their patience was endless, but his, being mortal, was not. At length, he tired of watching it dance, and determined to set it upon its task. He summoned the creature from the dish with a thought; obedient to his will, it hovered above a pristine sheet of cream-laid vellum. This was special paper, and more exclusive than it seemed, pressed with his own watermark and not that of the maker.

He spoke out of the darkness of his velvet-covered, wingback chair, his voice rising from the shadow like the voice of the dragon Fafnir from its cave. He *was* Fafnir; like the giant, now utterly transformed to something no one who knew the former self would ever recognize.

Time to construct his letter, while the Salamander and all its kin considered his requirements. *"Dear Sir,"* he said, and the Salamander danced above the vellum, burning the characters into it, in elegant calligraphy. *"I write to you because I am in need of a special tutor for my — "*

He paused to consider the apocryphal child of his imagination. A son? A lonely, crippled waif, isolated from the laughter and play of his peers? No, make it two children. If the crippled boy was not bait enough for his quarry, an intelligent, inquisitive girl would be. *" — my children. Both are gifted intellectually beyond their years; my son is an invalid, crippled by the disease that claimed his mother, and my daughter the victim of prejudice that holds her sex inferior to that of the male. Neither is likely to obtain the education their ability demands in a conventional setting."*

He weighed the words carefully, and found them satisfactory. Appropriately tempting, and playing to the "enlightened" and "modern" male who would be the mentor of the kind of tutor he sought. He wanted a woman, not a man; a male scholar with the skills he required would be able to find ready employment no matter where he was, but a woman had fewer options. In fact, a female scholar without independent means had *no* options if she was not supported by a wealthy father or indulgent husband. A female had no rights; under the laws of this and most other states, she was chattel, the property of parents or husband. She could take no employment except that of teacher, seamstress, nurse, or domestic help; no trades were open to her, and only menial factory work. There were *some* few female doctors, some few scientists, but no scholars of the arts, liberal or otherwise, who were not supported in their field by money or males. He wanted someone with no options; this would make her more obedient to his will.

"My needs are peculiar, reflecting the interests of my children. This tutor must be accomplished in ancient Latin, classical Greek, medieval French and German, and the Latin of medieval scholars. A familiarity with ancient Egyptian or Celtic languages would be an unanticipated bonus."

The Salamander writhed, suddenly, and opened surprisingly blue eyes to stare at its master. It opened its lipless mouth, and a thin, reedy voice emerged.

"We have narrowed the field to five candidates," it said. "One in Chicago, one in Harvard, three in New York. The one in Chicago is the only one with a smattering of ancient tongues *and* some knowledge of hieroglyphs. The others are skilled only in the European languages you required; less qualified, but —"

"But?" he asked.

"More attractive," the Salamander hissed, its mouth open in a silent laugh.

He snorted. At one point he would have been swayed by a fairer face; now that was hardly to the point. "Have they relatives?" he asked it.

"The one in Chicago is recently orphaned, one of those in New York was raised by a guardian who cares nothing for her, and her trust fund has been mismanaged as she will shortly learn. Those that do have families, have been repudiated for their unwomanly ways," the Salamander told him. "They are suffragettes, proponents of rights for women, and no longer welcome in their parents' homes."

Tempting. But relatives and parents had been

known to change their minds in the past, and welcome the prodigal back into the familial fold.

"Show me the one in Chicago," he demanded. She seemed to be the best candidate thus far. The Salamander left the vellum page and returned to its obsidian dish, where it began to spin.

As it rotated, turning faster and faster with each passing second, it became a glowing globe of yellow-white light. A true picture formed in the heart of the globe, in the way that a false picture formed in the heart of a Spiritualist's "crystal ball." The latter was generally accomplished through the use of mirrors and other chicanery. The former was the result of *true* Magick.

When he saw the girl at last, he nearly laughed aloud at the Salamander's simplistic notion of beauty. Granted, the girl was clad in the plainest of gowns, of the sort that a respectable housekeeper might wear. He recognized it readily enough, from a Sears, Roebuck and Co. catalog left in his office a few years ago by a menial.

Ladies' Wash Suit, two dollars and twenty five cents. Three years out-of-mode, and worn shabby.

She wore wire-rimmed glasses, and she used no artifice to enhance her features. In all these things, she was utterly unlike the expensive members of the silk-clad demimonde whose pleasures he had once enjoyed. But the soft cheek needed no rouge or rice-powder; the lambent blue eyes were in no way disguised by the thick lenses. That slender figure required no over-corseting to tame it to a fashionable shape, and the warm golden-brown of her hair was due to no touch of chemicals to achieve that mellow hue of sun-ripened wheat.

"She is orphaned?" he asked.

The Salamander danced its agreement. "Recently," it told him. "She is the most qualified of them all, scholastically speaking."

"And possessed of no — inconvenient — family ties," he mused, watching the vision as it moved in the Salamander's fire. He frowned a little at that, for her movements were not as graceful as he would have liked, being hesitant and halting. That scarcely mattered, for he was not hiring her for an ability to dance.

From the look of her clothing, she had fallen on hard times — unless, of course, she was a natural ascetic, or was donating all of her resources to the Suffrage Movement. Either was possible; if the latter was an impediment to her accepting employment, the Salamander would have rejected her as a candidate.

"We will apply to her — or rather to her mentor," he decided, and gave the Salamander the signal to resume its place above the half-written letter. *I am willing to pay handsomely for the services of any male or female with such qualifications, to compensate for the great distance he or she must travel. The tutor will be installed in my own household, drawing a wage of twenty dollars a week as well as full room and board, and a liberal allowance for travel, entertainment, and books. San Francisco affords many pleasures for those of discriminating taste; this year shall even see the glorious Caruso performing at our Opera.* Clothing he would have supplied to her, having it waiting for her if she consented to come; easier to supply the appropriate garments than to hope the girl had any kind of taste at all. He would *not* have a frump in his house; any female entering these doors must not disgrace the interior. While his home might not rival Leland Stanford's on the *outside*, the interior was enough to excite the envy of the richest "nob" on "Nob Hill." There would be no cotton-duck gowns from a mail-order catalog trailing over the fine inlay work of *his* floors, no coarse dark cottons displayed against *his* velvets and damask satins.

"*I hope you will have a student that can match my requirements,*" he concluded without haste. "*Your scholarship is renowned even to the wilds of the west and the golden hills of San Francisco, and I cannot imagine that any pupil of yours would disgrace the master. To that end, I am enclosing a rail ticket for the prospective tutor.*" It was not a first-class ticket for a parlor car; such might excite suspicion. A ticket for the common carriage would be sufficient, and a journey by rail would be safe enough, even for a woman alone. "*I am looking forward to hearing from you as soon as may be.*"

"The usual closing?" the Salamander asked delicately. He nodded, and it finished, burning his name into the vellum with a flourish. It continued to hover above the paper, as the paper itself folded without a hand touching it, and slipped itself and a railway pass into a matching envelope. The Salamander sealed it with a single "hand" pressed into the wax, then burned the address into the obverse of the envelope.

"Take it to Professor Cathcart's office and leave it there," he instructed, and the Salamander bowed. "If she does not take this bait, we will have to devise something else."

"She would be a fool not to take it," the Salamander replied, surprising him a little with its retort. "She has no other place to go."

"Women are not always logical," he reminded the creature. "We were best to assume that the initial attempt will be balked at, and contrive another."

The Salamander simply shook its head, as if it could not understand the folly of mortals, and it and the sealed letter vanished into thin air, leaving the Firemaster alone in the darkness.

CHAPTER ONE

Rosalind Hawkins answered the door with her entire being in a knot of anxiety; expecting yet another aggressive creditor, she schooled her face into a calm she did not feel. Outside, the dreary, drizzling day was giving way to another dreary night. The home that had once been her sanctuary was now under siege — and no longer hers.

How long must I bear this? How long can I bear this?

"I'm sorry," she began as the heavy oak door swung wide, "But if you have a claim, you will have to apply to Mr. Grumwelt of Grumwelt, Jenkins and — "

But the figure outside the door was no hostile stranger. "Do I need to apply to a solicitor to visit, now, Rose?" asked the short, slender, grey-haired man on the front porch in surprise. She started, and began to laugh with relief at seeing a friendly face for the first time since the funeral, her emotions making her briefly giddy — and she hoped she did not sound hysterical. "Of course not, Professor Cathcart!" she exclaimed, "It's just that I've had Papa's creditors at the door all day, and I've gotten into rather a habit of — " She stopped at the sight of the Professor's confusion. "Oh, never mind, please come in! I'm afraid I cannot offer you any refreshment," she added, ruefully, "but the grocer came with a seizure notice and a policeman and carted away everything edible in the house before breakfast."

A week before, that simple admission would have been unthinkable. Too many unthinkable things had happened since then for her to even think twice about this one.

Professor Cathcart, Ph.D. and expert in medieval and ancient languages, her mentor at the University of Chicago, widened his colorless eyes with shock. He took off his hat as he entered the door, and stood in the entryway, turning it in his hands nervously, twisting the soft felt. Rosalind closed the door behind him and led him into the parlor. She had all the gaslights on, burning in reckless abandon. After all, why bother to save the gas? The bills were already too great to pay.

He sat down gingerly on the horsehair sofa — which tomorrow would probably be gracing someone else's parlor. His elongated face was full of concern as well as shock, and he appeared to be groping for words. She felt a stirring of pity for him; after all, what *could* one say in a case like this?

He licked his lips, and made an attempt. "I knew that Hawkins was not well off after those speculations of his, but I had no notion that things had come to such dire straits!"

"Neither did I," Rosalind said simply, as she sat down on the matching chair, groping behind her for the arm of the chair to assist her. "While he was alive, his salary at the University paid the bills, and the extra tutoring he did for those brainless idiots in the Upper One Hundred kept the other creditors at bay. Now — " She turned her palms upward in her lap and examined them, unable to meet his eyes and the pity in them. "Now they descend."

Professor Cathcart sounded dazed. "He left you nothing, then?"

"Nothing but a stack of unpaid bills and this house — which has been seized by the creditors," she replied wearily. "They have graciously allowed me to retain my personal possessions — excepting anything of value, like Mama's pearls."

"They're taking the pearls?" Cathcart was aghast. "Surely not — "

"*Took*, the pearls," she corrected, pushing her glasses up on her nose with a cold finger, trying not to remember how she had wept when they'd taken the only inheritance she had from her mother. "Yesterday. And other things — " She gripped the arms of the chair, trying to hold off the memory, the horror, of watching strangers sort through her belongings, looking for anything they might seize as an asset. "The books in Papa's library are already gone, the furniture goes tomorrow, and the house itself whenever Mr. Grumwelt finds a buyer, I suppose. They say I can stay here until then. I could camp out on the floor until the buyer appears, if they'd left me the camping gear — "

She was saved from hysteria by a wave of faintness that made her sway a little and catch at the arm of the chair to keep from falling. The Professor was instantly out of his seat and at her side, taking her hand and patting it ineffectually. But his words showed a surprising streak of practicality.

"Child, when did you eat last?" he demanded. She shook her head, unable to remember — and that, in itself, was disturbing. Was she losing her memory? Was she losing her mind? "I haven't had much appetite," she prevaricated.

He snorted. "Then that is the second order of business; the first is to get you away from here. Go upstairs and pack your things; I'm not leaving you here to be jeered at by tradesmen a moment longer."

"But — " she protested, knowing his own resources were slender. He cut her off at the single word, showing an unexpected streak of authority.

"I can certainly afford to put the daughter of my old

friend up in a respectable boarding-house for a few days, and take her to dinner too. And as for the rest — well, that was what I came here to speak to you about, and that would be best done over dinner, or rather, dessert. Now, don't argue with me, child!" he scolded. "I won't have you staying here! The next thing you know, they'll probably cut off the gas."

At just that moment, the gaslights flickered and went out, all over the house, leaving them in the grey gloom of the overcast day, the uncertain and haunted hour before sunset. Suddenly, the house seemed full of ghosts. If nothing else, that decided her.

"I'll just be a moment," she said, truthfully, since most of her belongings were already packed into a carpetbag and a single trunk, with only a valise waiting to receive the rest. Mr. Grumwelt had watched her with his nasty, beady eyes, like a serpent watching a bird, the entire time she packed; presumably to make sure that she did not pack up something that no longer belonged to her. Fortunately he did not recognize the value of some of the keepsakes she had managed to retain, or he would doubtless have confiscated them as well. He had made it very clear to her that anything she carried away, she did so on his sufferance. The trunk already stood in the hall; she had only to finish packing her valise and carpetbag. "I find myself in the position so many philosophers like Mr. Emerson profess to admire — unburdened by possessions."

"I'll get a cab," the Professor replied.

Bergdorf's was not crowded at this time of the early evening; the theater crowd had not yet begun to arrive. Fortunately, the German restaurant had never been one of her father's choices for dining out, or the memories the place evoked would have been too painful to permit her to eat. No, she had no sad ghosts waiting for her here, and Bergdorf's was clearly Professor Cathcart's favorite, for the waiters all recognized him and they were shown to a secluded table out of the way of traffic. She wondered what they made of her; too plain to be a member of the demimonde, too shabbily dressed to be a fiancée or a relative. Did they assume she was his housekeeper, being granted a birthday treat?

Perhaps they take me for a suffragette relation, or one who has a religious mania and has given all her worldly goods to Billy Sunday. No matter. The respect they accorded to Professor Cathcart extended even to such peculiar females as he chose to bring with him; service was prompt and polite, and the headwaiter treated her with the deference that might be accorded to one who wore a gown by Worth, rather than one from the cheaper pages of Sears and Roebuck.

She had once worn fine gowns — not by Worth, perhaps, but by one of the better Chicago seamstresses. That had been before her father's run of bad luck with his investments, and she had chosen to economize on her gowns as well as in other household matters. It had not mattered to her teachers and fellow students; they probably would not have noticed unless she had donned the chiton and stola of an ancient Greek maiden, and perhaps not even then. Her economies had gone unremarked, which had saved her pride. Since another of her economies was to abjure eating out, she was not forced to parade the slender state of their purses in public.

The Bergdorf was comfortably warm, lit softly with candles and a few well-placed gaslights. The only sounds were those of conversation and the clink of silver on china. The Professor was one who gave a gourmet meal all its due reverence, so they ate in silence. Rosalind was not loath to do so either; the peculiar sour-savory tang of the sauerbraten awoke a hunger of intensity she had not realized was possible, and although she seldom drank, she joined the Professor in a lady-sized stein of the Bergdorf's excellent beer. The food vanished from her plate so quickly she might have conjured it away, and the attentive blond-haired, blue-eyed waiter brought her a second serving without being asked.

"*Vielen dank,*" she said to him, surprising a smile from him. He winked at her, and hurried to answer the summons from another table.

She devoured her second helping with a thoroughness that would have embarrassed her a month ago. Now her capacity for being embarrassed had been exhausted, and her pride flattened like a sheet of vellum in a press.

The waiter returned at the Professor's signal, and cleared away the plates as the Professor ordered Black Forest torte for both of them. Rosalind did not even make a token protest; it might be a long time before she ever ate like this again. Her torte was long gone before the Professor had finished his, and she settled back in her chair with a sigh of melancholy mixed with content.

I must think of some way to earn my way. She had a vague idea that she might take a position as a governess somewhere, or even as a schoolteacher in some Western state. Any thought of achieving a Ph.D. in the classics and medieval literature was out of the question now, of course. She only hoped that she could convince someone that her unconventional education had made her fit to teach the "Three Rs."

The waiter arrived to clean off the dessert plates, and with him came coffee. Professor Cathcart settled back in his chair as she sugared and creamed hers liberally, cradling his cup in both hands.

"You must forgive your old friend and teacher his bluntness, but how did you come to such a pass?" he asked. "I had not thought your father to be the improvident sort."

She shook her head, bitterly. "You may lay the cause of our loss at Neville Tree's door," she replied, with bitterness not even the savor of her dessert could remove from her mouth. The Professor had the grace to blush, then, for it was he who had introduced that scion of prominent politicians to the elder Hawkins.

He said nothing more, for indeed, there was no more to be said. For all of Neville Tree's illustrious parentage, the man was no better than a common sharpster. He had come looking for investors in his bank, and he got many, including Professor Hawkins; he then ran the bank into the ground with his poor management — all the while drawing a princely salary — leaving investors and depositors alike holding nothing but air and empty promises. Not content with that, he concocted another scheme, with many promises that he would get the money back and more — he would go and find oil and make them all rich. Throwing good money after bad, Professor Hawkins and others had fallen for his plausible tale a second time, and once again found themselves with shares of useless stock in a company that had drilled for oil where no geologist would ever anticipate finding any. Presumably he had taken himself to another state with more schemes designed mainly to allow him to draw a handsome wage at the expense of others.

Under the table, Rosalind's hand clenched on her napkin. When her father had told her of the loss of all of their savings and more, she had not had the heart to reproach him. *"I only wanted to give you what you should have had, Rose,"* he had said plaintively. . . .

"But the History Department — " Cathcart began again.

"You know that none of them have ever approved of

my 'unwomanly' interests," she retorted sourly. "Doubtless, if they knew, they would be pleased enough, and advise me to go and get married like a proper female."

As if any young man had ever, or would ever look twice at me. Plain, too clever by half, and with the curse of always saying what I think. That latter habit had gained her no friends among her fellow students, who could look elsewhere for romantic interests. *Any man at the University can find himself a nice, stupid girl with good looks or money who will assure him he is the cleverest creature on earth. Why should he take one with neither who will challenge him to prove he is her equal?*

"Your mother's people — " Cathcart ventured.

He knew nothing about her parents' relationship with her maternal grandparents — Professor Hawkins had been careful to keep that unsavory situation very private. It was natural for Cathcart to bring them up, but only the fact that she had already borne with so much already made it possible for her to bear this as well. "They appeared the day of the funeral," she said. *I will* not *call those — creatures — my grandmother and grandfather.* "They insulted my father, slandered my mother, and told me that if I admitted some specious sort of guilt, agreed to be a good and obedient girl, and gave up my nonsense about a University degree, they *might* consider permitting me to take up some position within their household. I assume they meant for me to come be a drudge to Uncle Ingmar, and be grateful to them for the opportunity."

Cathcart's expression grew horrified. "Even when he was still sane, Ingmar Ivorsson was *not* fit company for a female, and certainly is not to be left alone with one!" he blurted.

She only nodded. "I told them what I thought of

them, what Mother had thought of them, and what they could do with Uncle Ingmar, and showed them the door." *That might have been what brought Mr. Grumwelt down upon my head with such uncanny swiftness. They probably went off and alerted every one of Papa's creditors. Did they expect me to come running to them as soon as the vultures arrived, begging forgiveness?*

Cathcart gave her the ghost of a smile. "So you have burned all your bridges, then. That was brave of you. Not necessarily wise, but —"

"Professor, *that* bridge is one I would not cross under any circumstances. I had rather take Charon's boat than the Ivorssons' offer." She set her chin resolutely, but could not help a shudder of fear. *Charon's boat . . . it could come to that.* She had contemplated suicide that very night, alone with her despair in the echoing house. She had more than enough laudanum in her valise to suffice. . . .

But now the Professor's expression turned — calculating? Definitely! She had seen him look precisely like this when he was about to prove some obscure point, or had found a new research trail. She felt interest stirring in her, a feeling she had not experienced in days.

"I wanted to ascertain whether or not you had any other prospects," he said, quietly, but still with that calculating look in his eyes. "I have had a — well, a rather peculiar communication from a man in the West. It is *so* peculiar that I would not have advised that you consider it, unless you had no other recourse."

Now her interest was surely piqued. "Professor, what on earth are you hinting at?" she asked, sitting up a little straighter.

He reached into his coat pocket. "Here," he said,

handing her a thick, cream-colored envelope. "Read this for yourself."

Obeying, she opened the envelope and set aside the thick railway ticket, and read the single sheet of thick vellum contained therein with growing perplexity. "This — this is certainly strange," she said, after a moment, folding the sheet and returning it to its paper prison. "Very strange." She slipped the railway ticket to San Francisco in beside it.

Cathcart nodded. "I've had the man looked into, and from what I can find out, he's genuine enough. He's something of a rail baron on the West Coast and lives outside of San Francisco. The ticket is genuine; I telegraphed to his office to be sure that the letter had truly come from him, and the offer is genuine also. He's said to be as rich as Croesus and as reclusive as a stylite, and that's all anyone knows of him. Other than the fact that he has phenomenal luck."

"He might have been describing me, precisely," Rose said aloud, feeling again that little thrill of apprehension, as if she was about to cross a threshold into something from which there would be no escape and no return.

"That is what was so peculiar, that and the offer itself." Cathcart flushed. "I thought of all manner of other possibilities; one does, after all — "

"Of course," she said vaguely. "White slavery, opium dens — " She noticed then that Cathcart's color had deepened to a dark scarlet with embarrassment, and giggled; she could not help herself. *Really,* Professor! Did you think I was that sheltered? After all, it was you who let me read the unexpurgated Ovid, and Sappho's poems, and — "

She stopped, for fear that the Professor would have a stroke there and then. It never failed to amaze her that the scholars about her could discuss the hetairai of the Greeks, Tristan and Isolde, Abelard and Heloise, and the loves of the girls on the Isle of Lesbos, and then blush with shame when one even mentioned the existence of certain establishments not more than a dozen blocks from the University.

"Don't decide at once," he urged her, swiftly changing the subject. "I'll take you to Mrs. Abernathy's boarding house; rest and think for a few days. This should not be an act of impulse."

"Of course not," she replied —

But she already felt the heavy, cold hand of Fate upon her sleeve. She would go to this man, this Jason Cameron. She would take his job.

After all, she had no choice.

Rose woke with a shock, startled out of disturbing dreams by sounds she did not recognize. For a moment, as she glanced around, she panicked with disorientation, her heart racing with fear as she groped for her glasses. This was not her room! Nothing was where it should be — why was that rectangle of light at the foot of her bed, and not off to the side — and why was there only one, not two? Why were the walls white, and what was that huge, looming object at her left?

And *why* weren't her glasses on the stand beside the bed, where they should be?

Then, as the bed beneath her creaked in a way that her bed never had, the steadying knowledge of where she was and why she was here came flooding back.

Nothing was where it should be, because she was not at home, and never would see her room again. She was in a narrow, iron-framed bed in Mrs. Abernathy's boarding house for respectable young ladies.

Rose had met a few of them last night, and had immediately been reassured as to the solidity of this establishment. Several of the ladies were nurses; one worked at the Hull House with the indigent. Another was a typist for Professor Cathcart at the University. Her own shabby-genteel clothing fit in perfectly here, giving her no cause for embarrassment.

Mrs. Abernathy was a stolid woman who had not been at all disturbed when they appeared on her doorstep after dark. She had taken in Professor Cathcart's whispered explanation and the money he pressed into her hand with a nod, and had sent Rose to this room on the second floor, just off the common parlor. Her trunk was still downstairs in a storage closet, but she hardly needed what was in it. She'd brought up her carpetbag and valise herself, and had attempted to be sociable with some of the other boarders, but fatigue and strain had taken their toll, and she had soon sought the room and the bed.

She stopped groping for her glasses, preferring the vague shapes of furniture and windows to the stark reality of this sad little room. She closed her eyes again, and lay quietly, listening to the sounds that had awakened her. Down below, someone, presumably Mrs. Abernathy, was cooking breakfast; from the scents that reached her, it was oatmeal porridge and strong coffee, cheap and filling. Other girls in tiny rooms on either side of her were moving about. By the very faint light, it could not be much past dawn — but these young women were working girls, and their day began at dawn and ended long after sunset, every day except Sunday.

That was when the full impact of her situation hit home. Within the week, she would join them. She had not realized just how privileged her life had been, even with all the economies she and her father had practiced these last several years. She had always been something of a night-owl, preferring to study in the late hours when she would be undisturbed; her classes had always been scheduled in the afternoons, allowing her to enjoy leisurely mornings. Now she would obey someone else's schedule, whether or not it happened to suit her.

Everything was changed; her life, as she had known it, was over. It lay buried with her father.

The rest of her life stretched before her, devoid of all the things that she cared for — the joys of scholarship, the thrill of academic pursuit, the intellectual companionship of fellow scholars. She would be a servant in someone else's house, or a hireling in someone's employ, subject to their will, their whims. Very likely she would never again have access to a resource like the University Library. Her life, which had been defined by books, would now be defined by her position below the salt.

Professor Cathcart had insisted that she think Cameron's offer over carefully before deciding, but her options were narrower than he thought; the choices were two, really. Take Jason Cameron's job (or search for another like it) and become a servant in the household of a wealthy, and probably autocratic man — or take a position teaching in a public school.

The latter actually offered fewer opportunities. It was unlikely that she would find such a public school position in Chicago; there were many aspiring teachers, and few jobs for them. She would have to seek employment out in the country, perhaps even in the scarcely-settled West or the backward South, where she would be an alien and an outsider.

In either case, as a private tutor or as a teacher, she would be a servant, for as a schoolteacher she *must* present a perfectly respectable front at all times, attending the proper church, saying the proper things, so as to be completely beyond reproach. Neither a schoolteacher nor a child's private tutor could even hint that she had read the uncensored Ovid. Neither would dare to have an original thought, or dare to contradict the men around her. The days of her freedom of thought, action and speech were over.

She had not wept since the funeral; she had remained dry-eyed before the Ivorssons, before Mr. Grumwelt, before his greedy minions. She had stood dry-eyed for days, but now something broke within her at the realization of how much a prisoner of society she had become overnight.

Her eyes burned, her throat closed, and she bit her knuckle trying to hold back the tears. She was unsuccessful, and quickly turned her face into the pillow, sobbing, smothering her weeping with the coarse linen so that no one would overhear her. How could any of the women here hope to understand her grief? This prospect of life that she found intolerable was the same life that they had always led.

One born to slavery finds nothing amiss with chains. . . .

She curled up into a ball, forming herself around the pillow, as she cried uncontrollably. She had never believed that a heart could be "broken," but hers certainly felt that way now.

Oh Papa — why did you have to die and leave me like this?

Then came guilt for thinking such a terrible thing, which only made her weep the harder as she realized she would now face the rest of her life without his dear, if absent-minded, presence. Finally, she could weep no more; she huddled around the soaked pillow, muscles and head aching, eyes swollen and burning, throat sore with holding back her sobs, nose irritated and raw. Her physical discomfort did nothing to distract her from her sorrow.

While she had cried out her grief, the noises to

either side of her disappeared, leaving only the sounds of activity below-stairs. She did not feel that she could face anyone, and as for breakfast — the very notion made her ill.

Evidently either no one had missed her or Professor Cathcart had indicated that she was to be left alone, for no one came to disturb her. Despair held her in that hard, narrow bed in invisible bonds; she could not even muster the strength to reach for her glasses. Once again, the presence of the laudanum in her valise beckoned temptingly. She need only drink down the entire bottle, and all her troubles would end in a sleep with no waking.

Would that be so bad? True Christian doctrine told her that suicide was a sin, but the ancients had held it no more a sin than healing a wound was. When the soul was wounded past bearing — when life became intolerable — why tolerate it?

Why, indeed? Why spend the remaining years of her life in an existence that was less than life? Why must she smother her very soul to see her body fed? Surely that was no less a sin than simple suicide!

How many grim, gray spinsters had she seen in her schools, withered creatures who had ruthlessly rooted out every vestige of intellectual curiosity in themselves and now sought to do the same to the pupils beneath them? Life as one such as they would be less than life.

Better to end it all now.

She spent a moment in fantasy, imagining what the news of her death would mean to those around her. The Ivorssons, of course, would cluck and shake their heads, and say that they had expected nothing else from her — she knew better than to anticipate remorse from any of *them.* She could leave a note, blaming her despair on Neville Tree — a subtle sort of revenge, since the stigma of having caused a girl's death would ruin him, especially if she did not say precisely why he had driven her to this. People would assume the worst; they always did.

She uncurled herself from her pillow; felt for her glasses and put them on, since she could not write a suicide note if she could not see. But her hand fell upon something else as well; Jason Cameron's letter. Almost against her will, she found herself drawing the letter from the envelope and reading it again.

But this time, reading it carefully rather than skimming it, she got a much different sense of the writer's personality than she had in the restaurant. There, she had been startled by the strangely accurate description of someone with precisely the same accomplishments as her own. Now she was drawn to the paragraph about the children.

In particular, her eyes were drawn to the statements about the daughter.

" . . . *the victim of prejudice that holds her sex as inferior to the male. . . .* "

Surely the man who wrote such words was not the uncouth tyrant she had imagined! And surely he would not object to her continuing her own education — even if she had to choose an area of specialization other than her first choice —

Perhaps she would not be treated like a servant after all. This letter seemed to have come from the pen of a man who cherished scholarship, and would accord a scholar honest respect.

Shouldn't she at least *see* if he was the enlightened man his letter promised?

After all, the bottle would still be in her valise. She could end her life at any time; it did not have to be here. She could make the journey to the West Coast first; see the vast hinterlands in between. She had never personally seen a buffalo, a cowboy, or a Red

Indian. She had never seen a mountain, or an ocean. She had lived all her short life in Chicago; surely before she committed any rash act, she ought to see more than just one city.

Besides, if one ended one's life — the setting ought to be something less squalid than this.

The ancient Romans called in all their friends, gathered their most precious belongings about them, and had a great feast complete with poetry and music. Then, in the midst of splendor, they drank their bitter cup.

She should take more thought to the setting of her demise.

Besides, it would distress those pleasant girls if I did away with myself here. It might even cast a stigma upon poor Mrs. Abernathy, and neither she nor they have done anything to harm me. No. It would be impolite and unpoetic to drink my cup here.

If she waited until she reached the West Coast, however —

I could go to the Opera House when Caruso sings there.

That would be a setting worthy of the Romans, and a properly poetic ending as well.

If I saved — I could have enough for a fine gown, and a private box. Even if the promised wages come to less than he states, I could save enough.

Yes; *that* would be the way. To drink the dose at the first intermission, perhaps — drift away into death with glorious music accompanying her — be found dressed exquisitely, with her letter of farewell lying beside her on the table —

She might be thought to haunt the place afterwards, which would do the Opera House no harm, since every good theater should have a ghost.

Not in squalor, but in splendor; turning her back on this world in a way that could not be ignored or pushed onto the back pages of a newspaper.

I seem to have decided to live. For now, at least.

But now she was impatient to be gone. The sooner she was on her way, the sooner she would find out if the promise of the letter was true gold, or dross.

She managed to get herself out of bed, and went to the washstand, to pour cold water from the pitcher into the waiting basin. Just as well that it was cold; her ablutions succeeded in removing the outward signs of her despair from her face. She dressed in an odd combination of luxury and penury; her most intimate underthings were silk (though much-darned), but her stockings were of the coarsest and cheapest cotton at five cents the pair, and they were as heavily darned as the silk. The one thing that she never regretted about losing her maid was that she never again had anyone about to tie the laces of her corset as tightly as a human could manage; she had not retied the laces in a year. She donned that garment by letting out her breath and hooking it up the front, and tolerated being that much more out of fashion by not having a fifteen-inch waist.

Petticoats were the same mixture of luxury and thrift, depending entirely on whether or not she had been able to mend them. Her shoes were still good, although they would need resoling soon; her walking-skirt and shirtwaist ready-made, from a store that was far from fashionable, and of fabric that could be laundered at home. All of her expensive gowns had been sold long ago to dealers in second-hand clothing. Much of her own wardrobe had come from the stores of those same worthies.

I told Papa I didn't care about dresses, that I would rather have books . . . I wonder if he believed me. Did he ever guess how much I missed the silks and velvets?

She wondered, too, what her new employer would

think. Or would he even notice the sad state of her wardrobe?

She arranged her hair — her one real beauty — into a neat French braid, and set a pathetic little excuse for a hat squarely on the result, securing it with a dagger-like hatpin. Putting Jason Cameron's letter into her reticule, she stepped out into the hallway.

She would need to contact Mr. Cameron to let him know that she was accepting the post, so that he didn't hire someone else while she was making the arduous journey across the country. Her ticket was really a series of tickets, a rainbow of colored pasteboard, each of them for a different pair of cities. Evidently one did not simply "get on" a train in Chicago and arrive at San Francisco to "get off" the same train. From Chicago, one went to Kansas City; there one boarded a train from a second rail company bound for Los Angeles. Once there, a third and final change of rail companies took one to the final destination. But within the three stages, there were other options, other changes of trains, depending upon what day one traveled. It was all very bewildering.

No doubt — she must get in touch with Mr. Cameron, and the only one who knew how to do that was Professor Cathcart. So she must venture back into the beloved and hallowed halls of learning and endure a veritable barrage of memories in order to find the Professor himself.

She bundled herself in her old wool coat and slipped down the stairs and out the front door without meeting anyone. She walked to the University, since she could not afford street-car fare, much less a cab. It was not much more than a mile, and she was used to walking. It was going to be another grim, grey day, but at least it wasn't raining anymore.

What would the weather be like in San Francisco?

Wasn't California supposed to be hot, even tropical? She occupied her thoughts with such speculations until she reached the University campus, ignoring the shouts of a group of young men playing football in the Quadrangle.

Every step brought out another memory that hurt, and she felt like the little mermaid in the Hans Anderson tale, who felt as if she walked upon knives with every step she took on her conjured legs. Somehow she found Professor Cathcart, who took one look at her and insisted that she sit down while he sent for some coffee. She had always ignored his secretary before this; now, acutely sensitive to women in subservient positions, she watched the drab woman carefully. *I must learn to move and talk like that,* she thought, paying careful attention to the little things that made Cathcart's secretary so inconspicuous. *I will have no choice but to learn.* . . .

"Are you certain that you wish to pursue this offer?" the Professor was saying anxiously, as he pressed a cup of coffee into her cold hands. "Are you positive?"

Beneath his questioning, she detected something else, and after a moment, she identified it with some surprise.

Relief. He was already regretting his hasty impulse in setting himself up as her protector and rescuer, and he wanted her off his hands as quickly as possible!

Resentment built, and was quickly vanquished by weariness. This should have been expected. The Professor, a confirmed bachelor, had suddenly found himself burdened with an unwanted female who was not even related to him. Yes, he was her mentor and teacher, but he had never expected to find himself caring for her mundane needs, only the intellectual ones. Now that he had the time for second thoughts, he was probably cursing himself for last night's visit. If he had waited a few days, she would have been gone, and he would not have felt the need to find out what had happened to her.

If she should take Cameron's offer, she would not only be off his hands, but halfway across the continent. He would never have to bother about her again. He could soothe his conscience with the content of Cameron's letter, which promised a secure and fulfilling position. He had urged thought and caution, she had taken both, and he was under no obligation to interfere further — or to assist her in any way.

"Yes," she said, with weary resignation. "I am sure. I would like to notify Mr. Cameron that I will accept his position, but there was no address on the envelope."

"I can take care of that," Professor Cathcart replied — a bit too eagerly. "I'll have him wired that you're coming, in fact, so that he doesn't hire anyone else." There was no doubt; he was unhappy about his current obligation to her and wanted it done with.

"I don't want to put you to any trouble," she began, hiding her bitterness at his reaction.

"It won't be any trouble," he said heartily. "I'll just send a message to the rail office, and they'll see to it all. While I'm at it, I'll have them check the timetables for the correct schedule — you *do* want to leave tomorrow, don't you?"

She shrugged. It was obvious that her welcome here was at an end. "Why not?" she replied, which sent another look of relief across his face. "It's not as if I have anything to stop for. My research — well, what's the use in pretending? I'll never finish the degree, so I'll hardly need my notes. Perhaps one of your other students could use them."

Professor Cathcart made a token protest, but she could tell his heart wasn't in it. Not when both of them knew that she was only speaking the truth. The sour taste of anger and despair rose in her throat, and she stood up, hastily.

"I'll go back to the boarding-house and set things in order," she said, suddenly feeling as if she could not breathe properly in the dusty office. "If you could have that railway schedule sent over — I know you are busy, Professor, you can't be spending all your time with me when you have students who *will* be completing their degrees to help — "

He flushed, but did not contradict her; he merely fumbled in his pocket and pressed some money into her hand. "This is for a cab in the morning, and one now," he stammered hastily. "I'm sorry it isn't more. Your ticket entitles you to meals on the train, so you should be fine. . . . "

He babbled on for a little longer, and she finally fled his office to avoid his embarrassment. And she did not take a cab back to the boardinghouse; every penny in her purse was one more than she had expected to have, and she was not going to waste those pennies with frivolities like cabs. She had no choice, though, in the morning; there was no way that she was going to get herself and her heavy trunk to the train station without a cab — unless she was lucky enough to find a cart and driver for hire at that hour.

When she reached the boardinghouse, not only was the schedule waiting, but a telegraph from Jason Cameron himself. In the terse words required by telegraphy, he expressed pleasure that she had chosen to take up the position, promised her needs would be met on the way, and assured her that she would be greeted by his people at the Pacifica switch.

What, she wondered, *is a "Pacifica switch?"*

It must mean something to a rail baron, she reasoned. That would have to do for now.

After missing breakfast, she did not intend to skip

any other meals although her appetite had vanished again; she managed a luncheon of tea, wafer-thin ham and thick toast, and joined the other girls for a dinner of potato-laden stew with astonishingly little meat in it, more thick slices of bread, and a bread-pudding. On the whole, if this was the daily fare here, she was just as glad not to be staying. A diet so starch-heavy would quickly bloat even the slimmest person.

She took to her bed early, like the nurses who had awakened her, for her first train left the station almost at dawn. After so much walking and emotional turmoil, she was exhausted and drained.

Her last thought before sleep finally caught her was actually one of wonder — wonder at herself, for having made so clear and final a break between her past and her future. Perhaps it was true that despair could drive people to heroism and daring.

But she went into sleep, not with a feeling of excitement, but of resignation. She might be stepping off into the unknown, but it was not with a sense of adventure.

Perhaps that, too, had died with her father. She had once greeted each day with anticipation. Now, her only hope was that the new day would not be worse than the old.

And when all was said and done, for that, too, she had an answer, in a small bottle in her valise. . . .

CHAPTER TWO

Rose ignored the rocking of the railway car and the steady, vibrating rhythm of the wheels as she ignored the stares of the rude man across from her and kept her eyes firmly fixed on her book. This fellow had gotten on the train at a stop outside Los Angeles; with his "snappy" checked suit and well-oiled hair, pomaded with brilliantine, he evidently thought he cut quite a fine figure and that she should be well aware of the fact.

She wasn't certain why he had fixed his attention on her, but she wished that he would go away. He had been trying to attract her attention for miles, and she could not imagine what attracted him to her. She was grimy with days of nonstop travel; she hadn't had a bath since Mrs. Abernathy's boardinghouse. Her hair felt so greasy that she thought she must resemble one of those outlandish aboriginal people who coated their locks with oil. Perhaps it was only that she was the only unaccompanied female in the car below the age of sixty. By the huge leather case under his seat, she suspected that he was a drummer — a traveling salesman.

Whatever he's selling, I want none of it.

She was weary to the bone with days of hard traveling. Mrs. Abernathy had awakened her before dawn on the day she had left, with the welcome news that the man who carted away boxes and other "clean" rubbish was willing to take her and her trunk to the station for half the cost of a cab. She had also given Rose some sound advice in the matter of traveling attire.

"Whatever you put on," she had warned, "make certain that it won't show stains, and that it is something you will be willing to throw away at the end of your trip. Believe me, child, you won't want it after that."

Rose had followed her advice, wearing the dreadful black Manchester-cloth street-skirt and sateen waist she had bought for her father's funeral. The clothing was cheap, but serviceable enough to last the journey and look respectable. She had thought that Mrs. Abernathy had meant that after wearing the same clothing continuously, riding and sleeping in it for days, she would simply never want to see it again.

That might also have been true, but what Mrs. Abernathy had been too well-bred to explain was that the floor of the common railway-carriage—particularly in the West — was filthy. The uncouth men who shared the carriage with her chewed tobacco, and often did not bother to travel to the end of the carriage to use the spittoon. They brought mud and worse in on their boots, and the dust of the plains blew in at the window. The floor was sticky with the residue of tobacco juice, and coated with the ashes that often floated in through the windows. The outsides of the carriages gave no hint as to the state of the floors; the carriages were kept as clean as possible given the circumstances. Try as she might to keep her hem free of the floor, it dragged whenever she sat, or when the carriage lurched as she walked, and she was forced to drop her skirt and clutch at the backs of the seats for balance. She did not think that she was ever going to get the skirt clean again, and she only hoped she could prevail on some hardy soul in Mr. Cameron's employ to clean her boots, for she was nauseated by the notion of having to touch them, sticky and odorous as they were.

She had observed the travelers in the parlor cars and the occasional private carriage with raw envy. The hard wooden bench-seats of the common carriage were too short to lie down upon, and *if* one could sleep, one woke with a stiff neck and a headache from being wedged into an unnatural, upright position. The most comfortable naps she had taken had been in stations, on the benches reserved for waiting passengers, as she also waited for the next train, guarded by the watchful eye of the curiously paternal stationmasters.

At least she had not starved, although she had expected to spend at least part of the time hungry. Her meals were, indeed, taken care of, and she ate as well as anyone else taking the common carriages. Those same stationmasters saw to it that when there was no dining car attached to a train she was provided with a packet of thick ham or cured-tongue sandwiches and a bottle or two of lemonade. This, evidently, was on the orders of Mr. Cameron, since she saw no one else being so provided for, and occasionally her preferential treatment aroused glances of envy akin to those she bestowed on the wealthier travelers.

There had been sights she would never forget: the fury of a prairie thunderstorm, as lightning formed a thousand spidery legs of fire beneath the heavy, black clouds; the brilliant skies at night, with more stars than she had ever seen in her life; the mountains — every day held its share of natural wonders, more astounding than any of the seven wonders of the ancient world. If she had not been so exhausted, she probably would have been able to appreciate them more.

She had been looking forward to her first sight of the Pacific Ocean, but with this boor trying to catch her attention she was unlikely to be able to appreciate this particular vista.

At least she never tired of this book, *The Odyssey* in

the original Greek. The advantage of having the original before her was that she need not be confined to one particular translator's view of things; she was able to discover nuances and new interpretations every time she read it. It never mattered that she was tired, that the long stretches across the empty plains had seemed interminable. Even with the eyes of another upon her, she was able to reach beyond this journey, to a strange and wondrous journey of a different sort, infinitely more perilous than her own, fraught with the machinations of gods and terrible magics, with —

"Well, excuse me, missy!"

The boor, seeing himself spurned in favor of a mere book, had elected to take things a step further and try to gain her attention directly.

She pointedly ignored him, turning away a trifle, although that cast the pages of the book in shadow. *Surely he won't persist if I make it clear I want nothing of him.*

Undeterred, he persisted. When he got no response from his verbal attempts, actually poking her foot with his toe so that she looked up at him in shock and affrontery before she could stop herself.

"Well, there, missy," the rude fellow said, in a falsely hearty voice. "You sure have been buryin' your nose in that book! What's it you're readin' that's so interestin'?"

She stared at him, appalled by his impoliteness, then replied before she could stop herself, "Homer's *Odyssey.*"

He wrinkled his brow in puzzlement. Evidently his sole exposure to literature had consisted of what lay between the covers of the *McGuffy's Readers*. "Homer who? Say, missy, that's all Greek to me."

"Precisely," she replied, lowering the temperature of her words as her temper heated, and she turned her attention back to the book. *He's been snubbed, surely he won't persist any further.*

Only to have the book snatched out of her hands.

Her temper snapped. Outraged, she jumped to her feet while the lout was still puzzling over the Greek letters.

How dare *he!*

"Conductor!" she shouted at the top of her lungs, and in her most piercing voice.

The lout looked up at her, startled in his turn by her anger and her willingness to stand up to his rudeness. The conductor, who fortunately happened to be at the other end of her car collecting tickets, hurried up the aisle, walking as easily in the swaying car as a sailor would on a swaying deck. Before he could even voice an inquiry, she pointed at the miscreant with an accusatory finger, her face flushed with anger

"That man is a thief and a masher!" she said indignantly. "He has been bothering me, he would not leave me alone, and now he has stolen my book! *Do* something about him!"

But the cad was not without a quick wit — probably a necessity when confronted with angry husbands, fiances and fathers. "I don't know what that woman's talking about," he protested, lying so outrageously that her mouth fell open in sheer amazement at his audacity. "I was just sittin' here readin' my book, when she jumps up and screeches for you."

That wolf-in-sheep's-clothing! Her hand closed into a fist as she restrained herself from hitting him. Any other woman might have shrunk from confronting him further, given that it was her word against his, but her blood was up — and besides, the book had been a birthday gift from her first Greek teacher. She was not going to surrender the book, the truth, or the field without a fight. "Well, then," she said with venom-dripping sweetness, "If it's *your* book, I presume you can read it. *Aloud.*"

As it happened, he had the book upside down — not that it would have mattered to him. If he did not recognize the name of the great poet Homer, he could hardly recognize one Greek letter from another. He gaped at her in shock of his own, and she neatly plucked her prize from his nerveless fingers, turned it rightside up, and declaimed the first four lines on the page in flawless tones. By now, everyone in the car was staring at the drama unfolding at her end.

"Translated roughly," she continued, "It says, 'The One-eyed giant howled his anguish as his bleeding eye burned and tormented him. His fellow giants rushed to learn what had befallen him. "No man has blinded me!" he cried to them. "If no man has blinded you," they replied, "Then it must be the punishment of the gods."' Anyone who has the faintest knowledge of the classics will recognize that scene."

The boor was not to be so easily defeated. "Why, she could make any gabble, say it meant anything!" he cried. "She's a crazy woman!"

She put the book into the conductor's hands. "Look inside the front cover," she ordered imperiously. "On the flyleaf. It reads, 'To little Rose, one of the greatest flowers of literature, from a humble gardener. With affection, Lydia Reuben.' If this is his book, then how could I know that? And while I may or may not be a scholar of Greek, I have never yet met a man named *Rose.*"

Those sitting nearest her giggled at that, as the rogue flushed. The conductor read the dedication, his lips moving silently, and looked up with a nod. "That's what she says, all right," he rumbled, and turned a stern gaze on the masher.

The man coughed, and turned pale, and looked around hastily, as if searching for a way to escape.

Rose felt a bit faint, but she was not going to show it in front of *him*. "Conductor," she replied, in more normal tones, "Do you normally permit thieves who compound their crime with an attempt to molest honest women to continue traveling on this train?"

The man turned paler still as the conductor seized his collar. "That we don't, miss," the conductor said, handing her book back to her and pulling the man to his feet. "Sometimes, though, we let the train stop before we throws 'em off."

He blew a whistle, which brought two burly train-guards from the next carriage up, and together they removed lout and baggage, hauling both off towards the rear of the train, as he protested every step of the way at the top of his lungs. Curious stares followed this procession down the aisle, and more curious stares were directed at her after they left the car, but she no longer cared about what anyone thought. Now she let her shaking knees give way, and lowered herself back into her seat, holding onto the back with her free hand, precious book clutched in the other.

Now she let the reaction set in. How had she *dared* to face that man down? She'd never done such a thing before in her life! Oh, she had argued with men, and told them what she thought; she had made free with her opinions on paper, but she had never actually stood up to anyone who was not a gentleman. She had *never* confronted someone who was obviously prepared to do whatever he wanted, and determined to get his way. No lady would ever have faced down someone like that.

The conductor returned to make certain that she was all right. She murmured something appropriate at him, and he went back to his duties, evidently satisfied. She did not ask him what he had done with the boor. She really didn't want to know.

Probably he'd been escorted to a dank, nasty corner of a baggage car and put under lock and key. But she was a bit appalled to find that she hoped he and his case really *had* been pitched out of the back of the train.

Despite the bent heads and murmurs of delicious shock up and down the car, she must have convinced the conductor that she was properly helpless, for he kept a solicitous eye on her after that. And her first glimpse of the ocean was not marred by any unwelcome and uninvited presence, for no one else would sit with her. Or even near her.

She looked out across the endless expanse of water for as long as it was visible. She had seen Lake Michigan, of course, but this was so much *bigger!* She forgot her weariness, forgot everything. Huge — and fierce — even over the cacophony of the train, she heard the roar of the waves against the cliff below.

The train rounded a curve and scrolled away from the ocean, which vanished behind the hills. With the vista blocked, the tossing of the train threw her back to the sordid reality of the carriage. She turned back to her book, still feeling rather shaky inside.

And still angry and puzzled by the drummer's behavior. She simply could not divine what had driven him to persist, and that kept her worrying at the subject. *Did he really believe that I was only feigning indifference? Did he think I was trying in some perverse way to flirt with him by ignoring him? He was obviously expecting no resistance to his advances.* What had been in his mind? Was he so used to having his way with women that he saw everything she did in terms of what he wanted and expected?

What did *he think I was reading, anyway? Walter Scott? A dreadful dime novel? A romantic love story?* Wuthering Heights, *perhaps?*

Probably the latter, and the memory of his

expression when he tried to read the book sent her into a fit of giggles she tried to stifle with her gloved hand. *When he saw the Greek — oh my! I don't think I've ever seen anyone so surprised since — since I proved to Professor Smythe that I was just as conversant with Chretian des Troyes in the original as any of his other students.*

It did occur to her, however, that the works of the Bronte sisters would not have been inappropriate reading given her current situation. Or perhaps Jane Austen. *There is not much difference between going off to become a governess and going off to become a housekeeper. Perhaps reading the Brontes could prepare me for Jason Cameron.*

From a masher to her future employer — both male, both unfathomable. Neither responded to her attempt to analyze them. She simply did not know enough about either of them to grasp them and pin them beneath the white light of intellect.

She gave up trying, and read until darkness fell and it became impossible to read any further. There were oil-lamps suspended in each carriage, but they were too far away to cast enough light for comfortable reading — shadows moved as the lamps swayed, obscuring the letters and revealing them in a way that made her eyes ache. So she didn't bother to try; she just propped herself in the corner of the seat and half-dozed. This last leg of the journey, from Los Angeles to San Francisco, had begun before dawn and would continue until well after midnight. Perhaps her stamina had finally been exhausted; perhaps it was just the knowledge that the trip was nearly over and she was about to confront her employer and learn the truth or falsehood about him. Perhaps it was both, but she was conscious of leaden depression that weighed down her spirits.

She both dreaded the moment for the journey to end and longed for it. As the miles and the hours crept by and her fellow-passengers in their turn dozed off, she stared at her own reflection in the window, seeing only two dark holes for eyes in a ghostlike face which, because of her black clothing, seemed to hang suspended in the air, bodiless.

I am a spirit, wandering, without a home, and I shall wander bodiless forever. . . . I shall become a ghost in Jason Cameron's manor, long before I am truly dead.

What would Jason Cameron really be like? What could she expect as his employee? The comfortable and stimulating experience his letter promised? Or something out of a Bronte novel: poverty of spirit, repression and despair?

Would she find herself bundled up into a tiny attic room, waiting like a drudge on a pair of monstrous, spoiled children? Would the promised wage remain only promises, so that she remained trapped here, where she knew no one and had no way to escape, a virtual slave? Would she find herself confined to the grounds of the house unless she was escorting the children on some outing?

Or would Jason Cameron keep his word? Of late, her experiences had not done much to convince her of anything but the perfidy of her fellow man.

She stared at her reflection, and asked it a silent question. Why had she agreed to this?

Her reflection stared back in equal silence, for it had no answer for her.

A squeal of brakes broke into her melancholy thoughts. The train was slowing down, but why?

It had slowed before, of course, to pass around curves and over bridges. It had even stopped on sidings to let other trains pass, going the opposite direction.

But she hadn't felt the slight change in direction that meant a siding, and if there had been a curve ahead, she surely should have felt it by now. Yet the train was still slowing, and there were no lights beside the track, no buildings, nor any sign of habitation, as there would be if they had reached San Francisco.

The train came to a complete stop. In the strange silence, the engine panted, and some canine creature howled in the far distance. A wolf? Or only a farm-dog? She sat up and peered out of the window on her side of the train, and still saw nothing. Where were they — and why had they stopped?

Perhaps there is a blockage on the track? That would certainly be tiresome, adding more hours to the journey while they waited for the track to be cleared, even forcing them to get off and walk around it while their baggage was brought to a second train. During the course of the journey this had happened twice, both times in the mountains when land-slips had sent mud and gravel cascading down on the track. Those accidents had each added days to her trip, for it was no easy thing to get word ahead about the blockage and the need for a second train.

When she saw the conductor entering the car, she was sure he was going to tell them all that this was the case. But he did not disturb any of her drowsy fellow-passengers with a general announcement. He came straight to her, as she watched him in surprise.

"This is a special stop for you, Miss Rosalind," he said, when he saw that she was awake and aware of him. "We've already taken your trunk and bag off; if you'll just gather up your valise, we'll have you on your way in no time."

"On my way?" she asked, dazedly, as he picked up her valise from the seat beside her and offered her his hand to rise.

"Of course," he replied, as if this was a matter-of-fact occurrence to him. "Didn't Mr. Cameron tell you he was sending people to meet you at the Pacifica switch?"

"I — I believe so," she said, as he guided her to the end of the car and the stairs there. *There's no station here — who is Jason Cameron that he can have trains stopped in the middle of nowhere to let off a single person?*

The conductor handed her down as she gathered her skirts up in one hand for the jump to the ground. It was then that she saw what awaited her on the rails beyond a switch that joined a spur-line to the main track.

Lights cut through the darkness, from lanterns suspended on the rear of the vehicle ahead and from the headlights of both engines. The air was cold and damp, and she shivered as it penetrated her clothing. Overhead, the stars were not as huge and bright as they had seemed in the desert and on the open plains, but they were much more impressive than any stars seen from a city street. There were not many sounds besides the panting of the engines; a night-bird or two, some frogs or insects. Two men with lanterns and a hand-cart approached her from the odd vehicle on the tracks of the spur, and the wheels of the cart grated in the gravel of the right-of-way. Men from the baggage car met them, carrying her trunk and carpetbag. One of the two new men removed his soft cap deferentially and approached her.

"Are you Miss Rosalind Hawkins?" he asked.

"Yes, I am," she said, faintly, with one hand at her throat.

He looked relieved. "Good. Mister Cameron sent us to meet you, ma'am. We'll be taking you right to his door, practically." In the light from the carriage windows above her, and the lantern in his hand, the man smiled reassuringly. "Won't be long now, and you'll be all settled in."

He put his cap back on and offered her his arm. The other man loaded up his cart with all of her baggage, including the valise the conductor handed to him, and headed back to the odd vehicle without uttering a single word. Rose looked doubtfully at the conductor, who nodded and smiled, and made little shooing motions with his hands.

So she took the stranger's arm, and she was glad to have it. The railroad right-of-way was rough and uneven, and she couldn't see where she was putting her feet in the darkness. The conductor mounted back up to the platform of the carriage and signaled to the engineer with a lantern as soon as Rose and her escort were out of the way. Down at the end of the train, another lantern waved in the same signal from the caboose.

The engine, which had been "panting" slowly up at the head of the train chuffed out a great puff of steam as if sighing with impatience, and resumed its interrupted journey. The wheels rotated slowly, with a metallic screech, as the locomotive strained against the dead weight of the train, got it in motion, and gradually picked up speed. By the time Rose and her escort reached the spur, the red lantern on the back of the caboose was receding into the black distance, disappearing like a fading, falling star.

The vehicle they approached was like nothing Rose had ever seen before. A combination of two pieces, an engine and a passenger car, it was smaller than the locomotives that had brought her here, but quite large enough to be impressive. She could not see past the windows of the passenger section with their lowered,

red shades trimmed in heavy gold fringe, and it was too dark to see the exterior of the car clearly, but the carved molding, glinting softly with a hint of gilding, implied luxury and opulence.

"This is Mister Cameron's private vehicle," the man said proudly, patting the side of the carriage with his free hand. "We use her to get in and out of Frisco. Useta be, when he had to travel down to Los Angeles, we'd hook the car in with the regular train. I reckon you'll be comfortable enough in her, ma'am." He handed her up into the carriage, doffed his cap again to her. "Mister Cameron says, make free of what you find."

"How long will it take us to reach — where we're going?" she asked, feeling anxious, as he started towards the cab of the engine.

"Well, we'll be a-goin' fairly slow, ma'am, so maybe a couple of hours," he replied, over his shoulder. "This spur's a twisty piece, and we wouldn't want to take any chances. You ought to go inside and make yourself to home."

Since he was reaching for the handhold to haul himself up into the cabin of the engine, she decided she probably ought to take his advice.

Strange, how this rough-seeming man could be so polite, and the one who had dressed like a pseudo-gentleman had been nothing of the sort.

She turned and opened the door, stepping into a world she had thought was lost to her.

The color-scheme was of red and gold, the gold of polished brass fittings and gilded fixtures, the red of scarlet leather, velvet and satin. The car was fitted out to resemble a comfortable parlor, with three small tables covered with red damask cloths, real chairs, a Roman divan couch, and a bed-lounge. All the furniture was deeply padded and upholstered in red velvet or leather. The floor was covered with a deep red Turkey carpet, and the furniture was discreetly bolted to the floor through the carpeting. Mahogany bookcases full of leather-bound volumes decorated one wall, and a handsome mahogany sideboard laden with bottles and glassware graced another.

Enough oil-lamps burned from fixtures set between each window that the interior of the car was illuminated as cheerfully as anyone could ask. There was even a porcelain stove in an alcove at the back of the car to heat it.

A serving-plate covered with a silver dome sat on one of the tables, but as the "train" began to move, Rose's attention was drawn to a door on the end of the car. A discreet brass plaque announced "Lounge" in square script, and she made her way to that door, wondering if it contained what she hoped.

It did. A brass and porcelain oil-lamp lit the tiny room softly. Her valise sat in a clever tray bolted to the top of an oak washstand, to keep anything placed in it from being overset. The washstand — or rather, vanity — boasted a graceful porcelain basin inset in the top; the basin was even equipped with a drain-hole and a stopper to close it so that one need not try to find a way to empty it in the moving train. A bar of castile soap lay in a porcelain cradle next to the basin. Above the basin was a matching porcelain ewer with a spigot in the bottom. She touched the spigot and was rewarded by a stream of fresh, warm water.

Without hesitation she took off her sateen waist and washed and rinsed her face, neck and arms — twice, because she was appalled to see that after the first washing, the water was gray with grime. She could not wash her hair, but at least she could damp it down a little and comb it out — and she did, bracing herself against the basin as the train twisted and turned on its journey. She rebraided it and wound it about her head in a kind of crown rather than making the French twist and pompadour she usually wore.

There was one clean waist in her valise; she had been saving it, in the faint hope that she would find a way to change before she met her employer. A remnant of her former fortune, it was of much-mended taffeta silk in a deep rose. In the soft light of lamps and lanterns, the mended places would not be too obvious. She also had fresh stockings, but it would be impossible to change the rest of her underclothing without somehow extracting herself from petticoats and corset.

She put the stockings and the waist on, and immediately felt much better. To finally don clean clothing after so many days in the same outfit was pure bliss. She procured her tooth-powder and brush from the valise, and completed the process of cleaning at least the upper portion of her body.

She regarded her reflection in the mirror beside the basin, and decided that it could have been worse. She was exhausted, and looked it, but she also looked respectable now, and not as if she had been sleeping in her clothing, in trains and on benches in railway stations, for endless days.

She left her valise where it was, and re-entered the car, curious now to see what lay on that silver salver. She lifted the silver dome lid, and gasped with pleasure.

Fresh grapes, something she had not seen, let alone tasted, in weeks — and with them, two kinds of cheese, and bread with a chewy crust and, when she tore off an experimental bit, a curiously tangy flavor. She helped herself to a light wine from the cabinet and made an unashamed glutton of herself.

A nap would have done her a world of good, but when she reclined on the lounge, she discovered that her treacherous mind would not be quiet, manufacturing all manner of suspicions, coming up with reasons why the apparently benevolent Mister Cameron was in truth a monster.

This could all be some kind of trap. The food could be drugged. Cameron might be a white slaver. He could have brought you here to debauch you.

Nonsense, she replied to the slightly hysterical thought. Why go to all this trouble and expense to obtain one woman from Chicago, when there were hundreds — well, dozens, anyway — of "soiled doves" right at hand in San Francisco, all *much* more experienced at — at pleasing a man than she. Surely a man as rich as Cameron would not lack in charming companions of the demimonde, all eager to serve his every wish!

Yes, but perhaps he wants someone acquainted with the uncensored Ovid —

But the idea of the apocryphal Jason Cameron importing a scholar from Chicago to indulge him in Roman debaucheries was too absurd even for her suspicious nature.

He doesn't even know what I look like! she told herself, trying not to giggle. *He could be getting someone like Lydia Bullfinch, all bones and brains and hair!* And the idea of Lydia in a sheer Roman chemise, reclining sylph-like on a couch, *did* send her into hysterical giggles.

She must have finally relaxed enough to doze, for the next thing she knew, the little train was slowing with an unpleasant metallic squeal of brakes, quite enough to wake even the soundest sleeper. She sat up and smoothed down her shirtwaist and skirt, although she hated even to touch the latter, as it felt gritty and faintly gummy.

Once the train had come to a complete stop, there was a knock at the door of the carriage. She rose to her feet as a man entered, without waiting for her to answer.

He might well have figured as a creature from one
of the Bronte books. He was a little taller than she,
slender, and dark. His dark hair was long by the
standards of Chicago, just at his shoulders, and cut to
wave in a quite romantic fashion. His saturnine face
held a pair of brooding brown eyes above chiseled
cheekbones and a decidedly Romanesque nose. Only
in his chin did he lack true romantic grace — it jutted
just a bit too firmly outward, as if he was inclined to
use it as a ram against those who dared to get in his
way. He was impeccably dressed in a dark blue suit,
fine shirt, and tie with a conservative stripe.

"Mister Cameron?" she said, instantly, holding out
her hand. "I am Rosalind Hawkins —"

"I am pleased to meet you, Miss Hawkins, but I fear
I am not Jason Cameron," the man replied, taking her
hand and clasping it briefly before letting it go. His
voice was a deep tenor, with the intimation of power
behind it, but no discernible accent. "Master Cameron
is my employer also, and he sent me to bring you up to
the house. My name is Paul du Mond, and I am his
personal secretary and valet." Now he smiled, although
it was not an expression that brought any warmth to his
face. "You must call me by my given name."

"Of course," she replied, feeling rebuffed, although
she could not imagine why she felt that way. "Please
call me — Rosalind."

Dashed if she would let this cold fellow call her
"Rose"!

"Thank you, Rosalind. Ah, no — " he added, as she
made an abortive attempt to retrieve her valise. "No,
do not trouble yourself over your baggage. It will all be
seen to. Would you come with me?"

Seeing no other option, she descended the stairs of
the carriage behind him, not entirely certain what to

expect. She found herself stepping onto a marble landing, and looking up at a series of white marble stairs inset into the cliff, illuminated by lanterns, that seemed to rise into the stars. She backed up a step and put one hand to her throat, shivering just a little in the cold and damp. Fog wisped across the platform, and she thought that it might be very near dawn.

The staircase, however, daunted her. She was never going to be able to climb all *that!*

Paul smiled at her dismay, as if he was amused by it. "Do not be concerned, Rosalind. We will not be dealing with *that* tonight. The Master does not expect weary travelers to exhaust themselves at the end of their journey. The stairs are only for effect — and those who insist on showing how strong and fit they are."

He led the way to a door, hidden in the shadows, which he opened, revealing the prosaic iron grating of a lift door. He motioned to her to precede him, which she did.

The lift operated smoothly — disconcertingly so, with no noise or sound of machinery. If she had not been aware of the motion of the stone wall beyond the grating, she would have been sure they were not moving at all. Paul du Mond made no attempt at conversation, and neither did she, although the silence became very uncomfortable after a while.

Finally, a crack of light showed at the top of the lift door; it widened as the lift rose, and she saw they had reached their destination. This was a hallway; floored with black marble, with wallcoverings of wine-red brocade above half-panels of dark wood. Polished brass oil-lamps with shades of ruby glass lit the hallway clearly.

Paul opened the gate of the lift, but made no motion to follow her out into the hall. "I have some things to attend to, but I am certain that a competent lady like yourself will be able to find her way." His smile implied that he rather doubted she would be able to do any such thing. "Go to the right, take the staircase up to the third floor. Your rooms are the first door on the left."

She was taken aback by his brusque behavior. Before she could reply, he closed the lift door behind her, and the lift descended again, leaving her with no choice but to follow his instructions.

Not that they were especially difficult, really. It was only that she found the silence of the house rather unnerving. But that was only to be expected; after all, it *was* still night-time. It was not reasonable for her to expect that Jason Cameron or many of his servants would be awake to welcome her. It was enough that Paul du Mond — and whatever other servants were taking care of her baggage — had been here to greet her. At least they *had* a room waiting for her.

She had anticipated a dark, back staircase, a servant's stair to be precise, but the staircase proved to be both broad and handsome in dark wood and oak paneling, and well-lit with more brass lamps, this time with white porcelain shades. It boasted a red carpet, and climbed in a square spiral, with doors at each floor.

She opened the third of these — this time *certain* it would let out on a mean little hallway — to find that it did nothing of the sort.

The hallway here was papered in red-on-red fleur-de-lis, and the floor was of dark wood with a red carpet runner down the center of the hallway. Again, the lamps were of brass and ruby glass; red and gold seemed to be Jason Cameron's preferred colors. The door that Paul du Mond had indicated was a few steps past the door to the staircase; she had just touched the handle, when she noticed that the door itself bore a brass plaque. On it was inscribed a single word.

Rosalind.

Startled, she froze, but the handle seemed to turn beneath her fingers and the door swung open, as if under its own power.

She gasped as she saw the room; she could not help herself. In all her wildest dreams of what might be waiting for her, she had never imagined anything like *this*.

For a moment, she hesitated. Surely this was a mistake; this room could not possibly be meant for *her!* But her name was on the door — and Paul du Mond had sent her here. She stepped inside, hesitantly, and the door swung silently shut behind her.

If someone had given her free rein and an infinite budget to design a sitting-room that would best please her, this would have been it. There was a small fire in the fireplace to ward off the chill of the air outside, although a modern steam-radiator made it clear that the fireplace was mostly ornamental. Between the cozy fire and the two lamps, there was not a single corner that was unlit.

Unlike the red-and-gold opulence of the parlor-car and the rest of the house, this room was decorated in tones of deep blues and dark silver, both restful colors to her way of thinking. A Roman couch upholstered in teal-blue velvet stood beneath a huge window, curtained in matching material. Two wingback chairs in the same material flanked a small table with one of the lamps on it, and a combination bookcase and writing desk held the second lamp, with a matching armless chair positioned at the desk. The soft Turkey carpet was of a deeper blue than the chairs; the walls were papered in a lighter blue with a stripe of discreet silver.

A second door stood open at the other end of the

room, and she let her feet take her to it as in a dream. As she stood in the doorway, she could only stare, for this room was as perfect as the sitting-room.

It held not one, but three wardrobes, all matching and standing side by side, flanked by a pair of dressers; all were of dark maple with silver fittings. There were two chairs like the ones in the sitting-room, and a huge full-length mirror between them. Another radiator promised that *this* bedroom would never be cold. The carpet, wall-covering, and curtains were the same as in the sitting-room. The bed, which dominated the room, was absolutely enormous. Amazingly enough, it was of the medieval style she had always secretly favored, with curtains of blue-on-blue brocade, and a matching spread now turned invitingly down to reveal the snowy linens.

But there was more, and light through a third door drew her onward, until she found herself in a bathroom whose opulence matched the rest.

This room was tiled in pale grey, pale blue, and silver. A bath was drawn and waiting for her, steaming and fragrant with lavender bath salts. The tub, large enough to recline comfortably in, was of the square, Roman style — a huge marble basin enclosed in a tiled box. There were two sinks, an abundance of mirrors, a lounge and two chairs, a vanity with a framed mirror. The vanity held a wealth of green and silver bottles whose contents she longed to explore. Snowy towels hung from a heated towel-rack, and the "convenience" was of the most modern flush-type. The bathroom was as large as her bedroom had been at home, and had its own small wardrobe at one end, with the door opened to display a tempting selection of nightgowns and dressing-robes or kimonos.

Rose didn't even hesitate. Much faster than she had ever remembered undressing before, she shed her clothing down to the last stitch — shirtwaist, skirt, underskirts, stockings, corset-cover, corset, vest, drawers — all of them dropped from her body with a speed that was positively magical. She slipped into the hot water with a gasp of delight, and scrubbed and rinsed and scrubbed again until she was pink all over. She ran more hot water into the tub and rinsed again, then undid her hair and washed it as well.

She did not go so far as to appropriate any of the lovely night-things in the wardrobe, however. She was certain that they must belong to someone else, and had been left there by accident. Instead, she rebraided her hair, wet as it was, wrapped herself in a towel, and went to look for her valise.

The valise wasn't there — but *someone* had stolen into the bedroom while she was bathing, had drawn the curtains around three sides of the bed and had left a nightgown lying across the pillow, in an obvious invitation.

It was an invitation too tempting to resist — especially given that the mere sight of the bed had started her yawning.

She took the gown into the bathroom to change — just in case the unknown "helper" returned. It was silk, a luxury against her skin after the coarse cottons of her traveling clothing that made her dizzy with pleasure. She blew out the lamps in the bathroom and returned to the bedroom, to find that all the other lamps had been extinguished except for the one next to the bed.

She was too tired to be alarmed at the way people kept stealing in and out of the rooms without her noticing. In fact, she was too tired to think of anything other than falling into that wonderful bed — putting her glasses carefully on the bedside table and blowing out the lamp — pulling the bedcurtains around to shut out the morning light — and pulling the covers up over her head.

CHAPTER THREE

Rose woke in darkness, but this time with no sense of disorientation, no fear when she did not recognize her surroundings. She remembered precisely where she was; even if she hadn't, the faint perfume of some unfamiliar flower wafting from her hair would have reminded her.

She was at her destination, the home of Jason Cameron. She was in darkness because she had drawn the heavy velvet bed-curtains tightly around the bed, and not even the most persistent sunbeam was going to penetrate both velvet curtain and satin lining.

She stretched luxuriously in the warmth of the bed, taking an animal pleasure in the soft caress of the silk of her borrowed nightdress upon her skin. Tonight, of course, it would be plain cotton weave again, but for now, she could pretend to luxury.

Pretend? It would hardly be pretense, given the luxury of her quarters. While *she* might be shabby, her surroundings were palatial.

I wonder what time it is? Surely it couldn't be too late in the morning; she'd be expected to take charge of the children immediately, and her employer would probably insist on interviewing her first. Although she wished devoutly that she could wallow in this wonderful bed with a book, her hours were no longer her own. With a reluctant sense of duty she pushed back the curtains to find that oil-lamps had again been lit to augment the thin grey daylight coming in through the windows. Without her glasses, that was just about all that she could ascertain.

She reached for her glasses and the room sprang into sharper focus. She sat up, swung her legs over the side of the bed, and found that a pale-pink silk wrapper trimmed in soft lace that matched the lace-trimmed gown had been laid out on a chair beside the bed, ready for her to put on, even though she had not heard anyone come in. She frowned a little as she put on the wrapper and moved into the sitting-room, with the carpet soft as moss under her bare feet. Why hadn't she heard the servant come in? She didn't usually sleep that heavily.

Then again, those unseen servants had penetrated her room while she bathed last night, without her hearing them. They must simply be preternaturally silent.

Her trunk and bags had arrived while she slept — but to her dismay, when she opened them, she found that her clothing was missing! Searching frantically, she saw that not a single personal possession was missing — only the clothing!

She forced herself to calm down and think of a decent explanation. After all, there was still clothing here. Cameron obviously didn't intend to keep her a prisoner by taking away her clothes. *Wait. I'm being unreasonable. They've probably taken it all away to be cleaned.* Of course; that was the obvious explanation. She'd heard that this was the way such things were done in the homes of the wealthy.

Even for someone who is one short step above a servant?

She ignored the nagging thought, and turned to the small table beneath the window. The curtains had been drawn, showing her a view of a lush scrap of lawn, a wilderness of trees, and just beyond them, a hint of the sea. She couldn't see the shore itself; had this house been built on a seaside cliff?

On the table was one of those silver platters with a domed lid covering it, though this one was nearly the size of the tabletop. When she lifted the dome, she found a complete breakfast, hot and ready, as if it had just come from the kitchen. There was a pot of coffee wafting up a savor worthy of heaven; two perfectly poached eggs, golden-brown toast dripping with butter, fried shredded potatoes, and a slice of ham with the fat crisped and the lean moist and tender. Beside this lay another plate containing a piece of hot apple pie redolent with cinnamon and nutmeg, with a tiny pitcher of cream to pour on it. This was so unlike the pitiful bread and oatmeal of the boarding house that she could have wept. There was also a note, in an envelope identical to Jason Cameron's first missive, resting against the coffee-cup.

She opened it first, before touching the tempting breakfast, even though her stomach murmured its displeasure. The script was the same, in the same odd, sepia-toned ink.

Dear Miss Hawkins, it read. *Welcome. I have taken the liberty of ordering my servants to make away with your clothing so that it can be cleaned and pressed for you.*

There — the very explanation *she* had arrived at.

I hope that you will make free of the garments that I have had ordered for you, and continue to do so if they please you.

Remembering the envy she had felt on seeing the wealth of silken night-things, comparing the gown and wrapper she now wore with her own, and imagining what must lie in the wardrobes and chest, she was not inclined to miss her skirts and waists from Sears, Roebuck and Co.

Enjoy your breakfast at your leisure. I shall communicate with you when you have settled yourself for the day.

The note was signed, *Jason Cameron*. The signature was the same as the one she remembered.

Part of her was immediately suspicious. Part of her found this completely reasonable. Why *shouldn't* she be treated with respect and care? After all, she *did* have a set of completely unique qualifications. And Jason Cameron was obviously a man of extreme wealth, to whom all this expense on her behalf represented little more than pocket-change.

She seated herself at the table and picked up knife and fork, and found the ham was so tender she hardly needed the former. *Think of that lift alone!* she told her suspicious side, as she slowly savored her breakfast. *Not even a great hotel could afford a lift like that one! The man owns his own private rail-spur and train, and sends it to fetch someone the way I would call a cab! He is simply being a gentleman; he knows what the journey must have been like, and he is giving me a chance to get my bearings.*

As for the gowns and the accommodations — well, if *she* were in Jason Cameron's place, she would not want anyone in her employ to walk about looking as — as *shabby* as she was. *You purchase paintings to suit your decor — why not clothe your employees to match? Certainly there is no uniform for a governess the way there is for a maid or some other servant.* Certainly Paul du Mond had been clothed as elegantly as any gentleman of her acquaintance. Perhaps his garb was also the result of his employer's generosity.

Her suspicious side settled, though not without a grumble. She finished her breakfast, and returned to the bedroom to see what delights the wardrobes held.

She soon discovered that *someone* female had

assuredly had a hand in the selection of what lay within the drawers of the dresser and doors of the wardrobe. There was literally nothing lacking, from the most delicate underthings to fashionable corsetry to gowns, skirts, and shirtwaists of a style and fabric that shouted "Imported! French!" Any susceptible woman would have flung her good sense temporarily to the wind at the mere sight of such treasures, and Rose was no exception.

With much difficulty, she chose a selection that included underthings trimmed with real Brussels lace, and real silk stockings. To meet her employer, she picked a skirt of the softest wool she had ever touched in her life, wool as soft and as plush as velvet, in a deep sapphire blue, and a silk waist with a flowing jabot in pale blue with more lace, dyed to match, at the collar and cuffs. There were even shoes and boots in her exact size, and she had no hesitation in carrying off a pair of kid half-boots that matched the skirt.

She bore her prizes off to the bathroom, and spent a rapturous hour "putting herself together." When she was done, she surveyed the result in the mirror, and was more than pleased with the result.

Just as importantly, she was no longer self-conscious about meeting with her employer. Clothing was a kind of armor, really, and her armor had been patched, weak, and dangerously thin before. Beautiful clothing was, in a way, invisible — but people noticed when one was poorly or shabbily dressed, and acted accordingly. *Now* she could face any man or woman on the face of the globe and feel confident that she would be judged on her merit, not the state of her clothing. Her self-confidence increased with every passing second. *Now* she was herself; now she was Rosalind Hawkins, scholar and Doctoral candidate, and the equal of anyone in America, even Jason

Cameron! After all, *she* had something *he* wanted, and that made her the seller in a seller's market.

She left the bathroom and entered the bedroom — The silent, invisible servants had struck again. The bed was made, the havoc she had wrought among the clothing had been tidied away, her wrapper and nightdress whisked off to who-knew-where.

How are they doing this? she wondered, with mingled admiration and irritation. *I haven't been deafened by all the noise of the locomotives, have I?*

She moved on to the sitting room — and the breakfast things had vanished also. But there was a new addition; a pile of books lay on the table beside the couch, a reading-lamp had been lit, and the end of a speaking-tube was laid beside the books. On top of the books was another note.

Something about this sent a chill of apprehension running down the length of her spine, though she could not imagine why it should be so. She stepped carefully over to the table and picked up the note. Her hands shook as she opened it.

Dear Miss Hawkins, it said. *Now I must make a confession to you. You have been brought here under false pretenses.*

She almost dropped the note there and then, but something made her continue reading.

There are no children; I never had a wife. I do require the abilities of a remarkable scholar; the exact abilities and skills that I outlined in my missive to your mentor, Professor Cathcart. I am an invalid and an accident has left me unable to read the books that I require for my own research. In addition, I am imperfectly acquainted with medieval German and Gaelic. I desire your services, both as a reader and a translator.

She blinked at the letter, jaw dropping in a most

unladylike expression of amazement. Of all of the possibilities, *this* was the one she would never, ever have guessed at.

The salary will remain the same; the hours will perhaps be longer, and extend deep into the night, for it is at night that I require the distractions of work to free my mind from pain. I fear that you will not be able to make as many excursions into San Francisco as you would like, but that is only because the journey is of three hours in duration, and you would probably wish to stay overnight. At the moment my need of your services does not allow for this; in a month or two, I shall take pains to arrange such an excursion. In recompense for this curtailment of your freedom, I offer my apartment in the city for the eventuality of such a trip, and the use of my box at the Opera or Tivoli Gardens, whichever shall present the choicer entertainment for that evening in your mind.

She felt breathless, and hardly knew what to think, now.

I personally pledge that you shall hear Caruso, even though my own needs must then take second place.

How had he known how much she wanted to hear Caruso sing?

You have the freedom of the house and grounds, although I am afraid that you will probably find it rather dull. I entertain no one, and my servants are as reclusive as their master. You will, however, encounter my secretary, Paul du Mond, from time to time. He will see to obtaining whatever you need, if it has not already been provided. If you are shy of communicating some personal need to a strange male, simply write it down and leave the note with your meal-tray; my housekeeper will then attend to it.

She sat down on the couch, feeling suddenly dizzy. If this was a form of imprisonment, then it was the *oddest* sort of imprisonment anyone had ever imagined. And for what purpose? That she should read books?

My accident has left me disfigured in a way that I would not inflict upon one who did not know me before. You will therefore be reading to me through the speaking-tube, and I will make my requests by the same manner.

Not even the fevered and disordered brain of a Mary Shelley could have created a plot like this one! Surely even the publishers of dime novels would balk at such an unlikely situation!

You can, of course, refuse your services, and I will have you transported to San Francisco with all your belongings immediately. It was unfair of me to bring you here under false pretenses, and I apologize most humbly — but ask yourself this: if I had communicated the truth, would you have believed it? I think not. I believe that even Conan Doyle and Rudyard Kipling would have blushed to pen such a wild tale.

He had a point. If she had been presented with this situation in Chicago, she and Professor Cathcart would have discarded it as the fantasies of a lunatic.

She could leave, now, this moment. He had said as much. She did not need to stay here a moment longer.

But if she chose that escape, it meant to be set down, with two dollars to her name, in a strange city. That was not the best option open to her at the moment. Here — if Jason Cameron was more lunatic than this note suggested — she was subject to the will of one man, two at the most. Thus far there was no evidence that either Cameron or his man had any interest in any part of her but her mind. There was no reason to believe that she wasn't perfectly safe here. There *were* bolts on the doors, she *could* lock herself in — and although secret passageways and hidden doors in the walls were a hallmark of dreadful cheap novels, she knew enough about architecture to be aware that it was extremely difficult to construct such things, and even more difficult to conceal them.

I will be waiting to hear your decision in person, the letter concluded. *Merely say what you will into the speaking-tube, and I will abide by your decision. But please take into your considerations that if you accept this employment, you will be granting a crippled and disfigured man an entry into a world of scholarship he had thought was lost to him, and a way for him to forget, for a few hours, his pain.*

It was signed, simply, *Jason.*

Oh, that was manipulative! That last was clearly an attempt to win her sympathy; quite calculated to appeal to every noble instinct she might possess. And as such, it succeeded, even as she recognized it for what it was. She actually found herself admiring a man who had the strength and audacity to use his infirmity as a weapon. Most men would never have admitted to needing anyone or anything — Jason Cameron was clearly a craftsman who did not scruple at using whatever came to his hand, including his own weakness.

But she was also very much aware of the fact that of her two options — to go or to stay — this was by far the most attractive. There was no reason to suppose that this time, Jason Cameron was telling anything other than the truth. His tale was so fantastic that, strangely enough, it rang truer than the tale of the two precocious children.

He had treated her well up to now; why should that cease? He clearly *had* wealth; what would he want with her other than her services as a scholar? Money would gain the cooperative company of a professional courtesan for even the most hideous man in the world. He would not get *that* from her by any means other than coercion. All the arguments she had used back in Chicago to persuade herself to take this position still held true.

She put down the note; considered the room she sat in, the clothing she wore, the books on the table beside her. Her self-confidence returned, and she began to think that she might well be the equal of Jason Cameron, even in manipulation.

If this was a gilded cage, why not abide in it for a while? Where else did she have to go — and what else had she longed to do, but use her mind and her skills in pursuit of learning? He could not keep her if she was determined to leave. She was certain that she was clever enough to outwit any attempt to trap her here.

She picked up the end of the speaking-tube, coughed to clear her throat, and sent her first words into it.

"Mister Cameron?"

A moment later, the reply; hoarse, rather deep. And to substantiate the story, it did *sound* like the voice of someone who had suffered an accident of some devastation. "Miss Hawkins? Have you come to a decision, then?"

"I believe I have, sir." She took a deep breath, then committed herself. *I have what he wants and needs*, she reminded herself. *This is still a seller's market.* "I see no reason why I should not continue as your employee under the new requirements that you have outlined to me."

Another question occurred to her — *then why insist on a woman? Why not a male?* But the answer was obvious. He could not, dared not, trust a man. A male would be all too likely to take advantage of the situation, perhaps overpower the secretary and thus control Jason Cameron's life and fortune. Though Paul du Mond was not precisely robust, no woman would be able to physically overwhelm him. Thus, only a woman would be safe to trust.

Once again, then, I hold the cards.

A deep sigh, as if Jason Cameron had been holding his breath, waiting for her answer. "I should add something to this, in all honesty, Miss Hawkins. My path of research is very — *outre*. Very odd. You may find yourself reading books that are unpleasant to you. Perhaps even shocking."

Her self-confidence was soaring, to the point where she actually felt giddy. She surprised herself — and possibly him — by bursting into laughter. "Mister Cameron — I have read the unexpurgated Ovid, the love-poems of Sappho, the *Decameron* in the original, and a *great* many texts in Greek and Latin histories that were not thought fit for proper gentlemen to read, much less proper ladies. I know in precise detail what Caligula did to, and with, his sisters, and I can quote it to you in Latin or in my own translation if you wish. I am interested in historical truth, and truth in history is often unpleasant and distasteful to those of fine sensibility. I frankly doubt that you will produce anything to shock me."

There was silence for a moment, then a chuckle. It sounded like an appreciative chuckle. "Miss Hawkins, I am rightfully rebuked. You are a scholar, and there is nothing that shocks the mind of a scholar except censorship and falsehood. I confess that I was not aware that you were so widely read, and I commend you for your self-possession. You will find my research odd, then, but not shocking."

"Thank you," she said simply, glowing a little with pleasure at his words.

"I have, in the light of this, a new contract for you. You are evidently a lady of much stamina, and one who understands the need that drives the seeker of knowledge when the trail is hot. I had intended to ask you to read for a fixed number of hours in a day. I would like to change that — and ask you to read for as long in a day as I need you to. If you can put up with the whims of my research, and if you can bear with the fact that I shall need you for long and difficult hours, I shall see to it that you have all the resources you require to pursue your own goals of research, in addition to all else I promised you. In fact, I shall have all my recent book catalogs of rare and antique volumes sent to you for you to look through and make selections, and I shall have them purchased for you. Is that a bargain, scholar to scholar, equal to equal?"

If he had been Mephistopheles, he could not have offered her a bargain to tempt her more. If he had been able to read her mind, he would not have phrased it any differently. It was an offer she could not possibly reject. "It is a bargain, sir," she said, immediately. "And as I see you have had some books left here for me, I am prepared to begin reading immediately, to seal our agreement."

Was it her imagination, or did she sense elation on the other end of that long tube?

"Thank you," came the answer, "And — if you will forgive an impertinence, before you begin, I have a final question for you."

"You may ask," she replied, "but I will not guarantee to answer, if it is that impertinent." A bit bold, perhaps, but had he not just addressed her as equal to equal? Let him take what he had offered.

"Miss Hawkins — are you sentimentally attached to those garments you brought with you?" There was a plaintive, pained quality to his words that brought another laugh bubbling up out of her throat, which she suppressed only just in time. His poor, bruised sensibilities! It was the question of an aesthete confronted with an object of terrible banality stuck squarely in the middle of an otherwise matchless vista.

In other words — he really doesn't *want to know*

that there is anything shabby trailing about in his beautiful home. Poor man! He's probably afraid that I'll disgrace him if anyone should see me! She giggled again. He's probably dreading the censure of that terribly superior secretary of his if he permits a dowd to stalk his exquisite halls.

"Mister Cameron, I am not," she said firmly. "Provided that I may keep these replacements that you have graciously provided for me, you may do with them what you will. Burn them, bury them, use them for cleaning rags; I will not be sorry to see them gone. They are inferior specimens of their type, have nothing of grace or charm to recommend them, and deserve an ignoble end. Frankly, I bought them because I had to, not because I wanted to. My taste, sir, is better than that."

Another sigh of relief. "Miss Cameron, once again you please and surprise me. If you would take up the first volume in the stack and begin at the place marked?"

The leather-bound book was without a title or any other identifying marks; the ribbon bookmark within fell at a new chapter. Somewhat to her surprise, it was hand-printed, in medieval French. Within a few words, she knew what it was, although such books had never been of interest to her. It was a treatise on alchemy, full of maunderings about "Red Lions" and "White Eagles," "male and female principles," and allusions to "Hermetic Mysteries." Despite obvious flaws in grammar and syntax, she read it precisely as it had been written, for these tomes were often encoded, and to correct what was there might render it indecipherable.

Alchemy! I wonder what his "researches" are? Not a search for the Philosopher's Stone, surely; any man as acquainted with science and rational thinking as a man in his position must surely know what nonsense such things are! Besides, he does not need a Philosopher's Stone to render him wealthy; he already has wealth in abundance.

Then again — perhaps he *was* interested in the occult aspect of such things. He had suffered a terrible accident — would someone in his place not crave some supernatural remedy to his injury, since science could not supply one?

She came to the end of the section and was about to continue when Cameron spoke.

"No more," he said, sounding resigned. "I remembered that passage imperfectly; there is nothing there I can use. Pray, go on with the next volume. You will have to translate for me, if you would be so kind."

The second book confirmed her guess, as it was another treatise on an occult subject, this time printed in Gothic black-letter German, and of a more recent date. She read as she was accustomed to, given an unfamiliar text; when she encountered a phrase she did not immediately understand, she read it aloud in the original, then puzzled it through aurally. Cameron did not correct this habit; evidently he approved of it, for once or twice he suggested an alternative translation that made a great deal more sense in the context of the book — though not a great deal of sense in terms of the real world.

"The next section," she said, when she had finished the portion marked, "is entitled 'An den Seele' — if that is of any interest to you?"

She was beginning to enjoy her new duty, odd though the subject of her reading was. "Not particularly," was the response. "Pray continue with the next volume. May I say you have a particularly pleasant voice? This is proving to be as pleasurable as it is instructive."

"Thank you," she replied, surprising herself with a

blush. By this time, the light outside had faded into dusk, although she had not thought it that late when she broke her fast. She must have slept far longer than she had thought. On the other hand, if these were Jason Cameron's preferred hours, she might as well get used to them now.

She was halfway through the stack of books when Cameron himself called a halt. She reckoned that she must have read at least a hundred pages in that time, perhaps more. Her throat was certainly getting dry, and she was conscious of increasing hunger.

"Your voice is a trifle hoarse; I detect that you are in need of a rest. Have you any notion what time it is?"

"Candidly, no," she admitted. "I am afraid I do not possess a watch, and there doesn't seem to be a clock in these rooms." It had not occurred to her before, but that was a rather odd omission.

But apparently it was an accidental one, for he made a sound of chagrin. "I do apologize; I shall remedy both conditions immediately." There was a sound of scraping, as if something heavy had been dragged across the floor. It did *not* come from overhead, but rather through the speaking-tube only, which told her that wherever Cameron's rooms were, they were *not* above her own. "It appears to be approximately nine o'clock," he said after a lengthy pause. "Would you prefer to dine in your rooms or in the dining room? There are no other guests, nor, since my accident, are there likely to be, but you may care for a change of scene."

The thought of sitting at a long, empty table was a bit daunting. She shivered just a little; she would feel *precisely* like a heroine in a haunted romance. "In my rooms, if you please," she told him. "In fact, if it is convenient, I should like to take all my meals here, except for the odd *al fresco* picnic lunch if the weather is fine. I am in the habit of taking long walks," she added, warningly. "Exercise is valuable for sharpening the mind."

If he was going to try to keep her penned up in here, he would surely object at this point. But he didn't. "Healthy mind, healthy body, hmm?" he said with amusement. "The Greeks would approve, and so do I. It is quite convenient, actually, and I am sure my servants would prefer the arrangement. Simply let my housekeeper know with a note if you intend such excursions, and there will be a luncheon made up and waiting at the front door. I shall also see that you have a rough map of the area. You don't by any chance ride, do you?"

"Actually, no," she admitted. "I was raised in Chicago and never had occasion to learn."

"What, so you are not perfect, after all?" he replied with a hint of mockery. "A pity; my horse could use another to exercise him besides Paul and the stableman. Well, you shall have to content yourself with enjoying my little wilderness afoot. I am afraid I cannot recommend my steed for the inexperienced; he requires a rider who knows what she is about. And for now — I suggest that you might stretch your limbs in exploring the house a bit while I have Paul organize a dinner for both of us, and remedy the shocking lack of timepieces in your rooms."

"Thank you, sir," she replied, getting to her feet a bit stiffly. "I believe I shall do precisely that."

Just at the moment she felt a decided aversion to encountering the so-superior secretary; on the whole, if she met him, she would rather it was on neutral ground rather than in her own rooms. Besides, this was an open invitation to be as inquisitive as she cared to, and devil if she wasn't going to take advantage of it!

For one thing, she rather thought she would like to try and puzzle out just where her employer was

speaking from. It wasn't from overhead, and yet
the voice coming from the speaking tube was strong
and clear, so his own rooms could not be located too
far away.

Directly beneath her, perhaps? That would be
logical. It would also be reassuring. She really would
rather that he were not above or to either side. Secret
passages were one thing; peepholes, however, were
ridiculously easy to contrive. He might be able to spy
on her from any direction but below; even an occultist
would have difficulty seeing through a thick Oriental
rug laid down over carpet as the ones in her rooms
were.

She left her door standing open, so that Paul du
Mond would know that she was not in her rooms, and
considered her direction.

*Down the hall, I suppose. I might as well discover
what is on this floor before I go on.*

The hallway proved to be singularly devoid of
entertainment. The doors leading from it all opened on
suites as lushly appointed as her own, and all were
unlocked. Each had a unique flavor or color-scheme;
one was Chinese and a pale celadon in color, one East
Indian and done up in gold and brown, one appeared
to have a Russian theme, complete with icons and
massive samovar and the scheme there was red and
black. The remaining two suites were very nearly the
twins to her own, save that one was decorated in
stark green and silver, which she found rather cold
and repellent, and one was decorated in Cameron's
trademark red and gold, which she found uncom-
fortably lush. Living in the former would have felt like
living underwater, living in the latter like living in a
jewel-box. On the whole she was quite happy with the
choice that had been made for her.

That disposed of this floor. Where Paul du Mond

resided, she did not yet know, but at least there was no possibility of peepholes from either side.

Nor, it seemed, from above; the stairs upward terminated in a series of dark attics which she did not care to penetrate. So, that left below — and there were two floors to explore yet that she knew of.

The second floor was something of a disappointment, and yet it did tell her that this was, indeed, where Jason Cameron laired. Beyond the door on the landing was a kind of anteroom, decorated with black marble statuary in niches. Again the color scheme was red and gold, with three doors leading from it, one in each wall; all three were locked.

At least now I know where you are, Jason Cameron, she thought with satisfaction as she turned and descended the stairs to the first floor.

By the time she finished exploring that floor, she had the feeling she ought to be returning to her post, or she was likely to find a cold collation instead of a warm dinner. She was more than impressed by what she found on the first floor, which was much more extensive than the third floor would have indicated, as there were three single-storied wings off the main building. She guessed that there might be as much as twelve thousand square feet of floorspace here; she had been in museums that were smaller. Anything that a man of wealth and leisure could possibly have wished was in this house — from a grand ballroom and music room to a smoking room and billiard parlor. The library was enough to make her gasp and grow faint with envy and anticipation. She was doubly glad now that she had indicated a preference for taking her meals in her room; the dining room was echoingly huge, and decorated with the heads of trophy game animals. She was quite sure that she would have quickly developed indigestion with all those glassy eyes staring down at her while she ate.

There was also a conservatory and greenhouse, full of strange plants. That would be a pleasant place to sit or walk when the weather was uncooperative.

There was at least one lamp lit in every room except the ballroom and greenhouse; it must be the whole duty of one servant to see to them. It was a pity that this place was too far from the city to receive either gas or the electric main; she pitied the poor soul who went about cleaning, filling, lighting and extinguishing all those lamps.

On the whole, living here would be rather like living in a palace. She had *heard* that these western rail-barons had built themselves manors to rival the Medicis, and now she was certain this was nothing less than the truth. Why, the expense in lamp-oil alone must rival the total of all of the household bills of any normal household put together!

She hurried her steps as she turned back towards her own suite; the place was so empty it seemed haunted, and just at the moment she wanted the cozy walls of her own domain around her. Obviously Cameron did not ask the servants to keep his hours; they must all have retired for the night. Perhaps there was a separate building as servants' quarters. That might be where Paul du Mond resided.

When she entered her own rooms again, she heaved a sigh of relief, both because she had not encountered du Mond on the way, and because after the huge and lifeless rooms below, this suite seemed a very haven of warmth and welcome.

There were two additions immediately visible; a striking-clock on the mantlepiece, between two silver candlesticks, and one of the domed serving-trays. She seated herself at her little table with alacrity as her stomach had the bad manners to growl, hoping that she had not tarried too long.

Either she had somehow missed du Mond and the

servants by mere minutes, or Cameron's delving into alchemical processes had uncovered some arcane way of keeping food perfect and piping hot for hours. And perhaps he had divined that with a "masculine" mind her culinary preferences were "masculine" as well. This was no dainty lady's dinner of toast and lobster-salad; a savory and hearty platter of rare roast beef, new potatoes, and mixed grilled vegetables awaited her appetite, with caramel flan and a good red wine as accompaniments. There were also a pot of tea, sugar-bowl and a cream-pitcher waiting at the fire, presumably for the ease of her throat, later.

It occurred to her, as she finished her meal, that it was just as well that she was in the habit of taking hearty exercise. If she continued to eat like this without those long walks, she would soon resemble the plumply upholstered sofa!

Now would have been a pleasant time to settle in with a good history and read for leisure — but her duty called, and she would be reading in any case, though it was not what *she* would have chosen. She covered the remains of the meal with the domed lid and returned to her station.

But with the books, she found another new addition, so small she had initially overlooked it. There was a red Morocco-leather box on the table, and when she opened it, she found a lady's chatelaine watch within, complete with neckchain. Both were unique, and clearly from a fine jeweler's stock; the yellow-gold case of the watch was inlaid in white- and rose-gold, in a lovely pattern of climbing roses; the chain was a triple-strand of braided rose-gold, yellow-gold, and white-gold. This was no "gold-filled bargain" from Sears, Roebuck; it was an expensive piece of fine jewelry

For a moment, she was inclined to tell Cameron that she could not accept the gift —

Oh, why not? It wasn't inscribed with a sentiment; there was no note with it. *For all I know, this is the kind of thing he gives his housekeeper for her birthday.* Why balk at a trifle like a watch, when he had already given her an entire new wardrobe?

She picked up the next book in the pile — the ones she had already read were gone — and spoke into the silence. "Mr. Cameron?"

"Miss Hawkins?" the answer came, promptly. "I trust you enjoyed your explorations."

"Very much so. Your home is — is stunning beyond words," she replied honestly. "I cannot imagine that anyone in this area has anything to rival it."

A chuckle. "Oh, there are other homes in San Francisco that are larger — but I flatter myself to think that mine is in better taste. You would not believe the incredible pile my partner Crocker has constructed. I hope you will forgive the watch — I know it is a bit ostentatious, but I happened to have it on hand and could not resist the play on your Christian name. If you would rather have something plainer I shall have to have Paul look further in the safe — but this does suit your new wardrobe, you will have to admit."

"You have me at a disadvantage, for I must agree with you." Oh, she was enjoying fencing with words with this man! He was probably unprincipled in many ways, possibly without morals to speak of, but he was witty and intelligent, and he gave her the accolade of treating her as equal in intelligence. "There; now you know another weakness of mine, I am vain, and I fear, greedy as a child for pretty things. Greedy enough to accept your ostentatious gift. Thank you." *There. I have said it, so you cannot assume superiority.*

"You are welcome." Another chuckle. "It is very refreshing to find someone who knows when blunt and plain speaking can be as clever a weapon as dissimulation. Touche. Now, if you are ready to begin?"

"I am," she said, with a chuckle of her own, and resumed her task, pouring herself a cup of tea and adding cream and sugar in the English style, to ease her voice.

It was past one by both the watch and the clock when she finished, and she was suppressing yawns as she closed the last book. "Miss Hawkins, you give me cause to rejoice that you accepted my offer," came the harsh voice from the speaking-tube. "And now, I shall leave you to your virtuous rest. Good night."

"Good night, Mr. Cameron," she replied, as she drank the last of her tea. "I am looking forward with curiosity to see what you shall have unearthed for me to read to you tomorrow."

If he chuckled at that sally, she did not hear it; she had already moved to blow out the lamps and leave the fire to burn itself out.

Once again, a silk nightdress had been laid out for her on the invitingly-turned-down bed. She wavered between bed and bath, and finally her yawns overcame her. *I can bathe in the morning,* she told herself, as she stepped out of her clothing and left it lying, neatly folded, on the chair beside her bed. The cool silk of the nightdress against her skin only confirmed the rightness of her decision in her own mind.

This might have been a mistake — but she didn't think so. If Jason Cameron happened to be slightly crazed, well, then so were thousands of others, who went to Spiritualist meetings and flocked to hear Madame Blavatsky. What harm was there in his seeking some redress for an intolerable situation? And what harm was there in her aiding and abetting that search? Clearly, she amused him, and that in and of itself was healthy for him. Better that he should take amusement in her audacity than that he should sink into apathy and despair.

With that comforting thought, she fell asleep, with the bedcurtains drawn securely about her and the watch ticking quietly away beside her glasses on the nightstand.

CHAPTER FOUR

Cameron the Firemaster watched his newest acquisition in his mirror as she read to him, unaware she was being observed. Here in his own domain he had no need of the Salamander's aid to watch whomever he chose; the mirrors were his eyes, mirrors formed in the white-heat of his furnaces and enchanted before they cooled. Needless to say, he had mirrors everywhere, though he chose not to activate the ones in her bathroom. He was no voyeur, at least not of innocents.

And she was innocent, despite her intellect and all her reading. He found that both charming and touching. How like the Tarot card she was, of the Wise Fool, full of knowledge and utterly unworldly! How easily she could be led to a fall, unaware and unwary of the precipice, of the void gaping beneath her feet!

The Salamander watched her too, dancing above its volcanic mirror as he watched her in the mirror of man-made glass. "She is more attractive, properly dressed," it said, sounding surprised. "Even with the glasses."

"There is nothing unattractive about a woman with glasses," he snapped sharply. "A woman who is neither self-conscious about them, nor a prim and prudish old maid, wears such objects as any other accessory, and they become a statement of strength and character."

Now why had he leapt to her defense like that?

*Perhaps because she impresses me. I had expected a
mouse; I have been given a lioness. I prefer the lioness;
it will be a challenge to keep her tame and choosing to
come to my hand.*

She had certainly stood up to him with spirit and wit. *"I
know in precise detail what Caligula did to, and with, his
sisters, and I can quote it to you in Latin or my own
translation if you wish."* How many other women would
have *dared* to make a statement like that? How many
could have done so without stammers or blushes? How
many would have accepted his gift and laughingly told him
they were greedy for pretty things, daring him to think of
her as an opportunist? Oh, it was a valuable gift, but less
valuable than the furs and jewels he had flung at his light
ladies. Yet he could not have given her less, and what other
women would have faced him the way she had?

None, in his acquaintance. Rosalind Hawkins was
unique. And even when the passages she read held
nothing of value for him, he preferred to let her read
on to the end, enjoying the sound of her voice, the
cadence of her words.

Unfortunately, his memory had proved to be faulty in
regards to the books he had chosen for her to read today.
There were only one or two passages burned into the
oversized pages of the special book he'd had constructed,
a book with tabs at each page so that his misshapen paws
could turn them. He would do better tomorrow.

On the other hand, his choice of books was not
entirely due to his own needs. He would be educating
her in the ways of Magick as she read, tutoring her
with his selections. By the time she was ready for the
books he *truly* needed to have her read aloud, she
would no longer be surprised by anything she read to
him. She might well be repulsed, but she would not be
surprised, and she had already proved to him that she
could face what repulsed her without flinching.

"We like her," the Salamander said, unexpectedly. "There is Fire in her, though she is mostly Air. Fire and Air dancing together; it is a goodly dance."

Oh? It wasn't often that the Salamander volunteered anything. It wasn't in its nature to volunteer information, or even an opinion.

Now Cameron knew something he hadn't known before; Rosalind's Magickal Nature. That was useful; knowing her Nature would make it easier to predict what she would do, how she would react, what things would move her.

That also explained why she settled in so quickly, why she reacted so positively to the house. It also explained why she seemed to prefer the colors in the suite he had given over to her to the colors of the others. If she had been primarily a Water woman, she would have favored either the Chinese suite or the Emerald suite; if Earth, the Indian. A true Fire woman would have instantly sought the Russian or the Ruby suite, and asked for her rooms to be changed.

Interesting. Very interesting. What a pity he had not encountered her before!

Perhaps it was just as well. He could be amused and entertained by her without worrying about anything else. Attractions of the flesh had their place, but not when mixed with the Great Work.

"Paul doesn't like her," the Salamander volunteered again, surprising Cameron all over again.

"Paul's opinion was not asked for," the Firemaster said, coldly. "It is of no value. Paul believes that he will become a Master because he deserves to be one, not because he is willing to study, work, and sacrifice. Paul is a fool."

"Paul is dangerous," the Salamander warned, spinning a little before subsiding again.

"I know. A dangerous fool and therefore not to be

trusted, and I do not trust him with anything of importance." Cameron had once had hopes for Paul du Mond, but the man was lazy, and so had been given everything material he wanted, but no more power than any other menial. "Is he a danger to Rosalind?"

The Salamander laughed unexpectedly, a sound of tiny silver bells chiming. "She is too clever for him, and she does not like him. He can neither deceive her nor seduce her. He reminds her of someone unpleasant, but she does not yet remember who, so she does not know why she dislikes him."

"Good." He was relieved, and told himself that it was because this woman was too valuable to lose just at the moment.

"Why did you give her the watch?" it asked, with childlike curiosity and childlike candor. "It is very costly by the standards she is accustomed to."

He laughed at its boldness. "It is my collar of ownership," he told his creature. "Through it, I can follow her, no matter where she goes; I can hear what she hears and see what she sees. When she enters the city, if any of my rivals or fellows see her, they will know she is mine and not meddle with her."

"Even Simon?" the Salamander asked.

"Especially Simon," he replied, his voice turning as hard as tempered steel. Simon Beltaire was the only other Firemaster on this coast, and there was no love lost between the two of them. Fortunately, the accident notwithstanding, he had not lost any of his powers, or Simon Beltaire would not have hesitated to challenge him.

Just as, were their positions reversed, he would not have hesitated in challenging Simon. There could not be two Firemasters in the same city. He would rather there were not two in the same state. Eventually, one of them would go — living or dead, one would go.

❖ ❖ ❖

Rosalind was nearing the end of the last passage in the last book; soon it would be time to send her off to bed. He had enjoyed watching her as she read; she made a very pretty picture in the lamplight. How pleasant that she had turned out to be ornamental as well as useful! And possessed of good taste, fully the match of his own, he suspected. He had feared he would be forced to manipulate her choices of gowns; instead, she had made a choice that was as tasteful as anything he would have chosen, and yet was not what he would have chosen for her.

Should he order a Worth gown for her? He had never met a woman in San Francisco worthy of a gown from the house of Worth. *Perhaps, when I have been restored . . . when I am prepared to show myself to the city again, to take my box at the Opera. I wonder what sort of a companion would she make?*

Then he chided himself for even thinking the idle thought. This woman was no potential companion. She was no demimonde, not to be used only for pleasure.

And before I ended my Apprenticeship I gave up the romantic nonsense of finding a female to share the Work with me as well as my life. There is no such creature, and never can be. Rosalind Hawkins was a worthy *tool*, and as such, she must be cherished, honed, cared for, and put away when the task for which she had been brought was at an end. She must be sent somewhere as far away as possible. She herself might not know what she had done for him, but anyone who knew him would be able to deduce it with careful questioning.

She will have a sizable bank account, a fine wardrobe, possibly a generous bonus, and an excellent letter of recommendation. She will have the where-withal to do whatever she pleases. Perhaps it would even be wise to send her on a trip to Europe out of "gratitude." That would remove her — and her curiosity — from his life quite painlessly. He could arrange for the trip to return her to Chicago, where she could resume her studies. Or better yet, he could arrange for her to be admitted to one of the great universities of England or Europe. France, perhaps; with the example of Madame Curie before them, the French knew how to treat a woman scholar. Or Oxford; women were making great progress there.

That would be best. The one thing he dared not do would be to leave her where Simon might be able to find her and learn what she had been doing for him. It would tell him altogether too much about what had been going on in this house.

Definitely a trip to Europe. Perhaps I should arrange a romance?

He could do it; once he was back to his old self, his powers would reach that far — and the Firemaster held mastery over the hot passions.

No. No, she would be too wise to be carried away by an impulse, however romantic.

She finished the book and put it carefully down, taking care not to mar it. Interesting that he had seen her mostly in profile this evening. Most women turned towards mirrors as towards the light; she seldom glanced at the mirror in her parlor and then only by accident.

He bade her good night, then silently ordered the vision in the obsidian to fade.

On the whole, he was far happier with the results of this venture than he had any right to anticipate. Rosalind Hawkins was a redoubtable woman, pleasant to look upon, and quite self-possessed, although she had no idea of her real ability or her potential. He would not have to worry about keeping an eye on her every waking moment — not only because it was clear that she could amuse and defend herself, but because it was also clear that she was not the kind to be ruled by the busy-body curiosity that was the ruin of so many of her sex. He had watched her in his mirrors as she explored his house; when a door was locked, she left it alone. She did not try to force the lock, she did not stoop to peer through the keyhole, she did not listen at the crack. She assumed it was locked for a reason, assumed that the reason was no business of hers, and went on her way. Too many women made it their obsession to find out the heart of every secret. She was content to let secrets remain secrets.

It was a pity that she did not ride, though. He would have been happy to see her take Sunset out; Paul could not ride the stallion without a curb bit and he would not permit any such device of torture to go in Sunset's tender mouth. If a man could not guide a horse by neck and knee, he did not deserve to ride anything more than a mule.

Sunset can wait until I am myself again. He gets enough exercise in the field. He will not suffer for not being ridden.

"Well," the Salamander said, interrupting his thoughts. "Now what have you in mind?"

"See to it that those book catalogs I mentioned are on her desk in the morning," he replied. "Clean up the rooms as soon as she is asleep. I suspect she is going to want to look at the grounds tomorrow, so have a map waiting for her with the catalogs, and see that a luncheon is prepared for her if she decides to walk out. You know the rest."

"Have breakfast waiting when she wakes; tidy the rooms when she is gone." The Salamander spun lazily. "What books do we leave her?"

"I will choose them tonight, before I retire." That would be best. "I will tell you what chapters to mark."

It was a shame that the Salamander could not read; if it could, all of this nonsense could have been done away with.

Then again, he would not have had Rosalind here. The Salamander was occasionally amusing, occasionally surprising, but it took another living human to be a consistent challenge.

Rosalind Hawkins was a challenge; it would be a challenge to educate her, a challenge to keep her unaware of what she was capable of while nurturing that capability. It would be a real challenge to mold her while keeping her ignorant of the fact. It occurred to him that he had been in danger of losing himself to despair and ennui before her arrival. He was certainly in no such danger now.

He raised a glass in his clumsy paw to the obsidian that had so lately held her image. "Welcome, Rosalind Hawkins," he murmured. "May you never fail to surprise me."

When she woke, it was with a feeling of delight, of giddiness. She had thrown all caution to the wind; she had taken a position no prudent woman would have accepted. She might be mad — but she felt truly alive for the first time since she was accepted into graduate studies.

She reached automatically for her glasses —

And they danced just out of reach as the bed and nightstand shook.

She grabbed for them and caught them somehow before they hit the floor. Just as her hand touched them, the shaking stopped.

It took her a moment to realize that she had just been through an earthquake, and it was not her knowledge of the present that allowed her to identify what it was, but her knowledge of the past. *Vesuvius. Pompeii.* There had been Roman accounts of Pompeii, Herculaneum —

For a moment, her imagination took over. At least, she *thought* it was her imagination. The blue blur of the room vanished; she saw fires, people fleeing, screaming, and fire everywhere; for that moment, she even felt the flames hot on her own skin.

She saw herself on her knees beside victim after helpless victim, some crushed, some burned beyond recognition; saw herself trying desperately to help those who were beyond aid, or who perished beneath her hands. She felt the terrible despair of one who knows what she does is futile, and yet cannot, in the face of such pathos and need, stay her attempts to *do* something.

But no matter what she did, her actions were as chaff in the whirlwind. The destruction about her was too great, and her two hands too few. Still, defiant in the cause of life, she continued to try as the flames bore down upon her and those still trapped, screaming, in the ruins.

There are no volcanoes here, she chided herself. *I am not about to find myself in a hail of cinders! It was only an earthquake, and there are earthquakes here all the time. This is not ancient Rome! In this modern age, our buildings are proof against the worst that Nature can send.*

But there was a hollow place where her stomach should have been, and for long moments more, as she seized her glasses and settled them carefully on her face, her hands trembled.

But when she entered her sitting room to find breakfast waiting for her, she had regained her composure, and her knees no longer felt like water. She was looking forward to exploring the house and grounds further, especially the grounds, and to that end had donned a smart walking-suit of sapphire-blue silk-broadcloth, a pale blue silk waist with a hunting-stock tied about the neck, and low-heeled walking shoes. Beside the tray holding her meal were the pile of book-catalogs that Cameron had promised her, and a map showing the grounds. Beside the table was a basket just large enough to hold a picnic luncheon for one.

Just as he had promised.

A quick glance at her new watch told her that there would be plenty of time to explore before Cameron needed her services. The only question was — inside, or out? There was a great deal about the house she had only glimpsed last night; she would like to see it all in daylight.

But the sun shining warmly outside her window made up her mind immediately. If all she had heard was true, bright, sunny days were not all that frequent in this season. She should take advantage of this one. Tomorrow it might rain; she could explore the mansion then.

She hurried through her breakfast and took up the basket. The map showed her a side entrance not far from the staircase on the first floor, letting out near the stables for the benefit of those who wanted to take an early-morning ride; she would take that. She felt shy about confronting any more of Cameron's strange servants — people who could slip in and out of a room without her even hearing a footfall or people like Paul du Mond.

Especially people like Paul du Mond.

A breeze of no particular direction swirled around her as she stepped out into the sunshine, tugging her skirt around her ankles. She smiled and kicked free, turning at the same time to her right as movement attracted her attention.

The stable lay to her left, a building that could well have been mistaken for a fine home, painted in the traditional red with white trim and surrounded by white-painted fences. Behind it lay a forest of dark green trees, through which wind played, bringing her the scent of the woodland. In the middle of a lushly green field attached to the stable, surrounded by a wooden fence painted so pure a white that it hurt the eyes, a horse reared and danced with the breeze. Rose was not familiar enough with horses to know what kind he was, but it was clear to even the amateur eye that this was a stallion, and an extremely expensive one. His coat gleamed a pure copper, his mane and tail a fiery bronze; his muscles rippled beneath the shining coat with every move he made, and he was more alive than any other horse she had ever seen. He reared again, pawing playfully at the breeze, then glanced at her as she drew nearer the fence, attracted by his vibrant vitality. His dark eyes flashed, and she could have sworn he was laughing as he settled again on four hooves and whirled, neck curved in a perfect arch and tail flagged, turning towards her.

Fascinated and entranced by the beautiful stallion, she did not realize that she was walking towards the fence until she actually ran into it. The horse danced sideways towards her, as daintily as any ballet dancer, stopping just out of reach, where he posed as if perfectly well aware how lovely he was, and intending to show off for his appreciative audience.

"That's Sunset," said a dry tenor behind her. "Or, strictly speaking, 'Cameron's Fiery Sunset,' a pure Arab from a line that reaches back farther than your lineage and mine put together, imported at immense expense from somewhere near Mecca. Pampered beyond belief. Only Jason can ride him, of course."

She did not have to turn to know that Paul du Mond had once again approached her without her realizing it. Her shoulders tensed, and her hands clenched on the wicker handle of the basket. She did not know *why* she was developing such an aversion to the man, but every time she encountered him, that distaste grew more pronounced. "Oh?" she replied, without turning. "I wouldn't know an Arab stallion from a plowhorse, but even I can tell he's beautiful."

The horse stared at a point behind her, and gave a snort that sounded disgusted, although she would not ordinarily have attributed an emotion to an animal. He kicked up his heels and pranced away to the far side of the enclosure, where he resumed his dance with the breeze, glancing from time to time at her and ignoring Paul du Mond disdainfully.

Du Mond laughed, a sound with no humor in it. "He doesn't like me, and I'm afraid it's mutual. He was a gift from some Arabian chieftain, or whatever they call themselves. He was escorted here by a half a dozen of the nastiest-looking barbarians you ever could imagine, bedecked with flowing robes and great, curved swords, and evil expressions. While they were here, they lived in a tent on the lawn and took time out for praying to Mecca ten times a day. I'm told the horse had his own cabin on the boat that brought him to New York; he certainly had his own special car on the train that took him from there to here. Walnut and redwood interior, special spring-water to drink, and every strand of hay and oat he was fed examined by his entourage before he was given it."

"Really." If Cameron went to all that trouble for a mere horse — well, now she had some notion of her position in the scheme of things. Oddly enough, that was comforting. The less extraordinary Cameron's attentions, the better she liked the situation.

I am a pair of eyes and a voice, and that is all he needs of me. Good. She had rather be an object of utility than of interest. The one thing she did *not* want was for Cameron to take her for anything other than — say — a colleague.

Du Mond finally came up beside her and leaned on the fence, ostensibly watching the horse. "There are hundreds of children in the city that have less spent on their welfare than Sunset — and all for a horse that no one can ride since Jason's . . . accident." He cast a sardonic glance at Rose. "Jason is like that; if something benefits him personally, then he spares no expense on it, but if it's for anyone else's well-being, unless their welfare helps him in some way — well, that's just too bad." The man shrugged. "He's peculiar in other ways, too; he has odd interests and odder habits. He's got some notions many people would find unsettling. And some would say that he is dangerous."

"Oh?" She kept her attention on the horse. While she did not know a great deal about animals, she had noticed that they tended to reflect the way they were treated in the way they behaved. This was an animal that had never known a harsh word or a blow when young, and even now feared no one and nothing. He had never been mistreated, only controlled, which was interesting in itself. She knew many, many men who, to prove that they could, would have "broken" a horse like this one. She guessed that Paul du Mond was one of them.

Another of those oblique glances came her way. "He likes to own people as well as things; he likes to control them. When he can't, he prefers to make certain no one else ever can or will."

She echoed his earlier shrug, and said nothing. Du Mond waited for her to say something, then suddenly conjured up a charming manner and ingratiating smile.

"I'm sure you've met men like him before, so that hardly surprises you," he said, as he edged a little closer to her. She pretended to adjust her skirt to give herself the excuse to step away, keeping him at the same distance as before. "Powerful men tend to use their power without thinking it might crush those beneath them. We underlings have to remember our place, but it always helps to have someone about who knows how to handle an employer, don't you think? Jason has some strange talents, and stranger friends than that Arab to help him enforce his will; it's best to be warned in advance, it seems to me."

"I suppose so; I've never been an employee before," she replied without committing herself. *If I was as foolish as he seems to think I am, to be won over by a charming smile and a comradely manner, I might even believe what he's saying.* Now, finally, she realized who he reminded her of: a particularly facile graduate student who had been everyone's friend — and who had used his ability to ingratiate himself with people to crib shamelessly from their research.

She had heard things like this, before. Like Paul du Mond, Steven Smythe-David had also hinted darkly of conspiracies among the other students and even the professors, conspiracies aimed at "eliminating the competition."

She had been one of the first to be taken in, but fortunately she was quick to recognize her own researches when she saw them in someone else's presentation; particularly when she knew that *he* had never read a single one of the medieval letters he had quoted. All of her weeks of research had been for nothing, since he was as quick to write a paper as he was to steal the work, and beat her by a good week.

She might have allowed the friendship to persist anyway because he had also pretended to the beginnings of a romantic interest. She even started to convince herself that if his interest went far enough, marriage was an option. She toyed with the notion of making a husband and wife partnership with him. *She* would conduct the research, and he would write the papers. Of course, she would get no credit, but that was no new thing; many men of science and letters had similar arrangements with their wives, if the wife had a scholarly bent . . . and certainly, this was often the only way that a woman's research would ever be given credence.

Then she realized that such an arrangement would be nothing less than absolute falsehood. Her realization coincided with the point when her father's fortunes went into decline, and there were no more gowns, parties, or opera excursions, only economy after economy. When her money evaporated, so did Steven's interest in her. When he ceased to call, she was hurt for a while, but not deeply, and she soon got over it when she saw what a shallow creature he was.

She had thought about warning some of the other students when he began approaching them, but they had treated her so shabbily that she decided to have a subtle sort of revenge by letting them find out for themselves why this charming fellow had decided to cultivate a friendship.

And they did, as Steven presented paper after purloined paper, the spread of his subjects seemingly demonstrating a great breadth of expertise and interest. One of the professors even remarked in ignorance that Steven showed enough knowledge for ten people.

Of course he did, since he was cribbing from ten people. Once Steven had presented *his* paper, of course, none of those he had defrauded could present their own without it looking as if they had cribbed from him instead of the other way around. Eventually he was caught and expelled, but she guessed that he had probably gone on to another university to begin the same game all over again — and eventually, he would get his degree out of his machinations. And then — probably a professorship, where he would bungle his way through teaching unsuspecting undergraduates the rudiments of classical literature. Half of what he taught would be wrong, but they would never know that, having no interest in the subject beyond passing the course. He would probably woo and wed the daughter of a wealthy man or of the president of the college, and so settle himself comfortably for life. He would exert himself only enough to see that his life was comfortable with a minimum of effort required to keep it that way.

Physically, Paul du Mond *looked* nothing like Steven, who had been the tall, athletic, hearty and flaxen-haired collegiate to the core. That was what had kept her from recognizing the similarity at first. Perhaps it was his tone, perhaps something in the way he gestured; perhaps it was something else entirely — but now that she had the reference, her instinctive urge not to trust him had something she could base it on, and she was not about to let him charm her.

Much less seduce me, she thought grimly. But she allowed none of this to show, as she eased herself a little further away from him. "Well, although my duties will not commence until after dinner, I am sure I am keeping *you* from very important work, Mr. du Mond," she said lightly, swinging her basket in the hand nearest him to keep him from making the excuse to pick it up and carry it for her, and to force him to keep his distance. After all his hints about how important he was to Jason Cameron, he could hardly reverse himself and claim he had plenty of time to waste now! "I have a great desire to view the ocean, since I have never seen it this closely before. I'll be getting along now, so that I can be back before sunset. Good afternoon!"

And with that, she struck off down the path that the map said eventually led to the sea, leaving du Mond staring after her. Evidently he had never been cut dead quite so cleverly before; she'd left him speechless.

Perhaps now he thinks that I am even more foolish than I seem! She had no objection to that — provided he did not think that would make her easier to seduce.

Not that I have any illusions about my beauty — or rather, lack of it. But so far she had seen no other females about, and had certain knowledge only of the housekeeper, who was presumably of middle age or older. Hardly competition —

Assuming I was competing. She was not that desperate to change her single status.

Her path led beside the fence for a goodly way, and the horse left off his wind-dancing to trot along beside her, giving every evidence of enjoying her company. She had no objection, particularly if Sunset's presence would ensure du Mond's absence.

"I wish I knew how to ride," she said aloud to the frisking stallion. "I think you might let *me* on your back."

The horse bobbed his head wildly, for all the world as if he was answering her in the affirmative, and she had to laugh aloud. "Perhaps Mr. Cameron will get you a nice little mare to keep you company, and you can settle down together," she said lightly. "Be good, Sunset. I will try to remember to bring you an apple next time."

Her path left the fenced-in field and plunged into a stand of lush trees at that point, and she left the horse standing at the fence, watching wistfully after her. Doubtless, he was longing for a good gallop outside of the fences. She felt cooler air close around her as she entered the shadows of the forest, and was glad she had worn clothing appropriate to the chill.

The path was well-groomed and she had no fear of losing her way, although it turned and twisted so many times she quite lost track of where on it she was supposed to be. The noise of the sea grew louder, so she knew she had to be going in the right direction, but she did not know if she would come upon the shore in another few feet or another half mile.

But there was another surprise waiting for her, as she broke at last into the open. A stretch of perhaps twenty yards of closely cropped turf lay between her and nothingness. Although the path did, indeed, lead to the sea, it gave out on a cliff overlooking waves pounding the shore far beneath her.

Seagulls hung in the air at the level of her eyes, hardly bothering to move more than a wingtip to keep themselves aloft, as a strong wind along the cliff-face did all of the work of flying for them. Below her, at the foot of a rocky escarpment, waves crashed against tumbled rock and sent spray halfway up the face of the cliff. There was a scrap of a beach down there as well, and what appeared to be a path leading up. She was not adventurous enough to care to trust it.

She walked cautiously to the very edge and looked down. It was several stories'-worth, at least, in height. It felt for a moment as if *she* were swaying, and she backed hastily away.

"Well," she said aloud, "if there were ever a place for a picnic more picturesque than this, *I* have never seen it. What's more, I'm hungry."

She checked the map again to make sure that she wasn't inadvertently trespassing, before settling in. A group of rocks made a convenient shelter from the wind, and in their lee side, the sun had soaked into them until they were quite comfortably warm. She spread out her napkin and the contents of the basket, and proceeded to enjoy herself. Once again, someone had anticipated her taste. There were no ladylike cress and cucumber dainties in this luncheon, but a thick slice of honey-cured ham on more of that tangy bread, garnished with lettuce and a hearty mustard, and accompanied by good sharp cheese and soft rolls. A bottle of lemonade was more welcome than wine would have been with a long walk in front of her. The only concession to femininity was a delicate jam tart.

When she had finished, she amused herself by flinging the remains of the rolls to the gulls. Although they were probably unused to being fed by humans, it did not take long for such supreme scavengers to grasp the fact that she was throwing edibles over the side of the cliff. Before long, they were swooping in and catching what she tossed long before it reached the foaming sea below.

The edge of the cliff seemed quite open in either direction, although the coastline made such twists and turns that it was not possible to see anything past the nearest promontories. But if she followed the coastline north, she would, eventually, come to San Francisco. It would take a long time to walk there, particularly if she was burdened with a valise, but Jason Cameron did not have her trapped while she had two feet and shoe leather to cover them.

She did not need to consult the map again; there were no paths leading here other than the one she had taken. She lingered a while longer to give Paul du Mond ample opportunity to take himself about his business, then returned along the way she had come. There had been an apple among the luncheon things; remembering her promise to Sunset, she had not eaten it, but had tucked it back into the basket.

She was irrationally pleased when Sunset greeted her with a friendly whicker and trotted up to her *before* she presented him with the apple. Of course, he could have scented it —

Nevertheless, the feeling of his soft, warm lips on her palm as he gently took pieces from her made her smile, and when he followed along beside her like a puppy as she headed back towards the house, she smiled even more. If *only* she knew how to ride! But she was not foolish enough to dare putting a saddle on a stallion that no one but Cameron could ride, no matter how gentle and friendly the horse seemed!

It was just about sunset when she reached her room, leaving the basket just outside her door for one of the invisible servants to take away. There was a hot dinner waiting for her — one of the servants must have seen her feeding Sunset — and she found that she was starving although it seemed as if she had just eaten lunch. According to her watch, it had taken two hours to stroll down to the sea, but three to return, and the return trip had been all uphill.

It's just a good thing that I'm used to walking — and I am still going to feel the results of my bravado in the morning, she thought as she attacked her meal with zest. *Chicago is not known for its hills, after all!*

She had just enough time by her watch to tidy up before her evening session of reading. She found, once she had done so, that she was a hundred times more relaxed than she ever recalled being for the past three years and more.

Well, she thought, as she lit the reading-lamp and waited for the voice of her employer to request the first book of the night, *Perhaps there is something to be said for jumping off into the unknown, after all. What you cannot anticipate, you cannot dread.*

As always, the study was in darkness except for a lamp, glowing under its heavy red-velvet shade. Jason

Cameron folded his misshapen paws together beneath the shelter of his desk and regarded his employee and putative Apprentice with what he hoped was an icy calm. Of course, the lupine mask that was now his face was not well suited to expressing subtleties; if he was not in a deep and fiery rage, he tended to look calm and unruffled. But although Paul du Mond was a lazy fool he was not an unobservant lazy fool, and the less Paul knew, the better.

The younger man was dressed impeccably as usual, in an expensive tailored suit that Cameron's money had furnished, silk tie held with the diamond pin that was all that was left of his own "fortune." His handsome face bore an expression of dissatisfaction that he attempted to cover with an imperfect mask of deference.

Jason already knew about the encounter at the stable, but he was waiting to see if Paul reported it. If he did, well and good. If he did not — he would bear closer watching than Cameron had anticipated.

"Oh — and I met with Miss Hawkins just outside Sunset's paddock," du Mond said casually. "She was carrying a basket, so I assumed you knew she was going wandering and arranged for a luncheon." The slight rise of his eyebrow turned that into a question.

He nodded.

Du Mond frowned. "Do you think that's entirely wise? She might encounter one or more of your neighbors —"

Cameron laughed. "And what harm could that possibly do? What is wrong with my engaging another servant?"

But Du Mond grimaced. "She is not precisely a servant," the man pointed out. "Nor is she a guest. And she is unchaperoned."

The Firemaster shrugged. "She will style herself as such if she is wise and wishes to preserve her reputation.

She won't tell anyone that she is here alone and unchaperoned. If she's foolish enough to do so, she will brand herself as one of my *demimonde* ladies, and my very proper neighbors will have nothing whatsoever to do with her. If she does not make that mistake, they will assume she is here with the appropriate protections and will not feel any great impetus to place themselves in the position of protector. The one thing I cannot be accused of is taking advantage of an innocent. All of my light-of-loves have been well-known professional ladies, and while my neighbors may find this a bit fast, they also feel it is to be expected in a vigorous man in my position. Moreover, since they have persisted in flinging their daughters at my head, I assume *my* reputation as a gentleman is intact. They would hardly wish to wed their offspring to a rake."

Du Mond merely grunted, which Cameron took for agreement.

"Did you observe anything unusual about her?" Cameron persisted, curious to see if du Mond had taken note of how positively the stallion had responded.

Du Mond shrugged. "Sunset likes her to the point where he follows her like a puppy, but I don't see that as being very important."

As well not to tell him that Firemaster Prince Ibrahim had told him the stallion was supremely sensitive to personalities and would be a good way to measure whether someone could be trusted. "Animals dote on women," he said dismissively. "It is an indication of their more primitive nature."

When Paul actually smiled and nodded agreement at that piece of balderdash, he had to repress a sigh of disgust. How could he ever have thought the fool had the potential for the Great Magicks? He was facile, yes, and quick — but his fire was all on the surface, with no depth to his personality or his mind. Given fuel, it would burn out and leave no trace of its passing.

Jason Cameron was not going to waste precious fuel. Eventually, he would have to put some thought into finding a way to be rid of the man, but at the moment, Paul was his only access to the outside world.

But if he becomes too troublesome, that can change. I hired Rosalind Hawkins without his help; I could hire an appropriately close-mouthed and discreet manservant the same way. One of the other Elemental Masters might even be willing to help him with the choice of a servant; the local Earthmaster, for instance, who had no interest in Elemental power-struggles and wished only to tend his forest creatures and his garden, dispense herbal medicine, and pursue his charities. Perhaps Ho, the Master of Air — *he* had no love for Simon Beltaire, not after Simon had disfigured him in a quarrel over a Chinese slave-girl. *Or I could buy a Chinese boy, see that he learned English, free him, and educate him. Given the new freedom and luxury he would have with me, he would be more securely mine than if I bound him in chains, and as intensely loyal as a mastiff.*

Definitely a project for the future. And as for Paul — *If only I could interest Simon in him! They deserve each other. A pity that's too dangerous a prospect.*

"Is there anything else that requires my attention?" he asked. Paul shook his head. "Your elemental servants are performing well, your office can tell you how your investments are doing better than I. When are you going to begin teaching me again?"

He had been expecting this; Paul asked the same question once a week. "When you have mastered the Ninth Summons," he replied smoothly. "Until you do that, there is no point in going further, since virtually everything in the next stage requires that Summons or something like it."

Paul pouted; it was not an attractive expression on the face of a grown man. He could not deny the truth of the Firemaster's words, however, for he could see it in the hand-written tomes of Magick for himself, if he cared to look. Now, if Paul's troubles with mastering the Summons had been related to temperament, Cameron would have found an alternative to the course of study he had set for du Mond. But Paul's failures were due entirely to laziness, an unwillingness to sacrifice anything, not even a moment of leisure or a single luxurious meal. The Summons required a fast of seven days and total dedication for a month. Paul had tried numerous shortcuts; he had met with failure. Until he was prepared to conduct the Summons correctly, he would continue to meet with failure.

And since Jason Cameron would be willing to stake his entire fortune that he would *never* take the time and effort to conduct the Summons properly, Paul du Mond would never progress beyond Apprentice. And the most ironic thing of all was that in frantically seeking for the easy path he would waste a hundred-fold the time and effort it would have taken to do the Summons properly.

I hope I can rid myself of him without any . . . unpleasantness. Fortunately, du Mond had no living relations with whom he was still on speaking terms. He had alienated anyone who might ordinarily have felt concern if he vanished without explanation. It would, in fact, be only what most of them expected. Paul had been a clever "confidence artist" when Cameron first encountered him, alternating his time between parting fools from their money by sheer persuasion and by card-sharping. The latter was his court of last resort, as gambling cheaters, even in relatively civilized San Francisco, tended to find themselves facing guns or knives in the hands of very unhappy people.

Paul could not know what Cameron was thinking, but the Firemaster's steady and unflinching gaze clearly made him nervous. He began chattering — mostly making excuses why he had not yet completed the Ninth Summons successfully — and Cameron ignored him.

I believe it is time to persuade him to go away. With a whispered word, he caused the lamps on his desk to flare, so that he was no longer hidden in the shadows of his chair.

Du Mond started, and broke off in the middle of his sentence. A second later, he looked completely composed, but Cameron had seen the fear igniting his eyes for a moment before his mask came down. "I — still have some letters to write for you," du Mond said, his voice trembling ever-so-slightly, although his expression remained bland. "If that is all, I trust you will excuse me?"

Cameron nodded a gracious dismissal, and du Mond took himself out. Did he know, did he guess, that Cameron had Salamanders watching every move he made so long as he was on the grounds? Did he know that every mirror in the house was a pair of eyes for the Master?

Did it matter if he did?

I am bordering on hubris. *Time to remind myself of what that particular vice can bring.*

He stood up and turned towards the wall, reached out a misshapen, hairy paw, and pulled the red-velvet drapery away from the mirror behind his desk, staring unflinchingly into the yellow eyes of his reflection.

Into the face of the beast.

Hubris was what had gotten him here, what had led him to attempt a Magick that was no part of a Firemaster's Disciplines. Hubris left him with paws instead of hands, the mask of a lupine-human hybrid instead of his own face — and beneath the elegant clothing, a half-human body with a garnishing of heavy grey pelt, powerful shoulders, and the indignity of a tail. He stared into his own reflection until his stomach turned, and he let the drapery fall again.

What he had attempted, if it came within any Master's purview, would lie in the realm of the Earthmaster. But no Earthmaster would ever have defied Nature the way he had, in his pride and over-confidence, to warp and twist Nature herself with the most blasphemous spell in all of the grimoires of the medieval magicians of ancient France. If an Earthmaster wished to experience the sensation of being a wolf, he would have sent his spirit to share the body of a real wolf; he would *never* have tried to shape his own body into the form of a gigantic, man-sized wolf.

But Jason was proud of his power, certain of his ability, and had foolishly attempted the old French spell of the lycanthrope, the *loup-garou.*

There were two kinds of werewolves — those who were cursed to change with the moon, and those who could change at will. Jason was hardly likely to endure the first, but the second tempted him.

The spell called for — among other things — a belt made of the skin of a wolf, and Jason had trapped that wolf himself, just as he had gathered the other ingredients personally. There could be no question of their authenticity or purity. He had performed the spell as required — stark naked except for the belt — and he certainly had plenty of experience in correctly following spells.

But something went terribly awry.

He lowered himself carefully down into his chair; his joints did not work quite the same, and his balance was all wrong. Perhaps he would get used to this —

No! he told himself fiercely. *I will* not *get used to this form! I will regain my proper face and body! I will not permit myself to think otherwise!*

But the ghost of the pain of that night thrilled over his nerves as he sat. He had never felt pain so intense in all of his life, as his flesh writhed, melted, reformed — he had endured the pain of molten lava to earn his title of Firemaster, but this was worse agony even than that moment.

He had collapsed, half-conscious, on the floor of his workroom.

He had awakened to find himself, not in the form of a four-legged creature, but in this half-and-half hybrid. And he could not take the belt off to break the spell, because the belt had merged into his own body.

Paul du Mond had found him; Paul was the only human to know his true condition. Cameron had sent his human servants away once he regained his senses and replaced them with Elemental servants; had instructed his underlings to send all business to the house so that he need no longer go into the city. Rosalind was the only person he had told the spurious tale of an accident to — he had not wanted even a hint of his difficulty to reach his enemy.

Nothing he had tried when he awoke or since had broken him free, and he had exhausted his memory of anything even remotely related to the spell. He needed to do research.

And he couldn't even hold his own books, much less turn the pages. His eyes wouldn't focus properly; he had trouble reading even large print, much less the crabbed scrawls of many of the handwritten volumes.

But now he had Rosalind Hawkins to be his eyes and hands — and in fact, to translate those manuscripts he himself would have had difficulty reading. *Now* he could find a solution.

Now the real work could begin.

And as soon as he found his solution, his second act would be to find a way to be rid of Paul du Mond.

CHAPTER FIVE

Paul du Mond had never been so certain of anything in his life as he was certain that Jason Cameron had no intentions of teaching him anything further. As he left the Firemaster's private sanctum and heard the lock clicking shut behind him, he allowed his mask to drop and felt his lips contorting in a silent snarl.

He *knew* why Cameron didn't plan to teach him anything more; the man was afraid that once Paul advanced past the stage of mere Apprentice, he would quickly outstrip his teacher.

Paul's anger ebbed enough that a smirk passed over his lips. Cameron *should* fear him; he had more ambition than the Firemaster, and fewer scruples. Not that there were many who would say that Cameron was anything but *un*scrupulous, but Paul knew his employer, and he knew that there actually were things that Jason Cameron would not do. He would not take advantage of someone who was, in his estimation, truly innocent, for instance. So far as Paul was concerned, the world was against him, and anyone was fair game. No point in thinking anyone was innocent; even the tiniest children were supreme manipulators, using their big eyes and ready tears to extract what *they* wanted from unsuspecting adults. In some ways, the Catholics with their doctrine of Original Sin were more enlightened than the modern scientists.

That fellow Charles Darwin was right; it was a world of fang and claw, and not even infants were innocent, for they were as selfishly interested in survival as any adult. Only the fit survived, or deserved to survive.

The only way of succeeding in the world was to use every weapon at his disposal, use those weapons ruthlessly and without remorse, for without a doubt, given a change in circumstances, those weapons would be used on him by someone else. Paul had seen the truth of that in his own life, which was the surest measure of what was true.

So Cameron did well to fear him, fear what he would do if he ever became the Firemaster's equal. He would not, as Simon did, allow the situation to endure in stalemate. He would eliminate his rival, quickly, and efficiently. Cameron admired the horse — well, Paul admired the shark, the tiger, and the cobra, the most efficient killing machines in Nature. They wasted no motion, no time; if there was a chance to kill when the prey was unaware of the hunter's presence, *that* was the best moment to strike.

He retired to his own quarters and shut the door behind him. As luxurious as he cared to make them, they were no reward — everything in them belonged to Cameron and could be taken back at a moment's notice if du Mond failed to demonstrate the appropriate level of gratitude and servility. There was very little here that was his own, and Cameron never let him forget it. Everywhere he looked he saw Cameron's hand, Cameron's taste, Cameron's signature red and gold. He lived surrounded by those colors, even in his own bedroom, branding him as Cameron's property.

But Cameron was not God and he could not be everywhere; his sure influence extended only as far as the borders of this estate. Now that the man himself was confined, so was his power — and Cameron had taught Paul enough that du Mond knew how to make certain that influence did not follow him when he left the estate.

Cameron's business sent him into San Francisco overnight or for two or three days about once a month. He was due for just such a trip in another few days. With the addition of the girl to the household, the trip might be sooner than usual. There were bound to be things that she needed that Cameron had not thought of, and things that Cameron needed he had not anticipated. There would be "special" packages to deliver, and to pick up.

He would occupy Cameron's city flat most of the time; he would certainly sleep there. But during the day, he would carry out at least one errand of his own.

Just to be ready, tonight before he went to bed he'd pack his valise, so he could leave on a moment's notice.

If Cameron would not teach him, share the Power with him, there was someone else who would.

Paul du Mond went directly to the office attached to his suite. He did have work to do, as he had told Cameron, and he had better get to it in case Cameron could see him. There were books to order, routine business-letters to write, invitations to politely refuse, pleas from various charities to deal with, all the minutiae of a wealthy man's life to handle. Once or twice, something amusing would cross his desk — such as the time that one of Cameron's paid companions tried a spot of blackmail — but mostly it was boring work, which was precisely why Cameron had always left it to him. The important correspondence, such as missives from other Masters, du Mond never saw.

On the desk was one of the new type-writing machines, but tonight du Mond had pushed it aside in favor of pen and ink. Only completely trivial letters were written on the machine; Cameron preferred the personal touch for anything else.

Did the Hawkins girl have as elegant a hand as Paul did? He doubted it. He knew that his calligraphy was so perfect as to seem artificial, and he always knew how to choose precisely the right words, whether dealing with a hopeful clergyman looking for a contributor, or an equally hopeful socialite hoping to attract Jason to her soiree. Perhaps he could not read the manuscripts Cameron needed, but neither could the Hawkins girl replace *him*. Cameron needed his skills too much to be rid of him.

Especially now.

He had learned to keep his feelings hidden around Cameron a long time ago, but he could never look at that strange man-wolf mask without a mingling of fear and satisfaction. The fear was natural enough; how could any sane human look at what the Firemaster had become and not feel fear and revulsion? But satisfaction — that was a bit more complicated. There was certainly satisfaction in seeing how Cameron had at last overreached himself and come to grief. There was more in seeing that now the man's essential nature was reflected in his appearance. Cameron was a predator; well, now he looked like one. There was more satisfaction in knowing that Cameron could no longer be at the center of a glittering round of dinners, theater engagements, and parties. Paul had often seethed with resentment and envy as Cameron took his private railcar into the city for a weekend of amusement; now Cameron was bound more firmly to the estate than he. He held all the cards now, and all the control. Let Cameron go on pretending otherwise; it was Paul who would write the program for this little play.

When the end to this relationship came, it would come when Paul du Mond chose — and in the manner of *his* choosing.

With a smile, he sat down at his desk, removed an

engraved invitation from the waiting basket, and selected a piece of rich, cream-colored paper with Cameron's own watermark.

He dipped a pen into the inkwell, thought for a moment, and wrote the first word of Cameron's gracefully worded refusal of yet another dinner-party.

"I'm going to need you to go into the city for a few days."

Once again, the Firemaster's study was shrouded in darkness although it was a bright afternoon outside, and Cameron himself was nothing more than a darker form amid the shadows of his chair. Du Mond simply nodded.

"You'll take the private carriage," Cameron continued. "You'll be bringing back a quantity of packages for me, and I want you to have somewhere safe to keep them until you return."

That meant he would be picking up occult and Magickal supplies; otherwise he would have brought them to the apartment instead. But Cameron had greater protections on the railway carriage than on the apartment, now. In the past, that had not been the case, but since the accident he could not go into the city to renew the apartment's Shieldings himself, and he did not trust Paul to do so. Now, when he dared not take the risk of an enemy tampering with his belongings, he had Paul use the carriage as his storage-depot.

That was fine with du Mond, since the carriage was infinitely more convenient and comfortable than the small buggy he would otherwise have used. In a downpour, the buggy was decidedly damp and cold, and du Mond did not have the Elemental Mastery required to make it otherwise.

"There are a number of things that will be arriving

by train, so I will need you to remain in the city until they appear," Cameron went on. "You'll use the apartment, of course, and I trust you'll find ways of amusing yourself."

The sardonic tone of his voice said without words just how he expected Paul to amuse himself. It tickled Paul's fancy to know that Cameron hadn't the least idea how far his assumptions were off the mark. Not that he wouldn't have the *kind* of amusement Cameron assumed, but the style would be vastly different from Cameron's own.

Perhaps when he had broken free of Cameron, he'd make his amusements permanent. . . .

Then again, perhaps he'd better not. Slavery was illegal, no matter what the Chinese slave-dealers believed.

Too bad, too.

"These will be complicated errands, and they may take the entire week to complete, so I will not expect you to return for at least five days. If it looks to you as if you may be staying longer than a week, send a messenger, but otherwise don't bother."

Cameron didn't mean a human messenger, of course; Paul had mirror-mastery enough to send a message that way. Paul nodded. "Your correspondence is completely up to date," he offered. "I'm ready to leave."

"Good, then anything that comes in during the week can wait until you return," Cameron replied promptly. "I've already sent down orders to have the carriage ready; it will be waiting for you down at the siding at any time after two."

That meant, of course, "Be down there at two on the dot." The telegraph on Cameron's desk let him communicate with every stationmaster up and down the line and with the switchyard in San Francisco. The track would be clear of traffic at two, but probably not at two-thirty or three. If he wanted to get into the city rather than sit on the siding for hours, it behooved him to get himself down there and on that carriage at two, precisely.

He nodded again.

"That should be all, then, unless you have any questions." Cameron's voice told him the Firemaster had already dismissed du Mond from his thoughts and was on to other things.

"No," Paul replied, and took himself out. He wondered, as he opened the door to the landing, if Cameron had noticed the absence of the word "sir." Possibly. But just at the moment, subservience stuck in du Mond's throat, and he could not bring himself to offer the word to someone who looked like a creature in a circus freak-show.

Now that he was out of the office and he could read the face, he pulled his watch from its vest pocket and checked the time — which was set every morning by the big clock in the hall, which in turn was always set by railway time. How like Cameron! It was barely one-thirty. He would have had just enough time to run upstairs and throw a few things into a bag, if he had not already packed.

As it was, he was able to go upstairs at a leisurely pace, get his valise, and make his way to the elevator without breaking into an undignified trot. The elevator deposited him at the siding-platform just as the train-carriage itself backed into view, huffing and hissing. The brakeman saw him and waved to him; he waved back. He made it a point to be on friendly terms with these men, who knew nothing of Cameron's Magickal activities. For one thing, the engine was a creature of Fire, and Paul was quite certain Cameron had a Salamander on board to see that all went well with his precious vehicle, which meant the Salamander could spy for him, too. For another, these men had it in their power to make his trips to and from the city less comfortable than they could be. They did not have to report difficulties with Paul back to Cameron; they had ample means of revenge in their own hands. They could "forget" to take on water for the carriage when they took it on for the engine; they could "forget" oil for the lamps or fuel for the stove. They could "decide" that they were not comfortable with the margin between scheduled trains, no matter what Cameron decreed; they could wait at the switch for hours until a "safe" margin occurred, with Paul sitting in a cold, dark, velvet-upholstered box.

Paul did his best to be cooperative and undemanding, which was the best way to deal with them. Rail people often preferred cargo to passengers; cargo didn't make difficulties. Paul acted like smiling cargo, which seemed to suit them.

The engineer applied the brakes, and the wheels emitted their metallic screaming. As soon as the train had squealed and screeched to a full stop, he swung aboard, throwing his valise up onto the top step ahead of him. That earned him a grin of approval; the one thing a railroad man hated worse than anything was a wasted minute. Paul had barely time to open the door into the carriage itself when the train was in motion again.

None of the lamps were lit since it was still brilliantly sunny, but a small fire was going in the stove to take the chill off the car, and Paul saw with approval that refreshments had been stowed in the proper places. Good; a whisky and soda would be just the thing right now, with perhaps a cigar and a light snack.

But first he checked the safe, cleverly concealed in the sideboard.

As he had expected, there was a slim, pale envelope containing his instructions, and a packet of banknotes. He raised an eyebrow when he saw that in addition to the banknotes there was a supply of gold coins. Evidently some of the people with whom he was to deal did not trust paper money.

He took out only the envelope; the rest could wait until he arrived in the city. He poured himself a whisky and splashed in the soda, making certain with long habit that both bottles went back into their respective "cradles" before he closed the liquor cabinet. He took the letter and the glass back to his favorite chair and sat in the sun, sipping and reading, while the train clattered through an endless sea of trees. The whiskey in his glass trembled and the vibration of the car made even his bones hum — but by now he was so used to it that it was merest background, like the humming of bees in the summer.

Some of his errands were routine, but there were three that were not — trips to three different Chinese emporia. This, according to his instructions, was where he was to take the gold. In one, he was to purchase books that were waiting for him, in the second to purchase rare herbs.

In the third he was to hand over a specified amount of coin for a sealed packet, and was not under any circumstances to break the seal.

Interesting. All three errands could only have to do with Magick, though this was the first time he had been instructed to pick up a sealed package. Presumably Cameron had always gone after such items himself in the past. Just because the package came from the shop of a Chinese did not mean that the Magick was from the Orient, however. The Chinese, like the Jews, had a remarkable talent for acquiring things, and this package could contain anything from an African artifact to the ceremonial dagger of Giles de Rais.

He would have to make inquiries about the shopkeepers. They might be a resource he would need later.

The rest of the errands were much like others he had run in the past, except for one small item; among the other items Cameron wanted from the apothecary was a remarkable quantity of laudanum, and for the first time since Paul had known him, a small amount of morphia.

So, Cameron needed opiates, did he? Perhaps that hybrid body of his was giving him pain. And perhaps that sealed packet was not Magickal at all, but was the pure opium, straight from the poppy-fields of China. It wasn't illegal, but Chinese White was much purer and stronger than the stuff doled out by pharmacists and mail-order houses. Du Mond smiled, for if Cameron was clouding his mind with drugs, the situation could only be advantageous for du Mond.

He made a mental note to watch Cameron for any signs that the man was at less than optimal condition, and to take advantage of it if he was.

There were new errands, but they were obviously at the behest of the new employee, the Hawkins girl. There was a second handwritten list, a short one, in a hand he did not recognize. It was not as good as his, though it was legible enough. It certainly would not do for writing to important or influential people. In this, at least, his position was secure.

An endless parade of trees flew past the windows of the carriage. The train did not slow or stop as they neared the switch to the main line; evidently the way ahead was clear and they would not have to wait for scheduled traffic to pass. That was excellent; as they rolled onto the main line with the distinctive click-pattern that heralded a switch, the engine accelerated. At this rate, they would be in San Francisco well before sundown, and he would be in Cameron's town apartment shortly after that. All of Cameron's employees were well-trained to a nicety; the personnel at the switchyard would have a cab waiting for him, the driver already paid and briefed on where to take him. The poor little Hawkins girl, should she take advantage of an excursion to the city, would probably be speechless, she would be so overwhelmed. But this was how the very wealthy lived; so surrounded and insulated by attentive employees that they need never think or plan for themselves.

Cameron hadn't allowed such luxury to soften him, at least not until now. But what luxury could not do, perhaps pain, and the drugs he took to conquer it, would.

The remainder of the journey passed uneventfully. Even when the trees gave way to a cliff-side view of the ocean below, du Mond ignored it. Paul had made this trip too often to be impressed by the scenery; he renewed his whiskey-and-soda, sipped it while he read a book from the innocuous selection provided in the bookcase at the end of the car. Jonathan Swift was acerbic enough to suit his mood, so he was pleasantly occupied until the abbreviated train pulled into the switchyard and was sent to its own special siding.

Moments later, he was in a horse-drawn cab on his way to Cameron's apartment in one of the fashionable sections of the city, up against the base of "Nob" Hill —which had gotten the nickname because so many of the "nobs," or members of the wealthy elite, had built their mansions there.

Cameron's "apartment" was not the type of dwelling du Mond would have characterized as such. It was one of a block of similar townhouses, all owned by those who either had manors in the country and did not want to duplicate them in the city, or were wealthy bachelors who entertained only a few friends at most and did not want the burden of an enormous house. They were built so closely together that there was hardly room for a cat to pass between them, and their fronts were virtually identical. They differed only in color, variations on chaste tan, rose, and brown, all trimmed in demure white.

The cab let du Mond off at the western corner of the block at the intersection of Powell and Pine; a most desirable location, since the setting sun could shine in the windows on that side. That gave Cameron windows letting in light and air on two sides, an amenity shared only by the other corner townhouses. Carrying his valise, Paul walked up the steps, to be met at the door by one of the two manservants here. A cook and a maid rounded out the staff; a pleasant change to have humans to wait on him, rather than Cameron's invisible Magickal servants.

The man took his bag at once, allowing du Mond the leisure to check and see what, if any, changes had been made to the downstairs dining room, parlor, and billiard room. He already knew that the study and smoking room would be intact; Cameron allowed no meddling there.

A few new ornaments and a new Chinese rug graced the parlor; the chairs had been replaced in the dining room, and high time, too. They had been old-fashioned when Cameron was an Apprentice himself, and sentimental attachment to a piece of furniture did not become a Master of the Elements. In the billiard room an additional game echoed an increasing Oriental influence — a chess set of carved ivory from India, in which each the pieces was graced with balls of filigree so delicate it looked like lace, balls that held carved balls within carved balls. Paul picked up the king, which had seven balls nested one inside the other; he'd heard of these carvings, which were made from solid pieces of ivory and carved by master artisans so that the balls moved freely inside each other, but he had never seen one. He marveled at it for a moment, then put it down. He did not lust after such things; his pleasures were in areas Cameron would consider less intellectual.

By now the manservant would have unpacked his valise and put everything away in the guest bedroom — which, to be honest, was every bit as opulent as Cameron's own. There would be time enough to refresh himself before dinner — and after dinner, he would see about a little of that entertainment he had promised himself.

He smiled, imagining what the Hawkins girl would think of what he found entertaining.

Du Mond knew better than to count his winnings; enough that he had won, there was no point in exciting the envy of those around him to the point that they might consider helping themselves to his good fortune. He hadn't even used much Magick to influence the outcome of the cockfight, which made the win all the sweeter. He'd simply observed that the bird he chose demonstrated a certain berserk rage when presented with the least glimpse of another rooster; it literally flung itself at the bars of its coop in an effort to get at the interloper, ignoring the possibility of injury. It demonstrated all the mad fury of a goshawk rather than a rooster, and pain obviously did not affect it when it was in a fighting rage. All he'd done was to work that temper up to the boiling point, so that when the birds were released, his launched itself without any preliminaries straight at his rival.

Well, now he had more than enough cash to ensure his amusement for the next week without depleting any of his accounts. He could have used Cameron's money, of course; the man had given him a generous allowance for entertainment. But he disliked the notion; Cameron could have a Magickal trace on the bills themselves, and du Mond did not want that kind of information in Cameron's hands.

Enough people had backed the same bird that his winning was nothing out of the ordinary, and no one paid much attention to him as he stood at the payout window for his reward. Behind him, another fight had already begun, and shouts, curses, and cheers rendered speech impossible. Paul paused to consider doubling his winnings yet again, but the effluvia of sweaty, unwashed bodies, stale beer, cheap cigars, and blood suddenly seemed too much to bear.

Du Mond stuffed his winnings in his inside coat pocket, and left the cockpit while his luck was holding. On the way out, he tipped the owner of his winning bird a generous ten dollars; the awkward country-bumpkin took it and made it vanish with a speed that told du Mond that the man was no more a country-clod than du Mond himself was. He stepped out into the street and moved aside from the door, out of the path of traffic. He gazed up and down the street, at the garishly-lit businesses, the river of men —

Now, the question was — should he go looking for a girl now, or later?

Now, he decided. Go while his luck was still in.

He shoved his hands in his pockets and assumed a slouch that changed his silhouette entirely, then set off down Pacific Street towards the docks and deeper into the district they called the "Barbary Coast." Here were all the things that the good women of the stately homes on Nob Hill despised — the cockpits and dogfights, the gambling dens, the hundreds of taverns, the bawdy-houses, bordellos, and brothels. But this was not to say the district was entirely poor — and many of those good women would faint dead away if they discovered how many of their sons and husbands visited some of the more discreet and luxurious of those Houses on this street. There were none of those in this end of the Coast; as Paul looked up, he saw plenty of second-floor windows with women lounging out of them, calling and beckoning to those below, something that *never* would happen at the better Houses.

Nor was it to say that the district was wealthy; down sidestreets were the opium dens, squalid, filthy holes where men (and sometimes women) paid for the privilege of lying on a wooden bunk stacked three high, leaning on one hip, and smoking a little sticky ball of gum-opium until they either passed into unconsciousness, nausea, or both. The smoke in those places was so thick that a man walking erect between the bunks stood a good chance of passing out himself from the narcotic fumes.

Down other alleyways were the cribs, the lowest places of prostitution in the city, tiny little closets just large enough to hold an excuse of a bed and a girl to lay in it. "Girl" was a euphemism; most of them were aged far past their years, riddled with disease, drugs, or drink, subhuman creatures a year or less from their own demise. Many, many of them were Chinese; they would strip to the waist and press themselves against the wood slats of their windows, calling out the only words of English they knew. "One bittee lookee, two bittee feelee, three bittee dooee!" The only thing lower than a crib-girl was a street-girl, one who would service her clients in the alley because she had nowhere else to take them.

What Paul sought was in between those two extremes, and he knew just where to find it. He had a selection of three merchants he patronized, though given the current interest Cameron was showing in things Oriental, it would be best to avoid the place in Chinatown. That left Giorgio's, or the Mexican's.

The Mexican's was nearer, which was what decided him.

The entrance to the Mexican's place was a single narrow door in between the entrances to a bar and a peep-show. Recessed in an alcove, a passerby probably wouldn't notice the door unless he was looking for it, which was how the Mexican liked it. The Mexican's given name was Alonzo de Varagas, but he didn't like anyone to use it. Except for this little venture, which was what had made him the money to become a respectable shop owner outside the Barbary Coast and still kept Senora de Varagas in silk and pretty jewelry, he no longer had anything to do with the clientele of Pacific Street.

Paul knocked on the door, which opened just enough to permit the suspicious eyes of the doorkeeper to examine him. Then the door opened wide, and Diego grinned whitely at him in the light from a gas-lamp, gesturing him inside with a flamboyant fling of his arms.

"Hey, Mister Breaker! You come on in, we got a special one for you!" the man said, happily, and spat on the sidewalk before closing the door. "Damn! Good thing you get here, boss begun to think he might have to break her himself!"

The door gave access immediately to a narrow staircase leading up, lit by three gas lamps. Paul went up ahead of Diego, half turning so he could talk to the man. "Is she giving you trouble?" he asked hopefully.

Diego shook his head, but to indicate that she was,

indeed. "She wake up from the happy-juice, next thing, she be prayin' and cryin' — you know how boss hates the ones that pray an' start callin' on the Virgin."

"I know." It was a constant source of amazement to him that a procurer like Alonzo had trouble with girls who wept and prayed. Perhaps they reminded him of his wife — who tolerated the fact that he had this little business on the side so long as he didn't sample the merchandise himself. Hence, Alonzo's dual quandary with "breaking" this particular girl.

Du Mond was a man with a talent, and it was a talent the Chinaman, the Mexican, and the Italian all found useful. He was a "breaker," which was the name by which they knew him. The procurers themselves were not brothel-keepers; they supplied girls to the Houses up and down the street. The Chinaman usually bought his back in his homeland; Alonzo specialized in bringing mestizos and Indians up from Mexico. The Italian ran his business a bit differently; he recruited bored country-girls from Illinois, Wisconsin and Indiana by promising them something other than a life of drudgery married to a dirt-farmer, or Chicago shop-girls tired of waiting on surly customers.

Given the Mexican's problems with "breaking" girls who cried and prayed, Paul would have expected *him* to be the one recruiting in the Grain Belt, but evidently Alonzo's conscience never bothered him about recruiting his own countrywomen for a life of sin.

The Chinaman's girls thought they were coming to America to be given to husbands; the Mexican women were told that they would find easy jobs in the households of gold-rich families. And as for the girls garnered from the fields of Indiana and the shops of Chicago, Giorgio posed as a businessman setting up a rival to the Fred Harvey chain on the West Coast; the girls expected easy work waiting tables with big tips in gold nuggets from men who hadn't seen a woman in months.

What they got, was a dose of morphia; they woke up to find their virginity had been taken by men who had paid highly to have it, even from a semi-conscious and unresponsive body. What happened then depended on the girl. The Chinaman seldom needed the services of a breaker; most Chinese girls seemed to resign themselves to their concubinage readily enough. Giorgio preferred to break his girls to the trade himself, but often enough he had more than one who was making trouble, and a man could only do so much in a day. The Mexican girls seemed divided into three types; the ones that gave up, the ones that fought, and the ones that prayed.

They would all end up in the same position in the end; Paul never could figure out why they didn't just resign themselves and make the best of the situation. If a girl played her cards right, she could end up a madam with a house of her own, or even married to a client. But she had to be smart and she had to learn how to play the game quickly, before her looks went. And she had to stay away from drugs and drink, or her looks would go even faster.

"So we've got a weeper, hmm? Well, maybe she'll turn out to be a fighter, too." He preferred it when they fought; they often thought that because he wasn't built like a prizefighter, he couldn't overpower them, and it increased his pleasure to prove them wrong.

It was his job to break them like untamed horses; to prove to them that not only did they have no choice in their new profession, but that *he* was infinitely worse than any customer they were ever likely to service. The unspoken threat was that unless they proved tractable, *he* would get them.

He was popular as a breaker because he didn't need

to slap the girls around and possibly damage them to break them. He had an infinite number of ways to hurt them that didn't leave any marks. Some of them used nothing more than words; he couldn't use those on the Chinese girls, but his Spanish was as fluent as Alonzo's, and it was words he most often used on the Mexican's girls. By the time he was through flaying them with his tongue, they were convinced that they had brought this life of sin upon themselves, that they were already so black with sin that God had turned His back upon them.

He would pay for this privilege, of course; the exclusive use of a girl wasn't something easy to come by on Pacific Street. But the cost was a fraction of what such a privilege would have demanded in a House. He would be only the second man to touch these girls, which vastly reduced the all-too-real risk of disease.

The girl looked up quickly as he opened the door, which had neither latch nor handle on the other side. She had been kneeling — obviously praying — as far from the bed in the corner as possible. In the light from the single dingy, metal-barred window, her face was swollen and tear-stained, and she tried to cover her nakedness with her hands. That was all there was in this tiny closet of a room; the naked girl, the undraped, iron-framed bed bolted to the floor, and four bare walls with bare wooden floor. There was a single gaslight, too high on the wall for her to reach.

He smiled. He would try words, first.

"Hello, little whore," he said, in clear Spanish, his voice smoother than honed steel and just as cold and sharp. "I am your master now."

The first session had gone quite well; Paul was pleased as he gave the special knock that alerted Diego that he wanted out.

"Well?" the little Mexican asked, as he closed the door on the semi-conscious girl.

"Five or six days," Paul said, truthfully. "Not more than that. Today she cried, tomorrow she might fight or weep more; maybe the day after, too. Then she'll begin wearing down, and she'll have it in her head that she's dirt and there's nowhere else that would have her but a whorehouse. She'll probably start drugging once she gets into a House, though. The religious ones usually do."

Diego shrugged. "Not our problem," he said, dismissively. "Whoever paid for her can worry about that. We'll be seeing you for the next week, then?" He held his hand out, palm up.

"Probably." Paul counted out enough cash to cover the week, then some over. "I'll need the usual."

"The usual," was for Diego to dig up well-used clothing in Paul's size, send it to the Chinese laundry, and have it waiting here for him. Even if Cameron "followed" him here, the man's fastidious nature would never allow him to keep a more direct eye on his Apprentice. And the moment Paul left here on errands of his own, clad in shabby clothing that had never come within Cameron's reach, there was no way the Firemaster could trace him further.

Besides, as long as du Mond's own clothing remained here, Cameron would probably assume he was with the clothing, if not in it.

"It'll be waiting," Diego replied, without interest. He and his employer had no curiosity about why Paul used their establishment as a way-station. That greatly endeared them to him. Add in the fact that this place was within walking distance of the Nob Hill apartment, and it was altogether an arrangement to du Mond's liking.

But for the moment, with all of his needs satisfied,

it was time to get back to his gilded cage. He bade the Mexican goodnight, turned up his collar against the damp and chilly night air, and shoved his hands deep into his pockets to foil petty thieves. Although it was near midnight, the establishments of Pacific street, from the meanest tavern to the Hippodrome, were barely getting warmed up. Some of them were even decked out in electrical rather than gas lights. He wondered what the Coast would look like when electrical lights became cheap enough to use for signage and shook his head.

It was a lengthy walk, but not bad for a man in the physical condition of Paul du Mond. He strode east, watching the traffic around him with a wary eye and wondering what secrets some of those faces held.

One day, soon, he would have the power to find out. And San Francisco herself, the biggest whore of them all, would have a new master.

When he had a number of errands, Paul always solved the difficulty of finding a cab by hiring one for the entire day. They were Cameron's errands, so Cameron's money might as well pay for them. He ran the more mundane chores first, and they took him all over town before it was finished. Among those was the list the Hawkins girl had supplied, and he took some savage amusement in wondering what her reaction would be if she ever learned it had been *him* who had purchased her requested supplies —

She'd probably faint from embarrassment alone. He'd like to see her embarrassed, or better still, humiliated. He'd imagined her prim little face superimposed on Lupe's last night. He'd like to have a chance to break *her.* Damned women, thinking they had a right to careers, taking money out of a man's pocket to do so, getting ideas about equality. . . .

Perhaps he'd have the opportunity, if things worked out properly. She was an orphan; there'd be no one to miss her or inquire after her if she vanished.

Among his errands, he contrived to drop a message in a certain tobacconist's when he bought his own Cuban cigars. Tonight, after Lupe, he would find out if there was an answer to that message.

Meanwhile, the day plodded along like the weary cab-horse, straining its way up the hill of time towards noon, then straining to keep from tumbling headlong down the other side. Why anyone had ever chosen to build a city here, in this maze of hills and valleys, was beyond him. The inhabitants suffered from enough back and foot ailments to keep every purveyor of quack medicine in the country happy. There were no real places to leave a carriage, and even if you found one, it wasn't one where he'd want to leave a horse standing for long. The cable car system that ran up and down the Slot on Market Street had been invented because the life of a trolley-horse in San Francisco was a fraction of one in any other city. They had dropped dead in their traces all the time before the mechanical traction device took over their chore.

Paul, of course, did not have to walk unless he chose, nor suffer the press of the Great Unwashed on the cable cars unless he wished to. He always hired cabs with strong horses with some draft-blood in them; horses that were up to a long day of traversing the streets.

He had stopped by the tobacconist's early; on impulse, on the way back from the final errand of the day, he had the cabby stop there again.

Much to his pleasure there was already a reply to his message — a single slip of paper with three words, none of which would have given the game away even to Cameron. *Twelve, the usual.* It could have been someone's order, picked up by accident, for boxes of cigars or cigarettes, or any other product the tobacconist sold, which was precisely the point.

None of the parcels he obtained today required the special handling Jason had specified, so he simply left them piled in the hallway with orders to have them sent to the waiting carriage. The cook had prepared an excellent meal, and du Mond settled in to eat it with full enjoyment, now that his duties were over for the day and the evening lay before him.

He had a cab take him as far as the end of Pacific Street that was only risque; what harm, after all, was there in his taking in a bawdy show? He even entered the theater, although he came right back out again as soon as the cab was gone. From there, he walked to the Mexican's, where events proceeded as he had predicted they would.

He was finished by eleven, and the man who left the Mexican's in no way resembled the man who had entered. Seedy cap pulled low over his forehead, hands stuffed in the pockets of his dungarees, warding off the chill with a shapeless, baggy flannel shirt, Paul would not have been recognized by anyone who knew him as Cameron's secretary, and he knew it. All of the clothing was old, threadbare, patched. He had altered his posture, even his gait. He did not bother attempting to find a cab — no one looking the way he did would have money for such a thing, and the use of anything other than his own two feet would only reveal that he was not what he seemed.

It was a long way to the docks at the end of Pacific Street, but that was "the usual." So near water — both in the form of fog drifting in off the Bay and of the Pacific Ocean itself — it was the last place one would expect to see a Firemaster.

Which was why Simon Beltaire had chosen this as a meeting site.

Even if, by some incredible ability, Jason Cameron was tracking Paul by means of the flames of gaslights all across the city, he would *not* be able to do so on the docks. Nor would a Salamander ever come *here*, where the Salamander's worst enemies, the Undines, held sway. Humans, of course, could go anywhere they chose, no matter what their Magickal Natures, and if the Undines resented the intrusion of a Firemaster into the edges of their domain, they were wise enough to keep quiet about it.

The docks were silent at this hour. Perhaps someday there would be work around the clock — but not until either science created brighter gaslights or electrical lights became cheaper. For now, this was a good place to meet someone when you didn't want to be seen — although you had to listen carefully, for some of the street-girls brought customers here for the little privacy that the darkness and piles of crates afforded.

Paul walked five steps, paused, and listened before walking five more; in this way he made his way to the end of one of the docks without interfering with anyone's pleasure. It didn't matter what dock he chose; Beltaire would find him easily enough. He chose one that didn't have any boats moored up against it.

He leaned up against a piling, folded his arms across his chest, and waited. Beneath him the water of the Bay lapped against the wooden pilings, and the faint smell of fish and seaweed rose to his nostrils. Fog obscured the surface of the water to a height of about four feet; above the bank of fog, the stars shone down unobscured. Behind him, the sounds of the Barbary Coast drifted down Pacific Street, jumbled together and rendered into mere whispers by distance. Snatches of tinny piano music, shrill laughter, the shrieks of women, the occasional breaking of glass;

they all seemed to come to him from another world, across a distance too vast to bridge.

He wished he'd thought to have Diego get him an old duffel coat or a pea jacket; it was cold out here.

"I hope you haven't been waiting too long, Paul."

He didn't start, since he'd been expecting Beltaire, but once again Simon had somehow strolled up behind him without making a sound.

"Not long." He turned; the flare of a flame illuminated Simon Beltaire's elegant face as the man lit himself a cigar.

Beltaire did not use a match, of course.

There was not enough light to grant more than a fleeting glimpse of Beltaire's countenance, but Paul didn't need any light; he and Beltaire were well acquainted with each other. Beltaire, while not circulating among the elite as Cameron did, was still sought after in his own set. While he might well have been as wealthy as Cameron, he preferred not to flaunt that wealth. He could easily have stood as a model for the hearty, football-playing, dark-haired and dark-eyed college hero. His square jaw and cleft chin had been known to cause palpitations in the hearts of shopgirls and jaded professionals alike, sculptural as it was.

"And what has my estimable lupine colleague been doing since last we talked?" The light from the glowing coal at the end of the cigar was hardly enough to show Beltaire's smile, but there was amusement in the man's voice.

Paul gave a basic summary of most of it; Beltaire listened without comment, since it differed little from the last time they had spoken.

Then he casually dropped his real news, and instantly felt Beltaire's attention riveted to him.

"Cameron hired a young woman to read his books to him."

Simon's drawl did not disguise his intense interest. "I assume you do not mean fairy tales."

"He's working up to the important tomes, but he began her with High Magick from the first word," du Mond agreed. "He's found a way around his handicap. She's fluent in several languages, including the archaic forms and supposedly even has a knowledge of hieroglyphics."

"This is going to force my hand; I had expected to have more time," Beltaire said under his breath. Paul smiled; that was what he had hoped to hear.

"Tell me what you know about her," Simon demanded.

Paul complied. "I don't know much," he warned. "Cameron found her himself, hired her himself, and made all the arrangements to bring her here. Her name is Rosalind Hawkins; she's from Chicago, and she has no living relatives. I have to assume she was in some advanced degree program at the university there, given her accomplishments. Perhaps she suffered some change in circumstance that left her destitute and willing to accept Cameron's offer —"

"Never mind that; I can find the facts of the matter out for myself, now that I know where she comes from." Beltaire waved his cigar dismissively. "Once I have the details of her life, *then* I can decide what to do about her."

"I could get rid of her for you," du Mond offered, hoping that Beltaire would accept the offer. The girl had taken one long walk already; who was to say that something might not happen to her if she made a habit of such things?

"No — no. I want to know what she's made of, first. She could prove to be a useful tool, *especially* once she begins to understand just what Cameron is asking her to read." Beltaire nodded thoughtfully. "If he revolts her, if he frightens her . . . that woman's weakness can be turned to serve us. She might even welcome such an opportunity."

He must have sensed Paul's veiled disappointment, for he added in explanation, "I prefer not to discard a possible weapon until it proves useless. It would make things much simpler for us if we can use her against Cameron and avoid drawing attention to you."

Paul nodded, still disappointed, but with his disappointment fading fast. It *would* be better to avoid Cameron's attention and anger. He might not be the magician he had been before his transformation, but he was still formidable.

"If she proves useless, you may deal with her as you choose," Beltaire continued. "In the meantime, I will find out what I can about her, and you keep me informed. I particularly wish to know if she is released for an excursion to the city. I wish to approach her myself and take her measure. If nothing else, she may give us information we need on Jason's progress." Again, the smile crept into his voice. "I do not believe that I flatter myself when I say that I am remarkably good at temptation."

Du Mond laughed dryly at that, for Beltaire had certainly discovered exactly what tempted *him*. "I cannot think of anything else that would interest you at this time, Simon."

"Nor can I, and it is getting quite late." Beltaire's voice turned solicitous. "Paul, I do believe it is more than time that I gave you some recompense for your assiduous labor on my behalf. Here."

He passed over a parcel; as du Mond's fingers touched it, he felt paper and string tied about what felt like a book.

"Don't allow Jason to see this, or he'll certainly know where it came from," Beltaire warned. "It is rather in my style. I told you that Jason's way was not the only method of Firemastery. This should get you started on an easier path."

Du Mond's heart leapt with exultation, and with a fierce joy that he had been right. He had been so certain that Jason was prevaricating, that there was another, easier way to become a Master of Elements — one without all the tedious memorization and the mummery.

"I have hesitated this long only because I have been waiting for something to occur that would take Jason's attention off you — and to make certain of your own temperament." Beltaire chuckled. "There are things required on this path that would be repugnant to a weaker man, but I am certain you have the stomach for them."

"I have the stomach for a great deal," du Mond promised. "Thank you. Now, I must continue to play Cameron's errand-boy tomorrow, so if you'll pardon me, I will take my leave of you."

Beltaire touched the brim of his hat with his cane in ironic salute, and faded into the darkness. Paul waited several moments for him to get well on his way, then made his own way across the docks, making certain not to retrace his footsteps.

Diego was still on duty at the Mexican's — du Mond wasn't the only breaker the Mexican used, just the most skillful — and sounds from some of the other rooms led him to believe that his counterparts were hard at work. Diego bowed him mockingly into an empty room where his clothing waited.

It was past one before he was out on the street again and hailing a cab, his precious book tucked into a pocket. It was a leather-bound, handwritten volume, like many of Cameron's treasured books of Magick, and small enough to fit in a coat pocket.

So many important things were small in size.

He hailed a cab, and took it back to Cameron's townhouse — which would not be Cameron's for very much longer — leaving the noise and garishness of the Barbary Coast behind him.

Until tomorrow.

CHAPTER SIX

Somehow, even though she had hardly seen Paul du Mond for more than a few minutes at a time, knowing that he was going to be in San Francisco for a week made Rose feel much more relaxed. She woke uncommonly cheerful, and knew immediately that du Mond's absence had a great deal to do with that cheer.

She stretched like a cat and blinked at the blurred beam of sunlight creeping past the bedcurtains. *I could almost believe in six impossible things before breakfast, like Lewis Carroll's White Queen. This is such an incredible home. . . .*

Last night, she'd had the oddest feeling while reading one of Jason Cameron's books, that this nonsense she was translating for him wasn't nonsense at all. She had gone to bed only to lie awake for some time, staring at a single moonbeam that had found its way past both her window and bed curtains to fall on a single carved rose on one of the bedposts. *At least, I thought it was a moonbeam and a rose. Without my glasses it's rather hard to tell what I'm looking at.* Magic . . . in this house, with its invisible servants, its incredible luxury, and its odd master, did not seem so impossible, especially not in the moonlight.

But that had been last night, well past midnight, with the wind rushing in the branches of the trees outside and moonlight shining in her sitting-room window. Now, with the scents of breakfast coffee and bacon drifting through the bedroom door, and sunlight replacing the moonlight, she had to laugh at her own fantasy. *Magic indeed! I might as well believe in Santa Claus or genies in lamps!* If Cameron wished to continue to deceive himself, that was *his* doing. She would collect her wages and continue to amuse him, and meanwhile, with the help of the books he was ordering for her, she would continue her own researches. Then, when he finally tired of this farce, she would take her savings and enroll in another university. Leland Stanford had founded one here, in fact, that was well thought of. Would they admit a woman?

I'll worry about that when the time comes, she decided. There had been one book among all the ones she had read last night that had been well-written and coherent — unlike most of the rest, which were written as if the author had been granted a Doctorate in Confusion and Obfuscation. She had saved that one out of the pile with an eye to reading it straight through from beginning to end. Maybe if she had some notion of what Cameron *thought* was real, she'd be closer to understanding what he was looking for.

She had not planned on going for a walk, and by the time she had finished breakfast she was just as glad, for she would have been greatly disappointed. The sunshine had given way to a drizzling rain that didn't look as if it was going to let up any time before dark.

Well, she could get her exercise by doing a more thorough, daylight exploration of more of the house, and then she could settle in with that book until Cameron needed her.

She took the book with her, thinking that it might be pleasant to spend some time reading in the conservatory, among the exotic hothouse plants.

She had already examined the ballroom, the dining

room, the music room . . . most of the rooms that a casual visitor would have seen. Now she decided to pry just a little, and take a good look around those bastions of masculine power, the smoking room, the billiard room, and the library.

I've never actually been in a smoking room. . . . Women, other than maidservants who cleaned them, were not welcome in such places. Cameron had very sensibly arranged his entertaining area with the billiard and smoking rooms to the right of the drawing room, and the ladies' parlor and "withdrawing room" to the left. The smoking room was disappointing; her father had never had one, and she had actually expected something a great deal more — well — decadent. She wrinkled her nose a little at the heavy scent of tobacco as she entered, but other than that slightly disagreeable and penetrating aroma, there was not much to distinguish this room from the ladies' parlor. Instead of cut-crystal bottles of genteel sherry on the sideboard, there was a bar holding a variety of glasses and hard liquors, but other than that, it was fundamentally identical. The real differences between the rooms intended for ladies and men were in the materials used to decorate; in the parlor, the furniture was covered in damask satin and velvet. Here, it was covered in leather. There, the lampshades were fringed and elaborately painted; here, they were plain parchment.

In short, it was a luxuriously appointed version of a little boy's clubhouse, with cigars and strong liquor replacing chewing gum and lemonade; the only thing lacking was the sign on the door saying "No Girlz Aloud." *No paintings of naked odalisques, no illustrated risque versions of the* Thousand Nights and a Night *lying about on the table. No opium pipes! I expected a den of iniquity, a recreation of Caligula's orgy-rooms, and I find a harbor of hearty male games-manship! What a disappointment!* She had to laugh at herself, and wondered what most *men* thought lay in the ladies' parlor! Did they have similar fantasies, or did they assume that it was a room of such overwhelming femininity that they were afraid to venture in lest they break or soil something with their mere presence?

The billiard room was not much different; besides the billiard table, there was a truly lovely chess set carved from black onyx and white marble, and a substantial round poker table with a sealed deck of cards on it. Other than that, it was furnished in the same uncompromisingly comfortable and unadorned style as the smoking room.

Perhaps the library would be more rewarding, although she had the suspicion that she would not be finding any of the strange books she had been reading on the shelves of so public a room. It was far more likely that Cameron had a second library in his own suite where he kept such things. But at least she would see what his casual taste ran to.

The room she sought now was on the other side of the dining room, and covered as much or more floor space than any other large room in the mansion. She already knew that the library was a big one — that is, it contained a huge number of books; the room was two stories tall with a balcony around the second floor to give access to the higher shelves and ladders on rolling tracks to reach the books nearer the ceiling. She strolled down the hallway and found the door already open, as if she had been expected. All of the curtains were drawn back from the windows, which were not just plain glass, but also beautiful artworks of stained and leaded glass. Interestingly, the furniture here was of a piece with the smoking room, oversized and not

particularly comfortable for women; evidently
Cameron did not expect many female visitors to this
room — or else, he had decorated it to suit his
personal taste.

Perhaps his fancy runs to women who don't read,
she thought, a bit acidly. *Just because he finds me
entertaining now, that doesn't mean I am the style of
female he is likely to wish to associate with socially.*

Of course not. No man of wealth wished to spend
any time in public with a bookworm, a girl with her
nose so deeply in ancient volumes that there was dust
in her hair. No, she had seen her share of the style of
girl he would associate with, in the fiancees of her
fellow students; wealthy, beautiful, schooled in the
proper manners and life of a lady of the upper crust
and often enough without a thought in their heads
beyond the latest mode. Lady scholars were not
among those invited to the opera. Why was she even
considering that this man, her *employer,* would spend
one minute of time with her if he did not need her
skills? Just because she was coming to like him, that
did not mean that the opposite was true. *With
his money, he must have dozens of girls flinging
themselves at him, and more whose parents are doing
the flinging, I shouldn't wonder. All with proper
womanly interests, who grow properly faint at the
merest hint of the excesses of the ancient Romans. And
no matter how disfigured he might be now, there are
plenty of women who would be happy to become Mrs.
Jason Cameron. Once he decides that his quest for
healing is in vain, he will dismiss me and get on with
his life. And even if that life does not include a bride, it
will hardly include me. I am an employee, not a friend,
and I must always keep that fact in mind.*

She should be planning on what to do with herself
after he dismissed her — and on how to keep that

moment at bay until after she had amassed enough money to make the future she envisioned possible.

Well, let me see what literary face Jason Cameron shows his visitors. Perhaps that can help me decide how to proceed.

There was a section of popular literature and poetry, light novels and romances in the bookcase nearest the door, all bound in matching leather with hand-tooled titles on the spine and the cover. *The Bronte Sisters, Jane Austen, Walter Scott, Kipling, Doyle . . . oh, Lord Byron — now there's something a bit racier! Cooper, Defoe, Melville, Emerson, Hawthorne, that was to be expected. How could an American tycoon not have the American literary lions in his library? Longfellow, of course. Verne, now there's a surprise! Dumas and Stevenson. Oh dear, what are Corelli, Alexander, Hodgson, and Braeme doing in such exalted company? Probably for those whose tastes are a bit more plebian.* After a cursory examination she moved on to more fruitful territory.

Fruitful territory began with the very next case, which held general history books, arranged in time-sequence by author. Many of them were, as she well knew from her undergraduate courses, as dry as the Sahara, and guaranteed to encourage a "proper" young lady to return to the first case! Following the general histories were general geographies, then natural history and the sciences. The farther she went, the more pleased she became. All in all, a person could acquire quite a complete post-graduate education just by reading the books on the first floor.

So what was on the second floor?

She picked up her skirts in both hands and ascended the spiral, wrought-iron stair with anticipation.

Her anticipation was rewarded. *Now this is a great deal more like it!* Excellent translations of the Greek and Roman classics met her eye first — multiple translations, in fact — housed snugly next to the same books in the original. Other ancient works followed in the same pattern; translations, more often than not, multiple translations, followed by copies of the originals. *Oh my — there is dear old Wallis Budge, all of his Egyptian translations! If ever I suffer from insomnia, I shall know where to find the cure for it!*

Then a surprise; English versions of virtually every book ever considered "holy" by any culture, East or West, again with copies in the original tongues. They were all here — from the *Mahabharata* to the *Koran*, from the *Talmud* to the works of the Zen Masters. She raised an eyebrow at that; Cameron had not struck her as being anything like interested in religion. Perhaps, once he came to the inevitable conclusion that his search for "magical" help was in vain, she might send him here for consolation. *Perhaps . . . Buddhism? Somehow I can't imagine Jason Cameron becoming a proper Christian lamb. But I can't imagine him seeking enlightenment with serenity either.*

She was halfway around the room when she came to the next subject-change; pure mythology, with interpretations and volumes of scholarly speculation. Then a surprise, in the form of medieval romances, ballads, and minstrel-tales.

Interesting. That certainly doesn't fit. Is this the remains of a younger, more romantic Jason Cameron? Or is this fodder for something quite the opposite? At any rate — there was more than enough material here for her to write several dissertations. *I wonder if the world could tolerate another analysis of the cult of the Virgin Mary and the reflection of that cult in troubadour-ballads . . . no, wait! What about something allied but different? What about reflections of* Mary Magdalene *in the "fallen heroines" like Kundrie, Guinevere and Yseult? That would be new —* She happily pursued this notion for some time, making mental notes on a rich lode of source-material Cameron had available here. Why, she might even be able to fashion a doctoral dissertation just from what was here!

And how "proper" it would be for a lady, too — pious reflection on sin and redemption — One of the problems with her previous research had been resistance by her professors to the "appropriateness" of the subjects she found interesting. They could hardly argue with this! *Not like the last one, where I was trying to prove that the "allegorical" nature of the courtly love-poems was anything but allegorical!*

That brought her all the way to the end, which proved to be all huge, unwieldy, handwritten volumes. Some were old atlases, some she couldn't make head or tail of, and some were rather laughable "natural history" works of the previous century, showing all manner of imaginary beasts and claiming improbable things about them. There was certainly nothing of any use there, and the volumes themselves were so musty they made her sneeze. She dusted her hands off on her skirts and descended.

The weight of the book in her pocket reminded her that she had intended to read it this afternoon. While there was still plenty of light, it would be a good time to look the conservatory over and see if there were any surprises growing in the linked hothouses.

The conservatory was heated by steam and was as warm in this late-fall day as the warmest summer in Chicago — which was quite warm indeed. The conservatory was quite an affair of glass, wood, and wrought-iron, with graveled paths to walk on and wrought-iron benches placed at intervals for seating. In the main greenhouse, the largest one, was the expected tropical paradise, this one complete with two fountains, a waterfall, and towering palm trees.

There was another aspect of this delightful place she had missed in the dark, however — the birds. There were dozens of tiny, brightly-colored birds about the size of a wren flitting among the trees and bushes, bathing in the shallow pools and basins, and helping themselves to half-hidden feeders full of seeds and fruit. She recognized canaries both brown and yellow, but the others were new and entirely baffling. Their twittering blended pleasantly with the falling water, and by placing the benches in open spaces, away from overhanging branches, the unpleasant but inevitable droppings at least were not lurking on the seats.

There were four greenhouses attached to the main one. One held vegetables, one was clearly a forcing-house for flowers, and one for more tropical plants, both to decorate the mansion and to replace others in the conservatory. But the fourth one held herbs — and most of those herbs she didn't recognize.

More of Cameron's obsession with magic? Perhaps; many of the books she had been reading specified odd plants and herbs as components of spell-casting and ritual.

Or he could simply have a very sophisticated cook.

She took her book back to the conservatory and settled onto a bench to read.

In part because the book itself was so well-written, and in part because the concepts were not altogether foreign to her, she finished it quickly and closed the book on the last page just as the sun began to set. She remained with the book closed in her lap, thinking.

If one simply began with the assumption that there is some power that can be tapped with these cantrips and incantations . . . there is a logic about all this that is difficult to dismiss out of hand.

It had not been all *that* long ago that the mysterious

force of electricity had been as arcane as any of this magic. Claims of what it could do — besides providing light and heat — were still being made for it that were similar to those made for spells.

Was she being logical, or close-minded? Until now, she would have opted for the former without hesitation. Her understanding of the world was firm — until she read this book that was as reasoned as any of those modern books on science back there in the library.

The sun set, the birds settled into groups to sleep for the night, some of them packing themselves five and six at a time into round basket-nests made of gourds. The fountains and waterfall continued to play, filling the usual silence of the house with welcome music.

And that, in itself, set off another train of thought. *Usual silence . . . I have become so accustomed to it, that I haven't thought about it. But there are no sounds of people, ever, anywhere in this place. No sounds of cooking in the kitchen, not even a whisper or a footfall. Yet this place is kept clean, meals are prepared, the animals tended — and the only human I have ever seen within these four walls is Paul du Mond.*

She might have said, jestingly, that it was all done by magic. But what if that was no jest, but a fact?

I feel very much as if I have been sleep-walking and have awakened to find myself in a foreign land! She had been lured by the isolation of this place, and by the fact that she wanted that isolation, into ignoring the fact that she did *not* want the company of others about her. She did not want anyone to know that she was nothing more than a glorified servant in someone else's home, especially not other servants. As long as she could remain in her beautiful, luxurious suite without anyone seeing her here, she could pretend she was not Cameron's paid hireling, but a guest.

So she had willfully put the inconsistency of a huge, well-run establishment without any sign of a menial about completely out of her mind. She had purposefully closed her eyes to things that should have been screaming at her.

Or was I "encouraged" to ignore these things?

The book had also hinted that the power of magic — or rather, "Magick" — could be used to influence the thoughts and even actions of others. Had Cameron been playing with her mind?

A chill ran down the back of her neck, and spread over her entire body. If that was the case, what *else* could he have been doing to her? Could he be —

Her vision of the world and her common sense warred with what she had observed in this place, and now she was no longer certain of what was true and what was false.

There could be an even more sinister, yet completely mundane explanation. Cameron might be drugging her food, keeping her sleeping so soundly that the noise of staff working in the morning didn't disturb her. Then, once she was awake, he banished the staff to somewhere else on the estate so that she would not come into contact with them. *Why* he would do something like that, she had no idea — but a man who engineered a plot like that one was hardly sane.

But the situation as it stood was no longer tenable. "I have to talk with him," she said aloud. "I have to confront him, and know the truth about this place." She almost expected to hear a reply come out of the shadows gathering in the dusk beneath the tropical trees, but there was no response but the twittering of sleepy birds.

In a way, that was comforting. If magic really *was* a

true force in the world, at least Cameron wasn't using it to spy on her every movement and thought.

Cameron was not paying a great deal of attention to the girl as she prowled the halls and rooms of his home; she was not being overly curious — she was not opening drawers or trying cabinet doors, for instance. He didn't see any point in giving her more than cursory attention, although he was too suspicious by nature to let her make her explorations unwatched. He noted with a bit of amusement her enthusiasm for his library, once she got past the first bookcase. She spent a great deal of time where he had expected her to, in front of the medieval section. After that, she retired to the conservatory with a book, one he assumed she had borrowed from those same shelves.

Probably more of those ballads the trouveres *created; I suspect my selection is as good as that in her university. Trust a woman to be fascinated by the roots of romance and ignore all the open descriptions of Magick as practiced by Masters!*

He simply dealt with the mundane affairs of his business while she read, telegraphing orders to his underlings in the city. It was very convenient, having his own telegraphy instrument on his desk; he didn't need to write down the code as it came in, for he was so fluent in Morse he could translate it immediately in his head. If he hadn't had one, he would have had to depend upon Paul to an uncomfortable extent.

It is a pity I cannot give du Mond a watch like Rosalind's — but even if I did, he would probably find a way to be rid of it. Even he is capable of sensing something of that nature.

Having paws instead of hands did not greatly interfere with his telegraphy. With his instructions complete, he turned his attention to shelving his books of Magick and making the selections for tonight. He often ordered the Salamanders to perform this little task, but only when he was busy with other concerns. Even with misshapen paws instead of hands, he could still manage to shelve and remove books —

Then, as he shelved the last one, he knew that there was something wrong. One of the books was missing; there should have been seven, and there were only six. He hadn't noticed because the light was kept so low.

He knew immediately which one it was: *The Arte and Science of Magick* by Dee. He'd chosen it for her to read, even though it was really an Apprentice's book, because of a partial chapter on transformations, a chapter he thought might jog some associations loose for him if he heard it again.

It was also one of the books he had planned for her to read in its entirety later — when she was ready to believe, to prepare her for the more dangerous books he would ask her to peruse. But he had not planned that to occur for several months at least.

Swiftly he spun, and with a gesture of his black-tipped claws, called the mirror to life. She was still reading, although by the thickness left, there were only a few pages remaining. It was certainly too late to stop her.

He knew her; she was a scholar, and if she had not already deduced that Marcus Dee was a descendent of John Dee, the personal Magician and Astrologer to Queen Elizabeth, she would soon make that connection. The modern Dee had written his book for the instruction of the offspring of High Magicians who also bore the Powers in their blood, offspring presumably under the tutelage and guidance of their parents. To that end, it was clear, concise and erudite, rather than reveling in obscurity. Because it was meant for the eyes of those who were already being competently guided, there was no need to shroud secrets in formulas that required other information from other sources to be decoded.

Even as he watched her, she finished the last few pages and closed the book. In the gathering dusk, she stared straight ahead, her blue eyes behind the lenses of her glasses focused deep within herself. As she sat there, thinking, a myriad of emotions crossed her face. Speculation, alarm, fear — she must be going through incredible turmoil at this moment.

Well, he was sharing those emotions! He clutched both paws in his mane and tugged with frustration. All of his carefully choreographed plans, set awry in a single moment! What was she going to do? More importantly, what was she going to believe?

As if she was answering him, she spoke. "I have to talk to him," she said aloud. "I have to confront him and know the truth about this place."

She stood up, clasping the book to her chest, and turned quickly. A moment later, she was well on her way to the staircase, her brisk stride unimpeded by her skirts, the silk petticoats whispering about her ankles.

Is she coming here? From the determined look on her face, he was quite willing to believe that she *would* march straight up to the door of his suite and demand entry!

But she went right past the second-floor landing without a pause, heading for her own rooms.

"Dinner for her, quickly, before she reaches her room!" he ordered his servants, harshly — thank Heaven he had already decided on the menu! It appeared, on his silver and china, as always, purloined tonight from the kitchens of the Palace Hotel. He always selected items that would not be missed — slices of beef off the joint rather than a steak; soup and vegetables from large batches, and so forth. His servants *could* have prepared food, of course, but cleaning up required water, which Salamanders were not inclined to touch. He could persuade them to lick the china and silver clean with their flaming tongues, but as for cleaning up pots and pans —

The dinner was in place as she opened the door to her rooms, and before she could say anything, he forestalled her by speaking through the tube. He used his most commanding tone, on purpose, hoping she would not be inclined to ignore his authority if he invoked it.

"I sense you are agitated, Miss Hawkins. Please, sit down and enjoy your dinner. You will feel better if you eat first."

She turned and faced the speaking-tube; he noticed then that she was nowhere near as composed as he had thought. Her knuckles were white, she was clasping the book so hard before her breasts, and her voice trembled. "Is it drugged?" she blurted, her eyes wide.

That was *so* far from his mind that he found himself laughing, and for some reason that seemed to relax her a trifle. "It is not drugged, I pledge you that," he said, when he could speak again. "Please, enjoy your dinner. I believe that you wish to speak with me on an important subject. You will think more clearly if you are not suffering hunger-pangs."

He bolted his own dinner while she ate hers — his altered body required only meat, as near rare as possible, and he ate it as a wolf would, bolting it down in large chunks. He was finished long before she was, but he did not take his eyes from the mirror even when he ate. His mind, raised to a fever-pitch of clarity by his own anxiety and alarm, analyzed her every movement. She evidenced none of her usual enjoyment of the food before her, chewing and swallowing it automatically, as if she was not even tasting it. She drank a bit more wine than was her usual wont, and he gathered that she was trying to find courage in the bottom of the bottle, as so many did.

She kept the book on her lap, as if by having it in contact with her, she reminded herself of her resolve. She ate quickly, either out of nervousness or because she did not intend to allow him too much time to contemplate her intentions.

She did not touch the sweet; instead, she emptied her wine-glass, poured it full, and emptied it again in a gulp. Then she pushed resolutely away from the table and stood up again, still holding the book as if it was a shield. "Mr. Cameron?" she said, her voice quavering a little on the last syllable.

"I am still here, Miss Hawkins," he replied. "There is, after all, nowhere else I am likely to be."

"Mr. Cameron," she said, her face pale but her mouth set and her eyes behind the glasses hard with resolution and fear. "When I accepted this position, I was not aware of — of the irregularity of this establishment. I believe you owe me an explanation."

He coughed, and prevaricated. "I do not take your meaning, Miss Hawkins. There are no opium dens here, no ladies of dubious repute; I fail to see what you mean by an 'irregular establishment.' Would you care to explain?" Perhaps, given this opportunity, she would decide against confrontation.

"Why are there no servants here?" she asked, flushing a brilliant pink, as the words rushed out of her. "The work of many servants is done, the mansion is cleaned, the lights lit and extinguished, the beds made, meals prepared, animals tended — yet there *are no servants!* In fact, I only know of two people besides myself who dwell in this place! I have not seen a single soul but Paul du Mond since I entered these grounds, and I have only heard your voice. Where are the servants? And why did I not pay attention to their absence before this?"

"Before I answer that — what is your solution, Miss Hawkins?" he asked, as she reached blindly for the back of the chair beside her to support her. *She is unused to confrontation. This is taking all the courage she can muster.*

"I — I — " Abruptly she sat down, deflated, her hair coming loose from its careful arrangement and falling in tendrils about her face. "I have no logical solution," she said flatly, after a long moment of silence. "And the illogical solution flies in the face of all reason. I do not want to believe it."

Should he be the one to grasp the bull by the horns? Well — why not? *If he could bring her to* believe in the reality of Magick he would be able to eliminate a great deal of beating about the bush.

And it will save me endless effort in hiding it all from her. It is worth the risk.

"And if I told you that the reason was because all work in this house, on these grounds, is accomplished by what you would refer to as Magick?" he asked, just as flatly.

She flinched, and did not answer him directly. "I must be mad," she said under her breath. "I cannot be hearing this — or discussing these things. It is not *reasonable.*" She was shivering, though she tried not to show it.

She's afraid. She's afraid that it might be true, yet at the same time she wants it to be true. If I told her it was because my servants were all working only while she slept, she might believe me. . . .

"You could make her believe you," hissed a voice in

his ear. "You could make up almost anything and make her believe you."

He did not have to turn; it was one of his Salamanders, and by the voice and assertiveness, the cleverest one. "I know," he told it, covering the speaking-tube with one hand. "I could have you cloud her mind again. She has drunk so much wine it would be child's play to make her believe me."

"But you do not want to do that," the creature said shrewdly. "You want her to believe, because if she believes, she can help you."

Now how does it know that? The Salamander surprised him more every time it spoke. "If she believes, I will no longer need to waste time and effort concealing your presence from her — and I will not need to depend so much on du Mond for assistance, for she could do some things for me that do not require either experience or her actual presence."

"That would be very good," the Salamander said with emphasis. "*Show* her, Firemaster. Give her facts. Give her the evidence of her own senses. She is practical, and where she might doubt a mere explanation, she will not doubt what she can see and test for herself."

Show her? Well — why not. She is so annoyingly logical, that just might be the correct approach to take with her. "Go collect her supper-dishes," he told the Salamander. "But leave the sweet, and bring coffee. I want the effect of the wine countered. She may need both energy and alertness before the night is out."

The Salamander spun with joy and uttered a breathy laugh. "Yes!" it said. "Warn her I am coming! Let her test *me!*"

"I will," he told it. "Now *you* be certain of your path and move slowly, so that she doesn't miss anything."

✧   ✧   ✧

"I must be mad," Rose muttered again.

"You are not mad, Miss Hawkins," came the hollow, grating voice from the speaking-tube. "Believe me, you are not mad. And if you will not believe me, then believe the evidence of your own eyes and watch your supper-table."

The last words were still hanging in the air as she turned again to stare at the table — and at the flickering shape of flame suddenly hovering above it.

A conjurer's trick, she thought, with disgust — but then the flame took more definite shape, the general aspect of a lizard, which blinked fiery blue eyes at her, and began to spin in place.

Then her supper dishes rose gracefully on their tray, levitating above the tabletop. The dish containing the sweet separated from the rest and wafted gently down to rest on the tablecloth and a minute later, a spoon floated down to lie beside it. She hesitantly touched the latter; it was noticeably warm.

The tray remained above the table.

"Test it, Rose," the voice urged. "Use your own senses to tell you whether or not this is fakery. Make every test on it that you care to."

With exquisite care, she waved her hand beneath it, and encountered no resistance, no hidden supports. She reached out further and waved her hand to either side, and finally rose to her feet to circle the table. She tested the air all about the floating tray, and then waved her hand above it. There was nothing, nothing whatsoever. She circled the table again, looking for any means by which the tray could be moved, and still found nothing. The tray was perfectly ordinary, except for the fact that it was floating in midair, about a foot above the table-top.

No supports, no strings, no wires. And she thought

she heard a giggle of delight from the spinning shape, which continued to hover about a foot above the tray. She had even passed her hand repeatedly between the creature and the tray to make certain it was not somehow attached to the tray, and had encountered nothing.

She sat down again, her eyes wide, biting her lip. The tray and the creature of flame sailed towards the door, which opened obligingly for them, then closed again.

But Cameron wasn't done yet, for a moment later, the door opened again, and a coffee service sailed serenely in, below the floating flame, setting itself down on the table. She stared at it. *I am seeing this, but I still do not believe it. There must be a way to explain floating trays logically! Surely he's tricking me.*

"I thought perhaps after all that wine you might like something to clear your head," Cameron said, with a touch of amusement. "Then you can be certain that you are not being tricked."

The coffee-pot lifted into the air and poured a precise and delicate cup. The cream-pitcher followed, and her usual two lumps dropped neatly into the cup, which lifted, saucer and all, and moved towards her. She put out her hand without thinking, and it settled down on her palm like a pet bird. Finally the creature above the table stopped spinning.

She drank the coffee in silence, glancing obliquely at the little form of flame still hovering in the air, looking down at her. Finally, she put the cup down and addressed it directly.

"What are you?" she asked it.

The voice, which came from everywhere, was thin, sibilant, and silvery. "Salamander," it said to her, and blinked benignly.

She knew the precise meaning of the word in the

mystical sense, which had nothing to do with the amphibians in the garden. The Salamander was a creature commonly referred to in the medieval manuscripts she had studied back in Chicago, as well as the more modern book by Dee. She said it aloud. "Salamander — the Elemental of Fire —"

"Very good. I see your memory is still working." That was Cameron.

"As Sylphs are of Air, Undines of Water, and Gnomes of Earth — " she continued. Did he control all of these creatures? "What about them? Can you — do you —"

He anticipated the question before she formed it. "I am a Firemaster, Rose. Only the Salamanders are my servants. The Sylphs and Gnomes might aid me if they felt like doing so or their Master demanded it of them, the Undines would flee me or try to destroy me if their Master willed it. Water is my opposite, Air and Earth my allies. Every sign is the ally of those next to it, and the enemy of the one opposite."

She remembered that now from the book. Earth and Air were the opposites, and Fire and Water. She recalled the sequence now. Earth supported Fire, Air fed it. Water nurtured Earth, and gave Air substance. Air was transmuted by Fire and Water. Earth received life from Air and Water. . . .

But according to Dee's book, a human could only aspire to be a Master of the Element of his own Magickal Nature, and only those few humans who had learned and mastered their Natures could become Masters of Elements and Elementals. It took years, decades, to become the Master of even one Element, but the resulting power —

"But if you are a Firemaster, why are you confined here — " she stopped herself with a gasp, her hand going to her lips as she flushed. How could she ask such an impertinent question?

But he didn't seem to think it impertinent. "I am confined here in my home, as I am, for precisely the reason I told you when you first arrived. An accident, brought upon by hubris. I attempted a Magick for which my Nature was ill-suited. I am as — disfigured — as I told you I was, but in a far different manner than you had been led to believe." The voice was calm, but under the calm was a welter of emotions. "I dismissed my servants, all but Paul du Mond who is aware of my Magickal ability, and have lived here as a recluse since it happened. I dare not permit anyone to see me as I now am. My Salamanders attend to most of my needs, Paul attends to those things which require an intermediary with the outside world."

"And all of this around me — the books, the reading — is this to help you find a way to restore yourself?" There was a logic to this madness that was irresistible, It was all beginning to fall into place in a tight pattern, one she could not easily refute. If one simply assumed that magic power was real. . . . "I take it that Mr. du Mond is no student of languages?"

"Paul is no student of anything," came the dry retort. "He is competent in modern French, English, and Latin, but as you have seen, most of my books are in other tongues, many of them obscure. I am unable by reason of my deformity to read them for myself. Hence . . . the ruse that brought you here."

She closed her eyes for a moment and digested that, then opened them again and poured herself another cup of coffee. *If I had been the meek little bookworm I suspect he wanted, what then? Would I have been kept mind-clouded and in the dark while I prattled his translations away for him?* "And if I had told you I would not stay here in the first place?"

A dry chuckle, one with a touch of cruelty. "For myself, there were other candidates besides you. As for you — there are many ways for a penniless woman to make a living in San Francisco, but I do not believe that most of them would have appealed to you."

She felt anger penetrate her bewilderment at that bald statement. "You used me, used my circumstances to put me into a position where I had no choice!"

"I never claimed to be a gentleman, Miss Hawkins," he countered, his voice even and in fact, indifferent. "I am a businessman. You should be aware what that means by now. It is my nature to use people, and I have no responsibility to those people to guide their steps then, or later. It is up to them to make what they can of the situation, to make it mutually beneficial. You are hardly stupid. Can you say honestly that you are not benefiting by being here?"

He has me there. Wages, fine food, beautiful lodgings, lovely clothing — I am certainly worlds better off here. Even if I am at the mercy of a madman. Or a magician. If they're not the same thing. "No," she admitted. "I am much better off than I would have been back in Chicago. But I do not like being used!"

"Then do something about it," he replied, flatly. "Decide to stay or go, decide to be used or decide to use *me* to get what you want. It is your choice, Miss Hawkins."

She didn't have to decide; she knew already. "I'm staying, of course!" she snapped — and perhaps the wine was to blame for her runaway tongue and temper. "Do you think I am so foolish as to abandon luxurious surroundings and congenial work just because my employer is suffering from the delusion that he is a feudal overlord with wizardly powers?"

That made him laugh, as she flushed again. "It is not a delusion, my dear Miss Hawkins! I *am* a feudal overlord with wizardly powers. The powers you have seen for yourself, and as for the feudalism, why do you think we are referred to as 'rail *barons*'? But I am glad that your good sense overcomes any fear you might have, knowing your employer is also dabbling in Magick."

It was her turn to laugh, for once again he had turned the tables on her. But she still had an arrow in her quiver to sting him with. "I am not afraid of your magic; I haven't seen anything but a convenient replacement for gossiping servants. If you were all that powerful, Mr. Cameron, you would not have needed a railway train to bring me here. For that matter, you would not have needed *me*. Flying dinner-trays are all very well, but you obviously are dependent on normal people for a great deal, or you would not need Paul du Mond, either."

Silence for a moment made her fear she had said too much, and angered him. He *could* send her away and find someone more tractable.

"She is right, Jason," the Salamander said merrily, making her turn her head so suddenly to look at it that she nearly overset her coffee-cup.

"I know she's right, damn it!" Cameron growled. The Salamander laughed.

Rose smiled triumphantly. "Can I take it then, that this is about to become less a relationship of overlord and serf, and enter a stage of cooperation? Or — at least let it be an arrangement of lord and knight!"

"Only if *you* are willing to abide by some rules," Cameron countered swiftly. "If you wish to be my knight, you must obey my decrees, true? I did not show you all this only to have you flout my authority in Magick. I *am* the authority there. If I am occasionally terse with you, it is because I do not have the time or the leisure to be otherwise. If I give you a direct order, I expect it to be obeyed."

She nodded, primly. "Of course. You are still my

employer, and these are deep waters. I may have the rudder, but you are both the navigator and the captain."

"Very well." He sounded calmer, more satisfied. "I shall accelerate your Magickal education, and I shall not trouble to hide the activities of my servants from you. In fact, I shall assign one to you to tend to your needs, the same one that has been cleaning and picking up after you. Simply speak what you want aloud if you have any request, and it will tend to the task."

As unnerving as the floating fire-lizards were, she actually was relieved. At least now she could *see* the presence in her rooms. And now she knew it wasn't du Mond. That was reassuring all by itself.

Is there a grudging admiration in his voice? At least he won't be tempted to take me for granted now.

"I will still be attending to the matters of my business during ordinary office hours, so you will still have your afternoons free," Cameron continued. "However, I must ask you not to discuss any of this with du Mond. I believe that Paul may be jealous of you, and this would only confirm that jealousy. He wishes more from me than he deserves — or than I intend to give him."

Interesting. What is he to du Mond, or du Mond to him? Master and Apprentice? Or prisoner and keeper? On the other hand, she would really rather not discuss *anything* with Paul du Mond if she could help it.

This entire situation had an air of such unreality that it should have been a dream. That must have been why she felt bold enough to say incredible things.

I will wake up in the morning, and this will never have happened. This is all a dream; I fell asleep over that book by Dee, and I am dreaming all this.

"I would just as soon see as little of Mr. du Mond as possible," she said slowly. "If it is all the same to you."

"That will suit me perfectly," came the reply, which only made her wonder. Was there something that du Mond might tell her that Cameron did not want her to know? But what could it be? Were there still *more* secrets to be revealed?

"So, I take it that our schedule is still the same?" she said, vaguely aware that she should say something. It was trivial, but at least it was something.

"Exactly the same," Cameron told her, and there was no mistaking the satisfaction in his voice, as if now he had decided that he had accomplished something that he was very pleased with. "The only difference will be that now I will not have to wait for you to be conveniently absent or asleep to send my servants about. And now that you have recalled the schedule, may I assume that you are prepared to resume that schedule?"

"I am not so frail that I am in need of a bottle of smelling salts after all this," she said sharply. She pinched herself sharply. She did not wake up.

All right. This is no dream. And I am reasonably certain neither of us is insane. Well, I'm sure I'm not. This is not medieval moonshine; it is only a new kind of science. Surely, if I had never seen an electric light before, I would find it just as Magickal as the Salamander. "Send me your book, sir, and I shall resume my duties this very instant!"

He laughed; he was *very* pleased with himself. He sounded just like one of her father's cronies who had soundly trounced another in debate. "You may relax and enjoy your sweet, Miss Hawkins," he said indulgently, as one would to a child. "The events of tonight prevented my selecting your books, and it will take a moment before they appear."

The Salamander giggled again, and vanished soundlessly. Rosalind Hawkins was alone again in her sitting-room, torn between fuming with anger and shaking with emotions she couldn't quite define. Surely Lewis Carroll's Alice had never found herself in quite so strange a situation!

Certainly she had never encountered a male creature quite so infuriating!

Caught between conflicting emotions, she finally did what any sensible person would do.

She ate her dessert, and sat back to wait for the books to appear.

CHAPTER SEVEN

So now we embark on the real undertaking. Cameron sent his Salamander down to Rose Hawkins with the night's set of books, and sat back in his chair. *My hands are shaking. When was the last time that happened?* He regarded his trembling hands with bemusement. He had negotiated deals that could have broken his fortune if they had gone wrong, he had faced dreadful ordeals in the course of attaining his Mastery, he had endured trials of his strength and nerve that few other men could have survived, and *none* of that had left him feeling like this. He had been tempted to tell the girl that the evening's duties were canceled, but if *she* could sit there calmly and insist on carrying them out, he was not about to admit to weakness.

I feel as if I have run for miles, as if I have faced a ravenous tiger with nothing but my bare hands and my will, and convinced it to go eat something else.

The Salamander — which seemed very pleased with the evening's events — opened her door and brought the pile of books inside. She concentrated every bit of her attention on it, exactly as a bird of prey would concentrate on a rodent, as if she was still trying to spot some evidence of trickery. But when the books were on the table beside the speaking-tube, and the Salamander had transported itself to its customary position at his elbow, she stood up and walked slowly over to her accustomed seat.

"You will find these books a little more difficult than the ones I sent you in the past," he said, leaning forward so that his voice carried clearly down the tube. "They are mostly handwritten manuscripts, copies of books still older than they are."

"I am quite acoustomed to reading medieval script, Mr. Cameron," she replied briskly, taking the top book without hesitation and opening it. "I see you have not marked a passage. Am I to read the entire book?"

"Precisely," he told her, with a touch of coolness. "You may begin now, in fact."

He really didn't need to hear all of that particular book — but *she* needed to read it. Although the author was not credited, it happened to be Doctor John Dee, the ancestor of the Dee whose work had precipitated tonight's crisis, and there was a certain symmetry in beginning her real education in Magick with this book, intended for the instruction of *his* Apprentices. It was a symmetry that John Dee himself probably would have approved of.

She read through it, unflinching, even when she encountered concepts as foreign to a well-bred young lady of this century as a fork was to an African Pigmy. Much of Dee's work was pure nonsense, of course; he often got results that were quite astonishing, and would correctly deduce the cause of some particular event — but he would arrive at that cause by some of the wildest twists of illogic! For instance — the admonition that to rid a village of Plague one must first rid it of rats was, of course, correct — but the *reason* was absolute bunk. Dee's assertion was that both Plague and rats came under the auspices of the Moon, and thus the rats carried the Moon's influence indoors, where it otherwise could not penetrate!

His notes on transformations were sound though, as far as they went. Dee had never actually attempted a transformation; he only related what he had learned from colleagues on the Continent. His tastes ran to the mystical, which certainly suited a Master of Air. The Sylphs were the least effectual of the Elements, and the most capricious. It didn't do to depend on them for much of anything, and they could not keep their attention on a task for more than an hour or two at most. They made tremendous messengers and information-gatherers, they could fetch something from anywhere in the world in the blink of an eye, but if their Master had an accident and sent them for help, chances were that without the Master's eye on them, they'd become distracted on the way and leave him to bleed to death.

Not that they were harmless, any more than a tornado was harmless, or a hurricane. No would-be Master of Air ever made *that* particular mistake twice. Very few ever made it once and lived to tell about it. Such was the case with each of the Elements and its Elementals. They had their strengths and weaknesses — and all were deadly and dangerous.

In the final section of his book, Dee described the first Ordeal an Apprentice underwent in the process of becoming a Master of Air, and Cameron felt it would be instructive for Rose to read it. *It should serve as a cautionary tale, as well.* He waited expectantly when she closed the volume and put it aside. She reached for the next book, but did not open it immediately. From the expression on her face, he deduced that she was making up her mind whether to say something or not.

She cleared her throat, self-consciously. "Clearly, some of that was flummery," she said.

"A great deal, actually, but anyone with a rudimentary scientific education would recognize what is nonsensical," he replied, quietly.

"But that final chapter — ?" She let the sentence hang in the air, ending it on a note of query.

"The final chapter is accurate, insofar as it describes the correct First Ordeal for an Apprentice seeking to become a Master of Air," he told her, as matter-of-factly as if he were confirming that the sun rose in the east. "The Ordeals for other Elements differ, of course. Each is determined by the Nature of the Elementals; the one thing they all have in common is that there is a cost to the acquisition of power. Nothing comes without a price."

She did not answer that, but he had not expected her to. After a moment, she opened the second book, and began reading it aloud.

When she finished, it was well past four, and he called a halt. Even if she was able to absorb the stress of the past evening without any overt problem, *he* had not been.

As she finished reading, he cleared his throat. "That will be all for tonight, Miss Hawkins —"

"You called me Rose, earlier," she interrupted.

He recalled immediately, much to his chagrin, that she was right. "So I did. I apologize."

"Don't," she replied, surprising him. "The use of Christian names or even nicknames to another has more than one interpretation. It *can* be the sign that one is far superior to the other, but it can also be the sign that they are equal, if the liberty is equal."

He felt the corner of his mouth pull in an approximation of a smile at her cleverness. "Very well, then. I freely give you permission to call me Jason. I never had a nickname."

"I frankly can't imagine anyone daring to give you one," she countered, the blue eyes behind the thick lenses of her glasses sparkling with a hint of mischief. "I have no objection whatsoever to you calling me 'Rose,' however. I never particularly identified with my namesake."

"The character from Shakespeare?" he said, surprised. "But whyever not?"

"Because I wasn't named for the character from Shakespeare, but the naughty wife from *Die Fledermaus*," she admitted, blushing. "My father's taste ran to music rather than theater."

She startled him into a real laugh. "Now *that* I understand! We have done a good night's work, Rose; a great deal has been accomplished. Thank you, and good night."

"Good night, Jason," she answered, setting the book aside and standing up, brushing her skirt as she did so. "May I say that, strange as this has been, I fervently hope that I do not wake in the morning to discover this has been a dream brought on by too many medieval manuscripts and too much imagination? Life will be so much more interesting if all this is real."

"It is real enough, Rose," he told her image soberly, though too softly to be heard. "Real enough to be more nightmare than dream — which I pray you never discover."

In the morning, Rose woke quite certain that she *had* dreamed all of the events of the previous evening. It was too fantastic to be believed, too ridiculous. A railway magnate with a double life as a wizard, with magic at his command that truly worked? Absurd. She laughed at herself even as she stretched and made ready to rise —

Right up to the point where she drew aside the bedcurtains and groped for her glasses, only to find them floating mere inches from her face, with a blurry globe of brightness hovering in the center of the room.

She seized the spectacles and fumbled them on hastily, and the blurry form resolved itself into a Salamander. There was no mistake; it was exactly as she remembered, a lizard-like creature that glowed a brilliant, flame-colored yellow, with fiery blue eyes. She could not tell if it was the one from last night or not, since she didn't note any real differences.

Then it spoke, and the voice was significantly different from the other; higher, breathier, like a small, shy child's. "What would you care to wear today, lady?" it asked. Its tone was deferential.

She blinked at it, and said the first thing that came into her mind; the slight chill in the air reminded her that it was November, and she identified the first warm ensemble she recalled. "The brown wool plush suit and one of the ivory silk blouses," she told it. The Salamander began to spin, and the wardrobe doors opened.

The suit lifted out, jacket and skirt together, looking uncannily as if it was alive. "This?" said the Salamander, as the suit turned for her examination.

"Oh—yes," she replied, still feeling rather stunned.

A bureau drawer opened, and one of the blouses rose from it, unfolding itself before her eyes. Even as she watched it, dumbfounded, the creases it had acquired from lying folded in the drawer smoothed out.

"And this?" asked the Salamander politely. "Or another?"

It was silk, it was ivory — the details of ornamentation hardly mattered at that moment. "I — yes, that will do nicely." She stared in wonder as the suit draped itself over the back of a chair, the blouse followed, and the appropriate underskirts, petticoats, and underthings followed it. Without prompting, the Salamander extracted a pair of fine brown kid boots that matched the suit from the special rack holding shoes, and those skimmed across the floor to join the rest of the ensemble.

"Will you have a bath?" it asked breathily. "Your

breakfast is here already, if you would care to eat while I prepare the bath."

"Please — " she said, still dazed. The Salamander, still spinning, floated off into the bath room.

She groped for the dressing-gown she had left at the foot of the bed, slid her legs out from beneath the covers, and put it on. She made her way into the sitting room in her bare feet; there were already fires burning in the fireplaces, warming the air.

Of course there are fires. This is a Salamander, a creature of fire. It would probably want a fire here.

The usual tray was indeed waiting for her. She sat down, bemused and a bit dazzled, but not too bemused to eat. Long before she was finished, the Salamander, no longer spinning, floated in through the door.

"Your bath is ready when you are, lady," it said. "Is there anything else?"

"Not — not at the moment," she told it, hesitantly.

"Only say what you need, and it will be here." The Salamander gave itself another spin, then vanished completely.

She put her fork down, still staring at the place where it had been. *At least now I know what has been in and out of my rooms, and how things appeared so silently. It could be worse, much worse. It could have been du Mond.* The very idea was enough to make her lose her appetite.

It also made her skin crawl, and the bath suddenly seemed very inviting.

There were distinct advantages to this new situation. The Salamander had laid all her clothing out, perfectly; had drawn the bath while she idled at breakfast. She discovered another, when the creature appeared as soon as she stepped out of the bathtub. It warmed her towels before she touched them, then brought her garments, one at a time, into the bathroom without her having to ask. She felt rather like a French queen with a hundred attendants before she finished dressing — and for once she didn't have to do up her corset herself as an approximation. The Salamander tightened it snugly for her — not fashionably constricting, but not so loose that it was uncomfortable and unsupportive. Not for the first time, she wished she did not have to wear the silly thing — but she was not the kind of wild and rebellious woman who would shed her skirts and corsets for a vest and bloomers, and stride off to march in a suffragette parade. Perhaps she was a rebel in her own way, but she preferred to keep her rebellion to paper and academia.

Sunshine outside beckoned, and she hurried down the stairs to see what her new change in status meant to the running of the household.

The change wasn't immediately obvious, but as she walked around the gardens, she did see the occasional spinning globe of light moving along a hedge or over a flower-bed. Where they passed, order appeared in their wake. And when she reached Sunset's paddock, the handsome stallion was enjoying the ministrations of three of the creatures; one giving him a thorough brushing, one cleaning his hooves, and a third slowly combing out his tail. Or rather — one hovered above his back while a brush passed over his flanks, one spun around the vicinity of his knee while a hoofpick cleaned his upturned hoof, and one spun above his tail while a comb ran carefully through the long hair. He seemed perfectly at ease with them, which surprised her, as she would have thought that such strange apparitions would have sent the stallion into a fit of fear.

But perhaps — if he came from a "friend" of Jason's,

perhaps that friend is also a Firemaster. Perhaps Sunset has always been handled by supernatural as well as human grooms, and they seem ordinary to him. Even so, he was remarkably steady with them; the little she knew of horses was that they were often restive even with human grooms.

She took the remainder of her "stroll" at a very brisk pace, trying to cover as much ground as she could, to get the paths of the gardens firmly in her memory. Before long, she intended to have a mental map of every path on the grounds. A need to escape was still a possibility; Jason's cordiality last night had not changed her mind on that score. If anything, she regarded him as *more* dangerous, rather than less, no matter what she had told him. If she no longer needed to worry about interference from human servants in an escape, now she had to be concerned with the even more dangerous Salamanders. If she had to flee, she would have to get off the estate before they were sent to search for her, for she would never be able to escape them.

That set her to wondering just what Jason's accident had involved. *Is he terribly burned, I wonder? That would make sense — the little I remember about Salamanders is that they were employed to smelt ores, fire up crucibles to incredible temperatures, and make fine steel by alchemists.* Perhaps he had slipped, or somehow angered them, and they had burned him. *But if that was true, would he still have such control over them now? I thought he said that his accident was because he attempted something foreign to his Magickal Nature. But I can't imagine that Sylphs or Gnomes could do much to him — and what kind of deformity could an Undine inflict?*

The question kept part of her mind occupied as the sun slowly sank and she hiked her way through Jason Cameron's extensive complex of gardens.

For he had more than one. There was the Formal Garden, with its mathematically precise flower-beds and its carefully sculpted topiary trees in geometric shapes. This garden featured roses extensively, but also rhododendrons and other blooming shrubs. There was the requisite privet-hedge Maze, which she very quickly reasoned out to be a Fibonacci series and had solved the same afternoon she entered it. There was what she privately thought of as the Pleasure Garden, after the gardens mentioned in the poem "Kubla Khan" by Coleridge. This was a place of nooks and bowers, artificial grottoes and other places suitable for romantic tete-a-tetes, all planted around with bushes of fragrant leaves or flowering vines, all planned in such a way that each was invisible to the next or the one behind.

There was a Water Garden, a series of ponds graced with waterfalls and fountains, planted with lilies and other water-loving plants, and stocked with enormous, gracefully-moving fish of gold, white, and black.

A Kitchen Garden clearly supplied the estate with herbs and salads, and there was even a small orchard. But by far the largest part of the grounds had been sculpted into a clever imitation of a wild forest, complete with an artful "ruined tower," rustic swings, pretty little "forest huts" for shelter, and sculpted seats beneath the branches of some quite magnificent trees. A masterful hand had been at work here, keeping the best of the wilderness that had been here intact, leaving pockets of completely wild brush to preserve the illusion of absolute wild, while taming the rest so that it was inspiring rather than intimidating.

Cameron had walls around the gardens, but they were decorative rather than functional. At the extreme of his property, he had a single wire strung as a token fence. It was not even barbed wire — he had no near

neighbors, and there were supposedly no dangerous
animals about, so all that this "fence" did was to define
his property-line. Once she got this far — if she had to
flee — she could make her way down to the coastline
and follow it to San Francisco, or follow the fence-line in
the other direction to the rail-spur and follow it to the
main line. It would be a long and grueling walk; it might
well take two or even three days. But she had no doubt
that she could make it, provided she could avoid pursuit.

Perhaps it was foolish to think about a need to
escape from this place —

*But it would have seemed ridiculous to think that
Jason Cameron was a magician, two days ago,* she
reminded herself, as she made her way back to the
mansion itself. *I believe in the next day or so I will try
to find where the rail-spur crosses the property line.*

And if nothing else, this was certainly ensuring that
she got her exercise!

"Do you try again this afternoon?" the Salamander
asked, watching Cameron lay out the lines of a
magickal diagram in specially enchanted chalk on the
floor of his workroom. He had stuck the chalk itself
through a potato so that he could manipulate it, for
otherwise his paws did not have fine enough control to
hold something the size of a stick of chalk.

"Yes," he replied in a grunt that betrayed his pain;
his body was poorly suited to bending over, and the
position was causing him more difficulty than usual. At
the same time, he dared not take any narcotic for the
pain; he could not afford to make a mistake in this
diagram.

"Are you certain this is a good idea?" the
Salamander continued. "You have not found out
anything new in what the girl has read to you."

"Nevertheless — I think — I have — a new — insight,"

he grunted. Perusal of his notes this afternoon had given him a slightly different perspective into the spell — or rather, the counter-spell — that was *supposed* to have reversed his condition. He thought, perhaps, he might have deduced a piece that had been deliberately left out of the original manuscript. If he was right, he should be able to enact the altered spell and return to human form.

The main question in his mind now was if the spell would be effective on his hybrid form. It was possible that the only way to make the reversal would be to transform all the way to wolf first, then return to his human state. If that was true, his task was doubly difficult, for he would first have to find out what had gone wrong with the transformation to wolf, then make corresponding changes in the reversal-spell, then perform both.

I must have been insane. The medieval spell of the *loup-garou* appeared often in tales, but in only one real grimoire that he had ever discovered. That alone should have made him extremely cautious. He *knew* that most medieval Masters held things back from their written records, kept key points secret in order to maintain their power over their Apprentices. He should have assumed that this grimoire would have been no exception.

And he should never have trusted the grimoire of an Earth Master who created such a thing as a lycanthrope spell. What use was it, except to terrify or spy upon one's neighbors? If one wished to experience life as a wolf, there were many spells to place one as an observer within the mind of a real wolf. Earth Masters in general were the mildest of creatures, much taken up with the health and fertility of the regions in which they lived, with studying the flora and fauna, and tended to be very conservative in their Magicks. The Master who had written the grimoire must, therefore, have been something of a "maverick," unusual in his interests and in his approach to Earth Magick. Cameron knew now that he should have taken warning from this.

Instead, he had felt a cocky kinship with the long-dead Master, and confidence in his own ability to be as much of an innovator as the man who had penned the spells in this grimoire.

Stupid, foolish, over-confident . . . all those described Cameron, and well he knew it. After all, overconfidence was what had led him to accept Paul du Mond as an Apprentice, so certain he had been that he could make a silk purse out of that particular sow's ear. But up until now, he had never gotten himself into a difficulty he could not manage to get himself out of with a profit.

Up until now. Eventually the odds catch up with you, and pride goeth before a fall. He finished chalking the last of the sigils and straightened with a groan. His bones ached whether he remained still or moved, and he walked slowly to the table to deposit his chalk, listening to his joints pop and snap with each step he took. The muscles in his neck were so knotted and painful it was hard to hold his head up.

Fortunately, what he was about to attempt would either work, or not, within a half an hour.

"Guard me," he ordered the Salamander shortly. "If this is to be successful at all, it will be immediate, and whether it succeeds or not it will all be completed quickly."

"If it is over quickly, it will strain your resources." The Salamander sounded disapproving. "Your resources are thin enough, with very little to spare."

"If so, it is my decision to make." He turned to look at the creature with half-closed eyes. "You yourself know that your kind are no longer my servants, but my allies. I no longer need to guard myself against your rebellion, nor to use my Power to force you to obey me. I have not *controlled* you for years; you obey me because you wish to, not because I must coerce you. Unlike Simon."

"Unlike Simon," the Salamander agreed. "Still. You have limits, and you have enemies. There are other things you must guard yourself from, and Simon is one of them."

"So I will rely on you to accomplish some of that for me," he retorted. "Guard me now. This will require but a half an hour of both our time."

He stepped into the center of the diagram, being careful not to scuff any of the chalked marks.

Half an hour later, he stepped out again, unable to raise his feet enough to prevent scuffing the lines. But by then, of course, it didn't matter.

The modified spell had not worked, and as the Salamander had warned, it had left him in terrible pain and so exhausted that the mere act of breathing was an effort.

He ached in every joint and every muscle, and shivered, chilled to the bone, as if he was in the grip of a high fever. His mouth hung open, his parched tongue lolling out, dog-like, as he panted. His lungs burned, his stomach churned, there were shooting pains running down his spine and into both legs with every step he took. His head throbbed with agony. He got as far as his chair before collapsing, which was better than he had expected. He caught the arm of it as he fell, and turned enough so that his body slumped into the chair without further mishap. He wanted to close his eyes, but he knew that if he did, he would lose his grip on consciousness.

The Salamander was already beside him as he collapsed, and a goblet containing a mix of herbs and opium powder levitated into his hand before he could ask for it. He made the supreme effort it took to raise his hand, and lapped up the bitter mixture in thirsty gulps.

He lay back in his chair, as the goblet whisked away from his limp hand. Though bitter, the liquid did a great deal to ease the torment of his burning and dry throat and tongue. A second goblet followed the first into his hand, this one full of milk, one of the few liquids besides water he had any taste for in his altered body. As the initial exhaustion faded, he managed to bring it to his mouth as well; he lapped it up more slowly, and felt his stomach settling from the combined effect of some of the herbs and the warm, soothing milk.

The empty goblet lifted from his hand before he could put it down. He leaned back into the chair, and closed his burning eyes.

"Can you eat?" the Salamander asked. He raised his lids, and gazed at it. It had stopped spinning and now perched on the asbestos pad he'd placed on the desk for it to rest on.

"I shall have to soon — but not just yet." His voice sounded hoarser than usual to his own sharp ears. "Let the drugs take effect first."

"Yes." The Salamander cocked its head to one side, and regarded him closely. "You are not yet in danger from them."

"But I will be soon, if I am not careful." He filled in what the Salamander did not say. "And therein lies the dilemma, does it not? Do I take opiates for my pain, and risk addiction and muddle-headedness, or do I endure the pain and the attendant distractions and weakness? Both put me at risk, no matter which I choose."

"It is a difficulty," the Salamander agreed. It did not offer any further opinion, for which Cameron was grateful. He was not in a forgiving mood at the moment, and he did not want to hear any more criticism from what was essentially a creature under his command.

He slumped back in his chair and tried to relax into its cushions and support, consciously working to loosen those knotted muscles, to get them to release some of their tension. Gradually, the pain that was centered between his eyes began to ebb, the aches of his muscles and joints to subside, as the opium exerted its power. Finally, the pain receded altogether, and he opened his eyes, carefully assessing his physical state.

He was just a trifle light-headed, but no more than the equivalent of a single glass of wine. The Salamander was quite good at judging his need and the strength of the drugs he would require to deal with his difficulties.

And it was quite good at judging when those drugs would take effect. Within seconds, there was a plate of barely-seared chunks of beef on the desk, and another goblet of milk beside it. Obviously, his caretaker was going to see to it that he *did* eat.

The lamps had been trimmed, and the shades were thick, amber-colored glass, so that the light was clear, but not hard on his now-sensitive eyes. He was familiar with the physical effects of drugs; they were something a Master of any Element *had* to know, both on the rare occasions when he himself might have to resort to them or prescribe them, and in case an Apprentice resorted to drugs to make up for inferior ability. Cameron knew that the opiates had made his pupils widen, and that if he looked at himself in the mirror, he would see that there was nothing visible of the iris but a thin, brown ring around the dark, wide pupils. That would make him even more sensitive to light than usual, and his lupine eyes were very sensitive indeed.

He bolted the chunks of meat without chewing them, and washed down the salt-sweet taste of the blood left in his mouth with the milk. The Salamander said nothing during the whole time he ate, but whisked the plate and cup away the moment he had finished.

He yawned, and felt his jaw muscles stretching and his tongue extending, though he tried to prevent the latter. "I am just as glad that Paul was not here for this," he said.

The Salamander stirred restlessly. "Are you certain that you can trust him for a week alone in the city?"

It occurred to him that this Salamander was uncommonly intelligent and articulate, and growing more so all the time, as if continual exposure to its Master was making it into something akin to a highly intelligent human. *Well, all to the good. I certainly need an intelligent aide, and if it is a Fire entity, why should that matter?* He shrugged, or tried to. "I am reasonably certain that I cannot trust him, beyond trusting that he *will* follow my orders. But I have not yet detected the touch of Simon Beltaire on him, so whatever mischief he is getting into, it is probably nothing more serious than finding ways to cheat me. Or to cheat others," he added as an afterthought. "He has enough Magickal knowledge now to ensure that he wins at any number of games of chance. I am *quite* certain that whatever else he is doing, he is increasing his personal fortune illicitly, no matter how many times I warn him that such is a dangerous game to play."

"He would never believe he could be caught," the Salamander pointed out.

"And he might be correct," Cameron mused. "Who else would catch him but a Master or another Apprentice, and what others are there in the city that would stoop to cheating at games of chance for mere money when there are surer ways of obtaining a fortune for a trifle more work?"

He considered his own fortune, obtained by using his growing control and knowledge of Magick to be certain *what* commodity would be needed *when* and *where*. With that knowledge, and with the ability to see to it, through his Salamanders, that no one else beat his goods to the market, a relative pittance carefully invested doubled, redoubled, and doubled again. Within a year, he was well-off; within two, wealthy, and within five, in very near the position he held today. After that, he needed only to find competent underlings and he could settle back and concentrate his attentions on Magick, which was precisely what he had done.

It had been easier to accomplish all that out here in the West, where fortunes were made and lost overnight, where one's status depended, quite simply, on how much wealth one had, and no one questioned what a man did as long as he appeared to be a perfect gentleman in genteel company. In the East, he might have run into difficulties, not the least of which were the vastly greater number of Masters there. Here he had no one to contend with but Simon Beltaire, for the Masters of other Elements had no reason to interfere with him out here, where there was so little in the way of competition. The local Masters of Water invested in shipping concerns, knowing that they could *ensure* their ships arrived safely and ahead of all others. Those of Earth had made all of their fortunes in gold and silver; who better to know where the strikes would be? And those of Air invested in entertainment, and were paid back handsomely, for there was no place on the face of the earth as pleasure-loving as this West Coast, and no one better able to manipulate the emotions of others to induce pleasure than a Master of Air.

He closed his eyes, felt himself "floating" just a little with the effect of the drugs. It was the closest he came these days to a moment of pleasure himself — a moment when he allowed himself the luxury to be free from pain at the expense of mental alertness. He would not permit himself to fall asleep like this — his training made that much possible — but he could relax, just a little, and let his thoughts meander where they would.

He drifted further, and did not trouble to fight the drugs. The last time he had felt like this, it had been the effect of fever rather than drugs. . . .

Typhoid. So medieval. Incredible that I survived. With opium between himself and the memories of what some might call a tragic childhood, it seemed as if they might belong to someone else entirely. He let the memories flow past him, surveying them with drug-induced detachment.

Not so tragic. Not as tragic as an early death, certainly. There are sadder stories than mine playing out in the streets of every large city every day.

How ironic that he and the Hawkins girl should have come from the same city. But a span of fifteen years separated her birth and his, and he doubted that she even thought a great deal about the event that had been so pivotal in his life and the lives of most other natives of Chicago born before 1871.

How incredibly ironic that he should have become a Master of Fire when Fire had been instrumental in obliterating his past and changing his future beyond all expectations. How even more ironic that this same Fire had been caused by two now-dead Firemasters.

He had only been four years old when the Great Fire in Chicago had taken his mother and destroyed his father's home and business. That was what he had been told, at any rate — during the few times his father had been drunk enough to talk, but not too drunk to be incoherent. He himself had no real memory of her or of the times before the Fire; vague feelings, even vaguer images, but no memories. And as for the Great Fire itself —

Even the opium could not cushion that memory, and as usual, he shied away from it.

He and his father had wandered for days before someone had taken them to a charity shelter run by some church or other, but when his father began to drink, they were turned out. His father had no real heart for anything after his mother's death; despite the generosity and charity of many, he never bothered to look for help outside of a bottle again.

Cameron could, if he chose, conjure up a Magickal vision of his father as the man had been, but all that remained in his memory was the drunk.

I can't even think of him with any positive feelings; he was never more than someone I had to obey — and sometimes take care of. The only time that Ronald Cameron was not drunk was when he was suffering from a hangover and trying to scrape together the cash for his next bottle of rotgut whiskey. He dragged himself from one odd job to the next, hauling his young son behind him like so much unwanted, half-forgotten baggage.

It was life on the edge, but children are flexible, and he had endured it because it was all he knew. Such a life could not last for long, but it had been long enough to ensure his father's complete descent into a state where nothing mattered to him but the next drink.

The two years Jason spent trailing about after his father should have been a century for all the misery they contained. Always cold, hungry, filthy — fighting with tramps who tried to steal the little he and his father had left, always sleeping with one eye open for trouble — small wonder he had gotten sick.

Small wonder father abandoned me as soon as I became a real burden.

As so much of his memory was fragmented, he had only bits and pieces of memory from his illness, but the pieces he had were extraordinarily vivid. The first was of the hour before dawn, and his father literally *tying* him to the front gate of a brick house so that he would not try to follow, or wander away in his delirium. He recalled that he was cold, but as light-headed as he was now, and as he shivered, he could not make himself move so much as a finger. The second sequential piece was of an amazingly ugly man peering down at him, then glancing up at someone out of Jason's line of sight. . . .

"Sick as a dog, sir." Then, in a tone of acidic irony, *"Someone must've mistaken this place for a charity hospital. I'll call a policeman."*

A second voice. *"Wait a moment."* A second face, thin and ascetic, peering at him through the lenses of a pince-nez. *"No, bring him inside, clean him up, and send for the doctor. I can use this one."*

And *that* was his savior. Jason grimaced sardonically. Not surprising that "clean him up" was the order before "send for the doctor." Alan Ridgeway was not a cruel man, but he was not a compassionate man either. He could have stood as a model for anyone wishing to study the morals and manners of the pure intellectual. There was very little warmth in him, which was rather ironic considering that he was the most powerful Firemaster in Chicago.

He had not *been* in Chicago at the time of the Great Fire, or it might not have gotten as far as it had.

Might. He might have been able to separate the combatants before they burned down half of Chicago and thousands of acres around Peshtigo....

One Firemaster had lived in Peshtigo, a lumber town in the heart of the Wisconsin woodlands, and one on the South Side of Chicago. They had always been rivals, but one day in October, something happened to make them deadly enemies. And a few days later, the battle began that claimed twelve hundred lives in Wisconsin and an additional three hundred in Chicago.

The only other Masters in the city at the time of the Fire had been of Air and Earth, and precious little use in the face of an inferno. There were no Masters of any kind in the lumber-land of Wisconsin. And when it was over, both Firemasters were dead.

The Masters of Boston had been horrified by the carnage, and in an unprecedented burst of public-spiritedness, those of Fire decreed that one of their number *must* relocate to Chicago to see to it that there were no outbreaks of fires caused by Elementals set free by the deaths of their Masters. He had been told the Masters of Water of New York had sent a similar representative to counter any actions of Salamanders. The Firemasters had drawn lots to determine who should go, and Alan Ridgeway had lost.

A true Boston Brahmin, Ridgeway had changed his name when he achieved his Mastery and had vanished from the ken of his family, who would have expected certain duties from him that he was no longer able or willing to fulfill. Magick was his mistress and his wife, and no mere female could ever interest him enough to make him want to make even a token effort to satisfy her. That would not have Done in the circles he was born to, so he removed himself from those circles.

It hardly mattered that he was no longer even

part-heir to the family fortune, since no Master was ever without money for long. He soon made a modest fortune of his own — a modest fortune was all he wanted — and when he was chosen by fate to go to Chicago, he went without too much complaint.

But the Fire that had claimed so many lives seemed to have claimed a disproportionate number of those with the Magickal Nature of Fire itself, for the one thing Alan Ridgeway had not been able to find in the year he had been in the City was an Apprentice. For some, this would have caused no great trouble, but for Alan, brought up to always strictly follow the rules, it was very disturbing. He *was* a Master and a Master needed an Apprentice. He had left his previous Apprentice with another Master, since the boy was not able to make the move with him. And Alan Ridgeway, unlike many Masters, loved to teach. Without a pupil, he felt truly incomplete.

So when a filthy, sick, penniless child, *with the purest Magickal Nature of Fire Ridgeway had ever seen,* had been abandoned at his front gate, it must have seemed like the hand of a beneficent Providence at work.

Not that Ridgeway believed in Providence. A true Cynic of the ancient Grecian school of philosophy of that name, he believed in nothing he could not see or experience himself. Perhaps that had been why Magick had claimed his soul with such strength — for although Magick was mystical in nature, it was also something he could see, measure, and control.

Dear old Ridgeway. Once I was clean and fit to come into his immaculate house, he did his best for me.

For a Firemaster, of course, the work of augmenting the doctor to ensure a cure was fairly simple. The reason for fever was to burn out a disease. In a child whose Magickal Nature contained even a hint of Fire,

Fire could be used to complete the process before the child became too weak and debilitated to recover. In a child like Jason, Ridgeway could work a cure even the doctor pronounced as miraculous, though the illness be the deadly typhoid fever itself.

Jason had awakened in a place that, at the time, seemed compounded from fever-dreams — in an oak bed with clean, fresh sheets, in a fine room, with the ugly man sitting in a comfortable chair beside the bed, watching over him.

The ugly man was Ridgeway's trusted manservant, Barnes; beneath Barnes' gruff exterior beat a heart of solid granite. He was in that chair because he had been ordered to remain until Jason awoke, and not out of any humanitarian concern for a sick child.

Barnes never showed any sign of caring for anything or anyone; his acidic wit burned as wickedly as any Salamander, and he spared no one, not even himself. He treated Jason as an adult from the beginning, for he had no patience with children, and he reasoned that if Jason was treated like an adult, he would soon become one. If Jason did something childlike, he was scourged with the whip of Barnes' wit until he often thought that a physical beating would be preferable. *But as long as I behaved like a responsible adult, I had nothing to complain about. Certainly there was nothing lacking in my physical and intellectual surroundings!*

Ridgeway knew nothing about children or their needs, and left Jason's care up to Barnes. But as for Jason's education — *there* Ridgeway had an interest. He had his own theories about the way a child should be taught, and applied them with a vengeance.

It was a good thing I came out of that fever with all my intelligence intact. He had needed every scrap of it. Ridgeway's notion of a proper education was to rush the child through the tedium of learning to read, write, and figure, and then go straight into the *real* meat of learning, beginning with the classics of Grecian and Roman literature. Ridgeway had a sound background in history, and saw no reason why a modern child couldn't emulate an Elizabethan child like Lady Jane Grey, who could read and write in several languages competently enough to correspond with adults in them by her ninth birthday.

I would have been a severe disappointment to him if I'd been a dolt. Not likely, though. Not with such a strong Magickal Nature. Children of that sort were generally the brightest and best.

Ridgeway kept him at his books from dawn to dusk, with time out only for another passion of his, physical exercise of the classical Greek sort.

Cameron had actually enjoyed poor Ridgeway's attempts to replicate the exercises undertaken by the athletes of ancient Greece, with the addition of equitation, for Ridgeway loved riding and there was nothing he could not ride. *Sound mind, sound body, and all that.* They were the closest he came to being able to play. The time or two that he had feebly objected to the strenuous intellectual regimen, both Barnes and Ridgeway had pointed out that he had been taken from the gutter, and they had no obligation to him. If he wished to return to the gutter, he could do so at any time.

Memories of near-starvation were a potent goad to keep him from voicing any further objections.

Ridgeway was even kind in his own way. He never uttered a rebuke that was not justified, and while he did not demonstrate affection physically, he was certainly ready enough with warm praises as Jason rose to meet his high expectations. Before long, Jason never even thought of his former life.

Soon enough, Ridgeway treated Jason as the Apprentice he would be when his powers settled at about eighteen, rather than the child that he was. Such treatment included one-sided "discussions" of Ridgeway's observations.

"What do you think of people, boy?" The Master puffed on his pipe and regarded Jason speculatively.

"People, as in humanity, sir? Ordinary people, you mean?" At Ridgeway's nod, the boy shrugged. *"I don't think of them much at all, sir. I mean, we're so different from them, why bother thinking about them?"*

"People are sheep, boy." The Master made this pronouncement with the finality of a physical law. *"But it's in our interest to protect the flock. If we don't, the wolves will eat them up, and there'll be nothing for us. Just because they're sheep, it doesn't follow that they have no value. Always remember that, boy. We aren't the wolves. We're the shepherds, and the sheep can be of great benefit to us."*

Cameron had never seen anything in all his years to contradict that particular piece of wisdom. Ridgeway had used that analogy often during Cameron's education.

Once it had come up in an odd circumstance — when a stained-glass window in a church had caught Ridgeway's eye. It depicted Jesus with a shepherd's crook and a lamb over his shoulders, and Ridgeway had begun to laugh.

Jason had been puzzled at the reaction to a church window, and Ridgeway had been in a good enough mood to explain it to him.

"I have to laugh whenever I see the sheep talking about Jesus as 'The Good Shepherd' without thinking about it. What does the shepherd do?" Ridgeway waited for the obvious reply, smiling a little.

"He protects the sheep," Jason had replied promptly.

"And why?" Ridgeway chuckled. "So he can take their wool twice a year, take their milk if he's so inclined, and butcher lamb and ewe alike when the flock is big enough that he can afford some meat out of it. Do you think that's the image those good people in there really have of their God?"

Even at ten Jason was far more aware of the illusions people cherished than most adults. "No," he had answered promptly. "They don't want to think of God that way."

"But it's a truer view than they know," Ridgeway had replied, sardonically. "A truer image than they want to contemplate." He chuckled again. "Barnes keeps asking me if the correct translation of that passage in the Bible 'feed my sheep,' shouldn't read 'fleece my sheep.'"

Jason's mouth twitched with amusement at the recollection. No doubt if anyone had overheard them, Ridgeway would have been publicly vilified, perhaps even attacked.

But Ridgeway was too clever to say any such things where he might be overheard. He had made a concerted effort to portray a perfect humanitarian and man of letters. He contributed generously to charity, in part because the "sheep" had to be fed, and in part because people who were starving tended to make trouble. In his capacity as a Firemaster, he helped to keep the common people of Chicago safe from a repetition of the Great Fire, though that was hardly public knowledge. He was considered a fine gentleman and a model citizen, and he saw to it that Jason was formed into the same pattern — but also that Jason knew *why* such a pose was necessary. When Jason passed his Ordeals and became a Master in his own right, Ridgeway was as proud of his accomplishment as he had any right to expect. If Ridgeway and Barnes had never attempted to become substitute parents, they also never pretended that they were trying to do so.

He had never found his father. He'd gone out, now and again, to look — but his quest was as fruitless as it was futile. What would he have done if he'd found the man, anyway? He could hardly have taken a drunk back to his Master; Ridgeway would rightly have refused to have anything to do with the situation, and might have thrown both of them out. Any money he had supplied would quickly have turned into little bottles of spirits.

At least Ridgeway and Barnes wanted him. Ridgeway wanted him because of his potential as a student, and Barnes because having him there pleased the Master and because Jason assumed some of Barnes' duties. It wasn't *love,* but why should that matter? It was tolerance and welcome, and that should be enough for anyone.

Well, it didn't matter, and there's an end to it. My own father didn't want me, so I'm lucky I found a place where I was needed.

But after he became a Master in his own right, things changed, as Ridgeway had known they would. It was uncomfortable to have two Masters of the same ardent Element as Fire in such close proximity to each other — the more so, since one was a former Apprentice of the other. There were bonds of respect and pride there that would not permit them to become enemies, so one of them had to go, and since Jason was the younger, he opted to leave. Besides, he had just discovered the amazing potential for wealth that the railroads represented, and it had seemed to him that it would be foolish to compete for a territory when so much of the great West remained unclaimed. Ridgeway provided him with the seed money for his own fortune and sent him off with blessings, and Cameron began his investments in the Chicago Commodities Exchange. It did not take him long to build up enough that he could be considered a serious investor in larger projects. That was when he left Illinois entirely, and became an entrepreneur in Steam and the Railroads as only a Firemaster could.

"Rose is in her room again," the Salamander said, interrupting his reverie. "She's just finishing her dinner. Are you fit enough for her to read tonight?"

With an effort, he raised his eyelids, and waved a clumsy-feeling paw at the obsidian mirror. Rose Hawkins' image appeared in it, laughing at something.

"She has just found out where her meals come from," the Salamander told him. "She asked her servant. She seems to find it very amusing."

She looked as if she was beginning to take all of the strangeness of her situation in stride, which was a definite relief to Cameron.

"Where was she today?" he asked the Salamander. "What was she doing?"

The Salamander could not shrug, but its indifference was clear. "Walking in the gardens."

That was harmless enough, and surely would have bored the Salamander. But the girl did more walking than any woman he'd ever met; not even the women who made a living on the streets covered as much actual distance in a day as she did!

"She must be used to walking," the Salamander continued. "She seemed to walk a great deal in Chicago."

There was that. Given the shabby state of her wardrobe, she probably had not even been able to afford street-car fare regularly.

He pulled the mouth of the speaking-tube over to his face, and spoke into it. "If you are ready, Miss Hawkins —"

"Rose," she interrupted. "We agreed to use Christian names, Jason."

"Indeed we did." He felt a flicker of amusement at her boldness. "Very well, Rose, we can begin where we left off last night."

He was not paying a great deal of attention to anything but the cadence of her reading once she began. He allowed the chair to take all of his weight, and stared into the obsidian mirror at her image as she slowly puzzled her way through the complicated German grammar of the first of the night's volumes. It was not an easy task to wade through this book, and Cameron was impressed by her fluency.

As she paused to decipher a particular word, she evidenced a flash of humor. "I beg your pardon for taking so long with this sentence," she said without looking up, "But I sincerely hope that this fellow's grasp of Fire Magick was better than his penmanship and skill at writing, or I fear he came to a *warm* end."

Cameron was surprised into a dry chuckle. "I believe you can be easy on that score," he replied. "I am given to understand that he died peacefully in his bed at an extreme old age."

She continued on for a bit further, then frowned, flipped ahead a few pages, then stopped altogether. "Excuse me, Jason, but I think the reason you wish me to read this next section is for my benefit, and not yours."

Once again she surprised him with her acuity. "Your point?" he asked.

"While I have no objection to the principle, this man's handwriting is wretched, his spelling worse, and his grammar, even for a German, worse still." She looked at the speaking-tube directly, as if she was looking straight at him. "I think you would do your ears and my eyes a great deal of good if *you* would give me your understanding of a person's Magickal Nature, since that seems to be the subject of this particular segment of the volume."

"She has a point," the Salamander chuckled. "You hated that book when Ridgeway wanted you to read it, and for the same reasons she dislikes it."

Only too true. He considered his own state for a moment. Was he personally fit to give anyone a coherent explanation of anything?

Possibly. Just possibly. "I will try, Rose," he acknowledged, "but you must bear in mind that my approach is modern, and tends to the rational and scientific, insofar as Magick can be either of those things. The solution I am searching for may lie in more mystical realms and if your understanding is purely modern you may not translate later documents with the appropriate slant."

"Then I will set this aside to read later, in stronger light," she promised, and marked the book, placing it back on the table. Then she settled back in her chair, but rather than folding her hands in her lap, to his surprise she took a leather-covered notebook from the table and picked up a pencil, preparing to take notes!

He almost commented on that, and caught himself just in time. He could not let her know that he was able to watch her, or she might be offended. Worse, she might be angry, angry enough to demand to be released from this position.

I need her skills. There is no escaping the fact.

"Very well, if you are ready — " He cleared his throat, feeling a trifle self-conscious. *Well, I cannot possibly bore her worse than those ancient professors she had to listen to.* "According to the System of Magick which we all use, as calculated by Pythagoras, all Magickal Power is embodied in the creatures of the Four Elements. If a human — or any other earthly creature, I suppose, but at the moment we are only concerned with humans — wishes to work Magick, he must do so through the intermediary of creatures of the Element which he commands."

She nodded as she made notes. "Just as an aside, *are* there any other creatures that work Magick?" she asked.

"For certain, I am only aware that the whales and dolphins have a few Magick-workers among their kind," he said. "They work Water Magick, of course. There are rumors of other creatures, Man-Apes in both the Himalayas and the forests of the Northwest, for instance, but nothing I can confirm. If they do exist, these creatures are extremely secretive and are rarely even glimpsed. It is believed that they would do anything to avoid contact with humans."

"I suppose," she said, touching the end of the pencil to her lips as she thought, "That if they *were* working Magick, it would be to hide their presence from our own species, so you never would find out for certain, would you?"

He coughed. "A point, I grant you. Well, to get back to the subject, as described by Herr Alexander Metzeger, whose handwriting you so despise —"

She flushed very prettily.

"— every human has all four Elements commingled in his Magickal Nature. Most of them possess exactly equal amounts of all four, and thus, command no Magick for themselves. It is *only* when there is an imbalance that one can work Magick, for it is only when there is an imbalance that a human comes near enough to the Nature of the Elemental that he can communicate with and command them."

She scribbled fiercely in her little book, and he paused to allow her to catch up. "Would that be — something like a blind man having acute hearing?" she hazarded.

"Good!" he applauded. "Yes, that is an excellent analogy. It may be that because the Magician has that lack in one Element, he becomes more perceptive in another, as the blind man does. There is a danger attendant in having an imbalance, which is that you are vulnerable in the area in which you are the most deficient, and most often, that is the Element that is the opposite of your own."

"How far can the imbalance go?" she asked. "How — how far can the sensitivity to one Element be taken?"

"To the point where only a Master would be able to find the traces of any elements other than the one that the Magician — or would-be Magician — in question commands," he told her. "That is why no one can command more than one Element. By simply *having* that surplus of one, you of necessity drop the rest below even that of a 'normal' man." He frowned, and thought of an analogy, since she seemed to favor analogies. "Think of a square table, with marbles rolling about on the surface. Tilt it towards any one corner, and only that corner will fill with marbles. That is the way Magickal Nature operates, and it is just as well."

"Why?" she asked.

He had been expecting that question. "Because the Elementals are jealous creatures. They would never tolerate sharing a Magician with creatures of any other Element. Even if a person somehow managed to get a surplus in two Elements rather than one, he would be much better advised to simply concentrate on the one he preferred. The Elementals of his two Elements would be constantly bickering with each other, wasting time and energy, and interfering with *his* plans."

"They sound like naughty children," she commented, with a smile she did not know he could see.

He snorted. "They *are* like naughty children," he told her. Actually, he had thought of another simile, but it was not a polite one. "Well, that, in essence, is what Herr Metzeger has written in the section of his book you wished to set aside for the moment."

She made a face. "He took forty pages to say *that?*" she responded incredulously.

"With more elaboration, which you can read if you choose. He goes on at some length about the characteristics of each Element, how you can tell if a child has that imbalance in his Magickal Nature that will make him suitable for an Apprentice, and how the characteristics of the Magickal Nature carry over into the personality." Cameron paused for a moment to let a wave of light-headedness pass. "You might find all that useful. If you pay close enough attention, you will be able to decipher a person's Magickal Nature without ever using anything but your wit and your five senses to do so."

"Is that what you do?" she asked boldly.

He barked a short laugh. "No," he told her truthfully. "I don't have to. I am a Firemaster, and I have my Salamanders do it for me. They can tell with a simple look what a person's Magickal Nature is."

She had that contemplative look again. *She's thinking of something. This could be interesting. I wonder if she is going to ask me what her Magickal Nature is, and if she could be a Magician.* But the question she asked was not the one he expected. "Could a Master of one Element teach an Apprentice of another?"

"Well, that is an interesting question." He thought it over for a moment. "In theory, I don't know why not — in fact, according to some of the old books you will be reading, the great Masters of the past did so. The discipline is the same, only the spells and Ordeals differ. The one drawback would be that if the Apprentice got himself into trouble the Master would not be able to *command* the Elementals of the Apprentice to return to their places."

"You stressed the word, *command.* Could he do something else to save his Apprentice from his own folly?"

Dear God, she was quick! "He might, if his command of his own Elementals was strong enough, be able to *persuade* his Apprentice's Elementals to leave the Apprentice alone." He shook his head, forgetting she could not see him. "I would not care to try such a tactic with any Elemental but the Sylphs, however. They are the most forgiving and tolerant, and the least likely to anger. Gnomes are slow to anger, but when enraged, they are implacable, and Undines I could not handle at all, obviously."

"Obviously." She picked the book back up. "Thank you, Jason. You have saved my eyes a terrible strain. On to the rest of Herr Metzeger's pearls of wisdom — however atrociously written they are."

He settled back again as she resumed her reading, but his mind was still on the last question she had raised.

Her Nature was Air; the Salamander would not have bothered to mention that unless she was powerful enough in Air to command the Magick. Should he make the experiment she suggested, and try training her himself? It would certainly obviate the problem that most Masters and Apprentices had, that as soon as the Apprentice became a Master, one or the other had to seek a new home. A Master of Fire and one of Air could even dwell side-by-side in the same building with no ill effects. . . .

Could I? Should I? Who would it hurt? I don't think she's stupid enough to do anything that would get her in real trouble; the only question would be if she could pass her Ordeals, and that would be out of my hands if she was an Apprentice in Fire rather than Air.

It was a question that continued to coil in the back of his mind through the rest of the evening, and even followed him into his dreams that very night.

CHAPTER EIGHT

From the moment that she had accepted Magick as a reality, Rose had leapt out of bed every morning with anticipation that was not in the least hampered by her knowledge that Jason Cameron was a dangerous and possibly unbalanced man, and that this situation might turn hazardous at any moment. That didn't matter — perhaps it even put a *frisson* of exhilaration into the arrangement, for there was nothing quite like skirting the edge of danger to put a certain zest in living. But this morning Rose awoke with her sense of excitement and adventure dimmed, and for a good reason. Today, so Jason had informed her last night, Paul du Mond would return to the mansion. Cameron had reiterated his request that she not reveal her new-won knowledge of Magick, and she had been quick to repeat her agreement. Paul represented danger too, but not of the sort she preferred to court. She was suspicious of his motives and his morals, and he was altogether too sly for her liking.

I know too much about men like du Mond, and yet I don't know enough to protect myself. I would prefer not to learn anything more the hard way. She sighed. *No, it isn't precisely danger that he represents, it's corruption, it's veniality. I can't imagine him doing anything magnificent, only petty — or anything really horrifying, only tawdry.*

She pulled aside the bedcurtains, which was the

signal for the ever-attentive Salamander to levitate her glasses into her outstretched hand. Oh, what an improvement *that* was over her former fumbling!

I wish there was a way to keep this Salamander with me when all this is over. . . .

As her fiery servant moved to the windows and the window-curtains pulled apart to let in the daylight, the thin, gray light from outside was an ample reflection of her own dampened spirits, for she knew, as surely as she did *not* want to encounter du Mond, she assuredly would. It had always happened that way; the people she most wanted to avoid were always the first to greet her and the hardest to get rid of. With only the two of them in the house, it would be difficult to avoid him, for he could always find her by listening for her footsteps.

Ah well. At least if the weather has gone all grey and grim, I shall have the excuse to retire to my own rooms. She swung her feet over the edge of the bed, slipped into a dressing-gown and sought the bathroom. *It's too bad that I was never the properly fragile type so I could plead some infirmity and get rid of him that way —*

— on the other hand, Paul du Mond doesn't know that.

She stepped out of her night-things and into the hot bath — which was, as usual, at the absolutely perfect temperature, just short of painful and hot enough to forcibly relax every muscle in her body and open every pore in her skin. Yet another advantage of having a Salamander as a servant. . . .

He saw me going out for a walk, but he cannot have any notion of how far I went. I could have gone for a genteel little stroll, rather than a healthy hike. That's the solution; I can be polite to him for a few minutes, then develop a headache and have to go off somewhere quiet! If I'm inside, I can either come back here or be in desperate need of fresh air. If I'm outside, I can manage a similar excuse! Just having a "polite" way to rid herself of du Mond's unwelcome company made her feel a fraction better. Her thoughts began to move a little more freely.

I wonder if I could discourage him in some other way? I didn't say very much the last few times I spoke with him. I could continue that; I could pretend I'm shy. But he might take that as a challenge; some men would. Can I also pretend to be rather stupid, I wonder? She thought that over, as the steam from her bath rose about her face and curled the loose hair into little ringlets.

Stupidity might disgust him, but then again, it might encourage him. Men generally didn't seem to mind stupidity in a woman, and besides, how could she be stupid and claim to have all the expertise in languages she did? *Not stupid, but silly. I knew plenty of girls at the University who were amazing linguists, and hadn't the least sense.* That might be a better ploy. She'd noticed that men with silly fiancees or wives didn't spend much time in their company. *If he won't leave me alone, I could babble endlessly. I never saw a man who could tolerate babbling for more than a few minutes at best.*

That should be a last resort, however. She didn't think she'd be able to keep up the pretense of being silly for very long.

She took a deep breath, and further relaxed. Now that she had a plan, she felt much better able to face the day and whatever it held. If only it didn't hold du Mond! She wasn't exactly afraid of him — but whenever she saw him, she was somehow acutely intimidated. He might not be all that prepossessing physically, but he *was* bigger and stronger than she was, and she had the feeling he was not averse to using that strength against a woman.

I wonder if it would be possible to convince Jason to send du Mond into the city more frequently — or perhaps to keep him there instead of here, and only summon him back if he truly needs the man. It was a nice idea, but she didn't entertain it for very long. *Probably not. He is Cameron's secretary, and I'm not going to attempt to take on that task as well as my own.*

In fact, she probably *couldn't*. Du Mond obviously had very exact orders from Jason Cameron, and a routine he accomplished without thinking. She would not be able to follow that routine as smoothly and invisibly. Cameron clearly expected and rewarded competence, and was just as clearly impatient of incompetence. If she tried to replace du Mond, she was doomed to failure, and she did not want to lose the respect she had so far gained.

Her own job had now spilled over into the daylight hours, for as of today, she would be busy reading the books Cameron suggested for her own education when she wasn't reading aloud to him. She had suggested that to him yesterday, pointing out that she was fully qualified to do *research*, and if he was not utilizing that skill as well as her translation abilities, he was not making the best use of her.

I'm doing quite enough as it is. It will be much easier to keep du Mond from finding out I know the truth about Jason that it would be to try to become, not only translator, student, and researcher, but private secretary as well. There are not enough hours in the day and night together to accomplish all four.

The grey light reminded her of winter skies back in Chicago, although she knew that once she actually looked out the window, the scene would bear no resemblance to winter as she had always known it. It was now nearly Thanksgiving, not that she expected that particular holiday to be celebrated in this household. The nearness of the holiday was just a measure of how long she had been here.

Only a week to Thanksgiving! It hardly seems possible.... Since each day was the same, with nothing to mark one day as different from another, they all tended to blur together.

It is so hard to keep track of what day of the week it is, much less what day of the month. They were not even near enough to the small hamlet of Pacifica to hear the church bells marking Sunday mornings, as she had heard every Sunday of her life in Chicago. And of course there was no question of actually attending church on Sunday, so she lost even that "event" to mark the beginning of a week.

She reflected on that as she dressed — warmly. It was too chilly for silk; the radiators in her rooms were operating and the Salamander kept a fire tended in each fireplace. *Odd. I suppose if I were a properly brought up person I would feel very badly about skipping Sunday service, but I don't particularly miss not attending church. Was I bored? I must have been; the Reverend wasn't an entertaining speaker, and the music wasn't ever what I would call outstanding. I don't remember Father ever being very fervent about religion either. We always attended University Chapel because faculty was expected to, I suppose.*

Once she had passed childhood, Rose could not remember ever turning to religion for comfort or for aid — quite probably because she had become too practical to expect either. There had never been any evidence that the religious leaders *she* knew were prepared to offer anything but lip-service to the concept of "feeding the hungry and comforting the oppressed." As for the Deity Himself, she could not imagine that God was so idle he had time to listen to each and every voice rising plaintively and pleadingly from the Earth, anyway. *I don't think I'd want to, if I was God. Half of the people are begging like spoiled children for another sweet, and the rest are wailing about the unfairness of life. Perhaps a small fraction are pompously pretending to thank Him when they are really gloating over their own good fortune. If I were God, I think I'd send them all a nice plague or barbarian invaders just to shut them up and teach them what real suffering means!*

Yesterday must have been Sunday, the last Sunday before Thanksgiving. *November. So strange!*

She finished buttoning her shoes and went out to the sitting-room where her breakfast was waiting for her as usual. If the Salamander had been there, she would have thanked it, but it had gone off to wherever the little creatures did go when they weren't needed. She sipped her coffee and buttered a roll, while she reckoned up the passage of time in her mind. *I left Chicago in late October and I must have been on trains for a good week or more before I arrived here; in fact, didn't one of the conductors mention something about Halloween? Then I was just doing the translations for Jason for about a week or so before I read the Dee book. Paul has been gone for a bit more than a week and a half. Yes, it is nearly Thanksgiving; I haven't reckoned wrongly.* She shook her head. *I would not have thought time could get away from me so easily.*

So strange, how much her life had changed in the course of a few weeks! *Magick, Salamanders — good heavens, a few weeks ago I was trying to think of some way to keep a roof over my head and food in my mouth, and now look at me! Silk and wool-plush gowns, the finest of food, a palatial set of living-quarters, and work I not only am good at, but which I enjoy above all else! And the opportunity to complete my degree! All this, and I am being paid handsomely for my time!* She shook her head. *I should be thanking Providence, not fretting because I am trying to avoid the company of a single unpleasant man!*

Yes, that was true — but Jason Cameron must have some reason to mistrust the man himself, or he would not have asked her to keep her new knowledge of Magick a secret. So perhaps it was not inappropriate to fret about possible meetings with him. With that in mind, the question before her now, as she finished her breakfast, was whether to go down into the house and grounds and chance meeting du Mond, or to stay up here in her rooms and avoid him altogether.

I probably ought to try to avoid him. But Sunset is probably looking forward to seeing me. She had begun visiting the stallion daily; he was as gentle with her as a pet dog, and her contempt for du Mond and his dislike of the horse only intensified with each visit. Poor Sunset seemed very lonely, despite the companionship in the next paddock of the two carriage-horses and an aged pony. She had gathered from Jason's conversations that he had spent at least an hour or two every day riding his stallion before his accident, and she had a vague idea that for a horse, running in the paddock was not a substitute for being ridden. At some point she must have been told that a riding horse needed human companionship to be happy; certainly Sunset's behavior with her bore that out.

However, *she* was not going to be the one to ride him, though she had no objection to going and petting him and talking to him. He might be gentle with her, but she doubted he would be forgiving of a rank beginner on his back. She'd taken some thought to learning to ride on the old pony until she realized what a prime dunce she would look, a grown woman trying to bestride a pony meant for a child, with both feet dragging on the ground and her skirts hiked halfway up to her waist. It would definitely not be dignified, and she did not want Paul du Mond to have the advantage over her if he caught her in such an undignified state. Besides, she would have to learn to ride astride; she doubted that Sunset was used to a side-saddle.

The Salamander appeared to take her tray away. "Is it going to rain today?" she asked it.

"Not until just before dark," it told her with authority, and neatly levitated the tray towards the door.

That decided her. First of all, she was not going to let Paul du Mond intimidate her into keeping to her rooms. And secondly, that poor horse needed company. She took an apple from the basket of fruit she now kept in her room, and slipped it into her pocket, then pulled on the warm walking-coat she had asked for when she found the lovely cloak Jason had supplied with her wardrobe to be dramatic, but entirely impractical for strolls through the woods.

There was no mistaking the fact that Sunset was looking for her; she caught sight of him before he spotted her, for the stallion was hanging about the house-end of the paddock, occasionally draping his head over the top of the fence to stare longingly at the house. And when he saw her, his ears went straight up, his tail flagged, and he actually whickered a welcome, pawing the ground and tossing his head a little as she neared.

She found herself smiling as she walked up to the fence. He put his nose into her hand immediately, and *whuffed* into it, without any hint of wanting to use his teeth on her. *Stupid man. Poor Sunset probably just wants to bite him because he senses du Mond is not to be trusted.* She scratched his brow-ridges, then moved her hand to scratch under his chin as he sighed in pleasure and tried to rest the weight of his head in her hands.

"You only love me for my apples," she told him. "It's pure cupboard-love, and don't think I don't know it."

He whickered, as if agreeing with her, and she chuckled. "It's all right," she told him. "You're so beautiful that it doesn't matter. That's what happens when you're beautiful, you know, you can do anything and people will forgive you because they don't want to believe that anything so pretty could be bad." She sighed. "But of course, when you're as plain as I am, they're perfectly willing to think you'd do quite vicious things out of pure mean-spiritedness. And every pretty girl is quite certain you are ragingly jealous of her, and envious of her good looks." She reached into her skirt pocket for the apple. "That was why they hung women as witches, you know," she told him. "They were probably all plain and hadn't a chance in the world of getting a husband so they could be proper ladies, so of course they *must* have turned to the Devil for consolation."

She fed him his apple, but he didn't seem disposed to leave when he'd finished it, so she lingered with him, scratching him and saying baby-nonsense into his ears.

"You're spoiling the brute," said du Mond, startling her so that she jumped. That startled Sunset as well; the stallion jerked his head up, his eyes rolling wildly as he danced in place. Then he caught sight of du Mond, set his ears back and bared his teeth for a moment, then shot off across the paddock to the opposite side. There he trotted in a small circle, watching du Mond as if he expected the man to jump over the fence and beat him.

"You frightened him!" she said, taking care to put a little whine into it, and when she turned to face the man, she managed a little pout as well.

"Not I. That beast isn't afraid of anything or anyone." Du Mond stared sourly after the trotting stallion. "He just doesn't like me, and it's mutual. Animals should be made to earn their keep — people certainly are. I think he's a waste of money; if Jason isn't going to ride him, he should at least be sent off to stand at stud somewhere. With his lines, Jason could command enough fees to at least pay back what he's costing to keep."

She blinked, and tried to think of an appropriately silly answer. "I suppose so," she said vaguely, "But he's very pretty. I like seeing him here; he makes me think of all kinds of things that are wild and free. It wouldn't be the same if he was gone. Is having him here any sillier than having those birds in the conservatory?"

Du Mond simply shrugged. "The birds eat the insects that get into the greenhouses, not that it matters. What you or I like does not matter, dear lady. It is what Jason Cameron likes that is important, and he does not want his precious horse out of his sight."

Suddenly he was all charm, turning it on as if he were lighting one of the new electrical lamps. "But I did not come down here to talk about Sunset; I came to find out how you were faring. Is Jason treating you decently? Don't be afraid to tell me if he isn't; he is inclined to run rough-shod over his employees unless I remind him that this is not a medieval castle and he is not a feudal overlord."

She was startled to hear an echo of her own words to Cameron coming out of du Mond's mouth. It was positively uncanny; she'd have suspected he had been spying upon them had she not known he was in the city at the time. But she managed a weak laugh, and waved her hand. "Oh, how could I not like this job? It is *much* better than having to teach two children! I have everything I want, and all the time I wish in which to read!"

Quick. Now is the time to say something that will make him disregard you. "There's a lovely lot of books in the first case in the library," she continued hurriedly. "I didn't get much chance to read that kind of book when I lived at home, I — *Father* made me spend so much of my time studying."

Du Mond gave her a peculiar look. "You were going to the University to please your father?" he asked carefully.

She nodded, making things up glibly as she went along. "It was what he wanted — I always did what Father wanted. He said if I was going to be a spinster I might as well be a scholar so he would have someone to talk to."

She watched du Mond's eyes flicker as thoughts passed behind them, and tried very hard to read his expressions. He was making no attempt to guard himself with her, which argued that he already was underestimating her.

He's looking at my face — evaluating how plain I am, and thinking that I'm very obedient, very pliant, and don't have much in the way of a will of my own, I expect.

Perhaps that was a better ploy than playing stupid.

"Father always had my best interests in mind, and I was very glad to be able to help him," she continued softly, knowing that this, at least, was the truth. "For some reason I have always been good with languages, so I was able to serve him in the same capacity that I am serving Mr. Cameron."

Du Mond smirked. "Indeed. Well, don't let him bully or frighten you, my dear. You're too pretty a girl to have to languish in a room, ruining your eyes to read to him for days at a time."

She almost laughed, and held it back only with a great effort. *He really is spreading the flattery on a bit too thickly! I suppose I'll have to play up to it, though.*

She fluttered her eyelashes and dropped her gaze modestly. "It's really not at all bad," she murmured. "I could be cooped up in a stuffy old office or library somewhere, working from dawn to dusk. At least here I get to go outside every day for a little."

He moved forward as if he was going to try to touch her; she managed to move away from him without — she hoped — making it obvious that she was avoiding his touch.

"What if I found another option for you?" he asked, and frowned, his concern so patently feigned that she wondered how he ever thought he fooled anybody. "I don't want to alarm you, but Cameron's not entirely sane, you know."

"The — accident?" she faltered.

He shrugged, scarcely wrinkling his suit. "It might have been. He has always been ruthless, but since the accident he's become quite callous about anyone and anything other than himself. I think he's dangerous, frankly. I don't worry about myself, but I'm not sure a woman is safe around him."

She made her eyes go wide and put her hand up to her mouth, hiding the grimace of distaste. "Surely you don't think he would — that I —"

"I think he would not trouble himself to keep you safe, although I doubt that he himself is any danger to you," du Mond told her, with false sincerity. "He never comes out of his own apartments, after all. But I have several friends in the city, and I might be able to obtain an alternate position for you if you wished to find other employment. The circumstances would not be as pleasant as these, perhaps, but at least your employer would be sane."

She dropped her eyes again and shook her head. "I cannot imagine leaving this position," she said. "I gave my word."

"At least keep it in mind if you feel Cameron is growing unpredictable," he urged.

She nodded, and put her hand to her temple, making a face. "This is all so — unpleasant. I believe one of my headaches is coming on, Mr. du Mond —"

"Paul —" he said, warmly, once again attempting to touch her.

" — this is all very upsetting, and if I do not go and lie down, my head will be splitting shortly," she continued, turning, as if oblivious to his outstretched hand. "You really must forgive me."

And with one hand pressed to her temple, she gathered up her skirts in the other, and hurried back into the house before he could offer to escort or assist her.

She felt altogether unclean, as if she had brushed up against something slimy. *The nerve of that man! Ugh! I would rather have the company of a hundred frogs than his!*

She was just glad that Cameron could not possibly have overheard this conversation. He might not have put the best interpretation on her responses.

I think I will spend the rest of the day right here, she decided, opening the door to her room, and closing it firmly behind her. *I have had more than enough fresh air for one day. Or rather — given that I had to deal with du Mond, perhaps the air was not so fresh after all.*

Cameron stared deeply into the mirror, his jaws clenched so tightly he expected to hear some of his teeth snap at any moment. *Just what is he up to?* he snarled savagely and silently. *Who does he think he is, lording it as if he is the master here! That interloper — I'll tear his heart from his body — I'll rip his treacherous little head from his shoulders —*

His thoughts dissolved into pure and incoherent rage; the scent of musk and blood filled his nostrils, and bile rose, acrid and sour, in the back of his throat. He began to pant and his vision darkened, narrowed to the mirror before him. He wanted blood, blood and the death of this would-be Master who *dared* to undermine him within his own territory —

The splintering of wood shocked him out of his madness.

He looked down at the desk, stunned, to see that he had rent the wood in four long parallel gouges on either side of the blotter, where his claws had dug furrows into the maple in his rage.

That brought him to his senses. Icy calm flooded over him, replacing the hot anger.

Du Mond is just being himself — I know his pattern, I saw it often enough with the pretty maidservants. He's no fool, he can see how attractive Rose is for himself. His "friends" don't exist; he just wants to ingratiate himself with her and get her to trust him, get her to leave my protection and put herself into his hands —

That made du Mond a bounder and a cad — which Cameron already knew — but nothing more sinister than that.

What *was* sinister was Cameron's own instant reaction, immediate rage in response to a perception that a rival was trying — trying —

Trying to *what?*

Trying to take over my "property," trying to challenge my authority on my own ground. I reacted, not as a man and a Firemaster, but as an animal, an animal being challenged for his territory and his females.

To be precise, I reacted as a wolf. A shudder convulsed him, as he realized just how close he had come to going over the edge. *Is the wolf taking over the man?*

Shaken, he dropped back into his chair and stared at the eight furrows in the top of his desk. For many long minutes he was unable to move or even think, sunk in a paralysis of shock.

Then he shook his head — *Like a dog shaking himself dry* —

No! That way lay madness! *Wake up!* he told himself angrily. *There is no point in looking for more signs of something you might well be able to control with a little exertion of will!* He sneered at himself. *You do remember using your will, don't you? You were ready enough to boast to Rose about it!*

No, the important thing now was to *exert* his self-control and that so-vaunted Will. He must *immediately* bring things back to normal. He must immediately begin to analyze matters as he would have in the past. *Think, man! What else about that conversation was important?*

He felt anger begin to rise again as he recollected du Mond's impertinence, but he throttled it down successfully.

What was important?

Then he had it. *Rose's reaction. She didn't act as if she believed him. She didn't act as if she was coming under the spell of his rather dubious charm. In fact, unless I miss my guess, she fled him as soon as she could.*

Suddenly he felt much, much better; felt tension simply draining out of him. Rose Hawkins was too clever for du Mond; she saw through his blandishments, and she did not trust him. That meant he need not look for treachery on her part. Whether or not she believed du Mond's claim that his Master was mad — *which, unfortunately, I cannot honestly ignore* — at least she had the sense to see *why* du Mond was attempting to charm her.

He spent several minutes in a deep-breathing exercise, calming himself, regaining complete control of himself, and only when he was certain of his own inner state did he call up Rose's image in the mirror.

She was reading; to his pleasure and gratification, she was reading one of the Apprentice-texts he had recommended. So, her suggestion that she at least engage in the theoretical side of an Apprenticeship so that she could help with research had not been a ruse. She really did intend to follow through on the idea, at least for now.

We will see what happens when she encounters some of the more difficult books. Then again . . . they couldn't be any more abstruse than some of the medieval texts she had already mastered.

She had arranged herself in a pose which would have driven a teacher of deportment to distraction; sitting sideways on the upholstered, high-backed divan, her back against one arm, with both feet braced against the opposite arm-cushion, knees bent, and skirts modestly tucked around her legs. No properly-bred young lady would *ever* have taken a seat on a divan like that! And no properly-bred young lady would ever slouch the way she was now. She frowned a little as she read, rubbed her eyes now and again, and adjusted her eyeglasses from time to time as if her eyes were bothering her. While this was a printed book, the print was very fine; he hoped she was not having too much trouble with it.

Perhaps I should suggest she visit an occulist in San Francisco at my expense? I doubt that she had the wherewithal to have glasses properly fitted these past several years — not with the state her wardrobe was in. That was probably one more economy she was forced to bear with.

Then he snorted at his own naivete. *Of course she hasn't seen an occulist; everything else in her wardrobe came out of the Sears, Roebuck catalog, so her eyeglasses probably did, too.* He clearly remembered his amazement at the pages devoted to eyeglasses and spectacles, complete with a so-called "test" to determine which of the eighteen available strengths one should order. *She tested herself, no doubt, with that same exact care she uses for everything else. The only problem is, the test itself is hardly exact, and what they offer even less so.*

He closed his eyes for a moment, and made some mental calculations. *Useless to send her there before Thanksgiving; no one will be able to fit her in, even with me as her patron. Besides, if she's going into the city, I want her to have some time to enjoy herself a little. If I have her read some of the more important works this week and next, I can send her in for three days in the second week of December — and that will give me three days in which to put some of that to the test. Hmm. Thursday through Sunday, I believe. There should be something playing at the Opera House, and I'll arrange for something on whichever weekend night the Opera isn't. Is she frivolous enough for an operetta at the Columbia Theater? Perhaps a recital, instead. . . .*

He started to summon his secretary, then realized his agent in the city could take care of everything. Somehow, he did not want du Mond to know precisely what his arrangements were going to be for her. . . . *I could use a Salamander to write the letter for me. No, wait, I have a better notion.*

So he reached instead for the telegraphy machine, and began tapping out his orders to his agent at the railhead. *Have the apartment opened for her . . . notify the servants . . . appointment with an occulist . . . tickets. . . .* She didn't know her way around the city; he added another order. *Snyder to have a carriage or cab and experienced driver for her.* While she might well enjoy the cable cars, he had better warn her to either take Snyder or the maid with her on any excursions, and confine herself to the paid conveyance after dark.

He felt altogether like an indulgent uncle arranging a holiday treat by the time he was finished. And he couldn't wait until after dinner to tell her; he had to see her reaction *now*.

He reached for the speaking-tube, and cleared his throat, remembering to act as if he did not know she was there. "Ah . . . Rose? Do you happen to be there?"

She jerked her head up at the first sound of his voice, and with a look of guilt, swung her feet to the floor, put the book down, and moved to the speaking-tube in her room. "Jason? Yes, actually, the weather is not as pleasant as I would like, and I stayed here. Can I help you?"

"Actually," he responded, his jaw dropping open in the lupine equivalent of a grin, although she could not see it, "I thought I might help you. You're going to be working very hard for the next few days, and I had promised you periodic rewards for hard work. What would you say to an excursion into the city in about a fortnight?"

Her face lit up with pleasure and an emotion he did not recognize. "Oh, that would be absolutely *splendid!*" she exclaimed. "There are some things I did not like to ask anyone else to get — "

She blushes so very prettily.

"It occurred to me that you were working very diligently and deserved one of those treats I mentioned to you." The telegraph was tapping a reply to his message, and he translated it effortlessly. "The Opera will have a Friday night performance of *La Giaconda*, the Columbia Theater is presenting *Babes in Toyland*, on Saturday, or if you are so inclined, you can go see that ham, young Barrymore, overact his way through Shakespeare. I am aware that you wear eyeglasses — "

She self-consciously pushed her eyeglasses firmly up onto the bridge of her nose.

" — and I thought that with all the reading I am asking you to do, it would be beneficial to both of us if I had you go to my occulist to be certain your lenses are strong enough."

She opened her mouth as if to protest, then shut it again. *Good girl. You know you need them; don't look the proverbial gift horse in the mouth.*

"No harm done if they are fine, but you have been faltering a bit and I would like to be certain that your eyes are not being strained," he continued. "I certainly need them to be in top order. At any rate, you may use my flat in town, I'm arranging for a conveyance, and you can use the rest of your time to shop."

"Thank you, Jason," she said warmly. "That will be — considerably more than I expected." Her cheeks were flushed with pleasure, and her eyes behind those thick lenses sparkled brightly.

Now he felt even more like an indulgent uncle arranging a holiday treat. "Would you prefer Barrymore or *Babes?*" he asked. "I'll have my agent get tickets."

Her mischievous smile lit up her face. "I suppose I *should* say Barrymore, but I have to confess that I —

oh, this is dreadful! — I adore Victor Herbert. His musical plays are like candy: terribly sweet, probably bad for you, but such fun!"

"And what better Christmas treat than *Babes in Toyland*?" He laughed, and tapped out his last order. "Sometimes a surfeit of sugar is just what one needs. I must admit that my opinion of John Barrymore is not shared by the general public, but — well, Shakespeare is not his forte. He is far too dissipated for Oberon, too bombastic for Hamlet, too shallow for Macbeth, too callow for Othello, too young for Lear and too old for Romeo."

"Prince Hal?" she suggested delicately.

He snorted. "Only the drunken Hal, bosom friend of Falstaff. Wait until he's appearing in something more suited to his style, then I can recommend seeing him." He shut the box on the telegraphy machine. "Well, that was all I needed to interrupt you for, if you are ready to resume reading at the usual time. Unless you had something?"

There. If she wishes to "betray" du Mond to me, there's an opportunity.

She hesitated, biting her lip. "I encountered Mr. du Mond today," she said slowly. "I said nothing about Magick, and he did not ask. However, he seemed — quite friendly." Her tone said more than that, and he was pleased that he had not read her wrongly.

"I should have warned you that he is something of a rake," he replied solemnly. "I hope he did not become overly familiar?"

"Not precisely, no." She grimaced. "But I did — guess — that if he had any encouragement, he might."

"He has his orders to treat you with respect," Cameron assured her, "but I would not believe anything he promised if I were you, nor anything he told you about himself. He once claimed to one of my maids that he was the rightful heir to the throne of Russia, and that if she would come away with him he would make her a czarina."

She burst into laughter at that, as he had hoped she would. "No! Not truly! Did she believe him?"

He chuckled. "She smacked his face and told him to take his fairy tales to children, who would find them entertaining. I do my best not to employ people with more hair than wit."

She was still laughing. "Good for her! Well then, if he is so easily put off, I shan't worry about him. Thank you again, Jason. My diligence will be all the greater for the promised treat, I promise you!"

"I counted on that," he said teasingly, and grinned again at her blush and wry smile.

She resumed her place and position on the couch, taking up in her book where she had left off. He watched her for a few moments more, then blanked the mirror.

He did not summon the Salamander, but it appeared anyway. "I assume you overheard?" he asked it.

It spun lazily, once, then came to rest on its obsidian plate. "Do you want du Mond to have free access to her?" it asked.

"He won't try anything physical — not here, at any rate," he replied. "Not while she is under my protection. And, quite frankly, if he intends to say anything more to her, I want to know about it, and I want to see if she says anything about it." He thought for a moment. "She didn't precisely report his conversation, after all."

"One does not tell one's employer that another in his employ called him mad," the Salamander pointed out. "Not only would that be rude, but it might reflect badly on her and her ambitions. It could be assumed that she was angling for *his* position, which is a permanent one, whereas hers is only temporary — and after all, it would be her word against his."

"True." That was an aspect that had not occurred to him, and he was glad the Salamander had pointed it out. "Making claims like that could actually get her dismissed if I believed him instead of her."

"And she is no fool; she would like to continue in this position as long as possible." The creature sounded smug. "She sometimes talks to herself in the bath."

Which was, of course, the one place where he would *not* spy upon her! Nor did he intend to start now, however relevant the information might be.

"You may continue to eavesdrop, and tell me if you hear anything interesting," he told the Salamander. "I would just as soon not hear girlish secrets, however."

The Salamander grinned. "As you wish." It acted as if it had something it was not going to tell him now, and however much his curiosity nagged at him, he was *not* going to counter his previous order!

"You might as well come with me since you're here," he told it instead. "I'm going to select more books. We are going to intensify the search tonight."

Because I dare not take the chance that the beast is overcoming the man, he thought, grimly, as he led the way to the bookcases. *Nor can I take the chance that I can control what is happening. Perhaps this is the result of pain, perhaps the result of the narcotics I am forced to use — or perhaps it is not. I have no options.*

By the time her holiday comes around, I fear that Rose will be in desperate need of it. But with luck — I may by then have found my key.

CHAPTER NINE

Rose waited on the platform for the train to arrive, bundled warmly in her new fur cape, but too tired to really feel the excitement that she knew was within her. The last two weeks had been brutal; Cameron was making her earn her holiday. She read the Apprentice books feverishly until after dinner, sometimes even reading them while she ate, then went on to read and translate *his* books until very nearly dawn and they were both having a hard time staying awake. She hadn't had *time* to encounter du Mond much; once every few days he would intercept her as she returned from visiting Sunset, but she could always plead duty to get away from him. Taking a short walk to visit Sunset was nearly the only exercise she was getting at the moment.

She wouldn't even have been doing that, but for two factors. The stallion himself was so pathetically pleased to see her that she couldn't bear to disappoint him of his daily visit (or apple; she wasn't sure which he was looking forward to) — and Cameron had asked her to make sure he wasn't being neglected, once he knew that she and Sunset were getting along. The concern in his voice had been unmistakable, and she had promised immediately. She'd even gotten so far as to have one of the Salamanders show her how to use a brush and comb, and did some of his grooming herself. It had been very strange, and just a bit frightening the first time, to stand *in* the paddock with such a big, strong beast, without even a single fence rail to protect her if he should take it into his head to dislike her. But although it had been frightening, it had also been exhilarating, and the more she handled him, the more confident he became with her, and vice versa.

Now he's just like a big dog; I believe he might even let me ride him in the paddock if I only knew how to ride.

She hoped he wouldn't be too disappointed that she did not come to visit him for three days.

She stifled a yawn behind her hand; this was actually *morning,* and she had gotten no more than four hours of sleep. Jason had been very clear about her instructions, though, and he had explained the reason for them. "There is only a given amount of time when the main track is clear," he had told her. "If we want to have the proper margin of safety between trains, there is only one time today that we can insert my private carriage on the track. You must be at the platform by ten, or you will be waiting until late at night to get into the city. You would be exhausted, and the area down by the station can be a bit rough after dark."

She rubbed her eyes with a gloved finger, and stifled another yawn, then smiled at the hand as she lowered it. Kidskin gloves! She hadn't had a pair of kidskin gloves in ages; she'd had to make do with knit woolen gloves that had been darned and redarned so many times there wasn't much left of the original material on the fingers.

She had a trunk, not a valise, and a brand-new trunk at that. A Salamander had transported it down here for her, and a human porter would presumably be taking care of it once she reached the city. Someone named "Snyder" would be waiting for her at the station. It had all been arranged effortlessly, so far as she could tell.

Wealth can certainly work miracles of efficiency. Well, she would enjoy all of this while she had access to it; there was certainly no reason why she should not. There was no telling when Cameron would find his answer — or decide that it was not to be found — and dismiss her. She only wished that she knew exactly what he was looking for.

A plume of white smoke above the trees and the distinct *chuffing* of an engine in the distance alerted her to the arrival of that odd abbreviated engine and carriage that Jason used for his own excursions. In a few minutes it appeared through the gap in the trees, and groaned to a stop with a creaking and squealing of metal. They were backing it into place — she knew there was a place where it could turn around farther down the line, but apparently they didn't want to take the time to do that today.

As it pulled into place alongside the platform, one of the men operating it jumped down out of the cabin to help her; the other peered around the side of the cab and waved. To her pleasure, it was the same two men as the last time, and they evidently remembered her.

The one who had been so friendly before aided her into the carriage with a bow and a flourish. "Glad to see you again, ma'am," he told her, grinning as happily as if he had arranged the whole thing. "I reckon you're getting along all right here."

She laughed. "Quite all right," she told him, as he lifted her trunk as if it weighed next to nothing and stowed it in the rear of the carriage. "But I am ready for a little holiday."

"We'll have you in the city in no time, ma'am," he

told her as he turned and headed back towards the engine. "Track's clear as a bell, and the weather's grand." He jumped up into his own place beside the engineer before she had a chance to reply, and she took that as a signal that she should get inside the carriage and take a seat.

She had wondered if fatigue and contrast had made her memory paint a much rosier picture of the carriage than reality, but she realized as she surveyed the interior that she should have known better than to doubt its luxury. It *was* Jason Cameron's, after all, and he never seemed to skimp on anything. The stove in the front part of the carriage was burning well, heating the whole interior until it was just as cozy as her own sitting room. The carpet and furniture were as clean and as free of soot as a proper dowager's parlor, and if anything, the levels of sophistication and luxury were *more* evident by daylight.

The vehicle began to move with a little lurch. She sat down quickly on the divan, and loosened the collar of her cape. Beyond the windows, as the train picked up speed, an endless wall of tall, green trees flowed by.

I wish the landscape was a little more varied here. She stifled another yawn. *I suppose it wouldn't do any harm to lie down. There isn't much to see, and I don't think I can keep my eyes open if I try to read.* She changed her position, lying down to rest her head for just a little —

And the next thing she knew, *something* had awakened her from a deep, sound sleep, and the train was slowing.

It might have been the increase in noise that had awakened her, for when she sat up and peered out a window, she saw that they had reached the station, and it was quite a busy place, fully as busy as the one in Chicago.

No more than half an hour later, she was seated in an open carriage across from the very proper gentleman who had introduced himself as "Snyder." The mysterious Mr. Snyder proved to be the butler and valet at Cameron's townhouse. He had brought with him this small carriage that had been hired for her convenience.

The fresh air managed to wake her up, and the rest in the carriage had certainly helped bring her back to her normal state of alertness. Snyder was no Paul du Mond; he was very proper in his manners, but gave her an impression of intelligence and shrewdness. She noted that he was giving her a very close, if relatively unobtrusive, examination as they rolled along, and she returned the favor.

He was a tall, thin man, balding, with the demeanor she would have associated with a "superior" servant from the East Coast, although his accent had the faint drawl she knew was characteristic of the Southeast. She wondered where Cameron had found him, for here was certainly a superior servant of the old school. And had he always been in charge of the townhouse, or had Snyder once been the ruler of the Cameron mansion as well?

"Master Cameron normally makes use of cabs when he is in the city, ma'am," Snyder said, breaking the silence. "But I thought that would be rather inconvenient for a lady wishing to shop."

She thought of a number of replies, but settled for the simplest. "That was extremely thoughtful of you, Mr. Snyder," she told him, hoping that she sounded appropriately sincere. "Thank you very much."

He eyed her a bit longer, then asked, hesitantly, "Forgive me. This is hardly polite, but — might I ask, Miss Hawkins, just what your position is in Master Cameron's household? It has not been clarified to me."

It's not polite, and he must be in agony over it! Poor man. I don't quite fit into the hierarchy, the way I would if I were the tutor I was originally told I would be. She raised one eyebrow to show him that she was conversant enough with proper manners to *know* the question was impertinent, then answered him with the same directness he had used. "I am Mr. Cameron's research assistant, Mr. Snyder; I have both a Bachelor and Master's degree and I am very close to achieving my Doctorate. I am actually closer to a colleague than a member of the household, although he is technically my employer as well as yours. I came here from Chicago at his request, interrupting my own studies, because he was in need of my specific skills. He has some various papers and books he needs translated, and I am an expert in ancient languages."

That was close enough to the truth to pass muster without making her feel guilty.

Snyder relaxed; as she had suspected, his unease had been caused by the fact that he did not know where to place her in the household hierarchy. Now he did.

I'm somewhere above a servant, just below a guest, and not a member of the demimonde, which I expect was what he was afraid of. She smiled at him, and was glad she had chosen to wear one of her more severe and business-like walking-suits. She *looked* like a serious scholar, and she knew it.

"Chicago! That's a cold part of the country, this time of year, ma'am," Snyder said. "Gracious, they must be knee-deep in snow by now! I hope you aren't missing the colder weather."

She shivered, and smiled. "Not at all, I assure you. If your university here accepts female students, I may well remain here when my work for Mr. Cameron is complete. I had not been aware that this part of the nation was so lovely."

Snyder beamed, an odd expression on that long, melancholy face. "It's a great deal like North Carolina, where I come from, ma'am," he told her, as if imparting a precious secret.

Well, that explains his accent.

He coughed. "Now, I hope you'll forgive me again. I've been asked to advise you that it wouldn't be wise to go out at night — except straight to the theater and back — without taking me as an escort. Parts of the city are pretty rough after dark, and you don't know where they are."

So are parts of Chicago — but I didn't go out at night much, and never without Father. She nodded an absent assent; the hills of San Francisco rose all about them now, covered with buildings — for someone used to a flat cityscape, the effect was both strange and delightful. She couldn't get enough of looking. The houses, rising in two, three, or four stories, all seemed to be painted in shades of sand, peach, pink, or pale blue. They were like something out of an illustrated children's book, vaguely hinting at the Arabian Nights.

"Is it safe to visit China-town?" she asked, trying to see everything at once, failing, and not caring.

"Only by broad daylight, and not without an escort," he warned her. "I know what parts there are safe, and what are not. Perhaps you could make up a list of what you are interested in, ma'am, and I can arrange excursions for you."

She sighed with a little regret; she *had* wanted to go exploring unencumbered, but —

But I also don't want to find myself stowed away in the hold of a ship bound for the Orient, either. Tales of white slavery might be lurid and sensational, but there must be *some* truth in them or they would not persist.

"That's probably the best," she admitted, and Snyder relaxed a bit more. Obviously he had been anticipating resistance on her part.

I can understand that, and I really hope that some day I will know the city well enough to walk about alone — but that time is not now.

She looked her fill, as the carriage-horses labored up and down the hills; poor things, this was not a very heavy conveyance, and they were still toiling in the traces.

Snyder removed a small, leather-bound book from his breast-pocket and consulted it. "Your occulist appointment is in the morning, tomorrow," he told her. "Around nine. Is there anything you'd care to see this afternoon before you dine? There's just time enough before the shops close."

"A bookshop?" she asked hopefully. "A really *good* bookshop? And a stationer's?"

I can select ancient books from a catalog easily enough, but how can I select contemporary books without browsing?

He nodded, as if that was precisely what he had expected. Perhaps it was, once he knew she was a scholar. "We'll just leave your trunk at the townhouse for Miss Sylvia, the maid, to unpack, and go straight there. It's Master Cameron's favorite store, Miss Hawkins, and the stationery-supply is right next door. We can certainly arrive there before they close." Implicit, though not overtly stated, was that for someone connected with Jason Cameron, both stores would gladly remain open long past their ordinary closing-times.

She bit her lip, wondering if she ought to change her mind. If the shop was Cameron's favorite, the selection would be extensive — and expensive.

"You are to put your purchases on Master Cameron's account, of course, at both establishments," Snyder continued, as if it was a matter of course. "He left orders to give you access to his shop accounts, just as Mr. du Mond does."

Another reason why Snyder was uneasy about my position in the household, no doubt.

"He's never seen me in a bookstore," she said wryly. "He may live to regret his generosity."

Snyder looked at her for a moment with open astonishment, then actually unbent enough to laugh, though he would not tell her why.

They stopped at the townhouse just long enough to leave the trunk with a burly fellow who appeared to do all the heavy work about the place, and then proceeded straight on. And the moment that Rose walked through the door of the bookstore, she was in heaven.

The interior of the shop was all of polished wood and brass, a reddish wood she could not immediately identify. The bookshelves, which ran from floor to ceiling, were placed as closely together as possible and still permit passage of customers. It was at *least* as large as Brentano's in Chicago, and just as well-stocked. There actually were a few "frivolous" writers whose work she admired — Lord Dunsany, for one, though she thought she might die of embarrassment if Cameron actually caught her reading one of his fantasies of the Realms of Faery — and if she ever got a chance to read for pleasure instead of research, she wanted to have a few things on hand. For the rest, there were some reference works she thought might come in handy that were not on Cameron's shelves. Then again, there was no real reason why they should be, for ordinarily one did not associate the works with Magick; not hard-headed things like engineering texts from the fifteenth and sixteenth centuries, nor herbals, nor some of the theological works she wanted.

But there were hints in there, clues to alternate translations, that she thought might be very, very useful. Cameron approached his texts as a pure Magician, but *she* thought the approach might be aided by attempting to replicate the world the writer was brought up in, and see possible meanings through *his* eyes. There were shades to the meanings of words and phrases then that might not occur to a modern man — and as for slang, it could be as much of a code as anything devised for the purpose.

She kept finding more books she wanted every time she looked at a new case. She simply gave up the struggle against temptation after a while; she consoled herself with the promise that many of her selections would be remaining in the Cameron library when she left. She collected quite a tidy pile of volumes before she was finished; it took two boys to carry them to the carriage, but Snyder didn't raise a brow over it at all. Evidently Cameron's expeditions to this place yielded similar harvests.

Perhaps that was why he laughed. She thought about the library, and realized that this must look like a perfectly normal shopping expedition to Snyder.

Next door at the stationer's, she purchased several blank, leather-bound books of the sort used for sketching and journals. Those would become *her* reference books, where she would organize her own gleanings. With them, she gathered up reams of foolscap and boxes of pencils; Cameron had nothing but pens available, and with all the notes she would be taking, she was *not* going to risk oversetting inkwells. Nor was she going to waste good paper on scribblings.

Then, strictly because she saw them and lusted after them, she acquired a supply of soft, colored pencils and watercolors for sketching. They were beautiful — "From Japan," the clerk said. The colors were fabulous, rich and saturated, and she craved them the moment she saw them.

And since color seemed to play a prominent role in Magick, perhaps they might be as useful as anything else she had bought today.

Then, since she had bought the art supplies, she acquired watercolor paper and Bristol board as well. She felt positively giddy as she led the shop-clerk out to the waiting carriage with the brown-paper-wrapped parcels, and settled herself back into her seat, surrounded by wonderful, heavy packages. *I haven't spent this much money all at once in — in my life!* It was intoxicating as strong drink. The idea, to be able to walk into a shop and order anything one pleased! Even at the best of times, she had never been able to do that!

"Shall I have these taken to the railway carriage, or do you need any of this now, ma'am?" Snyder asked, interrupting her reverie.

"Oh —" She rummaged about for two of the novels and one of the reference-works. "This is all I need for now; the rest can go. There's certainly no need to clutter up the house with them when I won't need them until I'm back with Mr. Cameron."

"I'll see to it." Snyder settled back into his seat with the air of a man who has done a good day's work; she clasped her hands over the books in her lap, and did the same.

Already the sun was descending into the sea, surrounded by thin, scarlet-tinged clouds, and the air was growing colder — and damper. She was glad of the fur cape; the dampness of the air made the chill more penetrating.

Snyder handed her out, and stayed to instruct the driver. She went up the steps of the townhouse unescorted, but the door opened before she could reach for the big, brass handle.

For a moment she expected to see a Salamander there, but it was only a perfectly human maid, who must have been watching for them. "Please follow me, miss?" the woman said — she was a little more mature than Rose had expected, actually about middle-age. Rose complied, going up the steps to the second floor, and a little ways down the hall, where the maid opened a door almost immediately at the top of the stairs for her. Behind it lay a very luxurious little bedroom, decorated in chaste blues and whites. The furnishings were neither masculine nor feminine, but struck a neat androgynous balance; it was obviously a guest-room, neatly calculated to make someone of either sex comfortable. There was a bright fire going in the fireplace —

But the illumination came from *electrical* lights on the wall! Rose stared at them as if they were Salamanders. She had not expected that — very few private homes were lit electrically. In fact, neither the bookshop nor the stationer's had been illuminated electrically, although they did have gaslight. *Oh, I wish Cameron had these back at the mansion — no flickering, nothing but bright, even light! It would be so much easier to read by these!*

But beside each of them, and on the bedside table and the dresser, was a reminder that electricity was not *completely* reliable; candles in sconces, and several small boxes of safety-matches.

Although the room was small, it was as comfortable as her suite back in Cameron's mansion. It held a divan placed perfectly for reading, a dressing-table and small chair, a bureau, a wardrobe, the bed and a bedside table. All were covered or upholstered in blue slub-satin that she suspected was raw silk; a deeper blue carpet covered the floor, and the walls were papered in blue and white stripes. A door in the far wall led to a bathroom; she peeked inside and saw it was shared with an identical bedroom on the other side. The maid had already put her things away in the dresser and wardrobe, and was hanging up her cape in the latter when she returned from exploring the bathroom.

"Dinner is at eight, miss, but if you'd like something now, I can bring some tea and something light — ?" the maid said, her tone rising in inquiry.

"If it's not too much trouble — " Rose replied, torn between hunger and not wanting to be a bother.

"Oh, it's not. I'll bring a tray right up." The maid smiled at her. "There's always a nice pot of tea going. Do you prefer your tea served in the English style?"

"English, definitely, please. And if it would be less trouble, I would really rather have meals in my room." She'd gotten into the habit of taking cream and sugar in her tea because of all the British scholars visiting her father, and had never dropped it. Somehow it always seemed a much more substantial drink that way.

Though I wonder why Cameron's servants always have tea going, when at the mansion he has always sent me coffee at meals?

When the maid brought the promised tray up, she got part of her answer; it was a proper English lady's tea — tea, and tiny watercress and cream-cheese sandwiches, and the tea was "pukkah Khyber," (which, roughly translated, meant "the real, genuine, Khyber tea"), as black as sin without the cream and absolutely impossible to drink without sugar. Only the British ever drank tea like that, fully as powerful as the strongest coffee. Evidently Cameron's cook was from the Empire. Hence, the "pot of tea."

The sandwiches weren't much, but they were enough to stave off hunger until the promised dinner hour. As she expected, it *was* less trouble for the servants to make up a tray and bring it to her; that meant they didn't have to set up the dining room for a single person. And when dinner arrived, she *knew* that the cook was not only British, he — or she — was from India, for the main course was a powerful curried beef dish. And she suspected that it was something of a test, to see how she would react.

It was just as well that she and her father *had* entertained so many British; she had acquired a taste for curry.

"Curried beef!" she exclaimed with pleasure. "And saffron rice! Oh, this is marvelous, I haven't had a good curry in so long!"

The maid actually beamed. "Oh, well, we're alone here so much lately that my Charlie tends to make what *we* like, and we've all gotten a taste for his curries. Master Cameron, *he* likes 'em fine, he even brags on Charlie to his guests. Mr. du Mond, though, he's got a tender stomach. He *says*."

From the tone of her voice and the expression she wore, Rose gathered that Paul du Mond was not beloved in this house.

"Charlie — that would be the cook?" Since the maid was lingering, Rose took the time for a bite. The curry bit back, precisely as it should, and the beef was so tender it practically melted on the fork. She did not have to feign an enthusiastic reaction. "Oh! Oh, this is *perfect!* This is pukkah curry! Please tell him I haven't had as good a meal since — since Professor Karamjit made curry for Papa with his own hands."

Now the maid blushed, and Rose knew then that she was definitely married to this "Charlie." She confirmed it with her next words. "Charlie's my husband; he's the cook, and he does the heavy lifting and all," she said, answering Rose's first question. "He's the one that brought in your trunk. He was in the Army in India, he was the orderly and cook for an English officer there, but there wasn't much to go home to when his duty was over, so he decided to try his luck as a cook here. It was come here to the States or Australia, and he didn't like the notion of sheepherding."

"Well, I'm glad he's here," Rose responded warmly. "Please tell him not to go to any great trouble about my meals; I'll have whatever you're having, because it's bound to be marvelous."

"Thank you, miss, I'll tell him. That *will* make things easier on us." The maid positively twinkled as she gathered up the tea-tray and prepared to leave. Her pleasure in Rose's compliments took ten years from her appearance. "Mr. du Mond, he's always so particular about special meals; it's not a lot of trouble when there's Master Cameron and his guests here, but when it's only one — " She shrugged. "If you like, you can leave your tray outside your door when you're done, and I'll be along to collect it when I close up for the night. Would you be having coffee or tea with breakfast?"

Pukkah Khyber was not something she really wished to face first thing in the morning, although it certainly *would* wake her up! "Coffee, please," she said with an apologetic smile. "I'm American enough to require my daily dose."

"Well, and so am I, though Charlie can't see how we abide it." She smiled as if the two of them were in a conspiracy together. "And if *you* want coffee, that means I can get *my* cup, for he'll have to make a pot. I'll be up around seven with your breakfast, miss. Would you like a bath tonight or in the morning?"

"Tonight, but I'm fully capable of drawing a bath, honestly!" she laughed. "Don't go to such trouble over me!"

"If you're sure — then I'll leave you alone, unless you need something." She nodded at the expected satin cord ending in a tassel that hung down beside the bed. "If you need something, just ring."

With that, she left with the tray, leaving Rose to enjoy an excellent — and very, very British — meal. It even ended with a bowl of trifle smothered in whipped cream!

With meals like these, it's a wonder the English can govern their Empire; I should think they wouldn't have the energy to do anything but digest!

She put the tray outside the door when she was done with a sigh of satiation. *It's a good thing I'm not staying here long. I would be willing to bet that Charlie puts on a full High Tea, complete with cream-cakes and Bath buns. I would need my corset pulled tight just to get into my dresses after a few of those!*

There was more than enough time for a bath and some reading before she slept, although after the "early" start she'd had, she expected that she would sleep like the dead. She was torn between her Dunsany novel and the book on Magick that she had brought with her. *Pleasure or duty? Botheration! This is supposed to be a holiday for me!*

But her sense of duty was too strong to abandon altogether; she compromised, reading the book on Magick while the bath filled, then taking *The King of Elfland's Daughter* with her into the bathroom to read.

But her immersion in the story was not as complete as she would have liked, for her new knowledge that Magick was a real and living force in the world kept intruding on what should have been a tale to escape into. If Magick was real, could elves be pure fantasy? Did Dunsany *know* that Magick was real?

What he had written certainly sounded as if he did.

So, with regret, she put aside the novel for her Magickal tome to read herself to sleep with. As an aid to slumber, it wasn't too far off from old Wallis Budge; she soon found herself nodding, and put the book on the bedside table, then turned off the unfamiliar electrical light.

If she dreamed, she didn't remember the dreams. Surrounded by the city, with all the night-time sounds she was used to back in Chicago, she slept more deeply than she had in Cameron's mansion. The next thing she knew, the maid was drawing the curtains and it was morning.

After a hearty breakfast — again, typically British, complete with thick oatmeal and cold toast, and she thanked Providence quietly that there were no kippers — she dressed and sat down to make out a list for Snyder of the places she needed to go. They included one that she thought might raise an eyebrow — a Chinese herbalist. That was the main reason why she wanted to go to China-town.

Among her father's many visitors had been a gentleman who was both an Oxford graduate and a traditional herbalist, and she had the feeling that if her father had actually followed his friend's advice and taken the medicines he had left, Professor Hawkins might still be alive. *If I am going to do as much for Jason as I need to, I am going to have to have more stamina, and it isn't going to come from pukkah Khyber tea and coffee.* And there was another problem; she simply could not afford to be incapacitated two or three days out of the month with pain, yet she also could not afford to be giddy with doses of laudanum. That same gentleman had left remedies for *her* that she had faithfully used, but they were almost gone. A "real" doctor would ascribe her problem to "typical female hysteria" and dose her with opiates; she preferred to see if one Chinese could duplicate the recipe concocted by another.

As for the rest — *I've had my bookshop. I still need a regular pharmacy. And a general dry-goods store, and a department store. Perhaps I should ask Snyder to suggest some sights, if there's time.* What else did she need? *I wonder if I ought to get Jason a Christmas present?* But what could *she* get *him?* What could she possibly afford that he did not already have twelve of?

Perhaps I could find something in China-town.

For the moment, she had enough on her list to occupy the rest of the day. Tonight — ah, *tonight* there would be opera! She would sit in a *private box*, a luxury she had never, ever indulged in! It would be glorious, and as she gazed at the dress she had laid out, she had to laugh as she recalled the last time she had imagined herself attending the opera in San Francisco.

One could have made that the culminating scene of an opera itself — the poor, embittered, lonely heroine, expiring to the glorious melodies of Puccini! The girl that had made *those* plans of despair was so far removed from Rose as she was now that Rose didn't even recognize her.

Strange, how much difference a little hope makes.

She gazed on the dress with unabashed pleasure and a little greed. What woman *wouldn't* revel in the prospect of wearing a silk-velvet gown of deep red, trimmed in sparkling jet beadwork three inches deep, with silk elbow-length opera-gloves and satin shoes dyed to match? Her gown for tomorrow night was simpler, suiting the venue: sky-blue silk with handmade lace.

With her list in hand, she ventured down the stairs to find Snyder waiting for her patiently in the front entry-way. "With your permission, Miss Hawkins, I have arranged for the driver to deliver you to the occulist and return here with you. On your return, we will have luncheon awaiting you, and afterwards I shall guide you to your various destinations." He held out his hand for her list, which she gave to him, quite impressed with his efficiency.

"We can accomplish all of these within a few blocks of each other," he told her. "I believe you will wish to spend the entire day in China-town, so we will save that for the morrow. I have arranged for your new spectacles to be delivered here tomorrow, should you require them."

Goodness, he has everything organized! No wonder Jason keeps him here!

She could not possibly be in better hands. With that assurance, she stepped out the front door and into the sun.

She didn't need the maid to wake her the next morning; she bounced out of bed on the strength of her own newly-found energy and enthusiasm. The opera had been glorious, everything she could have hoped for. Tonight would be pure confection. And between then and now, she would be exploring mysterious China-town.

She dressed quickly, and bolted her breakfast — and yet, by the time she skipped downstairs, Snyder was already waiting for her.

He licked his lips as if he wanted to say something. She waited, giving him a chance to speak.

"Master Cameron himself patronizes a Chinese apothecary, Miss Hawkins," he said at last. "He is said to be a very good one. Would you have any objection to visiting him, rather than seeking out your own?"

"Not at all," she replied, puzzled by the question.

Although she waited a little further, he did not elaborate, simply opening the door for her.

It did not take long for the driver to reach their goal, and even at this early hour the city was awake and functioning. By the time they reached China-town it was obvious that the inhabitants of this district were accustomed to rising before dawn, for they were already hard at work at any number of tasks.

Walking in China-town was like walking in another world entirely. Most of the Chinese here wore their traditional dress, though some affected European-style suits and dresses; she even caught sight of a few unfortunate damsels tottering along on tiny, bound feet. Strange aromas filled the air — incense, odd cooking-smells, odors she could not define. And everywhere, the twittering syllables of a myriad of Chinese dialects fell upon her ears.

Snyder led her to a tiny, dark shop with a storefront window displaying bones, dried fish, the preserved body-parts of any number of animals, and bunches of dried herbs. The gentleman behind the counter looked precisely like an ancient Mandarin noble — except that his fingernails were of normal length. He wore a round, blue brocade hat surmounted by a button, and a matching quilted, high-collared jacket; his thin, scholarly face was graced with a long, white moustache.

But when he spoke, he sounded exactly like Doctor Lee — his words were formed in a crisp, precise, Oxford accent.

"Mr. Snyder!" he exclaimed. "How good it is to see you! Has Master Cameron an order for me?"

He extended his hand across his counter-top, and Snyder shook it gravely. "Master Cameron does not have an order, but this young lady who is assisting him in his research does, if you would be so kind as to give her the benefit of your expertise." Snyder then turned and indicated Rose. "Master Pao, Miss Hawkins."

She extended her hand, and Master Pao took it with a smile that was neither servile nor ingratiating. His grip was firm and quite strong, and she had the feeling that if she had not been wearing gloves, she would have found his hand to be warm, the skin of his palm dry. It was, as her father would have said, a "proper handshake."

"I would be happy to assist a colleague of Master Cameron," the apothecary said politely. "How can I be of service?"

She explained her needs circumspectly, taking out what was left of her "special tea" and handing it over the counter to him. At once, his eyes brightened with interest. He examined the herbal mixture, stirring it with a fingertip, sniffing it, crushing some between his fingers and sniffing again, and finally tasting it.

"This will be no problem to replicate," he said, finally, looking up at her with his bright, black eyes, "Although it is not a recipe I have prescribed. Now, you said you also needed something for times of long and difficult research?"

She nodded, and clasped her hands together on the countertop. "I believe that there will be a great deal of work ahead of us in the next few months, and I fear I will be working long hours and sleeping little. If you can manage something, a tea perhaps, that will give me the ability to work these hours without falling asleep over my books, that is what I need. Something stronger than coffee, but not something that will keep me awake when I finally get a chance to go to sleep."

Master Pao pursed his lips and fingered his snowy moustache. "This could take a little time," he said, "and in addition — I should like to concoct an alternate recipe to the one you wished me to duplicate." He looked up at Snyder, and something unspoken passed between them.

"Miss Hawkins, if you will be so kind as to wait until I return before venturing further, I have an errand I must pursue," Snyder said unexpectedly. "If you will both excuse me?"

And before she could reply, he turned and left the shop.

"I beg your pardon, Miss Hawkins," the apothecary said apologetically, "But Mr. Snyder knows that if I am to fill your needs properly, I must ask you a few questions, some of which may be a trifle personal. That, no doubt, is why he left, to save you a blush at having a stranger party to your private matters."

She relaxed a little, for this was precisely the sort of questions that her father's friend had wished to ask her, and she was oddly certain that Snyder would never have left her alone with someone who might offend her, inadvertently or otherwise. "You are a doctor, of course," she replied, meaning to give him the accolade whether or not he "qualified" by Western standards. "I am sure you would ask me nothing without having a good reason for it."

"Ah — and not only am I a physician in the ways of my own people, I am also a physician trained in your western medicine," he said, with another of his warm smiles. "I have my diploma from Harvard Medical School, in point of fact, and I honor both the Hippocratic Oath and the vows of my own people regarding the sacred duties of the physician. Now — you will find a stool there behind the door. If you will take a seat, we can begin."

She found the stool, a high, backless affair, precisely where he pointed, and set it before the counter. The questions he asked were not all that "personal," and she felt no embarrassment in answering them —

although she thought of herself as being unusually candid for a female, and poor Snyder probably would have been embarrassed to be present. Finally Master Pao seemed satisfied, and began making up packets of herbs, his hands flying among the various drawers and jars behind the counter. He never seemed to measure anything, and yet she was certain he was portioning each herb with absolute exactness. She watched him, rapt with fascination.

"Do I take it that you are assisting Master Cameron with his Magickal researches, Miss Hawkins?" he asked, as casually as if he were asking if she preferred the color blue over the color green.

She started, then stared at him, quite taken aback, and not certain how to reply. Master Pao looked up at her and caught her in that dumbfounded expression, and laughed softly.

"I am the Earthmaster here in the Land of the Golden Gate, Miss Hawkins," he said, very quietly. "We have been colleagues, Jason and I, since the day he arrived. We exchanged services; I reinforced his townhouse and mansion against the earthquake, and he made my shop fire-resistant. The imprint of Magick is upon you, though you yourself cannot yet see it."

"But — I have done nothing but read in his books!" she exclaimed involuntarily. "How could I —"

"You have read the instructions of Apprenticeship, and thus have taken the first true steps towards Apprenticeship," he chided gently, as if she had missed something terribly obvious. "Whether you progress further along the path or not, any Master who knows of your association with Jason will see that invisible mark. Some, an exceptionally sensitive Master of Air for instance, would even see it without that knowledge."

She bit her lip, not at all certain that she wanted such a "mark" upon her. This was not something she had bargained for when she began this! Would she always be so "marked," or would it gradually fade once she disassociated herself from Magick and its practitioners? Would this cause her even more difficulties?

No use complaining now; I suppose. I volunteered for this. Jason only wanted me to read and translate specific passages in specific books, and I suspect that if I had stuck to that, there would be no such "mark" upon me.

"I only mention this, because you should know certain things," the old man continued, with an expression of gentle concern. "Master Jason has collected some powerful enemies, as all who traffic in Magick eventually must." He chuckled, then, his concern softening. "Even so inoffensive a creature as myself can collect enemies, I fear. But if these enemies become aware of your association with Jason, they will seek to use you against him."

"How?" she asked, suspiciously. *Now what is he at? Does he think to offer himself as my "protector" — for a cost?* Tales of evil Chinese "white slavers" flashed through her mind for a moment.

"Nothing coercive, at least, not in all likelihood," the old man said soothingly. "No wise Magician exposes his powers *too* much before the multitudes; when people, especially handsome young women, are suddenly missing, the police begin to look suspiciously about." He shrugged. "And at any rate, cooperation is much more easily obtained with charm, tact, persuasion and . . ." He paused, and raised one eyebrow. ". . . and gifts? You should know that this may befall you, and you should be wary of men with glib tongues and blandishments. Be even warier of those who offer you much for what seems to be very trifling information. If Jason has taken you even a little into his confidence, what you know already could conceivably harm him."

She flushed, and shook her head a little. "I doubt that anyone is likely to think of me as anything other than insignificant," she replied crisply. "What I am doing is mere translation; if I have been reading certain texts, it is only to assist my own ability to translate. Mr. Cameron could certainly hire another translator at any time, and with very little effort on his part." She strove to control her blushes. "Quite frankly, although I have seen just enough to make me a believer in the power of Magick, I very much doubt that Mr. Cameron has 'taken me into his confidence' at all."

Master Pao gave her an oblique glance, but said nothing. His hands, however, continued to fly among the drawers and boxes of his herbs, until at last he had made up a fourth packet, this one wrapped carefully in red paper.

"Here, in the blue, is the replication of your previous recipe," he said, pushing the packet across to her. "When you look to run short, you need only have an order sent to me, and I will send another supply." He pushed the second packet, wrapped in green, across the counter to stand beside the first. "Here is the recipe that *I* would recommend for those same complaints. Try it, and see if you find it superior." The third packet, in white, joined the other two. "And here are the herbs you asked for an increase in stamina. Now — these will not act precisely as you requested. They will not *keep* you awake when you need slumber."

"What will they do, then?" she asked, both a trifle disappointed and a trifle annoyed.

His face took on the expression of a stern teacher.

"They will do much better than forcing you to stay wakeful. Such medicines are dangerous, and easily abused, and I do not prescribe them unless there is no other choice. *This* recipe must be drunk faithfully at every meal and at bedtime, and it will enable you to have a full night's sleep in only four hours' time." He chuckled again at her reaction, a bitten-off exclamation of pleasure.

"I could wish I'd had such a wonder long ago!" she exclaimed. "I have never been able to function on less than eight hours of sleep! This is wonderful!" She reached for the packet; he held his hand on it, keeping her from snatching it up immediately.

"There is, as in all such things, a price to be paid," he warned her. "Your sleep will be — compressed, as it were. This will mean certain changes in your dreams, which may be unpleasant changes if you are not used to recalling your dreams. Your dreams will become very vivid, and very intense, impossible to forget. They may be very disturbing, and possibly — possibly you will see things that will cause you unease. And although you will only require four hours of slumber, you *must* have that time; you *will* fall asleep over your books if you attempt to stay wakeful for more than thirty-six hours. The final price, however, is one, I think, no woman would quarrel over." He actually winked at her. "You will find that you use energy as if you were exercising heavily. You will be very hungry, and you should assuage that hunger without fear of gaining weight. As the natives of the North say, 'Sleep is food, and food is sleep.' And you should do without this prescription when you are taking the herbs in the blue or green packet. They do not mix well together."

She nodded solemnly, and picked up all three packets. "I understand — but what, exactly, do you mean when you say that my dreams will be disturbing?"

He stroked his long moustache and beard for a

moment, as if he was taking great care in choosing his words. "Several of these herbs are known among the people of India for what is called 'opening the third eye.' They enable one to see the Unseen, the past, or what is yet to be. If you have any such abilities slumbering within you, they may well awake at the touch of these medicines, and you may not like the result. It is a hard thing to see the future; many find such knowledge a burden too great to bear."

For a moment, a chill lay across her shoulders, as if a cold shadow fell there. Then she laughed, if a trifle uneasily. "I doubt that I will have any such difficulties, Master Pao," she replied, with emphasis intended to convince herself as much as him. "I fear that I am as prosaic as a loaf of bread, and as psychically aware as a paving-stone."

Once again, he bestowed an oblique glance upon her. "You give yourself too little credit," he said. Then he shook his head, and passed over the last, red-wrapped packet. "This, however, is not for you. It is for Jason — *if* you can get him to take it. He is that most dangerous of patients, the ones who prefer to diagnose and dose their own ailments. He needs these medicines — I know what he is doing to himself, in part, at least, and he is as a wolf who is so intent on the hunt that he will run until he collapses."

She accepted the third packet dubiously. "I have no idea how I could ever get him to take medicine. I cannot possibly promise anything."

"I know that. I also know that you are more likely to try than that wretched creature du Mond," Master Pao said, with a touch of irritation in his voice as he mentioned the secretary's name. "If you have the opportunity, I beg you to use it. I fear that he is doing himself mischief, and I hope that these medicines will counteract that mischief."

She nodded, and put the packet beside the other three in her handbag. As she slipped from the stool, a thought occurred to her; how was it that Master Pao was so conversant with Western Magick? "I was not aware that the Orient had the same system of Magick as the West. I never heard of Chinese Salamanders, Undines, Sylphs and Gnomes," she offered, and waited for his reply.

"We do not," was his ready answer. "Or at least, our disciplines are quite different, although the ends are the same. We have something so *like* the Masters of the Elements that I simply use the title of Master of Earth for the sake of convenience. My true title is something — quite different."

The arch way he said that made her pause and turn to look him full in the face. He wanted her to ask, and so she obliged him. "Oh?" she said. "And what is that title?"

He smiled, and for the first time, she sensed the power that this man held, coiled tightly and invisibly, inside him. Irresistibly, she thought of the World Snake, the great Worm, who encircled the world, and whose restless stirrings caused the earth to shake.

"Why," he replied softly, "it is Master of Dragons, of course."

With Snyder at her elbow, she browsed the shops of China-town to her heart's content. Here she spent her own money, and since she had been spared many expenses she had assumed she would have — such as the books she had wanted — she bought things she would otherwise have only looked at, admired, and passed with reluctance.

Enchanted with the beautiful colors, she bought a Chinese robe of silk and another of quilted cotton, both beautifully embroidered. The silk robe was of a rose-pink, embroidered with peonies, and the cotton of pale blue, embroidered with butterflies. One couldn't wear them on the street of course — and that was a pity — but they would be very comfortable for lounging in. If she was to spend hours reading to Cameron, she was going to be comfortable!

She was so enchanted by scenes of trees, pagodas, and cranes made of delicately carved cork sandwiched between two sheets of framed glass and set on a stand that she had to have one for her desk. The tiny scenes were like something out of an Oriental fairy tale. . . .

At another shop, her sense of smell was intoxicated. Two fans of sandalwood, one of the natural brown and one of black, joined her purchases, along with a vial of sandalwood perfume, and also some sandalwood incense, for she had never smelled anything so wonderful before, the whole of her experience with incense being limited to the rather harsh scents burned at church services. She could have spent a small fortune in that shop, for the various perfumes there entranced her.

A fabric shop beckoned, but she resisted the temptations of the luscious silks contained therein. She did not have the skill to transform them into skirts and gowns, and she did not have the wherewithal for the services of a dressmaker.

She did indulge in luncheon in a tiny cafe, at Snyder's suggestion, eating willingly whatever was placed before her and enjoying the strange but savory tastes and textures. This place seemed to specialize in a hundred kinds of steamed dumplings with so many different fillings that she quite lost track, though there were one or two that were *so* good she quickly learned to recognize the shapes when the bamboo baskets came around, borne by a young Chinese waiter.

She actually found a Christmas gift for Cameron,

although she was not certain that she had the temerity to present it to him. It was shockingly expensive, and yet she could not pass it by when she saw it — especially once she learned that, as the Dragon was the Oriental Spirit of Earth, the Phoenix was the equivalent Spirit of Fire.

It was a carved statue of fiery carnelian, translucent, about the size of her hand, of a Phoenix in flight. The carving was as delicate as lace, and she sacrificed a hair-clasp of white jade carved in the shape of a butterfly in order to purchase it. She was quite certain that he had nothing of the sort; it was among many other carvings, similar, but nowhere near as finely made. She bought it knowing that if she did not, she would regret it later, and return only to find it gone.

There were so many things to see, to admire! In what must have been the equivalent of a grocer's store, she purchased candied ginger so fresh that the scent permeated the bag, while she covertly watched women with bound feet buying things she couldn't even begin to identify. One store was filled only with images of the Buddha, made of every substance imaginable, with every level of skill, ranging in size from a charm to be worn to a huge statue fit to grace a small temple. There were more apothecaries, more curio-shops, stores that specialized in porcelain, carvings of ivory and semi-precious gems, strange cookpots and implements, clothing. But she had spent the last of the money she had with her on that extravagant little Phoenix, and she was willing to look, sigh a bit at the things that caught her eye, and move on.

Snyder conducted her back to the townhouse in a carriage redolent with ginger, incense, and strange spices, leaving her to enjoy her dinner in solitude.

After dinner, she dressed again for the theater. And

in a blue-and-white confection of a gown, as sugary and sweet as the Victor Herbert songs, she went off to enjoy *Babes in Toyland*, feeling as happy and carefree as a child.

Tomorrow would bring the end of her holiday, but for tonight, she would play the role of the lady of leisure to the hilt.

CHAPTER TEN

Cameron's claws dug into the wooden arms of his chair. Paul du Mond had no notion just how close he was to infuriating his employer. Once again he had come to Jason Cameron's study to make yet another importunate demand for further Magickal education.

No. That is not true. He does not want education, he wants the power without having to learn control, discipline, or method. He wants to be given power, as a child is given a toy.

Cameron held his temper in check and attempted to feign an air of complete nonchalance. "I know that this is a disappointment to you, but frankly, du Mond, until you master those specific techniques there is nothing more I can teach you." He hoped what expression was possible to his face was bland and calm. "I've told you that before."

But Paul du Mond frowned, and persisted in another vein. "Are you *quite* certain you won't be needing my help in your own work?" he asked. "Perhaps if I assist you, I will be able to overcome my own difficulties. And after all, that *is* the first duty of an Apprentice, to assist his Master."

And the Apprentice hopes to steal the easy path to power by observing the Master. Little does he know that there is no easy path to power, Magickal or otherwise.

"It may be the first duty of an Apprentice, but I'm

not doing any work of my own now," Cameron lied glibly. "How could I, looking like this? All I am doing is research, and you yourself are perfectly well aware that what you require is *practice*, not research. Now, your best option is to get that practice, and you can do so on your own." He carefully loosed his grip on the arms of the chair. "When you are not practicing, you do have needful duties. Why don't you just concentrate on catching up with your secretarial work for this afternoon? Perhaps you could go into Pacifica for dinner later; I know you tire of the fare here. You could have the Salamanders hitch up the light carriage for you."

Du Mond's frown deepened. "I would be the first one to admit that I have a great deal of correspondence to reply to, Jason. But if I leave the estate to eat, what will you do?"

"Bolt down a bloody chop, as usual," Cameron replied testily. "You forget that this form has needs that are not acceptable to polite society, needs that even you find distasteful. I shall be perfectly all right. I managed to survive your absence for an entire week, didn't I?"

Reluctantly, Paul du Mond nodded and finally left the study, looking backwards over his shoulder as if expecting Cameron to change his mind and call him back.

And for what? Cameron thought with irritation. *He's useful only as a secretary now. Rose is of more use as an assistant in Magick, and she has never set foot in my Work Room!* Somehow du Mond must have guessed that his Master was still attempting the reversal of his condition without the assistance of his Apprentice — perhaps he had even guessed that Cameron was going to make another attempt this afternoon. The stars were right, the spell itself called for daylight — perhaps to counter the lunar effect associated with lycanthropy — and Rose would not be back until nightfall. If he could just get du Mond out of the way, he would not need to fear interference from any quarter!

But du Mond would not go away until it was too late to start the ritual, and the auspicious time trickled away, inexorably, until there was no hope of making the attempt. Cameron's temper simmered and boiled, until he flung himself out of his chair and began to pace the room like a caged beast.

He finally turned to his mirror, as he had so many times in the past three days, and called up the image of Rose Hawkins, hoping that it would calm him. He had watched over her jealously during her excursion to the city: had taken vicarious pleasure in *her* pleasure. He had laughed, truly and freely, for the first time in many long days, at her childlike joy in the bookstore. He had reveled in the sights of China-town even as she walked through the crowded, colorful streets, seeing everything with a new interest as she discovered the places and people for herself.

He had been an invisible presence in the private box at the opera, and although the performance had not been an outstanding one, he had taken more enjoyment in it than if the singers had been gathered from the finest Houses in Europe. *She* had been so thrilled simply to be there that the music had an added savor for him. And as for the production of Victor Herbert, well, he had never once thought he would find such a childish, sugary musical even remotely entertaining — but she did, and her pleasure was infectious.

The only time he had not been able to watch her had been when she visited Master Pao. The old reprobate had magicks ensuring his privacy that his simpler spell could not pass. He wondered, though, why she had gone to a Chinese apothecary; some female complaint, perhaps? In this, she was better off going to the Chinese rather than resort to patent-medicines. At least Snyder had the sense to take her to Pao rather than letting her find her own man. Too many of these herb-sellers were inclined to lace their potions with powerful doses of opium, and such a treatment would render Rose useless for her duties.

The mirror showed her as he had expected; she was reading as the railway-carriage swayed with the rhythm imposed by the rails. She was lost in whatever it was she had chosen, immersed, completely oblivious to her surroundings. It was too dark to tell just where she was, but he did not think that she would be back soon.

Suddenly he was seized with the restless impulse to try his spell anyway, and hang the consequences. After all, it was only a variation on one he had tried many times before. Though the optimal time had passed, perhaps the optimal time did not matter. He had tried it before in bright daylight with no success; perhaps time of day was not a factor.

But the stars were a factor, and they were still in their proper configuration. He lurched to his feet abruptly, his mind made up. Very well then, he would make the attempt, and have it done with by the time Rose returned home. It was, at the bottom, a very simple spell, so what could possibly go wrong?

Rose left her luggage behind her on the platform, secure in the knowledge that all of it would be wafted up to her quarters the moment she issued orders to that effect to the "empty" air. It was well after ten at night when the train pulled up alongside the platform below the house; they had been forced to wait on a siding while a "special" went by, an order not even Cameron could or would countermand. Regular rail traffic must not be interfered with; that was the cardinal rule every rail-man lived by, and Cameron was too much a rail-man ever to violate it.

She took the elevator up to the house; she knew how to run it for herself now. Her heels clicked confidently across the floor and up the stairs; when she opened the door to her rooms, her luggage, books, boxes and all, was waiting for her beside the sofa.

But something else was waiting there, too.

A Salamander hovered in midair, throwing off sparks in its agitation. She thought she recognized it by the particular combination of its colors; this was not "her" Salamander, which was a pale bright yellow, but was the gold and orange one that seemed to be particularly intelligent and outspoken, the one that spent most of its time serving Cameron personally.

"Rose Hawkins!" it said urgently. "You must come with me! The Master is ill, and needs your help!"

Her first reaction was not one of alarm, but of incredulity. *Cameron? Sick? But — how would an inhuman creature like a Salamander know if a human is ill?* If Cameron happened to be drunk, perhaps the Salamander might mistake it for illness . . . if that was the case, he would hardly welcome her intrusion! Perhaps she ought to check first; despite the agitated dancing of the Salamander, she went to the speaking-tube and called Cameron's name several times. *This is surely a mistake. He was perfectly fine when I left him. The Salamander must be mistaken. How could he have fallen ill in less than three days?*

She was answered by silence — then, as she shouted more urgently, by a hollow groan in the distance, a sound she had to strain to hear that made the hair stand up on her arms and sent a shiver down her spine. It did not sound like a man who was drunk. It sounded like an animal, a dying animal.

She whirled, without a second thought, and picked up her skirts in both hands so that she could run. *Dear God, what could have happened? He was in perfect health! Could he have hurt himself? No, the Salamander said he was "ill," not "hurt." What illness comes on so quickly?* With her skirts hiked up above her knee, she burst through the door, ran down the hall, and took the steps of the staircase down two at a time. *Could this have something to do with his accident? Where in God's Name is du Mond? Why isn't he here and why didn't he know about this illness?*

The inevitable, guilty thought flashed through her mind as she clattered down the stairs. *Has he been ill all this time? Has he been lying there since I left, alone, in pain?* She reached the landing outside the door to Cameron's suite only to find the Salamander there before her, hovering before the open door, a door that had not once been open in all the time she had lived here.

"Hurry!" it said, and flitted inside, lighting the way for her with the illumination of its own body. Still clutching her skirts, with her heart racing and a trickle of perspiration trickling down the back of her neck, she followed it. There was hardly any light in here that was not already supplied by the Salamander.

He can't have been lying here unattended for three days, she told herself, as she ran through the apartment in the Salamander's wake, paying no attention to anything except her footing. *Du Mond was here all that time. The Salamanders would not have allowed him to lie there uncared-for. This must be something that just happened. But what?* The heels of her walking-boots made a muffled staccato beat against the carpeted floor.

And now her heart began to race with a different flavor of apprehension. *Now* she would see Jason Cameron, not just speak to him with a mechanical instrument; she would finally see the results of Jason's accident, see what dreadful disfiguration had turned him into a recluse. Surely it must be hideous to have made him close himself up on a single floor of his palatial mansion! She paid no attention to the rooms she passed as she ran down a hallway very similar to the one a story above. The Salamander knew where Cameron was; at least she did not need to search for him, rummage through rooms that must be very personal to him.

She steeled herself for the dreadful revelation as the Salamander darted into a doorway. She followed it, and stopped, seeing it hovering above the shadowed bulk of a powerfully-built man. He was lying huddled, face-down on the floor, as if he had collapsed there; the hood of the robe he wore enshrouded his head. The robe was similar to those worn by monks, except that it was made of crimson velvet rather than coarse, homespun wool.

There was something peculiar about this room, echoing and larger than she had thought possible, so barren of furniture that all sound reverberated hollowly, and with no sign of the carpets that softened the footstep everywhere else in this house. The floor itself was of slate or a similar stone, and inscribed with chalk-marks now blurred and half-erased. Behind the man bulked an object that could only be described by the word "altar," and to either side were two immense candlesticks, each holding a white candle as thick as her wrist. These, however, were not lit; the only illumination came from the body of the Salamander.

Jason lay at the center of the web of chalked lines. She recognized the half-obscured diagram at once —

by type if not the diagram itself. This was a Magickal circle, and Jason must have been attempting some procedure or other when, or before, he collapsed.

As she drew nearer, her skirts now held up to keep them from brushing against those chalked lines and perhaps causing some damage or releasing something better left bound, she revised her opinion. From the look of things, he had finished whatever he had been doing, and had been engaged in erasing the diagram when he was overcome and collapsed.

One thing, at least, was certain. Whatever else was going on, he was not drunk. Only a fool engaged in Magickal work when drugged or drunk, and of all things, Jason Cameron was not a fool.

He whimpered hoarsely, and stirred, though not enough to dislodge the hood, and she was reminded that some deformity lurked beneath that concealing fabric. She bent down and reached for his shoulder, touching it tentatively.

"Jason?" she said.

The body shook convulsively beneath the crimson velvet, and she pulled her hand away quickly, unable to stop herself. Suddenly she was terrified at what she might see, and the hand that had touched his shoulder tingled oddly.

Cameron heaved himself up onto his elbows.

"Get out!" Cameron snarled harshly, without looking up or revealing his face. "You foolish woman, what do you think you are doing? Get out of here! Leave me! Go back to your books where you belong!"

Every word was punctuated with a gasp, and the mere effort of speaking cost him dearly. He sagged back down onto the cold stone of the floor with a groan.

She was briefly tempted to do as he had ordered, but the agitated presence of the Salamander told her that no matter how much Cameron cursed her, he could not be left to himself. And presumably the Salamander could not help him itself. "No," she said simply, steeling herself for the inevitable. "Not while you need my help."

She seized both his shoulders in her hands, but before she could help him up, he writhed away from her, striking her hands away in the same moment. "Infernal woman!" he snarled. "Damn meddling Nosy Parker! I should have known! You won't leave until you have seen my face!"

Though still half collapsed on the floor, he reached up and jerked the hood of his cloak away from his head, twisting his head to stare up at her in defiance.

She leapt back with an involuntary gasp, the knuckles of one hand crammed into her mouth, the other hand at her breast — for what snarled up at her was not the disfigured visage of a man, but the mask of an enraged beast!

She could not even put a name to *what* beast it was; she had never seen anything to match it in all her life. The head was covered with coarse, gray fur; the snarling, toothy muzzle was certainly that of an animal's, but horribly, the eyes were all too human. Upstanding, pointed ears crowned the skull. The lips writhed, as if speaking was an incredible effort.

"*Now* are you satisfied?" the harsh voice rasped, a note of exhaustion and great pain underlining every word. "*Now* will you go and leave me to fend for myself in peace?"

At the very moment when she wanted most to turn and flee, it was the voice that steadied her, even when she saw that the hands were not hands at all, but clawed paws. Whatever else this creature was, there was no denying that it was *Jason Cameron*, and the man had not changed because she had finally seen his real face.

I must remember what I know about him; I must be like Tam Lin's lover, Fair Janet, and hold to what I know is within the monster, no matter how fearful it looks.

"Of course not," she replied, managing to keep her voice from quavering and her hand from shaking. "Your Salamander would not have summoned me if you did not need help. Where the devil is du Mond, anyway?" She couldn't help herself; her voice reflected her outrage that the man wasn't here doing his duty. "Why wasn't he where he belongs, helping you? I thought he was your Apprentice as well as your secretary!" She reached once again for his arm, and this time he suffered her to take it. As she helped him to his feet again, he pulled the hood back over his head, hiding his face from her so that she no longer had to look at it.

"I sent him away," Cameron replied, slowly, pausing to catch his breath. "He must have guessed I was going to try a Magickal Work, and kept trying to press his services on me. I — fear I no longer trust him. Precisely *because* he kept trying to persuade me, I was convinced it would be a bad idea to allow him to participate." He grunted with pain and effort as Rose helped him to a kneeling position, and waved at her to stop for a moment as he bent over, panting.

When he was ready again, she helped him to his feet, and with a vague memory of seeing sketches of firemen doing so, draped his arm over her shoulders so that he could lean on her. He was far heavier than she had thought, and she staggered beneath his weight.

But the Salamander flitted in front of them, leading the way, and together they managed to stumble into the hallway and on to the next room. This proved to be a bedroom, but Rose could go no farther than the chair nearest the door. Cameron's weight was too much for her, conditioned by long walks though she was. Weaving like a pair of drunks, they stumbled to that chair, a huge, leather-covered wingback. He dropped into it heavily, unable even to lower himself down slowly. She collapsed on the footstool, only now aware that she was perspiring with the effort of carrying him, pushing damp strands of hair out of her face. Her hair was coming undone, draggling down in untidy strands, and her suit-jacket had come unbuttoned.

She had a notion that the Salamander would know what was required now, and she turned to it as she fastened her jacket properly again. "Get him what he needs," she ordered it. It vanished, precisely as she had hoped it would, and after a moment to catch her breath, she rose to her feet again. Although feeling more than a little giddy, she set about lighting candles and arranging a table at Cameron's elbow while she waited for the Salamander to return.

It floated into the room supervising a levitating tray; somewhat to her surprise, the tray contained a large glass of milk as well as a piece of raw or near-raw meat and a collection of pills. She eyed the latter with misgiving, recalling what Master Pao had told her.

"Put that tray down on the table, then get me a kettle of hot water, a pair of tea-cups, a strainer, and the brown paper parcel in my valise," she ordered it, and picked up the glass of milk.

Milk! Well, I suppose it is strengthening. But it is hardly what I would have assumed a monster would drink.

She took it to Cameron who lay as one dead, oblivious to his surroundings; he sagged back in his chair with his head lolling against the side-wings. His hood had fallen back again, and she was once again favored with a view of his head and face. His eyes were closed, and he panted shallowly, his tongue lolling out a trifle. "Jason," she said, steadily, "I have something for you to drink."

The eye nearest her opened part-way. "Are you *still* here?" he rasped, rudely, without a word of thanks that she had gotten him this far.

"I am, and I have no intention of leaving just yet. Can you drink this on your own, or will you need help?" She held out the glass of milk.

His lips writhed, as if in distaste, but he brought a paw up to take it from her. His style of drinking was not elegant, but he managed without spilling it all over himself; his mouth and lips were more flexible than an animal's, which must have accounted for his relatively clear speech.

When he handed the empty glass back to her, though, his paw and arm were shaking. She set the glass down and began to cut up the meat for him, without asking if she should.

Perhaps his normal mode is to tear it apart, but I don't think I could sit here and watch that.

He glared at her, but said nothing as she put the plate and fork down on his knees. He picked up the fork, awkwardly, in a paw-hand that shook like a birch-leaf in the wind, and stabbed at a bite. He conveyed it to his mouth without mishap, and swallowed it whole, wolfing it down without chewing.

Wolfing his food . . . of course! If you somehow mixed up a man and a wolf, it might look the way he does! Now she knew — though she had never seen a live wolf, only stuffed specimens in museums and at the University — why those distorted features had seemed familiar to her. They were not wholly lupine, but they were certainly not canine. There was a feral ferocity there that no dog would ever display.

The Salamander reappeared with her kettle and the package of herbal medicines from Master Pao's shop. She extracted the white-wrapped packet from the rest, measured the proper amount into the cup and poured the hot water over it.

Cameron eyed her with misgiving. "And just what is *that?*" he asked sullenly.

She gave him the cool look of mingled superiority and pity that had quelled impertinent undergraduates many times in the past. "Medicine from Master Pao," she told him crisply. "*He* wants you to leave off whatever you're dosing yourself with and take this instead. I am inclined to see to it that you do, now that I have taken note of those quack nostrums you think necessary. Half of them are probably poisonous, and the others useless, and I intend to see that you at least *try* Master Pao's medicine."

He paused in the very act of conveying another bite to his mouth, and gazed at her with astonishment, his jaws still open. "And just how do you propose to do that? Pour it forcibly down my throat?"

She sniffed, and regarded the steeping tea with a thoughtful eye. "I dosed a puppy for worms when I was a child," she told him matter-of-factly, feeling rather like a governess with an unruly child to tend. "I don't think I would have any particular difficulty with you. *You* can hardly hold up your fork; the puppy was considerably more active."

He continued to gape at her, the paw holding the fork slowly dropping. "By George," he managed, finally. "I believe you would!"

"Whether you believe it or not is immaterial, for the tea is done and ready to drink." She poured it into the strainer held over the second cup, and waited while it dribbled into its new container. "There." She shook the last few drops into the teacup, and picked it up, handing it to him. "Do you take it yourself, or do I tilt your head up, pour it down your throat, and allow you to make the choice of drinking or drowning? I probably wouldn't have to rub your nose to make you swallow," she added thoughtfully, "But I might forget you aren't the puppy and do it by reflex."

"I might as well see what miserable potion that wretch Pao has decided I *must* have," he replied ungraciously. He looked as if he would have preferred to snatch the cup from her hand for effect, but it was all he could do to stretch out his paw and take it. With a face full of distaste, he sniffed it, then gulped it down.

"Pfaugh!" he choked, tongue lolling out exactly as that long-ago puppy's had. "And this is what I must have instead of my pain-killers?"

"If there is opium in them, as Master Pao asserted, *I* would consider it a better choice," she said steadily. "You ought to consider the notion that your so-called pain-killers might have been responsible for the condition you are in at the moment. Remember what all your books have said about working Magick under the influence of strong drink or drugs. However, it is up to you, of course, if you choose to be a fool and disregard all of the instructions to Apprentices that you have had me read so assiduously."

He gave her a look as sour as a pickled lemon, but said nothing, only went back to stabbing his pieces of meat and gulping them down as viciously as if they were personally responsible for his plight.

Or as if they were coming out of my flesh. She restrained a shiver, looking at those long, white teeth. How much of him was Jason Cameron, and how much the beast? *Would* he turn on her if she provoked him too much?

But if I lather him with pity and sympathy, he will

not pull himself together; if I treat him with fear he will disdain me. I must treat him as what he is — an equal who has made a great fool of himself, and deserves some sharp words.

He finished his meat, set the fork down wearily, and managed to get plate and fork back up on the tray. His condition improved moment by moment, and she felt cheered by that much at least.

"Since you already know that I am impertinent, I am going to be unconscionably rude as well," she said at last. "How on earth did you come to this pass? What happened to turn you into — ?" She could not find the words to describe him, but he answered her anyway.

"Hubris," he said bitterly. "I was already sufficient Master of every aspect of Fire Magick that there were no more challenges for me, and I began to experiment with other forms of Magick. One I found in a medieval grimoire, an incantation to enable a man to put on the aspect of a wolf at will and put it off again at will."

"The *loup-garou*," she breathed, nodding. "I remember it from the old legends."

I also recall the ferocity of the werewolf, and his insatiable hatred for humankind while in that form. How could he possibly want to take that aspect upon himself?

"Not exactly. The werewolf of legend has no control over his shape-change, nor does he retain a human mind in the form of the wolf. This would allow me to make such a shift safely and with my human mind and reasoning intact — or so I thought." He closed his eyes and leaned back in the chair, bitterness obvious even in so alien a face as his. "Something went wrong. I was frozen in this hybrid form. That is why you are here, to help me find the missing part of the formula — I *must* find a way to reverse this condition."

"Well, at least now I know what I am looking for." She

clasped her hands together on her knee and pondered, thinking in the back of her mind that this wolf-man hybrid was not so horrible, really. *If he had been disfigured, there would have been the ugliness of the wound, and that awful feeling I always get when I look at someone who's been hurt, that feeling that makes my throat tighten and makes me want to run away. This is just different. I expect I could actually get used to it in time.* "Forgive me for asking, but — how much of you is wolf?" She blushed as she realized just how that sounded, and amended it. "Has this altered your personality or your emotions, for instance? Are you likely to have to howl at the moon or go run with a pack?"

His laughter was very like a bark. "Hardly! And I pledge you, I am sufficiently housebroken!" But there was an uneasiness behind his words, as if he, too, was wondering how much he was subject to lupine instinct rather than human reason.

The unease hung between them, killing any conversation, and she decided to change the subject. "I can certainly understand now why you have been so reclusive, but surely we need not go on as we have," she told him, surprising herself a little as she spoke things she had only just thought of. "Now that I have seen you, there can be no reason why you must send books up to me and have me shout them at you through the speaking-tube. I believe it would be the most logical for me to come up here to read what you want — that way, if something in another volume occurred to you, we could pursue it immediately, rather than waiting until the next day for you to find it and send it down to me."

He licked his lips, thoughtfully, his red tongue passing across the sharp, white teeth. "You are not completely revolted by — this — ?" he gestured at his face, with his hand that was half paw.

She managed to look him in the eyes, steadily. "It is not pleasant, but neither is it unpleasant. Your appearance is rather startling, and I could imagine that to some of your former acquaintances, particularly those unaware of your work in the arcane, it would come as a shock. But I cannot say that I am *revolted* by it." And she discovered, even as she spoke the words, that they were true. "It has a certain striking quality, actually. Certainly ordinary people are most pleased when their beloved dogs look near to human — there is some of that in this hybrid form you wear."

He made a noise very like a snort. "You are a strange female, Rose Hawkins," Cameron said, rather rudely. "A most unwomanly woman by polite standards."

But she had been called that before, and the words had ceased to hurt. "Then polite standards are too narrow," she replied briskly. "Although I do not call myself a suffragette, I am completely in sympathy with most of their complaints. I cannot speak for the lower classes, but in *our* class of society, Jason Cameron, young ladies are forced to live atop pedestals, and let me tell you, they are *hideously* restrictive places to reside! *I* choose to live down upon the ground where I can actually accomplish something, and if that makes me an 'unwomanly woman,' well, so be it." She crossed her arms over her chest and gazed at him with challenge in her eyes. "Certainly my 'unwomanly' nature has stood *you* in good stead! A fainting, missish, hysterical *lady* would hardly have done you any good in your current predicament!"

He only waved a weary paw at her and settled back into his chair, half-closing his eyes. "Enough. I am not about to debate the cause of women's rights with you. But to take the subject of our reading, are you so certain you want to pursue our researches here, in my suite? I can make you forget that all this happened, if you choose to permit me to do so, and we can return to our former arrangement."

And have him messing about, planting whatever ideas he thinks fit in my mind? No thank you!

"I would not have made the offer if I did not intend for you to accept it," she replied. "What is more — is there any reason why I cannot take du Mond's place and perform the functions of your Apprentice? It does seem to me that you require *some* kind of help when you attempt Magickal Working."

"You?" he replied, turning at last to face her, with his eyes wide, aghast. "Help as an Apprentice? Have you any idea how dangerous that might be? Are you out of your mind?"

"I don't believe so," she said, with a little, forced laugh. "But if you won't have me, perhaps you ought to ask for someone else to help you? Some great Magician, for instance. Like — " she searched her mind for a name, hoping to think of someone who had appeared in the newspapers as an expert in the occult, and offered it up to him. " — like Aleister Crowley, perhaps?"

This time his bark of laughter was contemptuous. "Crowley? As soon trust myself to a circus clown! The self-named 'Wickedest Man in the world' offer *help* to anyone? I would extract blood from a stone before I got help from Aleister Crowley, my dear Rose, and any aid he gave would be so encumbered that my condition would be worsened rather than bettered by putting myself in his hands." He laughed again. "There are only two kinds of men who follow him; those who use others, and those doomed to lose everything including self-respect. He caters to the rapacious and the pathetic — and he uses both to his own ends, bringing satisfaction to none but himself." With great effort, he shook his head. "No, there is no one we can call upon for help at this juncture. Even my old Master would only say that since my own pride got me into this predicament, I must find my own way out of it."

Perhaps that is true, but — She grimaced. "That sounds rather harsh —"

"That is the way of Magick; only the skilled and fit survive, or deserve to." He managed a one-shouldered shrug. "You have read that for yourself, in more than one of the works I have sent to you."

She sighed, and repeated her offer. "Very well, then. You no longer trust du Mond and you cannot turn to any other of your own level of ability. I tell you again, truly; I will help you to the best of my own abilities as your assistant if you will have me."

He turned a blankly astonished gaze upon her. "You see this, you know that Magick brought this upon me, and *still* you persist?"

"I would make the same effort for anyone else I admired," she replied, with complete truth. "And although I do not care for some of your morals or your behavior, you have a first-class mind, and *that* I admire. I think it a shame that you have paid so dearly for so minor a sin as pride."

She held out her hand by way of sealing the bargain. He looked at it dubiously for a moment.

"I do not understand you," he said at last. "But if you are going to throw yourself into the breach this way, I would be an idiot to refuse to accept. You are old enough to be aware of the consequences and to live with them if need be." He hardly sounded gracious, but she didn't care. He also did not offer her his hand, but she did not press him for it. *In his position, I would be shy of offering a lady my paw, too.*

"Fine. We're agreed." She looked him over carefully, finding it easier now than it had been a few minutes ago. Perhaps she *was* getting used to the way he looked. "Well, logic suggests that you should be in bed, but I have no notion of how to get you there. Frankly, I do not believe I have the strength to carry you further."

Put him to bed! No proper lady would have spoken so boldly. She was truly changing. *If I continue to think of him as a naughty little boy, I believe I can say these things without blushing.*

"The Salamanders will help me," he said, with indifference. "Just at the moment, your assistance really isn't needed."

She glanced at the Salamander for confirmation, and it nodded, as if it understood what she wanted.

"Very well then," she replied, standing up and brushing off her skirt. "I will leave you to make your recovery. Master Pao directs you to drink his tea whenever you are in pain or fatigued, but no more than six cups a day."

His lips writhed in distaste. "I am not likely to endure that devil's brew more than twice a day! Be off with you, if you're so concerned that I get some rest."

She suppressed the urge to say something quelling, and simply nodded. She gathered up her package with the remaining packets of herbs in it, and turned, walking out the door of the bedroom into the hall.

He did not thank her, but she didn't expect him to.

Cameron watched Rose leave, seething with a mixture of positive and negative emotions. He supposed he should be grateful to her, but he didn't *feel* grateful, and he wasn't about to feign an emotion he didn't feel. He was angry, though not at her, and frustrated, though not *with* her. He was mortified that it should have been *she* who rescued him. He was relieved that the masquerade was at last over, and utterly astonished that she had reacted as well as she had.

His predominate emotion just at the moment, however, was disappointed exhaustion. All that work, and to have failed again! Perhaps Rose — and Master Pao — were right. Perhaps he should give over taking those pain-killers.

He listened as her footsteps receded, then heard the door at the end of the hall open and close again. "Don't bother to lock it," he told the Salamander wearily. "Now that I've given that damned interfering woman permission to 'help' me, if she finds the door locked against her, she'll probably batter it down."

The Salamander did not reply, but he sensed that it disapproved of his attitude. Well, let it!

The tea that Pao had so cleverly gotten to him seemed to be helping, at least. The aches in his malformed joints had subsided, and his energy was trickling back sooner than he would have expected. He sat up, experimentally, and found that his head was no longer swimming with every movement.

At least I can get back into my own bed by myself. The one thing that the Salamanders could not do — despite his assurances to Rose — was to touch living flesh without burning it. Only in the Conjured form called a "Firemare" could they actually, physically, touch and be touched. And they could not levitate more than — say — the weight of a fully-laden suitcase.

But I would crawl to my bed rather than have her assist me there!

It had grated on him, deeply, to find himself in the position of being unable to help himself. And then to have *her* appear and retrieve him from the results of his own folly — a subordinate, an employee, a *woman* — oh, it was ignominious! He gnashed his teeth as he

extracted himself from the embrace of his chair,
stopping often to pant with exertion.

*To have du Mond discover me in such a case would
be bad enough — but her! Why, two months ago she
did not even believe in the power of Magick, and now
she gives me lectures about how to conduct myself!
The cheek! I, who rescued her from abject poverty,
from that hovel of a boarding-house, from ruin! And
she sits on my footstool, in my private chambers, in my
home and dares to tell me that she will dose me like a
sick puppy if I do not voluntarily take some vile potion
that quack Pao has made up!*

Still, his conscience whispered, she was right, and
so was Pao. The opiates were affecting his judgment;
he would not have attempted tonight's exercise if they
had not been affecting his reason. And Pao's potion,
vile as it was, had certainly revived him. . . .

But that was not the point!

He clung to the back of the chair for a moment,
then got a hand on the wall behind it. Using the wall as
a prop, he worked his way over to the bed, still
stopping at frequent intervals to rest. The bed had
never looked so inviting; the covers were turned down,
and all he needed to do was to fall into it once he
finally reached it. He untied the belt holding his velvet
Working robe to his body, writhed out of it, and
dropped the long robe halfway along the wall for the
Salamanders to pick up later. He could have trousers
and shirt off in a trice, and today he had been in too
much of a hurry to bother with anything else.

*Working that damned tail through the right places
in the seats of my clothing takes twice as long as
everything else. Thank heavens this is no clime for long
underwear!*

It was with a groan of relief that he reached the bed,
and lunged for it, landing half in it and half out of it.

No matter; that was close enough.

He rolled himself onto the mattress, and with a growl of frustration, clawed the clothing from his body, ripping seams and popping buttons as he did so. It was not the first time he had done such a thing, and it would probably not be the last. The Salamanders could see it was mended, or he could buy new. He certainly didn't lack for the means to do so. Though everything else was falling down about his ears, his finances were prospering, especially with the Panama-Pacific International Exposition in the offing.

Naked now, he scrabbled the covers up over himself, and lay with his eyes closed. His head spun, but fortunately not in a way that made him sick to his stomach.

"Why don't you make me another dose of Pao's damned medicine?" he said, knowing he would be obeyed by the Salamander still waiting for orders. "You watched her do it, didn't you?"

"I did," the Salamander replied. He heard the dry ticking of bits of herb falling into the cup, then water pouring.

"I suppose *you* went and got her, didn't you?" he asked the Salamander.

"It is my duty to serve you," it replied calmly. "That was the best way to serve you at the time."

Trust the thing to tell him *that!*

"You have trusted her with everything else," the creature continued, and once again, he heard water trickling. "Why not this? She is worthy of trust. And she was not revolted by your appearance."

"Oh, she was revolted; she is just good at putting the proper face on things. She'd have to be; she grew up going to academic parties. If there was ever a hotbed of machination and deception, it is a sherry-reception given by a Noted Professor. I had rather swim with crocodiles; at least my reputation would survive." He opened his eyes as he felt the warmth of the Salamander near him, and saw the cup floating within grasping distance. He was pleased that his hand did not shake quite so much this time as he reached for it.

The medicine was just as appalling the second time, which probably meant that the Salamander had gotten it right.

For the first time since I was changed, I had a woman in my room — and I couldn't even touch her. His body's needs hadn't changed, and they reminded him urgently that Rose Hawkins was a *most* attractive, if annoying, woman. *What woman could look on me as I am and not be revolted? I could not* pay *a courtesan enough to serve me. Even the lowest, vilest woman in the meanest crib in the Barbary Coast would refuse to serve me. Good God, kissing me would be like kissing an Alsatian! And as for lovemaking —* He winced away from the thought. No healthy, sane woman would find him anything other than repugnant.

Although he did look mostly human from about the nipples to the knees.

Except for the tail, of course . . . but no one would ever look farther than his face and his hands.

The fur of his head and neck thinned and vanished altogether once it reached the middle of his chest, although his skin was paler now than it had been before. The fur did not resume until about the middle of the thigh, until it was a wolf's pelt again from the knee downward. He could not wear shoes anymore; his feet were more paw-like than his hands; he wore soft moccasins and slippers when he wore anything on his feet. The one place his torso was not bare was a ridge of hair that ran down his spine to the tail which had sprouted just above his buttocks.

A charming sight, that. Sure to inspire passion in

any red-blooded woman. Sure to inspire her to think of her pet spaniel, of course.

And of course, Rose had treated him exactly as any normal woman would, provided that woman had the ability to take what he had become in with a measure of composure. She had treated him like a puppy.

At least she didn't scratch my ears and tell me to be a good boy. He put the empty cup down, and curled up on his side. Not surprisingly, the "curled" position was more comfortable and felt more natural than lying on his back.

That damned tail again.

The Salamander was mercifully quiet. "Put out the lights," he ordered, and the light visible through his closed eyelids vanished.

That led to another thought — the behavior of the Salamander, in fetching Rose, presumably the moment she had reached her rooms. What had gotten into the creature? It wasn't supposed to act on its own initiative!

At least, he had never come across any references to Elementals that did. But then again, his relationship with his Elementals was not coercive in nature; perhaps they had never acted on their own initiative with other Masters because those coercions prevented such actions.

But why had the Salamander brought Rose? Why not du Mond?

They don't like du Mond, not any of them, but that isn't the answer. One of their primary functions is to guard me from danger. Could they see du Mond as a danger now? That was always possible; this particular Salamander had been warning him away from du Mond for some time now.

But again: why bring Rose here? Why not do the simple things they *could* do? They could have left him where he was, brought blankets and restoratives to help him regain his strength. Why bring Rose in at all?

The door below him opened and closed again, and he heard du Mond's steps coming up the stairs. The one good thing about this change was the alteration in his hearing ability: it had quadrupled. Not a pin dropped in this house without him knowing.

The man was whistling softly to himself; evidently, something had put him in a very good humor. *Well, since I permit it, he can command the Salamanders to hitch up the horses to take him in the carriage as far as Pacifica; perhaps that is the reason. It makes him feel like a Master.*

But if the Salamanders thought du Mond might be a hazard to him, he did *not* want du Mond to know of his weakness. *I can handle him when I am fit — but I do not want him to think he has the upper hand because I am incapacitated.*

The man paused on the landing, then tried the door to the suite. Finding it unlocked, he ventured inside, naturally. "Jason?" he called. "Is something wrong? The door is unlocked."

"What is that?" Cameron growled loudly, knowing that his voice would carry down the hall. "Paul, go to bed. I'm going over my books, what can you possibly want now?"

"Nothing — well, except to tell you that you really ought to have the Inn at Pacifica send some hampers up here. They have a new cook, a man from New Orleans, that does wonders with fowl." That was so trivial an excuse to bother Cameron that he at once suspected that du Mond sensed something was wrong and was trying to snoop.

"Fine. Start an account down there, and see to it," he replied, trying to sound as irritated as possible. "And if you won't go to bed, go find something useful to do."

"He's sniffing the air, trying to detect incense or burning herbs," the Salamander said calmly. "He must suspect that you attempted a Working without him."

Now how had the fool gotten so clever and observant, suddenly? And why couldn't he have done so when cleverness would have done Cameron some good?

Well, he won't find anything. The Working tonight required balsam and pine gum. He won't detect anything that a good fire in the fireplace wouldn't put out. His lips twisted in satisfaction.

"I'm trying to concentrate, du Mond, and I would prefer it if you weren't interrupting me. If you have anything else, keep it until tomorrow," he called, allowing his irritation to show in his voice.

"All right, Jason." Finally the footsteps receded and continued up the stairs.

"He's muttering something under his breath about opium, and he seems to think it is serious," the Salamander reported, evidently getting the information from one of the others of his kind that was keeping watch over the Apprentice. Interesting. So they *were* keeping a guard of their own on him. That meant they *did* consider him a hazard.

He must think I'm dosing myself too much. . . . He suffered a momentary pang of guilt, for that was exactly what Rose and Master Pao had said. If even du Mond was of that opinion, then he must have allowed pride to take him too near the edge again.

Oh, damn them all, every one of them! He was perfectly capable of assessing his own needs! He didn't need them to tell him what to do!

"Now he's talking to himself." That was a habit du Mond never had broken, despite the fact that it posed a danger of being overheard by Sylphs or Salamanders. "It's about Rose. He does not like her.

And yet he would like to have her to himself. He has plans for her that do not sound as if she would like them."

Cameron was well aware of what du Mond got up to when he visited the city, and his irritation turned to anger. "I can well imagine," he muttered. The man could have been the internal reflection of Cameron's exterior; he was a beast in spirit as Cameron was in body.

That cad. I should have had him horsewhipped out of here when I first found out about his hobby. I thought it didn't matter; after all, many Masters had little peccadilloes when they were Apprentices that they outgrew once they learned discipline. But he's not simply flawed, he's warped. He's another like that charlatan, Crowley. He's a malicious, filthy-minded, self-indulgent blackguard, and he thinks he has the right to besmirch any woman he comes across with his foul paws! And now he thinks he can take advantage of Rose because I am confined to these four walls!

Once again, his anger rose until his vision was red-tinged, filling him with such rage that if du Mond had been in the same room, he would have found the strength to rise from his bed and rip his throat out. Fortunately at the moment he did not have the physical resources to do anything.

He forced himself to simply lie still until his anger wore itself out. Logic asserted itself. *He dares do nothing under my roof or on my grounds, and Rose will not leave either without my watchful eyes on her. She is safe enough from him. But it is a good reason to be rid of him. The only question is — how to accomplish that without his realizing I have done so and seeking revenge?*

The easiest way would be to simply kill the man. The idea had its merits. No one cared about Paul du Mond; no one would miss him if he simply vanished.

Except for certain parties in the city for whom he performs his vile services, who will find someone else of similar disposition within a fortnight.

Still, murdering him did carry some risks. Not in his mundane circles, of course; he need only say he had dismissed his secretary for embezzlement and that the man had taken ship for the South Pacific in disgrace. No one would make any further inquiries, for men did frequently take passage to the Islands to lose a bad reputation.

No, murdering du Mond would attract attention only in Magickal circles. One did not go about incinerating one's Apprentices; he would probably be called to account for it before an assembly of Firemasters. If that happened before he managed to change himself back, his altered state would become public knowledge, and some of his deadlier rivals would know of his plight.

No. Much as I would like to, I cannot afford to kill him. Yet.

That left another option — find some place to put him that was out of the way. That would require a great deal of thought, more than he had put into it until now.

But until now, if I had come across a Working that required four hands rather than two, I would have needed him after all. Now, I no longer do. Now I can afford to think about getting rid of him.

Perhaps the Hawkins girl's impetuous offer was not such a bad thing after all.

She certainly can't be any worse as an assistant than du Mond.

He curled up a bit more and pondered the problem. If he worked hard at it, he could probably manufacture a situation that would require du Mond's presence in the city for some time. Perhaps that would be best.

I can always incinerate him after I have my proper form back. All I have to do is reveal the nature of his recreations and most of the Masters would second my action. Simon Beltaire would not, of course, but he would not second anything I did, even if it was to offer him the wealth of the Indies. Although few, if any, of the Masters would find those recreations in and of themselves reprehensible, since du Mond had up until now confined himself to women of the lowest class and intelligence, they *would* find his indulgence in them to be foolish and an indication of a fatally flawed personality, one that could never muster the will to properly command the Salamanders.

They already had a perfect example of how such a flawed personality could be detrimental to every Magician. Crowley had been one such — and look what he was doing now! The man was a perambulating disaster wherever he went; he couldn't touch something without destroying or fouling it. And as for his blatant publicity-seeking — he was doing more to discredit the entire world of Magick than the Spanish Inquisition.

His former Master must be spinning in his grave.

Still, he did serve a kind of purpose. Eliphas Levi had said as much in Cameron's first Assembly, when Crowley had been formally cast out and stripped of as much of his power as the Magicians of his Element had deemed he actually possessed. "He does us all a favor, in his twisted way," the old Master had said. "He gathers to him all those fools who believe that the path to power can be found through drugs and self-indulgence rather than study and self-discipline. Thus, he relieves us of the task of having to test and discard them. And in addition, he causes the common folk of the world to believe that *all* Magicians must be charlatans — which is just as well, for it enables us to do our work in relative peace and quiet!"

*Levi had a point. I do wonder . . . perhaps I could
persuade du Mond to go to Crowley? I would then be
rid of him and inflict a treacherous cur on Crowley as
well!* Now that plan had a real savor to it!

And with that pleasant thought in mind, he began
to relax, and his physical exhaustion caught up with
him completely. He had just enough time to remind
the Salamander to guard him while he slept, before
sleep itself overcame him.

CHAPTER ELEVEN

When Rose reached the haven of her room, she finally collapsed on the sofa, and allowed herself the luxury of *feeling* again — and of thinking, instead of merely accepting what she saw.

The result was an emotional collapse as well as a physical one. Shaking in every limb, she buried her face in her hands and let the reaction and tension play themselves out. She did not, as she had half expected she would, weep hysterically — though she did shiver until her teeth rattled.

It was a horrible moment, and it felt as if it would last forever. She had to keep reminding herself that Jason Cameron was more to be pitied than feared, and that he probably had no surer friends in the world than herself and Master Pao. *I can cope with this. I can deal with becoming his Apprentice. I can cope with his rudeness and his arrogance, and even handle his anger, if I must.* He *needed* her, however ungraciously he might act. She could not desert a fellow man who was in the state that he found himself.

As her shivering subsided, she forced herself to recall, as clearly as possible, every aspect of his face and figure, for there was still fear within her now that she was no longer caught up in the urgency and unreality of the emergency in his rooms. She confronted the monster directly, if only in her mind, contemplating it until it was no stranger than anything else she had witnessed in this strangest of homes. *I must make him commonplace to myself, so that I can concentrate on the work and not on him.*

The more she recalled, the less there was that seemed *outre*. Certainly she was able to think about working beside him without a shudder of fear. *Paul du Mond is more to be feared than he, I suspect. If the Salamanders do not like him, and if Sunset fears him, there is surely a reason.*

When it came right down to it, Cameron looked no worse than any of the animal-headed gods of ancient Egypt, and she had always thought *them* to be oddly attractive!

Yes. I will think of him as a kind of lesser Anubis.

Somehow that made everything fall into place; she had a "name" for what he was, and a category, and the world fell back into some semblance of order again. Once that happened, her feeling of disorientation vanished, and so did the last of her unease. That was hardly logical — *But then, as I am well aware, the emotions are not very responsive to logic.*

She took three deep breaths, and ordered the Salamander who tended her rooms to fix her a bath. She certainly needed one! *I was sodden with perspiration before the whole incident was over. My clothing will have to be cleaned before it is fit to wear again.*

She vaguely heard du Mond returning, heard a faint echo of him talking with Jason through the speaking-tube as she undressed. She was glad she had taken the precaution of locking her door. For some reason he seemed more than usually repellent to her. *Could it be because Jason no longer trusts him? I wonder why he was so insistent on helping Jason with his Magickal Working?* To do the man justice, he might simply have had the welfare of his Master in mind. . . .

But somehow, she thought, as she stepped into the steaming bathtub, *I don't think so. But what could his motive be?*

"Thank you for fixing my bath. Now take the clothing I left on the floor and clean it all thoroughly, please," she ordered aloud. She never forgot "please" and "thank you" with the Salamanders, and she had the oddest feeling that they appreciated the small courtesy.

But her mind kept turning back to Paul du Mond, in spite of her determination to enjoy her bath in peace. And a thought occurred to her that made her blood run cold in spite of the hot water she soaked in. *He is Jason's secretary, and he has had more than enough time to learn to forge Jason's signature. His reason could be strictly material! He could have been hoping for such an outcome as this one, hoping to catch Jason at a moment of extreme weakness and —*

And what? Murder his employer, perhaps? Her hands closed on the side of the bathtub, and it was all she could do to keep from leaping to her feet to run downstairs to warn Jason.

It was certainly a possibility. Cameron had been a recluse for long enough that no one remarked on the fact anymore. He communicated with his underlings by means of the telegraph set in his office, or by letters. *Anyone* could use a telegraph, and as for letters, du Mond already wrote the majority of them. Every secretary she had ever met was an adroit forger of his or her employer's name, and she doubted that du Mond was an exception to that rule.

He need only dispose of Jason, keep up the pretense that Jason is still alive, and enjoy all the fruits of Jason's wealth for as long as he cares to. She began shivering all over again, and hoped that Jason had not exposed his weakened state to du Mond. *Would he snatch the*

*opportunity, or would he wait for a surer time? I fear
he is the type to grab for any chance. . . .*

It would be all too easy for the secretary to cover his
employer's absence. Her imagination carried out the
scheme further, until Paul du Mond appeared to her
in her mind's eye as a very Moriarty of crime. *If
anyone suspected, he could purchase a ticket to Tahiti,
China, or Australia, hire someone to impersonate
Cameron for the trip, and then "Cameron" would
either vanish overseas or simply "send back orders"
now and again. The only person who would know that
Cameron was no longer among the living would be me
— I am the only person he could not fool, for I know
Cameron's voice.*

That made her grow even colder. Of course, du
Mond could always appear with orders for her
dismissal, but would he? Why should he let her go?
There was no one to miss her if *she* disappeared. If du
Mond balked at killing a woman, he could simply
overpower her and put her into the hands of a white
slaver. . . .

Or he could imprison me here, at his pleasure. Her
throat closed, as fear choked off her breath for a
moment; her chest tightened, and she feared that her
heart would pound itself into pieces. She clutched the
sides of the bathtub as to a lifeline, and willed herself
to fight the fear. *Logic! Think logically! Du Mond does
not know that Jason is indisposed. Nothing has
happened yet, and if I confide my thoughts to Jason,
he can be certain to guard himself —*

Guard himself! Of course! Suddenly her heart
quieted, and her breathing eased. Jason had his
Salamanders to protect him; if only half of what she
had read thus far was true, in defense of their Master
they could incinerate a man in the space of a
heartbeat! Du Mond was only an Apprentice, and not

a very good one, if Jason was to be believed. It was not likely that he would be able to defend himself against the attack of a Salamander.

The fear evaporated as quickly as fog at noon. She relaxed back into the hot bath, and sighed as a calm exhaustion replaced fear. *I will still tell Jason my concerns, but du Mond will not be able to overcome him now that Jason is wary of the man. Du Mond is no threat, not to someone as powerful as and wary as Jason is. I should concentrate on preparing myself to be a Master's Apprentice. I only hope I am as ready for that as I claimed I was.*

The mirror showed a face far more pleasant than Jason Cameron's wolf-visage, and Paul du Mond chuckled to his reflection as he prepared for bed. His trip into Pacifica for dinner had been a fruitful one, for he had no sooner settled down to a very satisfactory meal than who should stroll into the tiny inn by the sea but Simon Beltaire!

As if it had been planned ahead of time, the inn was crowded and there were no free tables available. Paul was able to offer the "stranger" a seat at his own without looking like anything other than a polite gentleman. The owner of the restaurant had been relieved and grateful that Paul was so accommodating. They had made mock-introductions to each other with perfectly straight faces, and Beltaire had ordered his own meal as soon as the waiter hurried up to tend to the new arrival.

"I believe that Cameron attempted a Working tonight," Paul had said casually, when he thought they would not be overheard in the general chatter.

"He will not get far with it." Beltaire had chuckled, stroking his goatee with evident satisfaction. "I have reason to believe that I hold the only manuscript with the key to his troubles, and needless to say, I have no intention of allowing him to have it."

Du Mond chuckled to himself at the memory of the cruel glint in Beltaire's dark eyes. The Firemaster intended to make Cameron suffer as long as possible before striking, that much was obvious to even a dullard. Not that du Mond blamed him for such intentions. Watching one's enemies suffer was one of the few totally pure pleasures in the world, and Cameron had been Beltaire's enemy for as long as du Mond had known of the existence of the Firemasters.

It had been a good dinner, and it had not been marred by Jason's surliness on his return. He untied his tie and put it and his collar away, fastidiously hanging the tie on a special rack and curling the collar just so in the wooden collar-box.

Beltaire's appearance was no accident; he had indeed arranged their meeting, for the Firemaster had told him so in as many words. "I have been waiting for you here in the town for some days now. I needed to speak with you urgently. I would like you to do two things for me," he had said. "First, I wish to repeat my request to plant as many doubts in that Hawkins girl's mind about Cameron as you can over the course of the next two weeks. And second, I would like you to find some way to persuade Cameron to lodge you permanently in San Francisco or Oakland before Christmas."

Nothing would have suited Paul better, but he had been both surprised and cautious that Beltaire should bring the second request to him. "Is there a reason?" he asked.

Beltaire had nodded. "I would like to have you available to me for an extended period of time. I wish to probe your memories of Cameron, his methods, and everything to do with his Magickal Work. If I am to defeat him, I need intimate knowledge that only you possess, and it will take time to plumb your memories for that much knowledge."

"And what do I receive in return?" Du Mond had not been at all shy in demanding that answer immediately. If he was going to be at Beltaire's beck and call, it had damned well better be worth his time!

The answer had been very satisfactory, and Paul smiled whitely at his reflection. Beltaire promised, with vows that no Firemaster would break, that he would initiate Paul into the paths that the noted magician Aleister Crowley had pioneered; he described the methods of Crowley's followers in detail, and Paul had been very impressed. These were paths that Paul found more to his liking, and along the same line as the book Beltaire had given him — the acquisition of Magickal Power by means of Sex Magick and the use of drugs to probe directly into the realms of the occult, rather than the tedious means that Cameron insisted upon. There would be no more memorizations or thumbing through half-legible manuscripts; this was the shortcut to Power that Paul had known instinctively existed, but that Cameron had denied him. There was no reason, in this modern day and age, to confine oneself to methods used by the ancients for no better reason than "tradition!" After all, it was "traditional" to light the night with candles rather than electricity, "traditional" to cross country by horseback rather than the railroad. Why should modern means be excluded from the pursuit of Magick? He had never been able to understand why a man like Cameron, so modern in every other way, was so stubborn when it came to modernizing Magick.

Beltaire had even hinted that use of such Magick did not confine one to the Mastery of only *one* of the Elements, but allowed the control of all four!

"I was able to subdue that Chinaman's Sylphs when he tried to hide the slave I had purchased," Beltaire had said. "I drove them away long enough to give him proper punishment for his impertinence. Cameron could not have done that."

I will be a greater Master than Cameron ever dreamed of becoming! he exulted in his mind. *There will be no limit to what I can do!*

But while he worked out the means to that end, he must somehow persuade that skittish Hawkins female to listen to him.

I can't imagine what possible reason Beltaire has for wanting her to desert Cameron, but he must have one. Well, I don't particularly care, either. That's his business, not mine.

He would do his best; but that was not *his* primary concern. The most important thing for him was to find a reason for Cameron to send him into the city for an extended stay.

"Find some reason to take an apartment of your own — and don't worry, I will arrange one that will be precisely to your liking," Beltaire had also urged him. "That way you'll have a place where Cameron's Salamanders cannot overlook you. I can make sure of that, in a way that will not make him suspicious." He had chuckled. "There are many things that Salamanders do not care for; I can arrange for your new dwelling to be in a haunt of Undines and they will not venture near it."

That had been altogether to his liking. *If I can have my own apartment, I will have a place I can bring a woman without that supercilious Snyder gazing down his nose at me.* Paul had not been at all loath to agree to this arrangement, especially since he and Beltaire shared many of the same interests. He would be able to indulge himself in his long-cherished fantasy of having a girl all to himself, for as long as he wished.

A Chinese, I think. They're cheaper for one thing; for another, if she's damaged or dies on me, I can dump her somewhere without anyone bothering to investigate. No one is going to bother about another Chinese whore turning up in an alley — they might *fuss a bit about a Mexican or a colored girl, and if anyone found a white girl in the same position, it would force a policeman to look around.* He felt a familiar tightening in his groin at the very idea of having his own little slave to do what he liked with. The only drawback to breaking girls for someone else was the need to keep them relatively undamaged. At last he would be free to indulge every fantasy. For that matter, if Beltaire was to be believed, he would be able to use a great deal of what he did with his women as a road to further Magickal Power. Beltaire was going to get him some texts and fiction by Crowley soon, so that he could see for himself what the potentials were.

Those will make better reading than Cameron's old fossils, by a damn sight!

He undressed carefully, as always; got into bed and turned off the light, and composed himself as if for sleep, but his mind was going at full speed. *What can possibly require my presence in the city for an indefinite length of time? It will have to be business matters. I must look through all the recent correspondence and try to find something appropriate, then blow it up out of proportion.*

Planting doubts into the Hawkins girl's mind would not be at all difficult. The circumstances under which she had been brought here were duplicitous; she should be ready to believe that Cameron had told her further lies. She was a scholar, and they were notoriously unworldly. And anyone who prided himself on being clever, the way she did, was an easy target for deception. People who considered themselves to be clever, to be more intelligent than those around them, simply would not believe that they could be fooled. *A large lie will be better than a small one. The best thing I can do is to hint that I have found things in Cameron's correspondence that indicate he is a party to the white slave trade. I can point to the nearness of his townhouse to the Barbary Coast as circumstantial evidence — also to his friendships with Chinese of dubious repute, and the presence of a man with connections to India in his very service.* Did Beltaire only wish her to flee, so as to remove the only potential witness to Cameron's destruction, or did he have some further goal in mind? Did he plan to offer himself as the girl's protector, in the most innocent sense? If she were frightened enough of Cameron — and if Beltaire presented himself in the guise of someone to be trusted, say a clergyman, he just might be able to pull it off. *Perhaps it would not do any harm to mention again that Jason is not mentally stable, hint at an addiction to opium.* That would give further connections, for the white slavers were also the men who supplied opium to the dope dens. Before he left, the wench would be terrified at the very thought of encountering Cameron in the flesh!

Now, how to convince Jason he should have his own apartment . . . ?

Whatever I choose to be my excuse for being in the city, I shall make certain most of the business will take place at odd hours and as far from the townhouse as possible. It will then be only logical for me to lodge where the business is, rather than disrupt the household with my comings and goings. He knew that the help at the townhouse had complained to Cameron in the past when he had come and gone at odd or late hours — they could not all go to bed until the last of the "guests" were seen to, nor could they lock the place up until everyone who should be in residence was safely in his bed. If some aspect of

Jason's business required him to be out late at night —

Then, all at once, he knew his answer. *I have it! The shipping company in Oakland he just purchased!* It had been part of a larger acquisition, but the relatively small company had proved to be unexpectedly key to much of his rail business up the coast into the great lumbering areas. There were bound to be problems with such a new purchase, problems that Paul could not only exaggerate, but even make worse by communicating ambiguous orders to those in charge. Cameron did not have an agent in Oakland; Paul could volunteer. Shipping companies kept late (or early) hours, for consignments must be on their way long before a "normal" business day began. And in addition, a daily crossing of the Bay would waste an intolerable number of working hours — *if* he could find a ferry that operated at such times!

This would be perfect. Beltaire had a home of his own across the Bay — placing him as far as possible from his rival Firemaster, and yet still remaining within the area. That home was probably where he did most of *his* Magickal Work, and being in Oakland would put Paul near enough to him to receive frequent personal instruction.

Beltaire has a private motor-launch, and I suspect he will be reasonable about my use of it if I want to visit the city after dark.

Yes. He smiled to himself as he put the final mental touches on his new plans. This was going to work out wonderfully well.

The last place that Rose expected to find du Mond was in the conservatory. She had taken to doing her reading there, soothed by the sound of the fountains and the twittering birds, but today, when she rounded a corner, there he was, sitting across from her favorite bench with a book in his hands. She doubted that he was reading it, since he didn't seem at all absorbed in it. He had never struck her as the kind of man who would find anything interesting about plants or small birds —

Except, perhaps, to find a way to do something unpleasant with them —

She shook the uncomfortable thought from her head. It was too late to turn around and leave; he had already seen her, as if he had been waiting for her, and was smiling that particularly false, bright smile at her, the one that made her feel as if she should check her hemline for an immodest display of ankle. She sighed, and continued to walk in his direction.

He stood up, and met her halfway. "I beg your pardon if I am intruding. I was not aware that you ever came here to read, Miss Hawkins," he said, before she could greet him. "And since I really should be getting back to my work, I shall leave you to the solitude you would obviously prefer and not inflict my company upon you."

Oh, drat. Did I make myself that obvious? Annoyed by her twinge of guilt, further annoyed by the fact that she had been patently impolite, she now felt moved to protest, even though she would rather have thanked him for being observant. "Oh, don't go on my account," she replied, doing her level best to cover her irritation. "Please. It is not as if you were practicing a trumpet, or something of the like. Surely two people can read quietly without annoying each other."

But he only laughed. "No, indeed, the only reason one could wish to come here would be to enjoy the illusion of summer and the quiet, and I will not spoil these things for you with my presence. I could wish you felt more comfortable with my company, but you do not, and I am not the kind of man to force myself upon you in any way."

The deuce you aren't! she thought rebelliously, feeling certain she had caught him in an outright lie, but he was continuing.

"I don't know what has put you off about me, and I do apologize. It may be that — that I am aware of many uncomfortable truths about our employer, and you are insensibly aware of this," he said earnestly, as if he actually meant every word of it. "Even hardened skeptics will admit that a woman's instincts are surer than a mere male's, and that a woman is far more sensitive to nuances. It could be that it is the burden that I carry that makes you uncomfortable in my presence, and not my presence itself."

She knew he was waiting for her to ask about the "uncomfortable secrets," and she was not about to oblige him. Instead, she bowed her head as if hiding a blush. "Most men of power have uncomfortable things about them," she murmured. "It is not my place to inquire about my employer, and still less to go hunting what may be nothing more than gossip."

But he took that slender rebuff as the invitation to confide! "I have recently learned some things that would make many people more than merely uncomfortable," he said, in a low, persuasive voice. "It is not gossip, I do assure you, but fact, and in his own handwriting."

Now I know you lie! Now that I have seen him I can understand why he cannot write anything for himself — those poor paws of his could never hold a pen!

But du Mond was hardly privy to all that Jason had revealed to her. He probably still thought that *she* believed she was translating obscure works for an eccentric invalid. Everything he told her was based on that assumption, and as a result, she was in a position to catch him in quite a few lies, if she cared to.

He continued. "They are — business arrangements

with Chinese and men with connections to the East that
are not only dubious, but may conceal truly illegal acts."
He contrived to look very earnest, a trifle worried, and
completely honest and open. "Miss Hawkins, I must
admit that I have no evidence of the sort that one would
take to an authority, but if I were you, I would think very
seriously about my situation. These are the things that
alarm me. Cameron has dealings with Chinese merchants
of doubtful reputation. He has in his employ in his
townhouse in the city a man of hardened mien who still
has contacts in India and beyond. His townhouse itself
stands dangerously near that terrible district known as the
'Barbary Coast.' And it is his habit to hire young women
with few or no living relations; women who would not be
missed if they suddenly were to vanish. And in addition —
I fear he is, in his illness, becoming extremely dependent
upon opium and similar drugs. At the least, this impairs his
judgment, and at the worst, it puts him in the power of
those who supply such things. Remember what infamous
activities this city is noted for, and please, be wary. Recall
my promise to help you, if need be. I still have many
worthy friends in the city, honest and honorable men you
could trust without a second thought."

It was all she could do to keep from laughing out
loud. Did he really, truly believe her to be so very
gullible? Did he believe she would so easily forget how
he had acted toward her when she first arrived? To
hide her twitching lips, she looked away, as if
profoundly embarrassed. "I shall," she said. It seemed
to satisfy him, and he went on his way after an earnest
glance of deep concern.

She sat down on her favorite bench with her book
clasped in both hands, thinking the encounter through.
Should I tell Jason about this conversation? In the light of
day, all of her fears of last night seemed foolish, the
childish nonsense of a woman terrified by imaginary

burglars under the bed and the scratching of twigs upon the window. She had decided not to say anything at all to Cameron of the plots and machinations her imagination had ascribed to du Mond. Why bother? There was not the slightest scrap of evidence, and she wanted to impress Cameron with her sense. Such nonsense would only annoy him.

But it seemed that du Mond had an imagination that was just as active.

She sat so still that one of the little birds landed on the back of the bench beside her, preened itself carefully, and then flew off.

She could hardly imagine the staff of the townhouse being involved in white slavery — but she also recalled that they did not at all care for du Mond, and the antipathy may have been mutual. It was always easy to ascribe a sinister purpose to someone you did not like — well, look at all the plots she had laid up on du Mond's doorstep last night!

She closed her eyes for a moment, trying to measure just how many of du Mond's accusations were true. There was no doubt that Jason *did* have dealings with less-than-savory merchants in town, Chinese and otherwise. He made no secret of that. He was a businessman, and one who cared very little about the morals of those he dealt with, although Rose found such an attitude reprehensible. So du Mond was right, in that much.

He was also correct in saying that Cameron was using far too much in the way of opiates. She had seen as much for herself, last night, in the number of pills he had planned to take before she intervened. Even Master Pao had known that he was in trouble so far as narcotics went — probably because he had relatives and informants all over China-town, which would be where Cameron got most of his opium and opium derivatives. And as for Cameron's propensity for hiring young women who would not be missed, she had only du Mond's word on that. . . .

But I am one such, and it is logical to think that there are others in his employ who could answer that description. There are far, far more men in San Francisco than women, even at this modern date, and those women who travel here are often those who seek their fortunes even as the men seek theirs, because they have no family ties to hold them, or family resources to fall back on.

She opened her eyes again, and licked her lips. It could be that du Mond was trying to frighten her into seeking *his* aid in escaping this place, for sinister reasons of his own. Then again, du Mond could simply wish her out of the house so that he alone had access to Cameron, and Cameron became totally dependent on him for his contact with the outside world.

She did not need to attribute sinister plans to him. His motive could be very, very simple, and that of any man hoping to preserve his position — drive her away so that circumstances returned to the way they had been before she arrived. He might even have sensed that he was about to be replaced in the Master's service as an Apprentice, but whether or not he did, he could hardly have missed the fact that *he* was not the only human in the house anymore!

So he sees me as an interloper and wants to be rid of me. A human and common enough motive! And nothing I need ascribe to sinister machinations. Who knows but what he may actually have those respectable "friends" he claims he has, who would be willing to help me find other employment. Well, why not? If she were as ignorant of the real situation as du Mond supposed, and if she were to find a better position than this one, she would never bother going

back, now, would she? It was in du Mond's purely
mundane interest to help her find good employment
elsewhere.

No, she was attributing far too much to him and to
his intelligence. There was no point in telling
Cameron about this — unless she could find a way to
do so that would amuse him and lighten his spirits.

Poor man! He could certainly use all the help he
could get in that regard, as in so many others.

She relaxed, and settled down to read her book,
grateful that du Mond had not seen it closely, for it was
Cameron's own Journal-*cum*-Workbook of his first
year as an Apprentice. She had found it on her
bedside table this morning, brought there, no doubt,
by a Salamander. She did not know if Cameron
himself had sent it, or if that one extraordinarily
intelligent Salamander had taken it upon himself to
bring it to her, but in either case it was proving to be
enlightening in many ways.

There was not a great deal that was personal in this
Journal, and what there was did not tell her a great
deal. She formed a vague notion of an extremely
intelligent child, quite a lone wolf, who spent no time
in the company of children his own age. Well, he was
hardly alone in that respect; most highly intelligent
children were isolated by their very intelligence.

I was, for instance. She had been shunned by other
girls her age for being a "bookworm," which hardly
mattered, since she had never found their games of
much interest. *I had more entertainment out of
re-enacting the beheading of Mary Queen of Scots
with my dolls than of playing at "house." And when I
dressed them, I made miniature costumes of various
historical periods rather than the latest fashions!*

Cameron had actually begun his work as a formal
Apprentice at the age of thirteen, and even at that

young age his penmanship had been impeccable. The one thing that this book had that others she had read had lacked was the reason behind every exercise that young Jason had been assigned. Evidently his own Master had been very meticulous about outlining the rhyme and reason behind the most trivial of Magickal exercises, and Jason had been just as meticulous about writing them down. The result of this was a very thorough education in the Magick of Fire, indeed, of Magick in general, and the equivalent of having a Master at her elbow to explain everything.

Now a great many things she had read in other books began to make sense — including the Ordeals. All of them were designed to ensure that the prospective Master could control his Elementals under any and all circumstances, so that even when the Master lay unconscious or near death, the Elementals would not revolt and break the coercions and restrictions binding them.

Here the young Jason had noted something very interesting. *'It would be better to make friends of the Salamanders than to force them,'* he had written in his unchildlike hand. *'This is how my Master conducts himself these days although he learned by the Old School; I believe his only friends are Salamanders, actually.'*

She smiled wryly at that. *Like Master, like Apprentice. I do believe that Jason's only friends are Salamanders.*

What would happen if an Elemental *did* revolt? She turned a page, and found that young Jason had asked the same question. *'Dreadful things happen until the Elemental's anger is spent. If an Undine turns against her Master, rivers rise, springs appear where they are not wanted, waters burst dams unexpectedly. If a Sylph, terrible storms, esp tornadoes. If a Gnome,*

earthquakes, sinkholes, and cave-ins, and if a Sala-
mander, fires everywhere that rage quite out of
control, and sometimes volcanoes. My Master says
that the Great Fire of London was because of angry
Salamanders breaking free from an unkind Master.
This is why he says it is better to make friends, tho it
takes longer.'

She shivered. Was *this* the answer to the fabled
destruction of Atlantis? Was this why Pompeii was
buried? What of the Johnstown Flood, the eruption of
Mount Pelee only three years ago that destroyed two
cities, or that mysterious earthquake that changed the
course of the Mississippi some fifty years ago? Could a
Salamander have caused the Chicago Fire her father
had talked about so much?

Then she chided herself for seeing a supernatural
cause behind every one of the world's woes. *Oh, surely*
some disasters are purely human or natural in origin. I
shall be suspecting a renegade Elemental behind
everything, if I am not careful! And what Elemental
could have caused the Irish Famine, pray — a Potato
Elemental?

Still, it was fascinating to think that there were some
otherwise inexplicable disasters that *had* causes. Now
the ancient Greek habit of propitiating Nature Spirits
whenever building or changing something began to
sound like a sound and reasonable idea!

She continued to delve into the book, as the
afternoon slipped away, lost to the world around
her and to any thoughts other than those of Magick.

Cameron was as nervous as any boy alone with a female
for the first time. He had ordered the Salamanders to clear
off the couch in his study and place the best lamp in the
house on the table beside it. There was a carafe of fresh
water and a glass on the table, and a pile of books awaited

Rose's perusal. She had appeared promptly when he called up for her, but she had not dressed as she usually did when reading — that is, casually. She'd donned a soft cashmere suit in a warm brown shade, and was as carefully and properly groomed as any prim female secretary. Although she did not seem ill-at-ease, she was not lounging on the couch as was her wont when reading in her room.

Of course she is not! She is not in her room, thinking she is unobserved. This is her public face, and she is not likely to show me her private aspect.

But he could not help thinking that she was so stiff because she was afraid of him — that despite her brave words, she could not help looking at him and thinking of him as a monster. How could she simply *accept* him? It was impossible, of course. It would take someone with more experience in Magick than she to accept something like him with equanimity.

"You're certain that you're quite comfortable?" he asked nervously.

"Absolutely," she replied, and raised one eyebrow. "Why do you keep asking?"

He was *not* about to tell her that it was because he had watched her in his mirror and knew that her posture was not one of ease and comfort! If she ever deduced that, he hoped she would be ladylike enough to pretend that she hadn't.

"I suppose it is because I expect you to be uncomfortable," he said, finally. "This situation you are in is — not a natural one. It is —"

"No stranger than reading to a disembodied voice through a speaking-tube, Jason," she replied firmly. "Now, I take it that we are *not* going to attempt anything more strenuous than reading tonight? Otherwise I assume you would have said something when you called me here."

"Probably not for the next fortnight, at least," he told her, rubbing the side of his head, where a dull and distant headache still resided. Along with the headache, he nursed a sense of self-righteousness. He had been very good about taking that damned tea of Pao's, and it did seem to him that he felt much more alert, but he missed some of the effects of his pain-killers already. He only hoped the headache would get better and not worse with time — or else he was going back to what he knew worked. "Conditions won't be quite right for at least that long. Did you find my Journal?"

She smiled at that; as always, the expression quite transformed her face, perhaps because she smiled so seldom. "Yes, I did, but I hesitated to say anything about it for fear that it had been your pet Salamander who had decided that I should have it, and not you." Her smile turned wry. "I did not want to have you annoyed at your pet when you are most likely to be irritable."

Damn. I didn't think that irritation showed. Or — maybe she's just guessing. I would certainly have cause to feel irritable after last night. He glanced at his "pet Salamander," who only spun a little in the Elemental's version of a quiet chuckle. "He is quite capable of doing just that, I suspect, but no, it was my idea. Do let me know when you feel you understand everything in that book completely, and I will get the next volume out of storage." *I do not think I will respond to that remark about being irritable. Unfortunately, it is too damnably accurate at the moment.* He clumsily opened his special book to the next blank page, and sighed. "The one thing my disaster of yesterday did was to suggest another train of investigation, so if you are ready, perhaps you could begin with the book on the couch beside you. Read the whole thing, if you please."

Taking that as the unsubtle hint it was meant to be, she picked up the volume and began to read aloud, as usual. And, as usual, he watched and listened, directing the Salamander to make notes occasionally. She was just a trifle distracted by this at first, but got used to it sooner than he would have expected.

So did he, for that matter. She sat in a pool of bright light in the otherwise darkened study. He sat off to one side, behind his desk with a dimmer light upon it, the Salamander hovering at his right, and the huge book of notes propped up before him, effectively screening most of his face from her. By degrees, she began to relax, and began to demonstrate the fact; first by resting her head on her hand as she read, then at last by tucking her legs up beneath her in the pose he thought she found most easy. It was a pity she felt she had to truss herself up in that infernal suit and corsets, but at least she hadn't bound herself up too tightly to breathe.

Once she relaxed, so did he. It was much easier on both of them for her to read in his study this way; he no longer had to strain to hear her clearly through the tube, and she did not have to read in a volume that strained her voice. She came to the end of the thin book and looked up in surprise as she realized where she was.

"Oh, excuse me — " she began, and dropped her feet back to the floor with a blush.

"Please, take whatever position you feel is less strained," he told her earnestly. "You read better when you are at ease. And I can certainly bear a few footmarks upon the furniture."

"It is a terrible habit from my childhood, and one my father never insisted that I break," she confessed. "It is hardly ladylike."

"I did not engage you for your deportment and

posture, Rose," he reminded her. "I engaged you for your knowledge and your mind. I would not care if you read like a contortionist in a circus, with both of your feet placed on the back of your head!"

She laughed, as he had hoped she would, and picked up the next book without prompting. She paid no more attention to him or to his terrible face than if he had been his old self — nor did she evidence any more fear of him.

I believe that this is going to work out after all, he thought with utter astonishment. *By George, she has surprised me again!*

It was just as well that the situation with Rose was going as well as it was, because within a week, Paul brought him a file on Golden Gate Shipping that was enough to fray his temper to the breaking point before he was through with it.

"How did things deteriorate like this?" he exploded, as du Mond waited patiently for him to finish going through the papers. The secretary just shrugged.

"It seems to have mostly blown up over the last week or so," the man said. "You've sent corrective instructions, but they seem to have bungled them. And quite frankly, it would never have gotten this way if you had an agent there. If you want my opinion —" he paused, waiting expectantly.

"Go on," Cameron growled.

"Well, I think the trouble is that the men over there are the kind that absolutely require someone watching them. Some people are that way; leave them alone for a moment, and they'll botch everything, but keep an eye on them and they do fine." He shrugged. "I can't explain it, but you must have seen cases like this before."

Unfortunately, he had, all too often. Why it was that

men seemed to take the absence of the boss for the signal to laze about and make mistakes of carelessness, he had no idea. "So the point is, I need an agent in Oakland, quickly," he growled in irritation. "Unfortunately, I haven't anyone to spare —"

Except that I have been trying to think of a way to get him out of the house so that Rose and I can Work without having to conceal it from him! I don't suppose —

"I — I suppose I could go," du Mond said reluctantly, in an uncanny echo of his own thoughts. "Quite frankly, Jason, there is very little secretarial work for me lately. Your circle of acquaintances seems to have gotten the idea that they are not going to pry you out of your reclusive retreat — and as for business matters, you have always taken care of most of them yourself, and your agent in San Francisco can handle what I have been dealing with. I believe I can straighten out this little tangle in fairly short order, and keep a new one from appearing with a firm hand on the reins."

Oh, this was almost too perfect to be believed! But why would du Mond, who Cameron knew was lazy by nature, *want* to take on something that would entail real work?

"Quite frankly, Jason, this quiet house is driving me crazy," the man went on. "Since your accident, there has been nothing for an active man to do here, and no company unless I go down into Pacifica for it. And that prim little stick of a scholar of yours is hardly what I would call *company*. I think that may be why I've fallen back on my Magickal studies. Perhaps if I can get out among people again, I'll be less distracted by boredom, better able to settle down to my Magickal work as well."

Not likely — but possible, I will grant that. And it gives me the excuse I have been searching for to get rid of the blackguard. Cynically, he would allow that du Mond's motivation for volunteering was probably the genuine one he had stated — he wanted *out,* back in a position where he had ready access to the city, the Barbary Coast, and the pleasures he was doing without. The presence of Rose Hawkins, who made no effort to conceal the fact that she did not like him, was probably salt in the wounds of his "deprivation."

"You'll have to live in Oakland," Cameron pointed out. "Assuming you could even get a ferry at the hours you'll need to travel, you'd waste more time traveling to and from the townhouse than is reasonable. My agent should be able to find an apartment for you."

"I should think I ought to take care of that." He squared his shoulders as if he was taking on a great burden. "And I should also think, from the state of things in these papers, that I had better start immediately. If you can have the train brought up for me, I can be ready to leave by tomorrow morning. I'll pack up enough for the next few months; I am afraid it will take that long to get everything set in order and convince these dullards that although their employer may not be present, he is watching them."

Cameron nodded, and tried not to look too eager to be rid of the man. "I hate to do without you, but you are right in thinking that my agent can probably deal with most of the work." *It won't hurt to remind him that the main reason I've kept him on was because he is my Apprentice.* "I'll telegraph my agent and have arrangements made to store what you bring until you notify him that you've found accommodations." He decided to be generous, and not name an upper limit on du Mond's spending. Frankly, there weren't *that* many expensive lodgings in Oakland! "You could take a small house rather than an apartment, if you find one furnished. You might as well hire yourself a servant and a cook as well — no point in you ruining your health by catching bad meals on the waterfront. Maybe a horse so you won't need cabs, if you find a place with stabling nearby. Once you've made all your arrangements, send the bills to me."

He didn't even want to name an upper limit; getting rid of du Mond was worth just about any price. In fact — if the man actually made a success of this, even a moderate success, there was no reason why he couldn't acquire another business somewhere and send him off with a promotion and a raise in the form of part-ownership of the firm! *Much* better than doing away with him — the Salamanders really didn't like to incinerate people, and he had a notion that Rose would hardly approve, though she didn't like the man either.

Perhaps I could buy a small rail company or shipping concern in the Far East or India? Or Tahiti or the South Seas? Something far away and in a place guaranteed to indulge all of his worst vices, and with a climate that will encourage him to his natural laziness. Then, when the venture fails, I will have the excuse to cut him off without a ticket back.

And if, against all probabilities, he succeeded, Cameron could reward him with full ownership, cutting him loose to work on his own. Why not? He could afford to be generous.

"Right, then — as usual, you'll find the cash you'll need for immediate expenses in the safe on the train," he said briskly. "You might as well take my leather luggage and steamer-trunks from the last ocean trip; I think they're in storage in the stable. I'll telegraph my San Francisco agent and authorize the rest of your expenses with him; he'll see to it that you have all the bona-fides you need to establish your authority with the Oakland firm. Can I expect you to be in the saddle by the day after tomorrow?"

Du Mond smiled thinly. "I don't see why not. I can

take a suite in a hotel until I find a permanent place —
but I don't really expect that to take more than a week.
Put your mind at rest, Jason. The situation will be
taken care of."

"Oh?" he replied. "You sound very sure of yourself."

Du Mond's smile widened until he looked very like
the proverbial cat who stole the cream. "I am," he said
softly. "In fact, I think you'll be surprised."

Cameron could no longer raise his eyebrows, but he
conveyed a certain skepticism in his voice. "Really?"

"Really." Paul du Mond chuckled and rose to his
feet. He stopped at the door for a parting shot. "I've
decided to take this as a personal cause, something to
be the stepping-stone to great success. I promise you,"
he continued, in a satisfied tone as he opened the door
and left, "I intend to use this as the opportunity to
show you just what I'm capable of."

CHAPTER TWELVE

Rose pulled a wayward strand of hair behind her ear and took a tighter grip on her piece of soft chalk. She had never much favored the rather risque costume for women espoused by Amanda Bloomer, but she had asked Jason for permission to order one on the chance that she might need it, and it was proving invaluable today. It might be immodest and not at all modish, but she could never have drawn these chalk diagrams on the slate floor of Jason's workroom if she had been wearing any kind of skirt. She would have found it difficult to get down on her hands and knees, and the voluminous skirts and dragging hems would have been in danger of erasing much of her work.

I do wish I could do this drawing unsupervised, however. I feel like a hoyden. Casting a glance over her shoulder, she noted that Jason was not looking at her, but at the last piece of the design she had finished. *At least all that he said was, "how very practical."* She consoled herself with the undoubted fact that she was no more exposed than if she had been wearing a modern bathing-costume. And certainly Jason had seen far more female flesh exposed on the stage in this city. Good heavens, the minuscule dresses worn by the corps de ballet at the Opera covered less than this! And those were prim compared to the tiny costumes espoused by the dancers in music-halls.

Besides, there was more at stake here than her modesty.

My knees, for instance. How they ache! Her knees felt bruised and sore, and her back and shoulders were stiff and painful. She had been at this task for hours now, and felt a strong kinship with those poor creatures forced to scrub floors for a living.

Jason himself stood to one side, coatless, and supervised the drawing, the overall diagram in one hand. She had a copy of the same diagram with her and had it lying open beside her bundle of colored chalks, but it helped to have someone outside it to see that she hadn't somehow overlooked something. They had laid out each portion with rulers, compasses, a carpenter's chalk-lines, and string; she had worked from the inside out, circling around the center of the room like a planet in its orbit around the sun. This Working Room of Jason's was a curious place; the walls featured inset panels of slate of the same kind as the floor, in case he might need to contrive a Work that required diagrams to be made on the walls as well as the floor. There were no windows, none at all. The room itself was not large, not as large as it seemed, since it contained no furniture of any kind. Between the panels of slate on the walls were ship's lamps, the kind that magnified the light coming from them, so that when they were all lit the room was as bright as possible. At the moment, every one of them was alight, making it easy to see if there were any mistakes in the diagram.

Rose was drawing the diagram, rather than Jason, for three reasons. He had trouble bending; his joints had been oddly warped by his transformation, and a half hour of drawing on the floor left him in agony. Drawing such diagrams was rightfully the work of the Apprentice, anyway, so that the Master could supervise the construction of the whole. She was the Apprentice, and when he had proposed this Work, she had taken it for granted that she would be the one doing the drawing, and had said as much. And last of all, she'd had a suspicion, which a quick test had proved, that the transformation had rendered Jason partially color-blind. Subtle colors — the pale colors of the chalks, for instance — all looked very much alike to him. It was only when hues were saturated that he could tell them apart. Taking them into strong sunlight helped, but he had not thought to do that before she pointed his deficiency out to him. She had further confounded him by proving to him that although he could, with concentration, tell the chalks themselves apart most of the time, he literally could not tell a chalked line of green from one of blue in even the strongest artificial light — and it was not possible to take the finished diagram out into the sun.

"That may have been what went wrong the last time," she had pointed out. "If you cannot tell blue from green, or green from yellow, and you did not remember to label them, you would have been drawing symbols in the wrong colors for their Quarters. You could have gotten the whole diagram so hopelessly mixed that nothing would have sorted it out."

"I don't know if that would have made a difference or not," he had said hesitantly. "The old Masters only had white chalk available for the most part, so that was what they used."

"I suspect that plain white chalk would not make a difference, but it would seem to me that the wrong color *would*," she had told him firmly. "Several of your sources are very firm about the importance of color to the Elementals. It is difficult enough for a Firemaster to gain the attention of Water Elementals long enough to convince them to leave his Work alone — only think how less likely that is if he uses the wrong color! The last time you attempted a Work, you got absolutely nothing for your pains, and that might well have been because you offended all the Elementals except your own."

He had nodded, reluctantly. And that was why *she* was on her hands and knees chalking out the four Quarters of his diagram *in the right colors* — pale red for Fire and the South, blue for Air and the East, green for Water and the West, and yellow for Earth and the North. If anything went wrong tonight, it would *not* be because the diagrams had been mismanaged!

And from now on, if he decides he must *work alone, I suspect he will take care to use plain white chalk.*

Oh, but her knees and her back hurt! If this was the lot of the average Apprentice, she had some sympathy with du Mond now for his alleged laziness. This was not something she would care to endure, night after night.

She was taking particular care with this diagram because there was not a great deal else she could control in this project. This was to be a Work that Jason himself had attempted only twice in the past, both times when he was working under the supervision of his own Master, both times for purposes less urgent than this one. It was common enough that every Magician of any sort knew it, or a variation on it, but the particulars were such that few ever attempted it.

For one thing, it required the presence of a virgin, male or female. Few Magicians remained chaste long past the age of majority, and the kind of women who tended to be attracted to Magicians — and that were also willing to be part and parcel of a Work — were generally not virginal. According to Jason, Magicians were of two varieties when it came to the opposite sex: either extremely charismatic and attractive, or ascetic and forbidding of aspect.

And I can imagine which of the two Jason was before his accident.

Yet Jason claimed even those who were ascetic tended to attract women, as if the power they held made them more appealing than they would otherwise have been. Nevertheless, the kind of woman so attracted was the sort that Rose would have styled "an adventuress," for whom the forbidden was as potent an intoxicant as anything sold in China-town. Such a woman would have been willing to take part in a Work, but for this Work would likely be utterly unsuitable.

And proper ladies would be horrified at the very notion. Since this Work requires that the virgin be alert and speaking, rather than drugged or screaming in terror, I can see why it isn't attempted very often.

They were going to attempt to summon — or rather, cajole — a Unicorn.

Now, as Rose had come to understand, the medieval Unicorn she had seen so often in illustrations and tapestries, was not *precisely* what they were going to get, if they got anything at all. As she recalled them, Unicorns both medieval and earlier, at least in the versions from Europe and the ancient world, all had in common a single spiraling horn protruding from their foreheads, and did not otherwise much resemble each other. She had seen Unicorns pictured as both the size and general look of goats, as antelope-like, as horse-like, and even Unicorns that looked, if they could be said to resemble anything, like a strange mingling of cow and hippo. In some, the horn was gold, in others, a pearly white, and in some, of three colors, black at the base, red in the middle, and white at the tip. And all this was without bringing in the Chinese *kirin*, which looked more like a dragon, so far as she was concerned!

According to Jason, the Unicorn was an Elemental

of a Fifth Element, that of the Spirit, and was the physical (if you could call an Elemental "physical") embodiment of Knowledge, Purity, and Wisdom. It had been known to appear as the medieval artists had painted it; it had also been known to appear as a prepubescent boy or girl in shining robes of white, as a burning bush, as a pure, white light, as a glowing cup, and as a white bird. It was shy and elusive, and yet curiously approachable, if one followed the proper procedure.

There were many kinds of Elementals inhabiting the realm of the Spirit; the Unicorn was just one, but it was one of the most accessible. But unlike the other four Elements, denizens of the Spirit realm could not be coerced, they could only be petitioned. *If* the Unicorn chose to appear, it would divulge only so much information as it cared to. This was probably another reason why Magicians did not rely on the Conjuration of the Unicorn as a major source of knowledge. Most Magicians did not care to conjure something they could not control. Conjuring a Unicorn was less like going to a shop and purchasing a book, and more like inviting a distinguished guest into one's home and hoping that pearls of wisdom would drop from his lips.

It is rather amazing that Jason has come to the point where he is actually willing to petition anything. *He must be the most arrogant male I have ever met!* The past few weeks had taught her a great deal about Jason Cameron, not the least of which was that his pride was his greatest fault as well as the cause of his downfall. In moments of extreme weakness, even he was willing to admit that, while still exhibiting pride in the fact! Nevertheless, she continued to find him just as intelligent and broad-minded as she had deduced from their conversations, and a certain amount of arrogance on his part was justified by his many accomplishments.

If I had done as much with my life as he has, perhaps I would be arrogant too. He has had a great deal of power, both Magickal and temporal, and people defer to him all the time. Perhaps that is why I amuse him; I do not. I must be something of a novelty to him. I wonder what he would say if he knew that I pity him? It would probably leave him speechless.

But the past few weeks had taught her a great deal about herself as well. She would never again allow herself to sink to the spiritual low where she had been willing to contemplate doing away with herself. For one thing, it was self-indulgent nonsense. For another, dealing with Cameron had shown her that a great deal could be gained simply by assuming that one *would not* be refused, and going ahead and pursuing what one wanted. Audacity often brought rewards; self-abasement seldom did.

She had been spending plenty of time with Cameron over these weeks. Paul du Mond had gone off to a position as Jason's agent in Oakland the week before Christmas. There had been no weeping on Rose's part, although the man had been uncommonly pleasant and polite with her. He had persisted in dropping those unsubtle hints that Cameron was not to be trusted, using real facts to bolster the case of something she felt in her heart was pure fabrication. That had made her very uncomfortable, but in the end it had been easier to pretend to agree with him, just so that he would leave her alone. She had promised him, just before he left, that the next time she was in the city, she would talk with one of his "friends," a promise she obviously did not intend to keep. With Paul du Mond gone, there had been no reason to maintain any kind of pretense about the close partnership she now had with Cameron; a great deal of energy and time that had been wasted in maintaining the charade was now free to devote to research and work. So much time was taken up now, that nearly the only time that Rose left the mansion was to make her twice-daily visits to Sunset, lest the poor horse pine away for lack of human contact.

At least the stallion now had some company. There was an old pony-gelding Jason had kept for harnessing to a small carriage — more like a plushly-appointed, covered cart — that du Mond had occasionally taken into Pacifica. Rose had persuaded Jason to allow her to bring this unlovely beast up to share Sunset's paddock rather than remaining in the smaller paddock nearby. Jason had feared that the fiery stallion might well attack and hurt the old gelding, but his fears had been entirely unfounded. Sunset was happy to see the poor old nag, and the old gelding was content to play squire to Sunset's knight. Now Sunset had some company and actually seemed much the tamer for it.

Rose had another notion about what could be done with the stallion — but that would wait until the New Year. Fortunately, that time was not far off, for tonight was Christmas Eve.

It had seemed rather strange to her that any procedure of Magick should take place on the very evening of the entire calendar considered holiest, but Jason had assured her that the one time this Work had any chance of success was Christmas Eve. There had been a reason that the ancient Church had appointed this as the titular evening of the birth of Christ — it was a day of great power, marking the turning of the year, as Midsummer marked its opposite. "Many doors are open on that night," he had said cryptically.

Fine. So long as the "door" that we want is open as well, I shall not quarrel with the time.

So here she was — instead of being attired in her

one new dress of the year, standing beside her father singing carols in the University Chapel, she was attired in a scandalous Bloomer outfit, on her hands and knees in a barren, slate-floored room, chalking diagrams she had a notion her old minister would have considered blasphemous on the floor. And yet, this was far more appropriate to the season than singing carols whose words had been debased to the level of the nursery, among the fat and complacent professors and their wives. Was this not the season of Hope and Renewal? And were they not searching for those very things, with Jason casting aside his arrogance long enough to actually *beg* for help?

She completed the last of the sigils in the outermost circle of the diagram, and sat back on her heels, critically comparing the chalked design to the one in her hand. A few paces behind her, Cameron was doing the same thing. She didn't think that he would find anything wrong — not unless he had somehow made a mistake on her copy. It was as perfect a copy as geometry could make it.

"I can't find a thing out of place," he said, finally, his ears twitching a little. "I don't wonder that your research papers were always well-received, if you put the same effort into them that you have into this."

She flushed with pleasure, and slowly got to her feet, taking care not to overbalance. As she straightened, she actually felt joints pop and muscles stretch out and uncramp. She winced. *Oh, my knees!*

But she showed no sign of discomfort. "Now what?" she asked.

"Now you go and change into your robe, while I set out the candles and the rest of the paraphernalia," he replied, and his mouth parted in what she now knew was a smile. "Don't be nervous. This will be very simple for you."

"I hope so," she replied, giving the room and its diagram one last examination, just to be certain they had not forgotten some small corner.

The center of the diagram was an immovable cube or table that looked suspiciously like an altar, made of white marble. Jason hadn't commented on the fact, but she had noted that a great many ceremonies seemed based on a religion, though not precisely Christianity, nor any other that she recognized. Cameron moved towards that, walking carefully along chalk-free paths that had been designed into the diagram, probably for that very purpose. In either hand he held a squat silver candlestick with a new beeswax candle in it, a creamy yellow candle as thick as her wrist. Candles of various colors also played major parts in the Work — as in religion. Curious. She moved back a little further, dusted her hands on the canvas Bloomers, and turned to leave the room.

When Jason said, "change into your robe," he meant a great deal more than that. There was an entire ritual she had to undertake before she put on the medieval-style loose gown of white silk, tied at the waist with a long belt of the same.

It began with a bath, but not just any kind of bath. She sifted a powder of various herbs over the water, and poured in a tiny carafe of fragrant oil before she took her place in the tub. When she emerged, she dried herself off and tied up her hair in a particular manner with a cord of white silk. Then she put on a simple set of underthings, brand new, and of unadorned white silk. She was not to wear a corset or stockings, and she anointed her temples, the hollow of her throat, and her wrists with sandalwood oil.

Then came the gown; it looked for all the world precisely like one out of a medieval Book of Hours, and it was made of a heavy white silk that she suspected was the literary "samite" that the Lady of the Lake was clothed in. The belt was totally unadorned in any way, and was wrapped three times around her waist before being tied in the front. The long fringed ends trailed down to the hem of her gown.

Altogether, she thought, as she surveyed the result in the mirror, *I am glad that I have seen the whole of this Work, or I should begin to suspect that I was a sacrificial virgin.* The effect was certainly "sacrificial." She expected at any moment to find that she was to be fed to a dragon!

Or — perhaps she would find herself carrying the Grail in a procession. The effect was just as ecclesiastic as it was sacrificial.

She probably should have felt immodest without the proper underthings, but the truth was that this gown was far more comfortable than anything of a modern nature, and she could not blame the women belonging to the Pre-Raphaelite movement for adopting such outlandish garb as their own. It was graceful, as well — and she certainly found it easier to breathe and move without a corset. The one drawback it had was that it was a trifle chilly; silk, however thick, was not as warm as wool. However, cotton or linen would have been chillier still, and that was what Jason had said that those of lesser means used for such robes. In fact, the two times before that *he* had performed this Work, when he had acted as the virgin for his own Master, his robe had been of plain, undyed cotton; she had found the first of those episodes outlined in his Journal.

That had given her a great deal of peace of mind, for if he himself had undertaken *her* role, not once, but twice, that was a guarantee that she would come to no harm. Silly of her, perhaps, but she found it comforting.

Tonight she stood in the role of the Summoner, and

the Summoner's clothing must be completely white, and made of a virgin fabric of non-animal origin. That meant it could not be woolen, leather, or made of any other animal hair or fur. The Petitioner — Jason — wore whatever his normal Working attire was; apparently that did not matter, since the Unicorn would not be coming in answer to *his* presence. She had eaten nothing but vegetables for the past three days, and drunk nothing but water. Everything about her must be free of the taint of shed blood, everything must be pure and unbesmirched.

Actually, I look rather like something out of one of Lord Dunsany's fairy tales, she thought, as she turned before the mirror. The only thing that spoiled the effect was her glasses. One did not imagine the Queen of Elfland with a pair of wire-rimmed spectacles perched on the end of her nose. They cast the only jarring note in the whole image.

Well, too bad. If the Elven Princess had eyes as bad as Rose's, she *would* have worn spectacles! She certainly would not have had any choice in the matter, if she wanted to keep her lovely gowns intact and her white skin unbruised. If Rose had to do without her glasses, she would be falling over something every few minutes.

By now, Jason must be finished with his preparations, and waiting for her. She picked up the skirts of her gown and walked carefully out into the hall and down the stairs — barefoot as she was, her feet chilled quickly, and she discovered all manner of drafts and cold spots she had no idea existed.

Jason was waiting, but not as impatiently as she had thought he might be; looking around the Working Room, she saw that he had been very busy indeed.

The lamps on the wall had been extinguished, and the only light came from the special candles Jason had lit and placed around the room. The barren room itself had been transformed. The "altar" was swathed in white silk and wreathed in flowers from the conservatory, with the two silver candlesticks standing on either side of a silver bowl filled with water, which was also surrounded by flowers. There were four silver candlesticks standing waist-high, one at each of the four cardinal points of the diagram. These each upheld another thick, beeswax candle identical to the ones on the altar. Each of the candlesticks was twined with two garlands, one of ivy and one of flowers. Flower-petals carpeted the floor outside the diagram. Mingled flower-scents perfumed the air, which unfortunately was a bit chill.

Jason was barefoot, and wore a hooded robe of thick red velvet — the same robe he had worn the night she had first seen him. The hood was up, keeping his face in shadow, although his eyes glinted at her from the darkness. If she did not look at his hands or his feet, she could believe that there was only a normal man beneath that velvet. The shoulders beneath that robe were strong and broad, and the belt confined the velvet about a waist that was becomingly narrow. *I wonder what he used to look like,* she thought, idly. *He is handsome enough now — I shouldn't wonder if he wasn't quite the dapper fellow then.*

She waited for his approval of her preparations. He surveyed her from head to toe, then without warning, reached out and plucked the glasses from her face.

She uttered an inarticulate cry of protest; now he was nothing but a red blur in the candle-light. "Jason!" she said. "What are you doing? I'm blind without my spectacles!"

"Don't worry, I'll keep them safe in my pocket," he said, sounding amused. "You've read the Work; you know you can't wear them into the circle."

"But I can't *see!*" she complained. "How will I get to my place? How will I know if anything is happening?"

"As to the first, I'll guide you," he told her. "Just take my hand and step where I tell you. And hold your skirts up. As to the second, believe me, you will know if the Summoning works correctly."

Reluctantly, she gathered up her skirts in her left hand and gave him her right. His paw-hand felt very strange, hairy on the back and dry and hot on the front, and a tiny electric thrill ran up her spine when she touched it. This was the first time she had ever actually *touched* him — his flesh, and not the clothing that covered him. But she did not wince away; instead she concentrated on putting her feet precisely where he told her, somehow managing to avoid scuffing the laboriously-drawn chalk lines.

"There," he said, dropping her hand, then taking her shoulders and turning her until she faced the right direction. She knew it was the right direction by the white blob which was the altar in front of her. Now she stood in the center of a circle just in front of the altar and to the North of it. Jason let go of her shoulders and stepped away; by squinting she could just make out a red blur, moving along a complicated path that would eventually take him to an identical circle to the South of the altar.

Drat. I can't see a thing. I might just as well be blindfolded. The Unicorn, if it came at all, would materialize above the dish of water on the altar. *And I won't be able to see it.* She could see the altar itself as a squarish white shape, with two soft, yellow lights above it that were the flames of the candles, supported by two streaks of white that were the candles themselves. The bowl was an indistinct smear of silver against the white.

For the first time since she had seen him face-to-face, there were no Salamanders about. She dropped her skirts to pool around her bare feet, and clasped her hands before her. Jason did not bother to ask her if she was ready, since she obviously was; instead, he began to intone the sonorous Latin verses he had memorized. This was to set the conditions for the Unicorn, transforming the Work Room into a place fit for such a being to appear.

From the moment the first word left his mouth, it was clear that *something* was going to happen. The first indication was a feeling, a very physical feeling, the kind of electric tension she had felt before massive thunderstorms. Her skin tingled all over, and the scent of the flowers intensified. The air warmed, until she might have stood in the middle of a blooming meadow in high summer, rather than the stone-lined room in the middle of winter. Then, as she looked down for a moment, the lines of the diagram began to glow with a soft, bluish-white light, as if she had drawn them with foxfire instead of chalk. She could only make out those nearest her feet — and then only vaguely — but the increased light at the level of the floor told her that all the rest of the lines were glowing too. There was so much light in the room now that the odd effect of a sunlit meadow was intensified. If she closed her eyes, she would have sworn she heard the lazy drone of bees.

And yet, with all of this going on about her, there was no sensation within her of fear, or even apprehension. Instead, a wonderful calm came over her, and a deep and drowsy peace. There was a surety that she was utterly, completely safe and protected, and insensibly she relaxed as Jason continued to chant. *I would be happy if this went on forever,* she thought in dreamy content.

Without her glasses she really couldn't see what else might be going on, although she had the impression from the moving lights that appeared over key points in the diagram and from the bright haze appearing over the altar that a great deal of activity was taking place. If she hadn't felt so peaceful she would have been immensely frustrated and annoyed; this was why she absolutely *hated* being without her glasses! No matter how she squinted and strained, she could not make out a blessed thing. *Drat. This is hardly fair. My first view of a major Work, and all I can see are moving lights and shadows. If I didn't know him better, I'd think he planned it this way.*

Jason came to the last quatrain of the verses, and she woke out of her dreaming; now, if at all, would be a sign that the Unicorn would accept a tendered Summons. She concentrated on the thin, bright mist above the altar and held her breath; hoping for his sake that he was going to get more than just some pretty lights.

As the last few syllables fell from his lips, a deep hush dropped over the room, and it seemed as if everything paused a moment — there was a feeling of imminence, of something *wonderful* about to happen. The mist above the altar dimmed — then suddenly flared, brightly, and even without her glasses, she made out a bright oval there, as if it was a window into somewhere where everything was made of light.

Now it was her turn, the time to issue the Summons, which more properly might be termed an invitation. She called out her own quatrain, the invitation to the Unicorn to come to her, begging the gift of its presence and its immortal wisdom to enlighten her.

The mist dimmed and flared a second time. Then there was something bright and — as far as she could tell — solid in the heart of the mist. And that was *all* she could tell; she could not even make out what shape it bore. But her inner peace did not desert her, although she knew, in the back of her mind, that when this was all over, she was going to be very irked with Jason Cameron for taking her eyeglasses away from her, ceremony or not. There should have been *some* way to allow her to retain them!

"It has been a very long time since I last heard the call of a Summoner." The voice from the white, blurry shape above the altar was bell-clear, sweet, silvery, and sexless. It caressed her like a light breeze, and made her heart dance. "You are fair in my sight, and acceptable, dear maiden. I feast upon your purity, and grant you your request."

It was a good thing that she already knew that the Unicorn meant these things in a metaphorical sense, or she might have been seriously alarmed by that particular set of phrases. That is, she would have been alarmed if the peace imposed upon her from without had not been so all-pervasive. "I thank you for answering my Summons, and I rejoice in the presence of your beauty and purity, O Brightest One," she replied, in what she thought might be the correct response. "My request is that you answer the question of the Petitioner, the Firemaster who stands in the South, O Unicorn," she concluded, and she felt, rather than saw, that it had turned its attention away from her. Its regard was like a brilliant sunbeam; so intense that she had actually felt it as if it was a hand, touching lightly upon her skin.

"And what is your question — as if I need to ask?" it said, and she was surprised at the amount of irony in its tone. It had never occurred to her that a Unicorn would indulge in such a thing. "You must wish to know how to reverse your current condition. I cannot imagine that you would care to remain in the state that you are now, Firemaster."

"My question is, as you divined, O Immortal Wisdom, that you impart to me the means by which I can reverse my condition to that of my wholly human former aspect," Cameron said, his voice a little breathless, as if whatever it was he saw left him shaken and hesitant. That surprised her as much as the Unicorn's irony; surely Jason, who had participated in a Summoning twice before, had known what to expect! "If, indeed, those means exist, I beg you to tell me where I may find them."

"The means do exist, but I am limited in what I may tell you. I cannot give you the whole answer, but I can tell you that it lies within a manuscript that is within your grasp, though not your possession," the Unicorn replied promptly. "It is no more than a few miles distant from this spot, and in the hands of someone you know."

"Who?" Jason gasped. "Where? Please, I beg you —"

The Unicorn interrupted him, and now the tone of its voice was stern and unyielding. "I cannot tell you more, and do not press me — you have brought this state upon yourself, as you are well aware, out of over-reaching pride and arrogance, and it has been judged that you must win free of it wholly by your own efforts, if at all."

Those clear, bright tones were utterly without pity, and Rose felt very sorry for Jason. Bad enough to *know* that was the case, but to hear it from such a being — that was hard, hard indeed.

The light above the altar brightened, and Rose's eyes began to water in reaction. And yet, at the same time, she could not bring herself to look away. The light drew her, even as it became impossible to watch.

"I have fulfilled your request, O maiden," it said, in a

voice of deep formality, and she felt its calm regard pressing upon her again. "I thank you for the Summons, and for the feast. And now — fare you well."

There was no sound, nothing to mark the moment that it departed. The light simply vanished so abruptly that the room seemed dark in comparison. She rubbed her eyes, which were still watering, and suddenly realized that she felt physically drained and exhausted, as if she had been working very hard for most of the day. And she wanted to *see*, so badly she shook with the need for clear sight. She reached out her hands, impotently groping for her spectacles, even though she knew that Cameron had them.

Jason was at her side before she realized it, as if he understood all too well her fear of sightlessness — of course, he had been only a few feet away, and no longer needed to worry about erasing the chalk-marks by striding directly across to her. "Here," he said, pressing the spectacles into her hand, as if he had sensed how imperative her need for sight was. "Are you tired?"

"Very," she admitted, fumbling the spectacles into place, and seeing the room leap into focus again with a surge of relief. *I would rather almost anything than not be able to see. . . .*

"It was the Unicorn, I think — " His voice sounded thoughtful. "I did not experience this myself, but the Unicorn I Summoned was not as powerful as this one, and it never said a word about a 'feast.' I believe that his 'feasting' was not entirely metaphorical, that he 'fed' upon your spiritual energy."

"My what?" she gasped. She turned to him with alarm, and he made a soothing motion.

"Don't worry, this *has* happened to me with other creatures, just not a Unicorn. I promise you, he hasn't taken anything irreplaceable; by his nature, he can't. In fact, he didn't *take* it at all; if you think about your quatrain, you offered it to him as a free gift. But energy has to come from somewhere, as the mathematicians say, and very often the Elementals find the energy *we* produce preferable to their normal fare." He chuckled a little. "Perhaps the reason that my Unicorn never 'feasted' upon my energies was that I was not sufficiently pure for it. You were obviously more to its taste."

"I suppose I should feel flattered," she said, hesitantly. "And if it really hasn't harmed me —"

"It hasn't," he reassured her. "You'll feel better after a short rest and a little food of less ephemeral nature."

She sighed, and gathered up her skirts. He offered her his hand in a particularly gallant gesture.

"You performed wonderfully, my dearest Rose; stronger Apprentices than you would have bolted from the room at the first signs of the Manifestation. I am very proud of you." He chuckled a little. "If my lady would care to return to the study with me, I believe my Salamanders have brought us just what we need." She sensed, rather than saw, that he smiled, and she was a little surprised that he should offer her so much physical contact. Heretofore he had avoided it, perhaps sensitive to his own appearance. She took the proffered hand, and once again felt that tiny electric shock pass between them. But this time, his paw-hand no longer felt so odd holding hers. She decided not to be annoyed with him. It might have been just as well that she could not see; if she had, she might have been too tongue-tied to make the proper responses.

Once they were inside the door of the study, he dropped her hand and plucked a warm and heavy brown plush cape from a hook beside the door. "I thought you might be cold after all that," he said, handing it to her, as he hesitated a moment, then resolutely pulled the hood of his robe back down onto his shoulders. "And there are two pairs of slippers warming beside the fire. I think you will know which pair is yours."

She wrapped the cape around herself, grateful for the warmth, and went over to the fire. It did not take the mind of a genius to deduce which pair of sheepskin-lined slippers were hers; she doubted that he could squeeze his feet into the smaller of the two, nor would he likely sport a pair of woolen slippers embroidered with white roses. She bent to pull them both on her half-frozen feet, and took her accustomed seat on the sofa, curling her legs up underneath her, just as the clock above the mantelpiece chimed midnight.

A moment later, he joined her, seating himself in a chair across from her, followed by a levitating table and floating tray, each accompanied by an attendant Salamander. The latter held covered dishes and service for two, and she was not at all loath to see them.

"A Christmas Eve dinner of the English sort for you, my lady," he said gravely, "courtesy of the Palace Hotel. Beef Wellington, roast carrots and potatoes, and plum pudding, of course. I can flame the latter, if you would like, but that is a custom I don't particularly care for. I've never found it improved the flavor of a dish, and it often makes sweets so hot that one runs the risk of burning one's mouth."

"I believe I'll decline," she replied cheerfully. "I think we have quite enough flame as it is." She waved her hand at the Salamanders, who danced in response to her sally.

He handed her a plate without further comment; *his* dinner, as usual, was rare (or raw) meat. It no longer disturbed her to see him consume it, since he had taken to cutting it up and eating it in a civilized manner. She had hot spiced cider to drink — probably a wiser choice than wine, as tired as she was. Again, as usual, he had a glass of milk, and a cup of Master Pao's tea.

Meat at last! I thought I was going to perish of longing for it before the three days were over!

She was too hungry to press him for his reaction to the result of their efforts, but as soon as she polished off the last of the plum pudding, and poured herself a second glass of the cider, she saw that he had finished his own dinner and was regarding her with an expectant air.

"Well?" she said. "Was it worth the effort?"

He nodded, slowly. "Quite worth the effort," he replied. "I was astonished at the strength of the apparition, to be frank. The ones that I Summoned appeared for only a moment or two, uttered a few cryptic words, and vanished again. This Unicorn practically engaged us in conversation, and it very clearly gave us all the information it was permitted to give us."

"Permitted by *whom?*" she asked. "That was what I wanted to know."

He shrugged. "When one deals with creatures like the Unicorn, one acknowledges the fact that there are higher powers ruling them. What those powers are, I have never attempted to discover. Because they are burdened, or gifted, with more knowledge than we, they are constrained more directly by those higher powers than mere mortals."

He stared down into his cup, and she said nothing, remembering what else the Unicorn had said. Finally, he shook his head, and looked up again.

"The important thing is that we know now that there is a solution to my problem, and what is more, the Unicorn made a very significant omission." He swirled the tea in his cup and drank the rest of it down, with his usual grimace. "Yes, it said that the means to reverse my condition existed in a manuscript. But it did *not* say that we would be unable to deduce those same means from our own researches, if we put enough effort into the task."

She bit her lip, and looked into his eyes. "You're right," she agreed. "What is more, it *did* say that you would find your answer by your own efforts, if at all. But are you not going to pursue the manuscript?"

"There is no reason why I cannot do both," he pointed out. "I can send out inquiries, while you and I continue to research. We can take whatever means presents itself first."

She nodded, feeling a great deal more comfortable with that solution. "I can't help thinking that in concentrating on this manuscript, wo might be chasing a wild goose," she confessed. "When you think that it might be in the hands of some antiquarian you know, someone who has no idea of the significance of what he has — someone who would just laugh at you if you even suggested the possibility of Magick —"

"That's all too possible," he agreed. "And now we *know* the most important part of any such secret."

"Such as?" she asked, stifling a yawn.

"We know the answer exists. We did not know that for certain before." He seemed very cheerful of a sudden, and his cheer infected her.

"That's true." She wondered if this was the right time to present him with her Christmas gift to him, and decided that it couldn't hurt. Better to give it to him now, while he still felt cheerful! That way, if he didn't like it, he would at least feel constrained to pretend that he did. If she gave it to him while he was in a bad mood, he might hurl it across the room in a fit of temper. He'd hurled other objects in her presence before — his temper could be as black and stormy as the worst tornado-weather, and she suspected that if he ever gave free rein to it, that temper could wreak just as much damage.

She beckoned to one of the Salamanders while his back was turned for a moment, putting a few logs on the fire, and whispered her request to it. It vanished, and came back in through the door a moment later with her wrapped package, just in time for him to see it as he turned back around.

"What's this?" he asked, puzzled, as the Salamander brought the package directly to him.

"I took the liberty of getting you a Christmas gift, Jason," she said, and surprised herself by blushing. "I hope you don't think me presumptuous. It isn't much — I don't know if you'll like it — but I thought of you when I saw it —"

He continued to stand beside the fire, staring at her, the package cradled carefully in both paws. "But I didn't get anything for you, Rose — " he stammered, as taken aback as if no one had ever brought him a present before. "How can I possibly accept this?"

"Gifts aren't given with the intent that the giver expects a gift in return, Jason," she replied, astonished that he would think that *she* expected a gift from him. "They're given because the giver thinks they might please the recipient — if you like it, I'll be quite rewarded enough by that. You don't *have* to get me anything. Everything I own now is something you gave me! I just thought this might grant you a little pleasure. Please," she prompted. "Open it."

He walked slowly to his seat, sat down carefully, and began, hesitantly, to open the package. She had taken special care to wrap it so that it would be easy for him to extract the box from the brightly colored paper and ribbons — no mean feat, so far as that went. She was rather proud of her wrapping job.

At length the box sat on the table, in its nest of shredded wrapping. He looked up at her, as if he had never seen her before, then slowly opened the box itself.

He stared down into it, then with trembling paws, reached inside and brought out the carved stone Phoenix.

The carnelian from which it had been made caught the firelight beautifully, seeming to glow from deep within. It could have been poured from liquid embers. She was altogether pleased with the effect — and with the statue itself. She had been afraid that in his study here, surrounded by all his expensive art objects, it would look shabby. In fact, it looked very much as if it belonged here.

He stared at it, and touched its carved surface gently. "This—this is magnificent," he stammered. "It's wonderful! Rose, you couldn't have chosen anything likely to please me more, and I haven't a single notion how you managed to deduce what I would like so accurately. What — what can I possibly say?"

"You might try, 'Thank you, Rose,'" one of the Salamanders said, impudently.

He shot a glare at it, but his expression softened as he turned back to her. "Thank you, Rose," he said softly. "Thank you very much."

"You're welcome, Jason," she replied demurely, not even trying to hide her smile of pleasure. "You are very welcome. I can't tell you how happy it makes me to have pleased you. Merry Christmas."

"And it is," he said, with a touch of surprise and delight. "It really is! The first time I have truly been able to say that in a very long time."

"Despite everything?" she asked, sipping her cider.

"Because of everything." He looked away from her for a moment, into the fire, and when he spoke, it was with the sense that he was revealing something he had not told to anyone else, ever. "Since I became an adult, my holidays have been spent either in the company of people I cared very little about, or alone. This is the first time that is not the case. It is the first time I have ever been given a gift without strings attached to it. I have hope now, which is something I have done without since the accident. There is literally nothing I would change about this moment, and that is not something I have *ever* been able to say."

"'Remain, for thou art fair?'" she said, quoting *Faust* with a wry smile and a faint laugh. "You should be glad that I am not Mephistopheles, or your soul would be mine."

He opened his mouth, as if to reply to that, then shut it again. She wondered what he had been about to say, for his face bore a very peculiar expression, one that she could not begin to decipher.

"Let me tell you what it was that you missed, being without your spectacles," he said, abruptly, and began to describe the events of the Summoning so vividly that she forgot that odd, yearning expression completely.

At least, she forgot it until she protested, laughingly, that she was too weary to stay up any longer, and he accompanied her to her very door, as if he was a gallant swain escorting his lady home. Then, as she turned back to bid him good-night, she surprised that expression on his face again.

And if she had not been as exhausted as she claimed, she would very likely have remained awake for hours, trying to decide what, precisely, it had meant. But tonight she had no choice in the matter; sleep claimed her the moment her head touched the pillow, and in the morning, she could not remember what had puzzled her so.

CHAPTER THIRTEEN

February was not Paul du Mond's favorite month, not even in San Francisco, where the winter was mild by most standards. But this February was proving to be a very good month indeed; one that marked a whole new high point in satisfaction.

As he left the front door of his small, rented dwelling, he waved a negligent hand at the handyman Beltaire had provided for him — a hardened man with double virtues. He did not seem at all surprised or disturbed by *anything* that went on around du Mond's rented bungalow, nor did he make any objections when he was required to dispose of the remains when du Mond entertained Beltaire, or indulged in a little private amusement of his own.

"I'm afraid this one didn't last very long, Smith," he said lazily as he took the reins of his horse from the fellow. "Do take care of it, will you?"

The latest Chinese slave had been surprisingly fragile — but that may have been due to the supplier's foresight. After all, if the slaves proved too sturdy, du Mond would not need one as often. The supplier didn't care what he did with them; there were always a dozen more where the last came from. And du Mond didn't care if his playthings didn't hold up through too many sessions; Beltaire was providing the money to buy them.

He had the feeling that he was being used as a way

to dispose of girls who had become difficult — girls who refused to cooperate without punishments even most Chinese would consider extreme — at least, if one intended to be able to sell the girl afterwards. Such girls were useless in the cribs and brothels, since few customers anticipated bruises and bites upon their person when they paid for an hour of pleasure. Most customers even preferred that their whores at least *pretend* to be pliant and cooperative. There had been some girls that du Mond himself, when he was acting as a "breaker," had been unable to sufficiently tame without inflicting damage the owners objected to. He had never asked what happened to those particular slaves; he had always assumed that, like the whores too diseased or drug-raddled to serve anymore, they were disposed of.

The slave-owners had an interesting custom for getting rid of useless merchandise; the slave was locked into a closet-like room containing a pallet and a single cup of water. Then they were locked in, without light or fresh air, for about a week. That usually took care of the matter, and if it didn't, well, the slave was in no condition to fight those who came to dispose of the body.

He had assumed something of the sort happened to the ones that continued to fight, but now he realized that there was a market for them, as well. Certainly he was not the only buyer for such slaves. Those fighters were the kind he got now; since he was paying for them, their purveyors did not care what he did with them, so long as the police were not moved to make inquiries afterwards.

Smith made sure that the police were not inclined to make inquiries. Paul was not certain what he did with the bodies, but evidently they never resurfaced in any condition to be awkward. Smith had remarked once that the police were amazed by the number of Chinese girls who killed themselves by jumping into the Bay with heavy objects tied about their necks, and thought it must be a form of suicide peculiar to the Orient.

When the man was not needed, he either tended Paul's horse, or spent the rest of his time in his room, injecting himself with vast amounts of cocaine. Paul was utterly astonished at the quantities Smith required to satisfy him — half the dose Smith used would kill an ordinary man. The other two servants that Beltaire sent him — a maid and a cook — paid no attention whatsoever to Smith or his habits. Aside from being amazed at the man's tolerance for drugs, Paul didn't, either. Smith did his job, and he did it well, and that was all that du Mond cared about.

Beltaire had told him the history of each of his new servants, and Paul had found it fascinating that Beltaire had managed to locate three such amazing felons *and* see to it that they had employment that would satisfy their cravings and the needs of their employer without drawing the attention of the law. Smith was a former jockey and a horse-owner — the horse Paul used now had been one of his own racehorses. Both had been banned from the track for drug use, and Paul suspected that Smith was still doping the horse as well as himself. Those were the sins that Smith had been caught at; according to Beltaire, he had also made a habit of sabotaging other horses and jockeys — one or two with fatal results, though he had never been charged with the fatalities.

The maid was a pretty case — she had gotten pregnant by a married man, given birth to and smothered the baby, and left it on its father's doorstep in that condition — with a note, made public, naming him as the parent. This had had the desired effect of not only destroying the man's reputation and ruining his business as a consequence, but of driving his wife into the divorce court. Then, with his life in tatters, the man mysteriously died. Some said it was because of the burden of his sins, and some even claimed he might have killed himself — but other women sometimes came to visit the maid, and men in their lives had a high mortality rate as well. . . .

And as for the cook — Beltaire had cautioned Paul always to specify the kind of meat he wanted, and never, ever to share what the cook made for himself. And du Mond had noted that when Smith disposed of one of the used-up slaves, he always paid a visit first to the cook. . . .

Still, they were all perfectly satisfactory servants in every way that involved du Mond, and that was all that mattered.

Du Mond mounted his horse, with its peculiarly glassy eyes, and guided it on its way towards Beltaire's home. The visible portion was modest by the standards of Cameron's mansion — but that was only what could be seen by passers-by. The building was much, much longer than it was wide; what appeared to be a small, two-storied building was an enormous, narrow, two-storied building, with the greater part of it concealed by trees and the angle of the hills among which it was nestled. Beltaire, unlike Cameron, saw no reason to advertise his prosperity. Then again, what transpired behind those doors was not something Beltaire would want anyone interested in.

The city of Oakland was hardly imposing on the surface, but in its way it held just as much to intrigue du Mond as San Francisco. Here was where Chinese slave-merchants brought merchandise in danger of being liberated by overzealous Christian missionaries. Here was where many imports difficult to pass by the eyes of the Customs agents in the harbors of San Francisco were brought. This place suited du Mond; beneath the middle-class respectability sheltered an entire culture that the law-abiding inhabitants of the town never dreamed of. And Simon Beltaire was the monarch of that community.

He had been as good as his word about initiating du Mond into a new Magickal path; Paul felt he had made enormous progress, and his personal feelings were confirmed by his new Master. In fact, he had at this point learned everything there was to know about every aspect of Sex Magick, delving right down into the darkest depths where Sex Magick met Blood and Death Magick. Tonight he would take another enormous step forward, he would begin exploring the avenues offered by the ingestion of potent drugs, and combinations of drugs. Then, under Beltaire's tutelage, he would combine the two, forging a potent weapon that would enable him to master not only his own Element of Fire, but Air, and perhaps Earth as well. The possibilities were astounding. . . .

And he had Cameron to thank for it all!

Of course, he thought cheerfully, as he guided his horse up Simon Beltaire's driveway, *by the time Simon finishes with him, there won't be a great deal left to thank. But I can certainly arrange for an impressive flower-arrangement to be sent to the funeral!*

December had given way to January; the short days of January had slipped through Rose's fingers like the beads of a rosary in the hands of a particularly fervent nun. Now they were halfway through February, and she had begun to feel as if she and Cameron had always been working together. She felt more completely comfortable around him than she ever had around any of her fellow graduate students at the University.

Now that she had a working knowledge of Fire Magick through his Journals, she joined him in searching through his personal library for more clues. Thus far, their attempts to find the Unicorn manuscript anywhere in San Francisco had been fruitless. There was nothing matching the little they knew in any of the collections of occult or esoteric writings in any of the collections, public or private, to which Jason had access. And the Unicorn *had* said that it was in the hands of a man that Jason himself knew. She had even made a foray into San Francisco to consult with Master Pao, and he had not been able to uncover any clues concerning it either. Pao had been somewhat distracted by trouble of his own, concerned with the "temper of the Dragons." He did not go into any great detail, but he had said rather abstractly that the Dragons were restless lately, and were growing more restless by the the moment. "They may dance," he had muttered, as if to himself, "they may yet dance."

She had known enough to feel a tremor of concern; if the Dragons were restless—the Elementals that ruled the Earth—then the Earth itself was restless. She had experienced several small earthquakes by now, and was in no great hurry to learn what it was like to feel a large one rock the ground beneath her!

But she must have shown her apprehension, for Pao had smiled suddenly and told her that she need not bother herself, for he would speak to the Dragons and lull them with his persuasion. "The Dragons cannot be ruled," he told her, "but they are capable of being soothed. And I am an old hand at soothing the restless."

He then changed the conversation, and she did not attempt to resume *that* subject, not when she had so many other things to concentrate on. And what could *she* do, if Master Pao was unable to quiet his dragons? Nothing, of course; and she had never envied the ancient prophets their foreknowledge of the future. She would rather not know than be aware of what was coming and be helpless to stop it.

It was from Master Pao that she learned something Jason had not told her; that her own Magickal Nature was not that of Fire, but of Air. Now, it occurred to her that as long as she was serving as an Apprentice, she might as well become an Apprentice in truth. So in addition to doing research for Jason, she was learning as much as she could of the Magick of that Element without the help of a Master of Air.

It was not all *that* difficult; the Work was very similar, the discipline required identical. The only real differences lay in the trappings and the abilities represented by the Elementals themselves. The framework of the Magick was absolutely identical; in many ways, the situation was similar to being an artist in glass; one could make a set of red goblets, or green, or blue — but they would all be goblets, in sets of four, or eight, or twenty. One could create the lead frame for a bird and insert the stained glass panels that made it a scarlet bird or a yellow — but the windows, in the end, would be identical except for color. Thanks to Jason, she knew what the framework was, and more importantly, *why* one did things thus-and-so. She knew the details of the Magick of Fire, and as importantly, she knew the reasons why, had *she* tried any of these Magicks alone, they would have worked poorly, if at all.

There is no Water in my Nature to negate the Fire Magick, but there is so little of Fire compared to Air that I doubt I would get very far.

Just as electricity would not flow through wire made of lead, the Magician's Nature had to be suited to carrying the "current" of the particular Element with which he was trying to Work. The purer the Nature, the better the Magick would flow.

She knew the theory, she knew some of the practice, and she had been learning the details of the Element of Air. But the time had come for her to stop simple study, and begin her real Apprenticeship — and that meant that the time had come for her to confess to Jason her "divided loyalties."

She always waited for him to call her by means of the speaking-tube before going down to his suite for the day. He was extremely sensitive about his appearance and the difficulties his changed form caused him, and she would not for the world embarrass him by bursting in on him before he was fully and correctly clothed and prepared to meet with her. This time, though, when she descended the staircase, she brought with her a basket of those things she would need that were not part of the Work Room of a Firemaster. *I might as well hang for a sheep as a lamb; if I am going to "tell all," I'm going to ask for permission to use the Work Room for my first conjuration of a Sylph.*

She was so used to his appearance by now that seeing her own face in a mirror sometimes gave her a little shock, because she did not have upstanding, pointed ears, nor a muzzle full of the sharp teeth of a carnivore, nor fur. He was so completely himself in any form, that the outward appearance was hardly worth noting. But today, she paused after her greeting to search his face intently, and acknowledged for the first time that not only did she not find him monstrous or repulsive — she found him remarkably handsome, in and of himself. *He* might consider his current form warped, but there was nothing misshapen about it to her.

"Rose —" he touched her shoulder to awaken her out of the little daze she had fallen into. "Are you quite all right?"

She shook herself mentally, and smiled at him. "Perfectly, Jason. But I have something of a confession to make —"

But before she could say it, he had taken the basket from her hands, and replied with a laugh, "You wish to tell me that you have been studying Air Magick in your free hours. And, I would guess, given this little burden of yours, that you wish to undertake your first Elemental Conjuration."

She froze with shock. "How — how did you know?"

He shrugged, as if it should have been obvious how he knew. "It was inevitable, my lady. Once you had a taste of Apprenticeship, once your need for Magick was awakened, you would never be able to deny the craving. And since your Nature is that of Air, even though there is no Master available to you, you would find a way to study it."

She stared at him, and he laughed teasingly, holding the basket just out of her reach. "Shall I continue to amaze you with my sagacity? Today, of course, you wish to undertake your first attempt at raising a Sylph, and you felt that you had to confess your activities but were afraid I would be offended that you 'stole' time from my researches for your own."

"But —" she spluttered, indignantly, her whole, carefully-rehearsed speech having gone up in smoke as he spoke. "But —"

Taking pity on her, he gave her back the basket, and placed one hand atop hers as she took it. "My dear lady, you could not help it, and I knew you could not help it. I have been attempting to guide your efforts as best I could without betraying that I knew your little secret. And since the first attempt at Conjury is best done in the presence of *a* Master, if not a Master of your own element, I was planning on overseeing you from the beginning."

Her indignation vanished; how could she be offended at such generosity? She had no reason to expect such understanding from him! "You were?" she said, astonished and relieved beyond measure. "But — your own work —"

"Can wait, my lady." He offered her his arm, and she took it. "To be quite selfish, it is entirely possible that our combined work will proceed much faster with the devotees of *two* Disciplines pursuing it. I will be the first to admit that my own Mastery may blind me to possibilities obvious to those of another. And —"

He hesitated, then shrugged. "Never mind," he ended. "It was not important."

But his expression said otherwise, and she raised a skeptical eyebrow at him. "You never look that way unless something *is* important, Jason," she chided, as they came to the door of the Work Room. "Now, out with it! Else I'll ask your Salamander to ferret it out for me!"

"You would," he growled, but not as if he was really displeased. "Well enough. I am perfectly pleased that you are not pursuing Fire. It is not possible for two Firemasters to remain together in the same area. That was why I had to leave my home and my Master when my Magickal education was complete. However, it *is* possible for a Firemaster and a Master of either Earth or Air to remain in close proximity. Even —" Was it her imagination, or did his voice grow just a trifle hoarse? " — even in the same dwelling."

She cast a sharp glance at him, but his expression was opaque, and she was not certain just what to make of that statement. But he gave her no chance to think about it.

"I have also sent a letter to that charlatan Pao, and gotten his reply," he continued. "The Orientals have slightly different Disciplines than us of the West, as you are aware, and I asked him if it was possible in his experience for a Master of one Element to serve as the teacher for an Apprentice in another." He pulled a set of folded papers from his breast-pocket and waved them, before returning them to the pocket. "According to him, not only is it possible, but it is quite the usual thing in the East. He even sent me suggestions as to how I might employ the Eastern methods in your Western education."

Now she stopped quite dead in her tracks, and turned to stare at him, her lips parted in utter amazement. He gave her a droll and triumphant grin over his shoulder, and tugged on her hand.

"So, Apprentice, as you can see, I am quite prepared to see you through this. You are, as you probably already know, far ahead of most Apprentices of your short experience, simply because you are used to conducting research and are possessed of formidable self-discipline and concentration." His grin widened at her reaction to that astounding statement. "I expect you to achieve Mastery within a year, quite frankly. Perhaps sooner. The Sylphs are gentler creatures than the Salamanders, and less wary; the usual weaknesses of one destined for Air Mastery are a lack of concentration and a general flightiness, and you suffer from neither — if you ever were burdened with such faults, you overcame them long ago. Now, come along, and you'll prove what I already know to yourself."

Once again he tugged on her hand, and she perforce followed him into the Work Room, taking the irrevocable steps down a path that would govern all she did for the rest of her life.

In the end, the conjuration proved just as easy as Cameron had claimed it would be for her. In fact — as she moved through the Work, with its studied gestures, poetic incantations, and all the attendant ritual, she felt a growing sense of joy, of rightness, as if she was doing something she had been born to do. By the time the moment arrived for the actual appearance of the Sylph, her happiness was bubbling out of her like an effervescent spring bubbling into life after being frozen over during the winter. It was all she could do to keep from dancing a little as she spoke the final words.

The Work as written in the reference she had used called for a circle of containment as well as invocation, but Cameron had advised against it, making the alterations in her copy of the diagram himself. "If you wish to follow my example, and persuade your Elementals rather than coercing them, you had better begin as I did, and do without the containment circles altogether."

"Isn't that — well — dangerous?" she had asked, doubtfully. "The book says it is. Without the containment circle, there is no way to be certain the Sylph will cooperate."

"Of course it is!" he had replied. "Friendship is inherently more dangerous than slavery. A friend always has the option to tell you that he will not do something, and that may happen, especially at first. My Salamanders disobeyed me once or twice to test my resolve not to coerce them, and I suspect your Sylphs will do the same, although they may simply confine themselves to impudence. But a slave will never offer his help unasked, and that is what you gain from persuasion rather than coercion."

So, she stood now before the marble altar, trembling with joy and nervousness, and spoke the last words of her invocation, as Jason watched her from outside the chalked diagram.

For a moment, she thought that nothing had happened — that she had failed.

Then, out of nowhere, a lively breeze whirled around her, a breeze full of a sense of laughter, tugging at her garments, teasing her hair until it fell out of its carefully pinned-up coiffure. It stole all of her hairpins and disarranged her clothing, twirling around her faster and faster until she looked as if she had been running up a hill in a strong March wind.

Then it gave a final tug on her sleeves, formed into a tiny vortex in which all of her hairpins danced, and dropped down onto the altar. Then it wasn't a vortex at all, but a creature that could have been the original for all of the illustrations in every children's fairy-book ever written.

She had not been quite certain what to expect, since the Salamander was so patently unhuman, but this ethereal, semi-transparent creature was *quite* human in appearance. It had a narrow face with a pointed chin, high cheekbones and almond-shaped eyes tilted upwards at the outer corners. It was androgynous, disturbingly pretty, more-or-less "clothed" in long, flowing, pale hair and what seemed to be a series of gauzy, ever-moving scarves, and even had a suggestion of transparent hummingbird-wings at the small of its back. The colors of the Salamander were intense golds, reds, and oranges — the colors of this creature were the palest of blues, violets, and pinks. The expression on its face suggested that its chief motivation was mischief, and now Rose understood why Sylphs were notoriously difficult to control.

"Well!" it said, quite cheerfully. "It certainly took you long enough! We thought you'd *never* get up the courage to call us!"

She took a step nearer, and the elfin creature widened its eyes playfully until its eyes were twice their original size. She stared into them, distracted and entranced; she had never seen eyes like those before, as blue as the skies over the desert, as infinite, and as hypnotic.

"So, what will you have of me?" it murmured, in a soft, silken voice, a voice that beguiled and bewitched her. "Shall I show you the world? Everywhere the Air goes, we go. I can show you anything, anywhere. Would you care to hear music? The Air carries all music — I can bring you the voice of Caruso, the piano of Rachmaninov, the violin of —"

Behind her, Jason cleared his throat. Only that, but it jarred her back to sanity and out from under the hypnotic spell of those eyes, that voice. And now she understood the danger the Sylph represented, the danger of the Lotus-eater, the opium-smoker, the one who dreams without direction and purpose. This was the first test — to see if she could withstand the temptation of the endless dream.

"I would really prefer if we made the Pact first," she murmured diffidently. "Please, it would really be better so. And once the Pact is sworn, you may depart if you wish."

That was a departure from the standard — if she had cast a containment circle, she would have said, "I give you leave to depart." But Jason's Salamanders came and went as they wished when he did not specifically need them, and he took no harm from them — if she was to follow in his footsteps, she must give the Sylphs the same freedom.

The books had all warned that when presented with the Pact that bound Magician and Elementals, the Sylph might turn angry and refuse to swear — another reason for the containment circle, which would prevent it from departing until it had sworn on behalf of all its kind.

But that did not happen, not this time; this seemed to be another example in favor of Jason's policy of cooperation instead of coercion. It laughed, long and merrily. "Too clever, too cautious, too disciplined to be caught!" it crowed. "You will be a good friend, and a good Master. Very well, Rosalind Hawkins, we will swear the Pact with you, for you will not abuse it, but neither will you be seduced by us!"

It remained solemn — although its eyes danced with merriment — just long enough to repeat the phrases that bound them Magickally together. But the moment the Pact was sworn, it became a laughing breeze again, and whirled around the room one more time, before vanishing.

And it took all her hairpins with it.

Rose sat down, all in a heap, right where she was, feeling completely drained of energy and emotion. Jason allowed her to remain long enough to catch her breath, then crossed the now-superfluous chalked lines to extend a hand to her.

She looked up at him without taking his hand. "It nearly had me," she said, reaction to what she had so narrowly escaped setting in. "It nearly pulled me in, and I would never have come out again."

"And depending on whether or not I could persuade the Sylphs to listen to my Salamanders, I would either have spent several days trying to bring you back, or regretfully sent what was left of you off to a lunatic asylum," he replied gravely. "Yes. I could not warn you; you had to face that danger, that temptation, all yourself. *Now* you see the danger inherent in treating with the Sylphs. The Salamanders invite one to unregulated passion when they first appear; the Sylphs to losing one's self in dreaming. The Gnomes tempt to the extreme of sloth, self-indulgence, and — if you will forgive me — sexual excess; and the Undines to the extreme of self-deception, particularly where one's own abilities are concerned. That is the danger with all the Elementals; they can entice the would-be Magician into fatal excess of the worst kind — the kind that always lives within him, because of his unbalanced Nature."

"You didn't tell me — the books didn't tell me —" She felt somehow shocked and betrayed.

"They hinted at it — though I will admit that I did not," he told her. "As I said, your Master is not permitted to give you an obvious warning; it is a test, and one you had to face without a real warning. You wouldn't *understand* it until you felt it for yourself. Now you do. And you will never fall prey to it, because you did not in your moment of greatest vulnerability." He shrugged. "From this moment on, your Mastery is largely a matter of increasing skill and practice. You have learned the trick of juggling; now you will simply learn to add more balls until you can juggle as many as I can."

He offered her his hand again; this time, she took it, but she was still shaken. "If you hadn't cleared your throat —"

"That is why *I* am the Master. It was my duty to remind you of yours." Now he smiled. "My own Master made a particularly cutting remark about fools who let their emotions get the better of them to one of his Salamanders when I was in danger of forgetting my priorities. You required a much subtler reminder, and that in itself is impressive. I cannot speak for every Apprentice, but I suspect most of them require prodding by their Masters at the moment of truth."

"Oh." She said nothing more, but felt immensely relieved that she had not done as badly as she had thought.

Now that she was on her feet, and the initial shock had worn off, she was able to think again. There would always be one Sylph about her now, waiting and watching. Whether or not it came when she called and did as she asked would be largely a matter of concentration and willpower — and her ability to persuade it. Jason no longer had to persuade his Salamanders, in no small part because they were in the habit of obeying him. She had to remember that although the Sylph had looked human, most of them were not particularly intelligent. Once they got into the habit of obeying her, they wouldn't think of doing otherwise.

It might also do things just because it thought she would like them done; and a rare, very intelligent Sylph would perform actions even because it thought she needed them done. Jason's "pet Salamander" was certainly inclined that way. It held intelligent conversations with him, and even contradicted him if he was wrong. Perhaps one of her Sylphs would develop that kind of intelligence.

She had not realized that Jason had led her out of the Work Room until she found herself standing beside the sofa in the study.

She started to turn to go back to clean up the mess she had left behind. "The Work Room — " she said, vaguely. "The mess — " She couldn't have the Sylph erase the diagrams and clean up the remains of the invocation — that was impossible, by the Pact that bound her to the Sylphs and vice versa.

He put both hands on her shoulders and pushed her gently down onto the sofa. "The Salamanders can take care of the mess," he said. "That is another aspect that is useful about having two Disciplines operating in the same household. My Salamanders are perfectly free to clean up after Air Work, and your Sylphs are permitted to clean up after Works of Fire. They will even enjoy doing so. Here — "

He handed her a cup of restorative tea, and she drank it down, thankfully. Her exhaustion was largely a matter of nerve and emotion — the effects of reaction after having successfully completed what really *had* been a dangerous task. In a moment or two, she would feel better.

But for right now, I believe I would really prefer to sit here on the couch!

Finally, after fifteen or twenty minutes, her nerves felt steady again, and her hands had stopped shaking. In all that time, Jason had not said a word. He simply sat in his chair and watched her carefully, as if he was studying her. Perhaps he was; after all, he was a Master, and it was part of his obligation to be aware of the mental, physical, and emotional state of his Apprentice.

"Did this happen to you?" she demanded.

He evidently understood precisely what she meant. "The reaction? Of course. But I am curious about something." He leaned forward, and focused on her intently. "When you became comfortable with your role — when you were thinking about nothing except the Work, how did it feel to you?"

"How did it feel?" she repeated. *It felt wonderful, but how do I describe that?* "It felt — I'm not certain. I think I must have felt the way an opera singer feels, when everything comes together in a perfect performance. As if I was born to do this, as if nothing in the world was more natural or right for me. There was a joy, a feeling of completion, a feeling of coming home — " She shook her head. "All that, and more. I can't describe it properly."

He sat back, and there was no mistaking the satisfaction in his eyes. "You don't have to. This was something du Mond *never* felt, and I should have known then that there was something wrong with him. The true Magician, the one who is born to it, comes to his work with pleasure, and not as if it is *work*. I suspect this must be the case with anyone who is doing what he is truly suited to, whether he be a Magician or a singer, a poet or a priest, or even a plumber. *You* had that joy about you; this *is* what you were born to do."

So he has felt the same way! She had thought perhaps that the feeling had been chimerical — or even simply the effect of her own imagination.

"You won't always have so pure an experience," he warned. "No singer has a perfect performance every night, after all. But some of that joy will always be there for you, reminding you of the moments when it does all come together into a perfect whole." He sighed wistfully. "The only other time I have ever felt that perfection was when I was riding Sunset. Now, I dare not go near him, for fear that I'll frighten him."

She put down her cup and got to her feet, extending her hand to him. "That reminds me — I have something I would like to show you," she told him. "That is, if you think we have time for a brief stroll outside."

"Outside?" He hesitated for a moment, then shrugged, and stood up. "Well, why not? After all, there's no one here to see me, is there?"

"Precisely." She said nothing more, but simply led him down the stairs to the side door — the one leading to the stables. He followed her as far as the walk, then stopped when he realized that she was heading towards Sunset's paddock.

"We can't go there — " he protested.

She stopped, and turned around to face him. She had not put her hair up after the encounter with the Sylph, and the wind flirted with it. "I have been doing other reading," she said, "but as a horseman, you can probably confirm what I read. Just how good is a horse's eyesight?"

"Not very," he admitted. "They tend to rely as much on scent and sound as on sight. That is one reason why they are so prone to shying at things they don't expect. They can sense movement very well, but they have to stare fixedly at something they don't recognize in order to identify it."

"And are you afraid that you would frighten Sunset because of the way you look — or because your scent has changed?"

"The latter," he said, puzzled. "But — "

"But I have had your Salamander bring me your shirts for the past month and more, and I have been leaving them overnight in Sunset's stall to familiarize him with your new scent!" she said triumphantly. "He was a bit alarmed at first, but evidently there was enough of the old 'you' in the new scent to reassure him. Now he is quite used to it. Won't you please at least *try* to see if he'll accept you?" she begged shamelessly, looking up into his troubled eyes. "He misses you so much — and I am simply no real substitute for you. Even the company of poor old Brownie is not enough to make up for your loss."

He looked away for a moment, and she sensed he was struggling with himself. She continued with arguments she had rehearsed almost as many times as the apologetic speech she had not had a chance to deliver. "Du Mond told me that he was a gift from another Firemaster, and although I have not had a great deal of experience with horses, it seems to me that he is truly quite out of the ordinary. Given that, don't you think you ought to give him the chance to prove he can tolerate more than any other horse you might have owned?"

"Perhaps," he murmured, but he did not sound convinced.

"He needs more exercise than he gets in that little paddock," she persisted, putting one hand on his arm. "And I *cannot* ride. I would not even dare to take him for walks, like a dog; I don't know enough about horses to keep him under control if he should take fright. He needs to be ridden, or he will be quite out of condition before long. He needs to see more than the paddock, or I think he will grow stale with boredom."

"Is he in the paddock now?" Cameron asked, still looking away from her, off in the direction of the stable.

He doesn't want to see my pleading expression! she guessed shrewdly. *He is afraid he would not be able to resist it!*

"Yes, he is — and you know, if he will not come to you, I think we could take that as the sign that he will not accept you as you are," she replied, as persuasively as she could. "After all, he hated du Mond, and the paddock seemed to provide plenty of room for him to feel safe when the man was anywhere near."

"That's true. . . . " Finally, after several minutes, he turned back to her. "All right. I will make your experiment on that basis." His tone turned wry. "I only hope he does not decide to attack me! That is what the lead stallion would do, in defense of his herd, if a wolf came sniffing about."

"He won't," she replied with confidence. Given Sunset's reaction to the scent of Jason's shirts, she was quite certain that Cameron's fears were unfounded. Perhaps if she had not taken the time to accustom the stallion to the scent, he would have been correct — but now whenever she brought a new shirt, Sunset drank in the scent, then looked to the direction of the house or the door of the stable expectantly, whickering as if he thought that Jason himself was about to appear.

It was her turn to take Jason's hand and lead him along the path to the stable and paddock area. He hung back, as though reluctant to go, and yet he kept straining his gaze for the first sight of Sunset.

I thought he missed that horse more than he would admit, precisely because he didn't talk about it. In fact, he had avoided the subject of Sunset and riding as much as possible, once he knew that she did not ride and could not give his beloved stallion his needed exercise. This was a part of his life that had been painful to give up.

As they came into sight of the paddock, she whistled shrilly — another unladylike habit that her father had never asked her to break.

"Whistling girls and crowing hens, both will come to some bad ends." How many times did bratty little boys quote that *piece of doggerel at me?*

Sunset whickered in immediate answer to her whistle, and soon came trotting into view. He broke into a canter at the sight of her —

And then stopped dead, staring at her companion.

Jason stopped as well, pulling his hand away from hers. "He sees me — he's afraid of me — "

"Nonsense!" she said briskly, seizing his hand again and tugging him insistently onwards. "He thinks you might be Paul du Mond, that's all! Good heavens, du Mond has been the only other human besides myself he has seen in months and months! Of course he doesn't know it's you yet. Call to him, or whistle, whatever you used to do so he knows it is you!"

Oh drat — can he whistle anymore?

But Jason cleared his throat, and made a series of very peculiar, high-pitched yipping sounds. "Sunset!" he called, as the stallion's ears pricked forward, and he took a tentative step or two in their direction. "Ho, Sunset!" Then he called out something else in a guttural tongue that Rose assumed was Arabic.

The stallion whinnied shrilly, and broke into a run towards them, pulling up at the last minute right at the fence, rearing a little in excitement. He continued to dance in place, ears up, tail flagged, showing far more excitement than he ever did when Rose greeted him. Jason ran too, dropping Rose's hand to sprint to the fence, where he met the horse, caught either side of the halter in his hands, and pulled Sunset's head down to his chest. The stallion made little rumbling sounds that Rose assumed were noises of happiness and contentment, as Jason rubbed and scratched his head, ears, and neck. Jason muttered things under his breath that Rose *knew* were words of affection and contentment, even though she couldn't understand a bit of it.

She made her way in a leisurely manner down to the fence, and stood beside them for several minutes. Stallion and Master were totally oblivious to her.

Which is as it should be, she thought, with great content of her own.

"His tack is all still in the stable," she said aloud. "And he's quite used to having the Salamanders about. I suspect you could have them act as stableboys. I'll be up at the library when you've finished your ride."

For a moment, she thought that he hadn't heard her. Then he turned to her with tears literally standing in his eyes.

"How can I ever thank you?" he asked. "You've given me back something I thought I would never have again — "

"You can thank me by saddling up and taking this poor, neglected horse for a long ride," she replied with a laugh. "You *both* need the exercise. Master Pao said that a great deal of your pain is, frankly, due to the fact that you never leave the house! *I* take my walks so that I don't turn into a fat little Milwaukee *bratwurst-frau* — now *you* go take your rides, or I fear you will do the same!"

And with that, she turned and marched back up to the house, sure that he would take her advice.

She stopped in her room long enough to put her hair and clothing back in order, and looked out the window at the unaccustomed sound of hoofbeats. Sure enough, she reached the window just in time to see Jason, feet somehow crammed into riding-boots, galloping off towards the cliff-top trail.

She wiped a tear or two of her own away, although she was smiling at the same time. *I don't think that I have ever seen him so completely happy before. I believe that this time I managed to give him an important part of himself back.*

She returned to her mirror, but once her hair was pinned back into place, she didn't rise. Instead, she sat at her dressing-table, staring soberly into the eyes of her reflection. She had not had a moment for contemplation of anything other than Magick in a very long time, but this had brought the question of the future home to her in a way that could not be ignored.

What will happen when he gets the rest of his life back?

Realistically, she already knew what would happen. He wouldn't need her anymore. He would return to his former social round, and there was no room in that for her. She was not the kind of woman that a man of his station would associate with, socially. The only time someone like her would encounter someone like him, perhaps, was as the wife of one of the university professors if he were given a reception following a generous endowment. Or if she somehow achieved scholastic notoriety, and he required advice about a manuscript or something of the sort.

More importantly, she was not the kind of woman a man like Jason Cameron would marry. It was not the thing to have a wife interested in anything other than being the hostess to one's guests, and looking attractive and charming on one's arm when one was a guest elsewhere. Her interests could be in genteel charitable work, fine embroidery, or even gardening, but they could not be scholastic. That might imply she was better educated, or even (heaven forfend!) that she was more intelligent than her spouse.

He'll marry an heiress, of course. Since he has plenty of money of his own, he'll have his pick of an entire flock, and since they have nothing much to do except groom themselves for prospective husbands, they'll all be beautiful, accomplished, and none of them will be as rude or outspoken as I am.

Before he married, of course, he would have to dismiss her in such a way that she would not take offense and cause an inconvenient fuss. He would, no doubt, find her a real Master of Air to Apprentice to, probably as far away as possible. She and all the things he had given her would be packed off — with Jason's heartfelt thanks, eternal gratitude, and a fat check besides her savings to cover any hurt feelings.

Or broken hearts? Oh, I expect he's well acquainted with paying for broken hearts. There. I've admitted it. I'm in love with him.

She sighed, and stared into the eyes of her reflection with resignation; her reflection stared back at her through the lenses of her quite unmodish spectacles. If this had been her first love affair, she probably would have been in tears at this point. But it wasn't, and the fact was, she had never *really* forgotten the vast social gulf that separated herself and Jason. That gulf was bridged only by the fact of his appearance, and there had never been any illusions on her part that when he got his old self back, the bridge would disintegrate.

And even if he actually proposed to her against all logic, it would probably be out of a sense of duty, of what he owed her. And perhaps out of a notion of avoiding possible scandal — which would not hurt him, but could ruin her. If she accepted, he would be chained to an inappropriate wife, and she would be aware, and resentful, that he had offered her marriage only because he felt he had to. The resentment they both felt would sour everything good that had ever happened between them.

So what does a woman in love with a werewolf do at this point?

The heroine of some popular romance would probably dissolve into tears, and be perfectly incapable of thinking. This would put off any need to plan whatsoever, since she would not be able to face the prospect of such a bleak future, and would live helplessly from day to day. And of course, romantic novels being completely divorced from reality, when Jason *did* return to normal, like the Prince in Cinderella, he would declare that no matter who or what she was, he would love her forever.

And pigs will doubtless fly before that happens.

But *she* was not the heroine of a silly romance; her mind seldom stopped working just because her emotions were involved. This was not a fairy tale — and even in the originals of the fairy tales, the ending was not guaranteed to be "and they lived happily ever after."

Well, the brave heroines of quite a few fairy tales sacrificed everything for the happiness of the one they loved. She thought about the Little Mermaid, dying so that her prince would never know that it was *she* who had rescued him, and not the princess he had come to love. Or the half-human, immortal Firebird, giving up Ivan so that the mortal Tsarina could have him. The thought of Beauty and the Beast occurred to her, but she was no Beauty, and her love for him would be no cure for his condition.

Very well, then. I shall be the Little Mermaid, and walk upon legs that stab me with a thousand pains, and in the end, fling myself into the ocean with a smile so that he can have his life again. I will still have my work, I will have a lovely wardrobe, and I shall have the financial means to complete my degree and pursue an academic career. I believe that I will make a fine Professor of Literature in a woman's college somewhere. I shall attempt to wake the intellect of silly young girls, most of whom will be occupying space until they marry men like Jason, and I will treasure and nurture the intelligence of those few who are different. I will be mysterious and enigmatic, respected, if not loved, perhaps a little eccentric, and I will continue to have Magick.

She practiced the bright smile in the mirror, until she was certain that she had gotten it right. At least she would do better than the poor Mermaid out of this. In the end, she would have a well-fattened bank-account and someplace to go.

And she *would* have Magick. Perhaps among those silly young girls, she would find another with a spirit like her own, to pass the Magick on to.

Jason's Master had never needed anything more than the Magick to make his life complete. Perhaps she could learn to feel the same.

Her throat closed over tears she refused to shed. *And pigs will surely fly the day I do. . . .*

Jason brought Sunset back into the paddock at a walk; the stallion was sweating from a good run, but not foaming, and his unstrained breathing told the Firemaster that his wind had not suffered in spite of his long idleness. For being confined to the paddock for so long, he was in remarkably good condition; better than Jason had any right to expect.

That he had accepted Jason, changed as he was — it was nothing short of a miracle, and it was a miracle that would never have happened if it hadn't been for Rose. It had *never* occurred to him to get Sunset used to the changed scent by bringing shirts down to the stallion's stall. It had never occurred to him that the familiar scent could overcome the unfamiliar sight.

Once again, Rose had given him a gift that he could never repay. What a woman she was! Compared to her, the daughters of his business peers were as shallow and empty-headed as the brainless horses *they* rode, or the idiot little spaniels they carried about with them.

Once, he had taken it as a matter of course that he would, in due time, marry one of them. He would, of course, continue to have an expensive courtesan discreetly kept in town for his real pleasures — a woman of wit and amusement, who would entertain him in more ways than the amorous. If the girl he married, as was all too likely, found her marital duties a burden, he would perform *his* duty just often enough to produce a family. He probably would have chosen the prospective bride on the basis of whether or not she showed any potential in her family for Magick; if he had children, he wanted them to be magicians if at all possible.

Frankly, now that I have come to know Rose, I would rather marry one of the spaniels. Fortunately, I don't have to marry one of those brainless debutantes if I choose otherwise. I am a self-made man, in a city of self-made men. I have no well-bred parents with familial expectations of my station. This is no monarchy, where I must wed for the sake of the country. There is no reason why, when all this is over, that I cannot marry Rose. There is no one I have to placate through marriage. I have a fortune of my own, and I do not need to wed another. And I need not explain my choice of bride to anyone. She is a Magician, of a Discipline compatible with mine. She will not need to be sheltered from anything, nor will I need to keep any secrets from her. And — I do not believe she will find the sensual side of marriage at all distasteful.

He had to laugh at that, after a moment. *Her? The woman who told me crisply that she had read* The Decameron *in the original? She might well force me to prove my mettle!*

But as he dismounted, and pain shot up his legs from his cramped feet, the reality of his situation came home to him.

He was still trapped in the body of a half-beast. And there was no real evidence that he would be able to reverse that condition any time soon. No matter what his dreams and plans, *that* was the current reality.

He led Sunset into the stable, and with the help of his Salamanders, removed the tack to be cleaned and began to rub him down and groom him.

Such a purely physical occupation gave him plenty of time for reflection, although his thoughts were far from pleasant ones. He was being very confident in her presence about the matter, but the fact was that they were no closer to finding a solution than they had been when he first hired her. And he had a shrewd notion just who owned that manuscript the Unicorn referred to.

Beltaire has it, I'm sure of it, and he'd burn it to ash if he thought there was even a chance that I might get my hands on it. He is the only person I "know" that I have not asked about it, and if he had any inkling of my condition, he is probably gloating over it.

What could he possibly offer her, trapped in this state as he was?

She was being very brave and very controlled, giving no obvious sign that she found his bestial form repugnant, and in fact, he thought that now and again she actually managed to forget the form he wore, at least as long as she was not looking directly at him. But how could any woman look at him without shrinking away? He was hideous, a nightmare, and he would be a fool to think otherwise.

She was willing to be kind to him, but he should not hope for love, could not expect it out of even this most generous-hearted of women.

Even though I am afraid I have actually fallen in love with her myself. She would have to be a saint to love me as I am, and Rose Hawkins is no saint.

What a damnable situation.

He bore down on the brush savagely, and Sunset snaked his head about and nipped him in protest. Not that painful, but a reminder that Sunset would not put up with mistreatment.

If the situation were different —

Then I might well find myself in an equally damnable situation. She is not some pretty fool to be swept off her feet as I impersonate a prince in a fairy tale. How could I possibly propose to her as myself without giving her cause to resent me? "Here I am, handsome, rich, powerful, and shouldn't you be pleased that I, in all my glory, have deigned to make you my bride?" Or she'll think I'm making the offer out of a sense of obligation, and that would make any normal human feel strongly resentful.

Perhaps, in time, he might be able to persuade her that he was sincere — but she might not be willing to grant him the time.

She had a life of her own before her father died. She

can resume her education, get her doctoral degree, and go on to a fine and respected career as an historical scholar and Lady Professor. She does not need me — or any man — to give purpose to her life, for she already had it, earned by her own effort and no one else's.

With a sigh, he put up the brush and currycomb, and saw to Sunset's dinner.

There was no answer; the prospects were equally bleak whether he reverted to his former self or remained as he was. She could not love him as a beast, and probably would not love him as a man.

The best he could do would be to conceal his true feelings, and continue on as they were. If he could not have her love, he would at least not spoil the friendship.

He left Sunset to his grain, and turned his steps back toward the house, prepared to hide his feelings forever, if need be.

Fortunately, the mask of the beast made it damnably easy to hide the heart of the man.

CHAPTER FOURTEEN

Paul du Mond watched in fascinated detachment as hands that did not seem to belong to him slowly drove a potent load of clear, pink-tinged liquid into his vein through the medium of the syringe needle. The hands squeezed the plunger hard as the last of the liquid entered his body; he wanted to be certain he got every precious drop. Beltaire was generous with his drugs, but du Mond was not going to repay that generosity with wastefulness.

"What did you say this was?" he asked Beltaire, as he removed the bandage from around his elbow, and felt the first rush of euphoria hit him. He sat back on his bed, and watched Simon through a sweet haze of pleasure.

"I didn't," Beltaire replied casually. "A little of this, a bit of that, actually, including a few things known only to The Great Beast's devotees. You've had most of them in single doses already. It is a blend designed to last longer than cocaine, yet one which will not send the partaker into a mindless dream-world like many of the opiates. Eventually, it will free your spirit-eyes so that you can see beyond what fools call the real world into the many worlds beyond this one."

Paul nodded wisely, although in his current euphoric state he probably would have nodded wisely had Beltaire recited a nursery-rhyme.

"I don't suppose you've heard anything more about

the virgin child your suppliers were supposed to get you?" the Firemaster continued, raising an interrogative eyebrow. "We really *must* have a virgin for the final ceremony opening up all four Elements to you." He sighed. "Best of all, of course, would be virgin above the age of puberty, but that's too much to hope for from these Chinese slave-merchants. They never can resist sampling their wares."

Du Mond shook his head, and a deep, hot anger awakened from the coals that were always glowing within his soul. He had paid, and paid dearly, well in advance of delivery — and all his supplier could offer him were excuses. There were shortages, due to high mortality in the shipments. It was harder to get people to part with children than with useless girls of marriageable age who had no dowries. The missionaries had confiscated his shipment. The missionaries had made it difficult to bring his shipment into port. Always difficulties, never anything but excuses.

He already had a Fire Elemental bound to his service, which was more than he'd ever achieved with Cameron. The trouble was hardly with his new Master. Simon Beltaire delivered everything he promised and more.

"I'll have words with them again," he replied, and added darkly, "I can always send Smith and Cook to them if they have nothing more to offer than excuses. I suspect the two of them could extract our money, at least."

"That should be your court of last resort," Beltaire warned. "It would be better to go to the extreme of doing your own hunting before you turned force on your suppliers." He raised a finger suggestively. "Remember that you have the use of my motor-launch when I do not require it. There are quarters in San Francisco — as you well know — where a brat might not be missed for several

days. Most would go with anyone who offered them candy
—and opium-powder mixed with taffy or fudge is a sure
way to keep an urchin sleepy and cooperative long enough
to get it into the launch across the Bay. Once it is in my
house, of course, it can yell as much as it likes. Under
normal circumstances I would not suggest this at all,
except that the matter is fairly urgent if you are to make
continuous progress. A local brat would at least be sturdy,
which is more than can be said for Chinese merchandise
that's just made a long voyage."

Paul licked his lips. "I'll consider it."

Beltaire nodded, and packed up his paraphernalia.
"I will leave you to your experience," he said. "This
first time, you might not be able to break through the
barriers to the Other Side; if not, be patient, for
sometimes your body needs to become accustomed to
these things so that your spirit can soar freely. And
sometimes your spirit is preoccupied with a problem
that must be solved before you are free to seek other
realms. If that is true, and you identify the problem,
solve it at once."

Paul did not notice him leaving, but after a timeless
interval of lying in a state of hazy, vague pleasure on
his bed, neither was he able to make the breakthrough
he had hoped for. Despite Beltaire's advice, this
frustrated him. Try as he might to empty his mind of
everything, one problem kept intruding; the need to
find his Vessel, the untouched female — or male, but
Paul preferred to use a female Vessel, and it was much
easier to tell if a female was a virgin than a male.

If only he could find an adolescent — or better yet,
an adult!

He stared at a spot on the ceiling, a water-stain
shaped like a cloud. *Scant chance finding a virgin past
the age of ten,* he grumbled to himself, his euphoria
flattening. *At least, not one I can get hold of without*

*getting the police on my trail. And as for an adult —
huh, there's only one that I know of, and —*

It hit him then, like a bolt of lightning. His Vessel,
his perfect Vessel, was right at hand and waiting for
him! That Hawkins harridan — *she* was a virgin, and a
fat lot of good her virginity was doing anyone, too! She
wouldn't be missed by anyone but Cameron — he still
had free access to Cameron's estate, and if he caught
her outside the mansion on one of those long walks of
hers, Cameron would never know what had happened
to her! Cameron wouldn't report her missing, he
wouldn't dare; he couldn't face police himself, and
there would be no one else who could answer
questions about her! He might even assume she had
run off, frightened by the things he was asking her to
read to him.

He levered himself up off his bed. Best to do it now,
as Simon had said, as if the Firemaster had somehow
known that this would be the solution to his problem.
If he waited, Cameron might get tired of the lack of
progress and send her off himself, or she might decide
that poverty was better than reading what must seem
to her to be the ravings of lunatics, and quit.

He had a moment of doubt as his hand fell on the
doorknob. Beltaire had said that the drugs would last
for many hours, and that they would have several
different effects on his mental and physical condition.
Should he do this while he was still under their
influence? *Could* he? They might slow his reflexes, so
that he would botch the kidnapping. They might send
him visions that would confuse him. They might
render him too euphoric to act. Or — they might give
him immensely greater strength and endurance, and
render him impervious to pain. He stood twisting the
knob in indecision.

But then, he saw that while twisting the doorknob,

the thing had come off in his hand. It hadn't simply fallen off, either; he'd wrenched it from the doorplate.

Well! So that *is one of the effects!* Beltaire had warned him to be careful around the house, and now he knew why! There were several drugs that had the effect of numbing the nerves and enhancing strength, and Beltaire must have put them in his mix.

Perfect. If I leave now, I can borrow the motor-launch and be in Pacifica in an hour. I can have the men drop me in the shallows, then anchor the launch just below the cliffs, and I can take the path up from the beach. I can wait there for her.

Neat, clean, and impossible to trace. She would simply disappear.

And there's no reason for Cameron to suspect me.

He would finally get Rosalind Hawkins, and she would finally get what she deserved.

Rose could hardly help but compare April in California with the same month in Chicago. There was nothing to choose between, to be frank. April had always seemed to be one of the most miserable months in the calendar to her — the weather was hideously distempered, changing every few moments, and all of the changes unpleasant. There was just enough promise of spring to raise one's hopes, but not enough to be convincing that winter's grip was loosened — and there was always the chance that a blizzard in the middle of the month would send everything into an icy winter freeze for another week or more. There could be no opera, no ballet, no concerts, even; it was Lent, after all, in a predominantly Catholic city, and if there *was* any music available, it was all religious, and dolorous. Menus at University were full of fish, a dish that Rose got weary of rather quickly, given the limited imagination of the University cooks. Their illiterate Irish cook had always insisted on honoring the Lenten custom as well, and her ideas beyond fish were limited to vegetable soups and stews, and Welsh rarebit. By the time Lent was over, Rose was generally ready to kill for a pot roast.

San Francisco did not seem to notice that it was the Lenten season. This was the month that Caruso and the Met were coming to perform at the Opera. Fish had no greater share in the city's menus than any other time of year. Flowers had been in full bloom for two weeks and more, and if it rained a great deal, well, the fresh greenery looked very pretty in the rain.

Rose had resumed her walks as a guarantee that Jason would ride Sunset at least once a day. She had no trouble encouraging him if she called out that she was about to get her exercise, but if she said "I believe I'll continue working, so why don't you go take your ride," he would always find some excuse to remain. As long as it wasn't pouring rain, a fast walk down to the sea and back was a good way to shake off discouragement and depression — it was very hard to think of one's self as a martyr when there were birds singing in every tree, and flowers filling the air with perfume.

And today it was impossible to think of herself as anything but incredibly lucky. Tomorrow she would take Jason's private train into San Francisco again, and she would listen to Caruso for the following two days from Jason's private box.

Cameron had asked her to consult Master Pao about some disturbances he had felt lately among his Salamanders that he thought might be Earth-related. She had resolved to tell Master Pao the whole truth about Jason's problem — for he still was unaware of the extent of the damage the "accident" had caused —

and see if there was something Eastern Magick could do that Western could not.

Perhaps we will never be able to undo what was done to him. That thought had occurred to her several times over the last two weeks, sounding what could have been a pessimistic note with overtones, for her, of hope. If Cameron remained in his half-lupine form. . . .

It would be sad, of course, but not the tragedy it might otherwise have been. He didn't need servants as long as he had Salamanders and Sylphs. He was able to get out on his estate again, atop Sunset. Granted, he could no longer entertain his old friends, but he didn't seem to miss them.

He does miss music, but there are gramophones, and there are inventions like the radiophone that hold some promise of bringing distant concerts to listeners. I should persuade him to get a gramophone and a collection of recordings. Soon enough, electricity would come to Pacifica, and thus to the estate; with electricity would come the telephone. He could conduct all of his business from his office here, and for what needed the personal touch, there was his agent, and there was Rose.

I don't need a degree to do research and publish. I certainly don't need one for Magick. I could stay here with him forever. . . .

Could her company — and yes, her love — make up for his restricted life? She liked to think so. Certainly he seemed to be enjoying himself more now than he had been when she first arrived.

She did not want to hope for something so selfish, and so tragic, as his continued imprisonment in his altered form — but it was difficult not to.

Time for research was at a premium with her departure so soon, and she thought seriously about turning back halfway down the path. But the distant roar of the waves lured her on, and she told herself that they would have plenty of research-time when she returned. *It is not as if we are pursuing this under some deadline, after all.*

Sunlight showing past the trees ahead of her pointed to the clearing at the top of the cliffs, and her turn-around point. *I'll just enjoy the sea and the wind for a moment, and get some sun, then I'll walk back at a faster pace —*

Her ears warned her a fraction of a second before it happened; there was the crackle of underbrush, and she had just enough time to half turn before something heavy hit her from behind, grappling her around the waist.

But her assailant did not get a firm grip on her, nor did he manage to pin her arms. With a shrill scream startled out of her by sudden fear, she clawed and struggled her way free, leaving her jacket in his hands. As she wrenched herself away, she let her momentum take her and staggered a few paces away in the direction of the cliffs.

That was *not* where she wanted to go — nor did she want this attacker between herself and the mansion! She staggered about to face him, her hands crooked instinctively into claws to tear at his face and eyes, her hair draggling down into her eyes, and one sleeve of her shirtwaist half torn off.

To her utter shock and horror, when he scrambled to his feet and glared up at her, she recognized the face of Paul du Mond. And to her deeper horror, she recognized by his dilated, glassy eyes, his pale complexion, and his fixed stare that he was not his normal self. She had already marked him with a long scratch down one cheek; he did not seem to notice it, not even to wipe the blood away. Nor did he speak, or alter his predatory stance in any way although he *must* have recognized her, and knew that she now knew him.

Her stomach knotted and her heart chilled. For some reason, known only to him, he had come to attack her. *If he is drugged — he won't feel anything I do. I could claw his face to ribbons and he won't feel it —*

He lunged for her again, his lips twisted into a snarl, a thin line of spittle drooling from one corner of his mouth. She tried to evade him, but this time his luck was better, or hers worse; he caught her by the skirt, and wrenched her off-balance long enough to take complete control of the situation.

She had no time to react; his reflexes were inhumanly fast. He seized both her wrists in one hand with an iron grip; she made herself go limp, landing on her derriere with a painful *thump*, determined to make of herself a dead weight that he could not carry. And once she was down, she began to kick at his knees and legs with the hard heels of her shoes. If she could break a bone, drugged or not, he would *not* be able to carry her off, as he seemed fixed on doing!

Her focus narrowed to her struggle; although her entire body thrilled with terror, she did not, would not, could not let it overwhelm her. She *must* fight; Jason was who-knew-where, and his Salamanders were probably with him. Only one person was going to save her: herself.

She didn't scream; she saved her breath for the fight. No one would hear her this far from the house. But inside, she was screaming in terror. Her arms burned with pain as he hauled at them; it felt as if he was tearing them out of her shoulder.

He ignored the vicious kicks at his legs, and began to drag her inch by inch toward the clearing. Twigs tore at her clothing, her face, her arms, marking her skin in fiery paths — she twisted and turned, trying to break that powerful grip in her wrists, until her arms were nearly wrenched out of their sockets. What did he want with her? What *could* he want with her? And why was he dragging her towards the cliffs?

The struggle went on in grim silence; the roar of the ocean covered the sound of her panting and gasping, and *he* seemed as impervious to everything as if he were an automaton made of clockwork and steel. She made one attempt to bite him, but gave that up when he used the opportunity to attempt to land a blow to her jaw that would surely have knocked her senseless had she not ducked out of the way. After that, she did her best to keep her head out of his reach.

Kicking and writhing, hooking her legs around trees until he tore her loose, forcing him to fight dearly for every inch, she was dragged inexorably towards the clearing and the cliffs. Her shirtwaist was in rags; her skirt, of sturdier stuff, hampered her attempts to get a purchase enough to throw *him* off-balance. Was he going to throw her over the cliffs? And why?

Whatever he wanted with her, the fact that he apparently wanted her *alive* for it made her even more terrified, if that was possible. Panic gave her new strength, and she twisted like a wild thing in his grasp, wrenching her arms back and forth. But some other force had given *him* incredible strength, and he continued to pull her onwards.

Only two or three yards of cover remained between him and the clearing. Once he got her that far, there would be nothing for her to hold on to, and he could simply drag her across the slippery grass unimpeded. Her heart pounded so wildly she thought it would burst.

Terrified past reason now, she screamed in hopeless terror, and fought with all her strength.

❖   ❖   ❖

"Firemaster!"

The Salamander popped up under Sunset's nose, startling the stallion into a fit of rearing and bucking. Cameron fought to control the horse with knee and voice; his heart hammered even as he hauled on the reins of the bitless bridle to force the horse's head down into a position where it would be difficult to buck.

"Help! Firemaster!" the Salamander shrilled again. *"Rose! Danger! Help, Firemaster!"*

What? At that same moment, he fought Sunset to a shivering standstill, and he twisted in his saddle to face the Elemental. "Where? What? How?"

"Du Mond has her!" it screeched. "Follow!"

It shot off like a streak of red lightning in the direction of the path to the cliffs; without a second of hesitation, he wrenched the horse's head around in the right direction. Digging his heels into Sunset's sides, and shouting, he gave the stallion his head. Already excited, Sunset needed no encouragement to break into a gallop. The horse pounded after the blazing Elemental, as Cameron's thoughts churned chaotically.

Du Mond — but why — the Salamanders can't protect her, I sealed him against their direct interference — the cliffs — what can he want — he wants her, he always has, he's been after her all along —

He urged Sunset to his fastest with shouts and slaps of a light twig he carried instead of a riding-crop, but his thoughts went from chaos to incoherence. Red, bloody rage built up in him, as it had once before, at the thought of du Mond putting his filthy hands all over Rose, *his* Rose —

I'll kill him — kill him — kill —

Bile rose in his throat, and the thick musk of rage in

his nostrils. His stomach knotted, and his vision misted.

Sunset thundered down the path to the cliffs, covering in minutes what it would take someone afoot a half hour to cross. His vision was narrowed to the path ahead, and filmed with scarlet. Sunset was tiring, slowing, but it didn't matter, for he saw du Mond ahead of him now, dragging Rose. Her clothing was torn and her face scratched, but she was kicking and fighting and screaming at the top of her lungs.

He might have been able to control himself, if it had not been for the sheer terror in her screams.

That sent him over the edge — and over Sunset's neck as the horse pulled up in startlement. He leapt upon du Mond like a wolf leaping for a rabbit, claws extended, and nothing in his mind or his soul but the need to destroy.

He caught a glimpse of du Mond's face as they both went down — which did not even show that the man registered his presence. Then they were grappling together.

Du Mond's strength was prodigious, far greater than the man should ever have commanded on his own. He managed to hold the wolf off for a few moments; long enough for him to realize, in whatever drug-fogged world he was in, that he was in trouble. He wrenched briefly away, and stumbled over Rose as she lay prone, stunned, where he had dropped her.

He still might have been able to save himself, if he had simply fallen flat and unresisting. Instead, he drew a knife, and tried to grab for Rose again, perhaps with the vague notion of using her as a shield.

He never got any farther than the motion.

With a growl that clawed its way out of his throat, Jason leapt for him again, swatting the knife out of his hands —

At that point, everything faded into a scarlet haze.

❖ ❖ ❖

He came to himself a moment later, with a strange, sweet, warm, metallic taste in his mouth. His claws held du Mond's shoulders to the ground; beneath him, the body quivered as the last vestige of life passed from it. Du Mond's head was flung back, and in his eyes was a look of sheer horror. Du Mond's throat was a red ruin.

With a shock, Jason recognized the taste in his mouth as blood. Fresh blood.

Du Mond's blood.

He had ripped out du Mond's throat with his bare fangs.

With an inarticulate cry, he shoved himself to his feet, and staggered back clumsily a pace or two.

A sound that was part sob, part wail of fear, and part gasp made him lurch about —

— meeting the horrified gaze of Rose.

The beast had won — and she had witnessed it all.

No — no!

He gave a howl of anguish, and ran, not knowing where he was going, and not caring, so long as it took him away, far away, from those fearful, accusing eyes.

Rose didn't remember how she came to be halfway up the path to the house, with the rags of her blouse gathered about her in one hand, the reins of Sunset's bridle in the other, and her hair straggling about her face. She only knew that at one moment she was staring into the eyes of a creature she had *thought* she knew — a creature with the blood of a man on its hands and fangs, which stared back at her with no sign of recognition in its face. She had been fighting for her life at one moment, and at the next had watched the man she loved tearing out the throat of her attacker.

Literally.

I'm in shock, she thought, dimly. _I must get back to the house —_

But _he_ had run off, howling, in that same direction. What if _he_ was lying in wait for her, his blood-lust unappeased by his first victim?

This is Jason _you're thinking about!_

But it had not been Jason who had looked at her with the uncomprehending eyes of a beast. It had been the werewolf, the _loup-garou,_ and she did not know it at all.

Sunset walked along beside her in utter exhaustion, head down, sides heaving, streaming sweat. She dimly recalled hoofbeats approaching before something had flown over her head and sent her sprawling into the underbrush. Had Jason ridden him here? Had the Salamanders alerted him? But why hadn't they attacked du Mond themselves?

She thought of the blood on Jason's hands, dripping from his abbreviated muzzle, and shuddered. She had never seen anyone die before, not even her father. How could he have done that to anyone, even his worst enemy?

How could she stay here? What if he snapped again?

She had once asked him how much of him was wolf, and he had seemed startled and uneasy at the question. Now she knew why.

How close to the surface is the wolf? And what if I am the one to make him angry next time?

As she emerged from the forest in front of the house, two Salamanders flitted up to take charge of Sunset. She dropped the reins listlessly, and stumbled on to the house, with both hands holding the ruins of her blouse over her chest in a vain attempt at modesty. Her hands, her wrists, her arms ached, and she was limping because the heel of her right shoe had broken off in the fight.

She found herself in her room, again with no clear idea of how she had gotten there. With a frightened gasp, she whirled, and with trembling hands, locked her door.

Only then did she stumble into the bathroom, where she knelt beside the toilet and retched until her stomach and chest ached and there was nothing left for her to be rid of.

She wiped her mouth on the back of her hand, feeling the sting of scratches there as she did so.

Shaking in every limb, she got slowly to her feet again, to find a bath waiting ready for her although she had not ordered one. She lifted her hands to look at them with dull curiosity; they were covered with deep scratches, and her hair, now loose and straggling, was full of twigs and knots.

She looked down. There was blood splattered on her skirt, on the remains of her blouse. There was too much of it to be hers.

In a frenzy of sudden horror, she ripped the rags of the clothing from her body without regard for fasteners, breaking a nail in the process. A Salamander appeared just as she struggled out of the last of it. She did not wait for it to ask what she wanted.

"Take it!" she wailed, shoving it away with her foot as far as she could. "Burn it! Burn it *all!*"

The Salamander levitated the pile of blood-stained clothing from the floor; still shuddering, she turned her back on it and its burden, and freed herself of her corsets and the rest of her underthings, just dropping them and leaving them where they fell. She plunged into the bath as into the waters of life, scrubbing frantically and hysterically to remove any taint, any hint of blood.

She blanked out again, and came to herself as she was dressing in entirely new clothing. Presumably the Salamanders had brought it all; she didn't remember. Something had combed out the tangles and twigs from her hair; perhaps she had, perhaps they had. Perhaps her own Sylph had.

She did not want to go out into the next room. She wanted to stay here, in the clean, white, safe bathroom.

Against her will, her feet walked into the bedroom, and from there into the sitting-room, and her body was forced to follow.

Her trunk and other baggage was waiting for her; she had not packed it before her walk, and could not have packed it afterwards. . . .

There was a note. Numbly, she picked it up and read it.

I have sent for the train. Go into the city, tonight. Stay long enough to see Caruso, if after all this you still wish to. I have engaged a room at the Palace Hotel for you so that you need not see anyone who knows you and who might require an explanation, and there will be a porter and a taxi waiting at the station. You must rest tonight. After that, if you wish to leave, I will understand; leave word with my agent where you wish to go and first-class tickets will be waiting for you at the station. After you have gone, I will arrange for the rest of your things to follow. My agent will arrange for your bank-account to be cleared, and add a generous severance-fee.

It was not signed, but it didn't need to be. Not with the copperplate script burned into the paper as only a Salamander could.

In a state of benumbed emptiness, she gathered up her gloves and her cloak, pinned her hat to her still-damp hair, dropped her veil over her scratched face, and left, without a backward glance.

❖   ❖   ❖

She told the concierge at the hotel that she had suffered an accident and a great shock and wished to be left alone. He stared at her scratched, bruised face behind the concealment of her veil, murmured polite words of sympathy, and had the porters usher her immediately to a first-class room with a private bath. Presumably, he did not want to take the of risk playing "host" to a young female having a case of strong hysterics in his hotel lobby, for he did not even require her to sign the register, but expedited her check-in himself. Immediately after, the concierge sent up a large bottle of brandy to her room.

She was tempted by it, but did not drink it, much as she would have welcomed the oblivion. Instead, she sent for a pot of hot water, and searched through her toiletries for her selection of Master Pao's herb teas. He had given her what he described as his "medicine chest": a tightly-packed box of herbal remedies, each packet with the purpose handwritten in his peculiar script on the front.

She found two, and hesitated between them. *Sleep*, said one, and *Calm*, the other.

But she was already calm; granted, it was the false calm of shock, but it was calm of a sort. Sleep was what she needed now, and that was the tea she chose.

She locked her door, checking it twice to make certain she had done so. Then she undressed, slowly, with a care for the hundred new bruises and aches she discovered with every passing minute. She put on the thickest and most enveloping of her night-dresses, drank down the bitter tea without bothering to sugar it, turned off the lights, and climbed into bed.

It was barely sunset, and her room had a westward-facing window. The setting sun made a red glow against the closed curtains, as if the entire city were aflame outside her window.

There were still those strange blanks in her memory; she also did not remember the train ride here. She must have convinced the men manning it that she was all right, or she suspected they would have delivered her to a hospital and not to the waiting taxi. Shock certainly did strange things. . . .

Her window was open, allowing the sounds of the city to drift into the room. She knew two men in this entire city, and one of them had just torn out the other's throat in front of her.

If I were a normal, rational woman, I would send for the police, she thought, abstractly. But she knew that she would not. What was the point? Cameron would dispose of the body in some fashion, probably by burning it to ash. The chances that anyone would inquire after du Mond were minimal; she had the impression from Cameron that the man had no relatives — or at least none who cared about him. If Cameron was clever, he would file a report with the police himself, describing du Mond as having taking flight to parts unknown with a large sum of Cameron's money.

And why should *she* say anything to the administrators of justice? Du Mond had clearly been planning something horrible for her; Cameron had saved her. Du Mond had died quickly; possibly more quickly than he deserved. If Jason had *shot* the miscreant in front of her, would the result have been any different?

That was what anyone else probably would have done in the same circumstances, and du Mond would be just as dead, possibly just as bloodily dead. In newspaper stories, in novels, and on the stage, men were applauded for saving women in danger from their attackers. When the villain met his end at the point of gun, knife, or bare hands, there was no one crying out in reproach — rather, the saviors were toasted as heroes, and basked in glory afterwards. The police, if this were made known to them, would probably give Cameron a medal for heroism, not an accusation of murder.

A *non sequitur* occurred to her. She had always railed at the heroines of stage or literature who, when confronted by villains, conveniently fainted dead in their arms, making it perfectly easy for the cads to carry them off. She had sworn that if *she* had been in that situation, she would have fought tooth and nail, and her friends had always laughed at her, saying that she would never know how she would react, and that *she* would probably faint dead away. *At least I proved them wrong,* was her peculiarly flippant thought. *And I have the bruises to prove it.*

The scarlet light outside faded, deepened to dark rose, the bluish-rose, then deep, twilight blue. The light within the room faded with it, and with the loss of vision, her hearing became more acute. She heard the murmurs of conversation in the room next to hers; water running somewhere, and the clink of china and silver as a room-service cart was wheeled past her door.

There were no werewolves here; no men with the faces of beasts. . . .

But there are men with the souls of beasts, and which is worse? Somewhere outside those windows, people who looked more human than Jason Cameron were doing terrible things to other people, things infinitely worse than simply killing them. Master Pao, although he was not a Christian, worked closely with some of the Christian missionaries who worked against the slave-traders and opium-suppliers. On her last visit, he had told her something of the evils they were combating; that there were hundreds of opium-dens in the Barbary Coast area alone, places where men took money so that other people could slowly destroy themselves. And he had told her that there were over a thousand "cribs," that *he* knew of; tiny, closet-sized rooms where Chinese girls as young as ten or eleven sold their bodies twenty times a night and more at the behest of their owners. *Ten or eleven!* She had been horrified — and more so when he told her gravely that this was *not* the worst thing that could befall a little Chinese child, brought to this country by the slavers. He had not told her what the worst thing was — and she had not really wanted to know.

Compared to that, Jason Cameron was a Saint George, a Sir Galahad. *She* had never seen the face of the beast until the moment when her life was imperiled; he had not lost control until that moment, which should tell her at least that he was fond enough of her to lose control at the sight of her being beaten and carried off.

But this fact remained — the beast had been ascendant, for that one moment. How could she trust that it would not happen again and again, until the beast was all there was left?

She was still mulling that over when Master Pao's tea went to work.

Cameron was dictating the most difficult letter of his life; Pao would surely repudiate him for it, but there was nothing he could do about that. Pao must know the whole truth now, for if Rose went to him for help, he must be fully aware of the situation she had faced. He had revealed the whole of his transformation and why it had happened, why he had brought Rose here, *her* growth in Magick, *his* growing love and need for her, and finally the murder at his hands — or teeth — of du Mond.

"She may turn to you; in any case, please, Pao, watch over her while she is within your sphere. If I had not been so certain that she *could not* remain here and also remain sane, I would not have let her go. She is probably in shock, and definitely vulnerable. Take care of her, if she will let you. I beg of you, for her sake, if not for mine." He fell silent for a moment, and the Salamander stilled. "Sign it, Respectfully, Jason Cameron.'" The Salamander burned the last of the letters into the page, and he took the missive and sealed it into an envelope, handing it back to the Elemental. "Now take it directly to him, and wait to see if he has a return message."

The Salamander nodded wordlessly, and it and the envelope vanished. Cameron hid his head in his paws and dug his claws into his scalp.

When he had returned to the house, he had locked himself into his chambers, then gone into a frenzy of telegraphing: ordering up the train, passing orders on to his agent. When all of his orders had been confirmed, he sent the Salamanders to Rose's rooms to put the rest of his hasty plan into motion.

She could not possibly want to remain here. That much was certain; what woman could have faced what he had done and have any shred of feeling left for the monster that had done it?

He must give her the means of escape from this place before she felt trapped, did something rash and tried to run away from him by herself. That was the only course of honor left to him. And after that?

Somewhere, at the back of his soul, there was still a tiny shred of hope. She might, possibly, consent to return — but only if he could guarantee that the beast would never break loose again, and only if he gave her this means of escape freely.

I will drug myself senseless if that is what it takes to bring her back. . . .

The body. He must get rid of the body —

"I have burned the attacker to ash, Firemaster." His special Salamander appeared at his elbow. "The ash is scattered. The train is coming, the woman is going down to the platform to wait for it. She seems unwell."

"She is unwell," he told it. "Watch over her. Protect her, if you can."

The Salamander vanished.

Was she still wearing his watch? She seemed to put it on automatically; he called up the link in his mirror, and saw to his relief that she was. She was at the platform, and more Salamanders had already delivered her luggage; she was sitting on the steamer-trunk. She was wearing light gloves and long sleeves that would conceal her mistreated hands; she not only had sense to do that, she had the sense to wear a modish, but very concealing veil, as well. He had telegraphed the men that an emergency had come up; that they were to insert the train as soon as the track was open, and make all speed into the city. He knew them; they were good men. They would not tarry, but would get her and her things into the carriage and get out on the main track as soon as the signals cleared. They would not plague her with questions — they probably would not look at her too closely. From now until the time she reached the hotel, she was safe.

The Salamander he had sent to Pao returned at that moment — and it had a folded sheet of Pao's handmade paper with it. He snatched it up and unfolded it.

The Dragons are restless; I am attempting to calm them, but fear the worst. I will help as circumstances permit, but cannot now. Trust in your courage and her heart. Pao.

His first reaction was relief so great it made him lightheaded. Pao had not cut him off! That was better fortune than he'd had any reason to expect —

But hard upon the relief came irritation — why the devil did the man have to speak like a damned fortune-cookie! *The Dragons are restless* indeed! Just what was *that* supposed to mean? He had never discussed Eastern Magick with Pao; didn't the old goat remember that? All they had ever discussed — in the rare moments when they were in a less-than-public place — was Chinese Herbalism as it related to *Western* Magick and *Western* medicine.

Trust in your courage and her heart. Charming sentiment, but not too damned useful.

All right, then; he would keep a watch over her himself, and if anything happened, either send word to Pao or deal with it in the form of his Salamanders. He could not leave her alone in the city without someone to see that she was safe, not in her current mental condition.

He called her image in his mirror again; the train had arrived, and the last of her baggage was being loaded. The men seemed respectful and sympathetic, but not at all alarmed, as she murmured something about a riding accident and an urgent telegram from Chicago. No, she had no details yet, but she wished to be in San Francisco in case she was summoned home. Yes, she was quite upset, but would be all right.

A riding accident! That is not something I would have thought of. It would be a reasonable explanation for bruises, scratches, even broken bones! How was she thinking of these things?

The same way I did, I suppose; part of her is having fits of hysteria, but it is not the part that is in control of what everyone sees.

He had not intended to watch her in the mirror

during the train trip, for after all, nothing was likely to
happen to her there — but he could not help himself.
There wasn't a great deal to see; she sat in her chair
with her hands clasped in her lap, and did not even
raise her head to look out the window. That alone told
him of her state of shock, for he had never once seen
her sitting idle. If she had nothing else to do, she
always had a book in her hands.

He knew that his own men could be trusted to care
for her properly, but he had not expected the same
consideration from strangers. Yet the driver of the taxi
that was waiting for her, the doorman of the hotel, and
the hotel concierge all seemed to sense her precarious
mental state and treated her with amazing delicacy.
And once she was safely in her room, with the door
locked, he felt himself able to attend to other matters.

More telegraphs went off to his agent;
arrangements for the transfer of a substantial sum into
her account, for someone to replace du Mond in
Oakland, for notices of termination to be sent to the
servants and his landlord. Cameron's lips twitched as
his hand sent further signals to ensure that no one
would inquire after the deceased; authorizing his
agent to have an audit done of the accounts du Mond
handled, and to report du Mond's disappearance
together with a large sum of cash and other valuables
kept in the safe of the townhouse. The police would go
to the townhouse, of course; the safe would be
opened, and there would be no cash there. That
would be because a Salamander took it, not du Mond.
The police would question the servants, who would
give them the evidence that although du Mond had
not been *seen* at the townhouse for many months, he
had every opportunity to make a key to the front door.
Cameron would post a reward asking for information
concerning du Mond's activities. People would come

to claim the reward, and although there would be nothing forthcoming about his whereabouts, his unsavory pastimes in the Barbary Coast would soon be uncovered. The police would eventually assume that du Mond had bought his way aboard one of the many tramp freighters that used San Francisco as a port-of-call, and advise Cameron's agent to that effect. A reward would be posted, which would never be claimed. And the trail would be neatly covered.

He sent off the Salamander to empty the safe, and leave a note warning the servants that du Mond might have absconded, possibly with valuables. They often received notes slipped in through the mail slot, which they assumed came by special messenger — and in a sense, they had.

He completed his arrangements, and looked in again on Rose. She seemed to have gone directly to bed, which was probably the best place for her.

He glanced longingly at the dust-covered bottle of narcotic pills on the corner of his desk. Oblivion would be very welcome tonight. . . .

But he dared not take the chance — what if he were unconscious and she awoke with the sudden conviction that she *must* leave the city? What if she awoke, disoriented, and wandered out into the streets?

No; she deserved the respite of sleep, but while she slept, he would remain on guard.

CHAPTER FIFTEEN

When Rose awoke, it was late afternoon again. For one moment, she thought perhaps she had not slept at all — but then she realized by the stiffness of her bruised limbs and the hunger-pangs in her stomach that she had actually slept the clock around.

She probed mentally at herself, expecting to trigger a paroxysm of weeping or hysteria. All that she uncovered, however, was a weary confusion. She stirred restlessly beneath the smooth hotel sheets, stretching a little while she thought.

While she had slept, something had resolved itself in her mind. While du Mond's death was horrid, he *could* have been killed by a fierce mastiff sent to protect her, and the effect would have been the same —

Except that once I got over my fits, I would have made that dog the most pampered canine on the face of the earth. No, the problem is not what happened to that cad. The problem is not that it was Jason *who did it. The problem is that it was Jason who acted like a wild beast in order to protect me. And I do not want to leave him — yet I am not sure I can trust myself with him anymore. I simply do not know what to do.*

She closed her eyes for a moment, then opened them again. There was only one thing she could be utterly certain of. She must not, under any circumstances, make any hasty decisions. For one thing, she did not have enough information.

I am in the city, as I planned, just not in the townhouse. I will proceed precisely as I had planned for today — for what is left of today, at any rate. I shall get dressed, have a fine dinner, and go to the Opera. And tomorrow I shall take a taxi to China-town and visit Master Pao. Perhaps he will have some ideas.

Perhaps there were drugs that could help; perhaps even the tea that had been intended to help Jason's condition had led to his berserk rage, who could tell? She realized now that she had made a serious mistake in not revealing all of Jason's secrets to Pao in the first place. It was as if she had described less than half of a friend's symptoms to a doctor, leaving out the most important ones, and expected him to work a cure with only that information.

She rose with a care for her injuries, and went directly to the private bath, already missing the presence of the attentive Salamanders who would have had a bath ready for her. As yet, she did not feel secure enough in her own relationship with the Sylphs to command them as servants. Perhaps that could come later, but she did not want to force anything now.

I particularly do not want to face them as emotionally unsteady as I am. If I lose them once, it will be the Devil's own time to get them back.

As she soaked in another hot bath, relieving the aches of her many bruises and examining the deep scratches her ordeal had left on her arms and legs, she reflected wryly that she might have saved herself a great deal of pain if she had just thought of calling up the Sylphs to help her against du Mond. In his drugged condition — for he must have been drugged, to act as he had — he could never have commanded Salamanders to counter them.

Unfortunately, it simply didn't occur to me. After

*all, I have only been in "command" of them for a
month or so. I am still very new to all of this. . . .*

She wondered what Master Pao would make of the
Apprentice of Air appearing in his shop to ask for help.
*Air and Fire are complements, but Air and Earth are
opposites . . . though not quite as deadly enemies as
Fire and Water. I wonder what his reaction will be to
me now?*

He would probably just smile, and utter something
ineffable, inscrutable, and utterly Chinese. *Something
about Yin and Yang, I suppose, or Dragons dancing
with Clouds.*

She dressed quickly, and not in either of her Opera
gowns; both revealed more flesh than she could cover
with cosmetics. There were bruises on both her arms
up to the elbow where du Mond had grappled with
her, and she looked as if she'd been dumped into a
briar patch and had to fight her way out. Out of the
steamer-trunk she pulled a heavy black silk moire
skirt, and a high-necked, long-sleeved black silk
shirtwaist trimmed in black silk embroidery and jet
beads. *It will look as if I am in mourning, but no
matter. Perhaps I am, in a way.*

At any rate, the evening-hat with the best veil was
also black, which would enable her to keep her
injuries secret, even in the well-lighted restaurant.

The restaurant staff were attentive without being
obnoxious; perhaps her look of mourning made them
so. They showed her to a secluded table for one, took
her order and brought it immediately, and thereafter
left her alone. Only once did anyone approach her,
just before her entree appeared. One of the waiters, a
young, red-haired boy, hesitantly intruded on her
solitude, a collection box in hand.

"We wondered, ma'am, if you or Mister Cameron
would be interested in contributing to the Palace

Hotel Vesuvius relief fund?" he said, very shyly, thrusting forward the cardboard box with a smudgy newspaper photo of a volcano in eruption pasted onto the front of it.

"Vesuvius relief?" she repeated, and shook her head in confusion. What on earth could the boy mean by that? "Why? Has something happened in Italy?"

He stared at her as if she had just crawled out of a cave, and she felt moved to explain lest he begin to suspect that something was wrong and start a train of gossip.

"I have just come from Mister Cameron's estate in the country," she told him, one hand going unconsciously to her throat where she touched the golden round of her watch. "It is very remote, and we have not even had delivery of newspapers. Please, tell me, what is it that has happened? If it is something serious, I shall have Mister Cameron told at once."

The boy relaxed, as if he had not been quite sure of her sanity. "That volcano, Mount Vesuvius, ma'am. It blew its top clean off. There's whole towns under the lava — hundreds killed, thousands hurt. Two hundred fifty people were killed in one market, buried under ash! It's bad, ma'am, there's people collecting all over the city, and the Palace has a special fund going and they asked us waiters to try and get up some of the fund money?"

He spoke the last on an uncertain, interrogative note. She smiled reassuringly, although it hurt one side of her mouth to do so, and dug into her handbag. She hadn't emptied it since the last time she was in the city, and she hadn't spent all the pocket-money Cameron had given her for that trip. Surely there was *something* in there she could give the boy!

Mount Vesuvius erupting — She remembered now, as from a time ten years in the past, how she had dreamed of fire, earthquake, and disaster the night she arrived here. Had that been a premonition of this calamity in Italy?

Then her hand closed on a thick wad of banknotes, and she froze, looking down into her lap.

There was a roll of bills in her purse at least an inch across. Under cover of the table, she opened the roll and stared at the result. None of the bills were smaller than a ten-dollar note. Beneath the roll, lying loose, were the scattered notes of smaller denomination from the last trip.

How had that gotten into her purse? Was it Jason?

Of course it was. How else could it have happened? As clever as the Salamanders were, she did not think they were clever enough to realize that one needed *money* to pay for things.

She extracted two bills, one of them a twenty, and handed both to the boy, whose eyes went wide as she placed them in his box. "There," she said, "The ten is from me, the twenty from Jason Cameron. It is the least that Mister Cameron and I can do."

He stammered his thanks and went on to the other patrons of the restaurant. She extracted another couple of bills and secreted the rest in a side pocket of her handbag so that she would not pull them all out inadvertently. *I am not such a gull as that; even here, I would not be certain of my safety if word passed that I had such a quantity of cash money on my person.*

She paid for her dinner — leaving a generous tip — and sought the concierge for aid in acquiring a taxi to the Opera.

Perhaps warned by the restaurant staff and in anticipation of a fine gratuity for himself he managed to find her one despite heavy competition. Although it was a Wednesday and a working-day, carriages full of opera-goers were already on their way to Mission Street in the cool breeze of the early evening. The fair weather tempted many out for an evening of entertainment, although the theaters would be dark by midnight. Besides the Opera, *Babes in Toyland* was still playing at the Columbia Theater, and John Barrymore held forth in Richard Harding Davis' play, *The Dictator.* And of course, there was vaudeville at the Orpheum, and the disreputable entertainments of the Barbary Coast, which never seemed to close for long.

The concierge handed her into the cab, and smiled his thanks when the gratuity was the size he had hoped for.

Rose hardly noticed the congestion; surrounded by all the bustle of a busy city street, she felt oddly isolated, as if she were not entirely centered in the real world, as if only part of her rode to the Opera, and the rest of her was elsewhere.

The journey from the Palace Hotel to the Opera House was not a long one; soon enough, she descended from the cab to join the rest of the three thousand music-lovers fortunate enough to have tickets to hear the great tenor in his San Francisco debut.

She settled herself in Cameron's box and asked the usher to draw the curtains partway closed. Tonight she had no wish to see or be seen by anyone in the audience. In honest truth, she wanted most to be alone with her thoughts, but the isolation of her hotel room was not the kind of isolation that she craved.

She settled back as the house-lights went down, and the first strains of the famous overture rose from the orchestra.

But music did not have the usual effect of taking her out of herself or even of removing her from reality to that fairy-land where the incredible events of a lifetime could pass in three or four hours. Not even Caruso's unbelievable voice could lift her spirits, even though the pudgy tenor seemed to grow in stature and nobility the moment he opened his mouth. *He* easily transformed from a fat little Italian with oily hair, to Don Jose, the noble soldier and tragic lover. Perhaps the problem was with his co-star, a Wagnerian soprano from Germany, normally found filling out the breastplate of a Valkyrie or donning the gold-horsehair braids of Elsa von Brabant. She was making her debut in the role of Carmen, and it was one she was ill-suited for. Instead of being transformed by the music as Caruso was, she seemed ill-at-ease in the role of the Gypsy temptress, as ill-at-ease as Rose herself was tonight. She switched her skirts as if she was chasing flies rather than trying to seduce Don Jose with a glimpse of leg and bosom. And as for the fight with the other cigarette girl — they looked like a pair of *hausfraus* squabbling ill-naturedly over a cabbage, rather than a pair of ill-bred Spanish cats ready to take knives to each other. The audience was as restless as she, and probably felt the same; when Caruso sang, a perfect hush filled the theater, but when the diva took the stage, she heard whispers, the rustle of programs, and other noises of inattention.

So at the interval, although Rose had enjoyed every note Caruso sang, she had not been distracted much from her troubles; certainly not as much as she had hoped to be.

When the lights came up for intermission, she decided to remain in her box rather than brave the crowd in search of champagne or milder drink. It seemed like far too much effort to squeeze through the mob just to obtain a single glass of indifferent wine or weak lemonade.

But a tap at the door of the box startled her, and she answered it before she thought. "Yes?" she called, revealing that the box did have an occupant.

The intruder took her tentative reply as an invitation, and opened the door.

She found herself facing a middle-aged man of relatively good looks; one whose figure suggested that he might be allowing good living to overcome the athletic physique of his youth. His dark hair was perfectly groomed, as was his small mustache. He was attired in perfectly-tailored evening-dress, and the cut of the suit suggested that the large diamond stickpin in his cravat was the genuine article and not paste.

He looks like some character out of an opera, but I cannot think who! Don Giovanni in modern dress, perhaps?

He held two glasses of champagne, and Rose was certain that he had mistaken her box for another.

"I beg your pardon, Miss Hawkins, but may I come in?" he said, disabusing her at once of the idea that this had been a mistake. "I hesitated to disturb you, but I had a perfectly good bottle of champagne and no one to share it with — and then I saw that you were occupying Jason's box, and hoped you might do me the favor of drinking half." He smiled, but it was a smile of confidence, rather than an ingratiating smile, as if he was quite certain of his welcome. "You see, it would be a very great favor. Half a bottle of champagne never hurt anyone, but to drink a whole marks one as quite the dissolute."

He apparently took her stunned silence for assent, and walked in, with an usher with a plated bucket of ice and the open bottle of champagne following behind. Before Rose knew what to say or do, the man had handed her a glass, given the usher a tip, and settled himself into one of the chairs opposite her. All of her old diffidence around a strange or powerful man had reasserted itself.

"I beg your pardon, I never introduced myself," the man said, acting as if he had all the right in the world to be there. "I am Simon Beltaire. I am not precisely a colleague of Jason Cameron's — more of — shall we say — a gentleman of his circle."

She found her tongue. "Oh, really?" she replied. She had hoped to make it sound sarcastic, but the words emerged weak and without intonation. Beltaire's black eyes glittered in a way she found both repellent and fascinating, she found it difficult to look away. *How did he know who I was? That can't be exactly common knowledge —*

"Jason and I share many, many interests," Beltaire continued, as she automatically sipped at the glass he had put into her hand. "More than you might think."

He managed somehow to draw her into conversation, although she could not imagine how; his probing questions prompted her to reveal more than she had intended to, and his eyes seemed to catch all of the available light as he spoke. She had never felt herself quite so maladroit at conversation before; she learned nothing of him, until their conversation lulled for a moment, and he sat back in his chair.

"I will be frank with you, Miss Hawkins," he said, finally. "Because I can see from what you have told me that Cameron has let you into more of his secrets than I had supposed. *Many* more. In short, he has trusted you with the reason why he needed your services."

"He has?" she replied inanely. "I can't imagine what you're talking about, sir —"

He waved his free hand in the air, dismissing her prevarication as precisely that. "Do not think you need to dissemble with me, Miss Hawkins. If he can trust you, why, so can I. You are probably wondering how it is I knew that you even existed, much less your name and your vocation, and your relationship to Jason." He leaned forward again and refilled her glass — a glass she did not recall emptying. "It is very simple. It is impossible for one Firemaster to keep many secrets from another."

His words sent an electric shock down her spine, riveting her to her seat. His next words shocked her even further.

"I know everything there is to know about his so-called 'accident' as well, Miss Hawkins. It was no accident that gave Jason Cameron the face — and the nature — of a wolf."

She had not even realized that the opera had started again, and the wild strains of the "Fate" theme served as an eerie punctuation to his words. The glass fell from her suddenly-numb hands to the carpeted floor, where it bounced without breaking, spilling its contents on the red wool beside her feet.

Was it her imagination, or did he smile for a moment at her reaction? Perhaps it was just a trick of the light, for in the next moment he was leaning forward, nothing on his face but concern.

"I know more — a great deal more — about this transformation Magick than he does. I have manuscripts dealing with it that he does not even dream exist. And I know what it can do to the inside of a man as well as the outside." He tapped his temple with one white-gloved hand, significantly.

But her attention was caught by his previous words. *Could he be the one the Unicorn referred to? The one who has the manuscript Jason needs?*

He went on, his voice low, and yet it somehow carried over the voices of the singers and the music from the orchestra. "Jason Cameron is half beast, Miss Hawkins, but it is the side of him that is the beast that is growing to be the strongest. The longer this goes on, the more the beast will be in the ascendant. His ability to think will fade, and the instinct of the beast will take its place. He will be given to ungovernable rages, and during those rages, he will not know who or what he attacks." He nodded solemnly as she gasped in recognition — and as her memory of Jason's face and eyes flashed before her mind's eye. "That is why the old tales of the werewolf told how the creature would kill the things it loved most when it was a man — because it knew nothing but the urge to kill when the rage was upon it, and it attacked whatever was nearest."

She clasped her hands together tightly, as her throat and chest constricted until it became hard to breathe. Beltaire caught her eyes again in his glittering gaze.

"He sent you away, didn't he?" the man whispered softly.

She shook her head, and found her voice again. "No!" she replied. "No — this was a trip we had planned since I arrived —"

But her denial sounded weak, even to her own ears, and Beltaire nodded as if she had answered in the affirmative. "He knows. He may not be aware of it, consciously, but he knows. He does not wish innocents to come to any harm, and he has sent you away where he feels you will be safe. I expect, if he has not already, he will send you an offer of severance."

The knowledge of the note back in her luggage burned in her heart like a guilty secret. Beltaire leaned farther forward, and put one of his hands on both her clasped ones.

"I would like to help you, Miss Hawkins," he said. "I sense that you are a brave young woman; I know that you are an accomplished woman, a resourceful woman, and a beautiful woman. I would like very much to help you, but I cannot unless you allow me to."

She found her voice again. "Help me?" she croaked. "How?"

He did not release her hand, and she could not look away from his eyes at all. "In a sense, you would come under my protection," he said. "You would do the same thing for me that you have been doing for Cameron. I could use a fine translator for the many works of Magick I have acquired over the years. My scholarship and knowledge of languages is not as great as his, but my knowledge is broader. If you have any personal interest in Magick, I could further it, easily enough. But I know that you have limited means, and that your position with Cameron is a precarious one. He is not a generous man, and he can be a vindictive one. He might even blame you for his own failures, and turn on you. If that were to happen, in the state that he is in, he might lose all caution and hunt you down like a frightened doe no matter where you happened to be — unless you accepted my protection."

It was so hard to breathe! She gasped, as if she had been running. "And then — what?"

Beltaire shrugged. "Eventually, something will happen. Either he will realize that he cannot reverse his condition and end his suffering by his own hand, or he will more likely revert entirely to the beast, break out of the grounds of his mansion, and go hunting. When that happens, someone will cut him down. It is just a matter of time."

"What do you have to do with this?" she asked, in a thin whisper.

"I? Well, for one thing, I am able to protect a fine scholar." He patted her hand. "I have seen your record; do not protest. If Jason reverts to the beast — it should be the hand of someone who knows him and will give him a quick and easy death that takes him down. I would also make certain it happens before he kills someone."

Was this a nightmare? It felt like one! But if it was a nightmare, why couldn't she wake up?

"If you are willing — and brave enough — you could make certain of that, Miss Hawkins, and I would see you had a reward commensurate with your risk," he continued, with earnest intensity. "*You* could serve as the bait in the trap for the beast. *You* could make certain that no one who was innocent and helpless became his victim. Think of it! Think of a child, or an innocent youth, or a harmless old woman being in the wrong place at the wrong time when he finally snapped! Think of him rending their flesh, tearing their throats out! And think of *his* horror when he realized what he had done! If you value his honor, if you have compassion for what remains of his humanity, you can save him from that, Miss Hawkins. You can make it possible for him to die with some shred of honor and dignity left!"

She shook her head, but the movement was so faint, he probably didn't see it. Or else he chose to ignore it.

She heard music, and recognized it as the fortune-telling scene in the gypsy camp. It seemed to come from a thousand miles away.

He released her hand. "Then — when it is all over — I can send you back home. Back to Chicago," he continued in silken tones as he sat back, releasing her from his eyes as he had released her from his grip. "That would be your reward. I can send you back with restored fortunes. I can make certain that you have all you once had before your father's ill-considered speculations — the house, the furnishings, the income — all. You will never need to worry about money again for the rest of your life. It will be a fitting reward for a brave heart and a gallant, self-sacrificing lady."

She licked lips gone suddenly dry. "I — I'll think about it," she heard herself saying, as from a vast distance.

Somewhere, out beyond the curtains of the box, the orchestra thundered as Carmen turned over the card for Death.

Her entire body jerked and her eyes closed. When

she opened them again, Beltaire was gone.

There was only the half-empty bottle of champagne, and a single glass lying on its side on the floor, to show that he had been there at all.

Jason Cameron fought the red rage as it threatened to engulf him and prove that everything Simon Beltaire had told Rose was true. He succeeded — barely — and sat literally panting in exhaustion with his paws clenched tightly on the arms of his chair. Meanwhile, in the mirror, Rose watched Don Jose murder Carmen in a scene that unfortunately more closely resembled Captain Ahab stabbing Moby Dick with a harpoon. Under other circumstances, he would have been howling with laughter, since he would not offend anyone with his mirth.

He was nearer to tears than to laughter at the moment. As his rage died, the stark truth of at least some of what Beltaire had told her chilled him even further.

This incredible rage *was* getting stronger; when it had first hit him, he had only scored claw-marks in his desk. Now he had killed one man, and if he had been able to get his hands on Beltaire, the total would have been two.

How long until he *did* lose out to the animal urge to kill even further, and slaughter those he loved?

Beltaire had confirmed what he had already suspected, that the other Firemaster possessed the manuscript that would free him from this hell. He would never release it to Cameron, however, nor could Cameron see any way of obtaining it by force or otherwise.

And there were other truths there. If persuaded to swear upon the Pact, he *would* do everything he had promised Rose, and Cameron knew that Rose was wise enough to make him swear that very oath. He could even help her; he could allow her to serve as bait in a trap, then evade the trap at the last minute. Her duty would be fulfilled, and by his oath, Beltaire would have to give her everything he had promised. Wouldn't that be the best thing he could do for her — to let her see for herself that he was the beast and no longer himself, then let her go?

If you really love her, you will, whispered a little voice, deep inside of him. *What she might not accept from you as a gift, she will accept from him as payment.* That had been one of his greatest fears; that she would recklessly throw away every parting gift he offered because it came from a tainted source, and escape with very little more than she had arrived with.

He struggled with himself for hours, as he watched her in his mirror, her face reflecting a similar struggle. She had not gone back to her room in the Palace Hotel; instead, she had the taxi-driver drop her at the front entrance, but had changed her mind and begun to walk. She did not go far; stopped by a concerned policeman, she had assured the worried man that she had many troubles on her mind, and simply wished to walk until she had thought them out. He suggested kindly that she simply circle the block so that he could keep an eye on her safety, and with a shy bob of her head, she had agreed to follow his suggestion.

Around and around the block she went; granted, it was a long city block, but she circled it many times in the next few hours, and Cameron held vigil with her while she did so. Down Market, across to Mission, up Mission, and back again; around and around she paced, beneath the bright street lights and the ever-watchful eye of the policeman. He expected her to finally tire and return to her room at about three in the morning, but she continued to walk as if she were tireless, or so restless that she could not have stopped if she wanted to. The city was very quiet at that hour and the noise of her footsteps was very nearly the only sound to be heard other than the chiming of clocks in towers all over the city. Four came and went, and still she kept her unchanging orbit.

What is it she is thinking about?

Finally, around five, the sun, behind the Berkeley Hills in the east began to lighten the sky, moving from the grey of false-dawn to the clear blue of another lovely spring day. The street-lights dimmed, then went out. Several carts passed, drawn by horses; the first traffic of the day was beginning. She paused, looked wistfully ahead to the entrance of the hotel and sighed wearily.

The chimes rang out the hour, and she looked at her watch to confirm it. She sighed again, and looked, first eastward towards the dawn, then south — in *his* direction.

Then she shook her head, and turned back towards the hotel. She had just reached the entrance at about ten minutes after five, and Jason stretched and relaxed a little, seeing the end of his vigil in sight.

All the horses on the street stopped dead in their tracks — and screamed in utter terror. She whirled, staring at them.

He froze, as out in the stable, Sunset and Brownie screamed in tones of identical terror.

Rose had made up her mind to go back to bed for a few fitful hours of sleep before visiting Master Pao. *She* knew nothing of Simon Beltaire, but he might, and she would trust his judgment. The man had tried to exert some hypnotic magnetism over her last night, of that much she was certain, but it had not lasted once she began to walk. Perhaps he had not counted on that; certainly, had she gone straight to bed, she would still be quite certain of the utter and complete truth of everything he had told her.

Now, she was not at all sure. In fact, given his behavior, and the arrogant way in which he had bullied his way into the theater-box, she was less and less inclined to trust him in any way. After all, the best way to tell a great lie was to salt it liberally with small truths. Just because he had been telling her things she knew were true, it did not follow that everything he told her was true. It did not follow that *most* of what he told her was true.

And if he knew Jason's problem, *and* possessed other manuscripts dealing with it, *and* was the "friend" he pretended to be —

Why didn't he offer help to Jason, rather than coming to me and asking me to be the means for Jason's demise? A very good question!

She had taken perhaps a dozen steps in the direction of the hotel entrance, when suddenly every horse in the street stopped dead, threw up its head, and screamed in mortal terror.

And with that scant warning, the earth rose up in revolt.

A terrible rumbling that made her stomach churn and her knees go to water began in the distance, and as she looked instinctively towards the sound, impossible as it seemed, she actually saw the earthquake approaching.

The whole street was rising, like an ocean wave, and more waves followed behind it. The street billowed as if it was a rug and a housewife was vigorously shaking it. As it billowed, buildings swayed and began to shake apart.

For some reason she herself could not have afterwards explained, she ran *into* the nearest hotel doorway, which was a small side-entrance that was almost certainly locked to the outside, and reached that spot just as the first wave struck.

She braced herself in the doorway with her hands and legs as the earth began an insane gigue. Around her, up and down Market Street, walls, chimneys, and entire buildings were toppling. Church bells rang with cacophonous fury, as if an enormous child had grasped each tower in its fist and was shaking it. Under the ringing of the bells, the earth roared defiance so deafening that Rose could not even hear herself screaming, although her mouth was open and she *felt* herself to be howling in fear. The cornices of buildings about her fell to the ground in a deadly hail of masonry; chimneys collapsed with killing force, crashing down into their own buildings or the ones next to them. There were no words for the terror that filled her; anything she had experienced before this was as nothing. There was only mind-numbing fear, and the sound of Judgment Day.

Then, finally, it all stopped.

She took a breath; another. She dared to think that it was over.

It began again.

She honestly thought, as the second quake struck, that she was going to die of fright.

Finally, after an eternity almost as long as the first quake, it was *truly* over. There were several small pulses, diminishing in strength, then — quiet. A hush as deathly as the roar had been settled over the street.

Then the screaming began.

The quake bucked and kicked like an untamed stallion, but Cameron's home and grounds had been made as safe as Pao's Earth Magick could make them, as Pao's home in China-town had been made as fire-resistant as a Firemaster could guarantee. All over the house, furniture and ornaments crashed to the floor in a paroxysm of destruction, but the house itself remained intact. With the sure instinct of one who had ridden out smaller quakes, Cameron dived beneath his desk, a sturdy piece of furniture that would shelter him if any of the rest of his possessions or parts of the ceiling came crashing down upon him.

The huge mirror flung itself from the wall and hurled itself at the desk just after he dove beneath it, shattering into a thousand splinters. Out in the stable, Sunset and Brownie screamed their terror, but they were safer than he was. There was no furniture in the stable to come hurtling at them.

There was a pause of about ten seconds, then the second quake hit, shaking the house with the fury of a dog killing a rat. If anything, the second quake was worse than the first.

Then, after an interlude of terror too long to be time, it was over.

Cameron had only a single thought, and it was for Rose. If she had, in her fear, run out into the street, she was now almost certainly crushed beneath tons of brick and masonry!

But he looked out from beneath the sheltering bulk of the desk, to see small fires everywhere there had been lamps or candles, and he put that thought aside for the few seconds it took to summon his Salamanders and send them all over the house and grounds, extinguishing flames wherever they found them.

Then he snatched up a shard of mirror, cutting his hand a little, and breathed his Magick on it.

He was just in time to see her getting slowly to her feet, sheltered in *precisely* the correct place, a sturdy servants' entrance to the hotel, her black clothing now grey with the dust that choked the air. The mirror was too small to give him much of a view, but she cocked her head to one side, then hiked her skirts up to her knee and began to run shakily up Market toward Third.

At that moment, he knew one thing, and one thing only.

It did not matter what he was, or who saw him. It did not matter what she thought of him, or about him. He had to get to her, if he died trying. And there *was* one way — on a horse that would not tire, would not stop, and would run faster than poor Sunset ever dreamed of doing. It would take his every resource, and would even require his own blood, but he could reach her within the hour. He had done this before, and it had left him with little in the way of resources, but it was his only hope.

Pushing fallen debris aside with the strength born of fear for her, he ran to his Work Room, to transform the most trusted of his Salamanders to a new form, the only one which could cross this now-broken country at the speed he required. And if his Salamanders had not been his trusted friends, but had been coerced, this Conjuration would, in these conditions, almost certainly be deadly.

He was going to Conjure the Firemare.

The screaming was coming from the area of Third and Mission; that was all she was certain of. Somehow she had retained her glasses through all of the heaving and tossing, but dust hung so thickly in the air it was hard to see clearly. But the buildings south of Market were mostly of frame or brick, and the earthquake had wrought terrible damage to them. From a block past the Palace Hotel on down towards the Waterfront and down Third to the south, the buildings were twisted and collapsed like so many constructions of paper and matchsticks. It was from there that the screaming of the trapped and injured came. Why there should be so much damage there, and so relatively little where she had stood, she had no idea. There must have been a reason, but it didn't much matter at the moment. Up ahead, people were trapped, hurt, possibly dying, and she ran to help them.

Other people were emerging, mostly still gowned in their nightclothes, from buildings on either side of her. They were shaken, white and subdued, talking in whispers, looking towards the distant sounds of screaming. She had not gotten far before another quake — smaller, but no less terrifying — sent her down to her knees again.

But she was on her feet as soon as it had passed, and the continuing screams drove her onward. Finally, though, hampered by petticoats and skirt, she stopped in the middle of the street. Oblivious to anyone watching, she pulled her petticoats off, and ripped the sideseams of the skirts to the knee. She started to discard the useless underthings, then thought better of the idea; she slung them over her shoulder and began running again.

Other people, mostly men, and some in shirtsleeves or nightshirts, began to respond to the sounds of terror. It was soon apparent what their goal was. Here, in the area that San Franciscans called "South of the Slot," the buildings were all wood and frame. Had been, rather — now they were twisted matchsticks and splinters. Many had been inexpensive hotels and rooming houses, and it was towards one of these that she and other people were running.

It was very clear the moment she reached the spot that *she* would be useless in rescue work, even with her skirts tied up above her knees. Rescue work consisted of clearing rubble and wrenching timbers loose until you reached a body — hopefully, a living body — then waiting until others took it away before beginning again. That was the job of strong men; even in a frenzy of hysterical strength she could not have lifted a single one of those splintered boards. But if she could not rescue, she could perform rough first-aid, and she did.

The living were laid out in the street, waiting for other folk to find a cart or some other means to get them to a hospital; she and two or three other women began to tend injuries better suited to a battlefield. A few folk were relatively uninjured, but the rest were bloody, battered, with limbs crushed or slashed by glass, heads gashed open. Blood was everywhere, and one woman, wiser in the ways of wounds than Rose, was going first from victim to victim, applying rough tourniquets to stop the bleeding.

Rose's petticoats were soon gone, torn into strips for rough bandages. This had been a rooming house, and as she ran out of bandaging material, she would dart into the wreckage to snatch another sheet out of the discarded rubble and begin again. There was no room in this terrible work for fear, revulsion, or horror. She lost track of how many people she tended, and a certain grim numbness began to set in as twisted and broken body after body was also pulled out to be set out of sight of the living. People emerged from their houses with more sheets to make into bandages for the survivors, and blankets to cover the still forms of the dead. She stopped for a dipper-full of water offered by a disheveled child to realize with a start that morning was well under way. She glanced down at her watch for the time.

It was only seven o'clock. It felt as if she had been working for hours.

She coughed a little, and drank another sip to clear

her throat — harsh, acrid smoke had begun to wreathe its way through the buildings. There must be fires everywhere.

Thank God the San Francisco Fire Department is one of the finest in the nation. They would have their hands full this day.

She handed the dipper back to the little girl, who was still in her nightdress, and just as she bent down to tear another strip of sheet for a bandage, a hand seized her wrist. She looked up again, sudden anger rising through her numbness at the audacity of whoever it was.

It was Simon Beltaire, and whatever words she was about to speak died on her lips as he stared down at her with those glittering black eyes.

He was dressed impeccably in a fine suit and hat, and looked utterly untouched by anything that was around him. Even the dust had not settled on him.

"Miss Hawkins," he said, with uncanny calm. "Please come with me. You can do nothing that matters here."

"Nothing that matters?" she spat, snatching her hand away from him. "Are you insane? Look in front of you! There are people trapped and dying in there — why aren't you helping rescue them? For God's sake — you are a Firemaster, at *least* begin helping to control the fires!"

He looked at the mass of wreckage, covered with men pulling away at debris like so many ants, and smiled cruelly, as if they meant no more to him than insects. The smile chilled her to the bone, for it was quite, quite unhuman. That was when she knew what it was — or rather, who — he reminded her of. Mephistopheles, from *Faust.*

"These strangers mean nothing to me," he said coolly. "I have no care for their welfare."

She rose to her feet and backed away from him a

pace or two. "So the well-being of strangers does not concern you?" she asked, with a curious detachment. "You have no particular interest in whether they live or die?"

"Of course not," he replied with a touch of impatience. "These are mere drones, their lives had no meaning before this earthquake, and have no meaning now. We should concern ourselves with our own welfare, not that of people we do not know."

Oddly enough, it was his words that freed her from his fascination, and confirmed what she had deduced about him before the quake. He cared no more for her than for these poor people. She was nothing more than a tool to him, to be used to destroy Jason, and then discarded. "Interesting that you should say that, Master Beltaire," she replied, just as coolly, "since you met me less than twenty-four hours ago, and spoke to me for scarcely more than an hour of time. I would hardly call us anything other than *strangers*. Surely even you would not pretend to a closer acquaintance than that!"

All this time she had been edging away, attempting to put as much distance between herself and the frantic rescue-work going on as possible. If Beltaire erupted into violence, she did not want to involve innocents —

Now I'm beginning to sound like Jason. . . .

He started, looked oddly shocked for a moment, then composed himself. He laughed, and held out a hand to her. "Oh, really, Miss Hawkins. Do be sensible. You are hardly going to equate yourself with these —"

"Less than a year ago I was living in a boarding house exactly like this, with people exactly like this, and looking forward — if it can be termed that — to a career very similar to theirs," she replied, her own tone icy cold now. She stumbled a little over some rubble and fell, but picked herself up and continued backing away. But the fall had been deliberate, and in her hand, hidden by her skirt, was a nice-sized chunk of brick from a chimney. "I think perhaps you had better leave me alone, Master Beltaire. I would rather take my chances beside Jason Cameron than with you. I have the feeling that I would be much, much safer."

It took him a moment to digest her words — then his face twisted into a snarl that absolutely transformed him. *Now* she saw what really lurked beneath the urbane mask.

She did not wait for him to lunge for her. She threw the brick at his face, turned, and ran.

Smoke had begun to billow in thick curtains through the streets; there were the signs that there were fires everywhere, and she hoped to use the smoke to hide her. She should have known better than to think that would help against a Firemaster.

She had run about fifty paces when he appeared before her, looming out of the smoke, his handsome face disfigured by a broken and bleeding nose. Somehow he had outflanked her! She tried to turn to run from him, but he grabbed her by the arm and swung her towards him before she had a chance to use the tactic that had worked with du Mond. His strength was enormous, and she felt like a rag in his hands.

He delivered a closed-fist, backhanded blow to her face that drove her to the ground and sent her glasses spinning away. The pain in her jaw was incredible, and he came very near to knocking her senseless. She fought for consciousness and held it, as her knees hit the ground with force enough to bruise and cut. Now all but blind, she could only try to scramble away on hands and knees, devastated by her sense of sudden helplessness. He strode over to her and grabbed her again, trying to haul her to her feet as her head spun.

Now, though, she could use what had worked against du Mond; she went limp and kicked out at his legs.

But he was quicker and stronger than du Mond. With an audible snarl, he snatched her up, then hurled her full strength against the wreckage of a building, knocking the wind out of her. She fell to the ground, trying desperately to get her breath, and he strode towards her, an angry black shape against the billowing smoke.

"You little hellcat!" he howled. "Du Mond was right! You listen to me, you worthless bitch! You either help me, or I'll beat you to death with my own two hands, right here in the —"

"Get away from her, Beltaire!"

The voice sent thrills down her back, but they were chills of fear rather than of joy. "Jason!" she screamed, jaw turning red-hot with pain, turning blindly towards the sound of the voice. "Don't! Leave me! He's only using me as a trap to get you!"

"I'm perfectly well aware of that, Rose." She couldn't make out anything clearly, but Jason Cameron was not alone. There was a large, fiery mass beside him and several small golden masses levitating all about him. The Salamanders — and what else?

"You come armed, I see." Beltaire was all coolness now — but he was also close enough to Rose that he could, if he chose, reach her before Jason could stop him. "A Firemare? You changed one of your Salamanders to a Firemare? Jason, that must have cost you dearly. Too dearly, perhaps —"

"Turn around and leave, and this doesn't have to be a confrontation, Beltaire," Jason rasped. "I've already taken du Mond out of the picture. You don't have an Apprentice to feed off of, now."

Beltaire chuckled. "The better to deal with *you*. Killing du Mond must have cost you as much as

Summoning the Firemare. Is that what brought your little wilted flower running into the city? I had hoped he would initiate some decisive action."

He took a step nearer Rose; without her glasses, she couldn't see to evade him. Between the smoke and her near-sightedness, she couldn't tell which way was safe to run, and which strewn with obstacles for her to stumble over.

"Now, here's a quandary, Jason," he continued in dulcet tones. "If you give in to that rage that's building inside you, you'll lose the Firemare and your Salamanders, and you'll cement yourself for all time into that rather unpleasant form you're in now, but you *might* reach me and kill me — very messily too — before I kill your little scholar." He took another step. "If you don't, I might kill *you* or her, or both. In fact, I probably will."

Rose shut her eyes and held her breath. She sensed Jason struggling against the terrible anger within him. "You're bluffing," he snarled, as Beltaire took another step.

"Oh no, I'm not. One of the reasons I went home last night was to obtain this little manuscript." She heard the rustle of stiff, old parchment as he handled it. He cleared his throat ostentatiously.

Keep talking, you cad, she thought, striving to weave her mind into a particular path without all the chanting and gesturing she was used to and fighting past a hundred pains that threatened to distract her fatally. *Give me more time!*

"Now it says here, quite clearly I might add, that each time you invoke a killing rage and shed blood, you make the man-wolf form more your own. The fiercer the rage, the more certain the binding." He chuckled. "In fact, according to this, if the blood you shed is *human*, you might have driven the nails into your own coffin, so to speak. It's possible that not even the little Magicks described here could get you back to your fully human form."

She heard the scrape of claws on cement, but Jason said nothing.

"So, what's it to be, Cameron?" Beltaire asked tauntingly. "Turn tail and slink away, and let me beat your bitch until she submits to me or dies? Meet me Firemaster to Firemaster, knowing that I'm stronger than you, and try to save her as well as take this manuscript away from me? Or attack me with your rage and your bare hands?" He laughed. "You must know that the third option is the only one where you have a chance of winning both her life and your own. You might even get the manuscript."

She heard Jason's growl — but now she was ready. Her eyes flew open — not that she could see much — and she spread her arms wide, calling on the Magick of Air within herself, spending it recklessly into the Realm of Air, leaving herself exhausted. She was not ready for this — but perhaps the fact that her Pact had not involved coercion meant that she would be able to Call not just her own Sylph, but one or two others, if she offered them enough of her energy.

And in that same instant, with a rush of wings, not one or two, but an *army* of Sylphs answered her Call. They hovered about her like so many angry wasps, buzzing in fury she didn't understand.

"Help him!" she cried to them, pointing blindly at Jason.

She couldn't have described the sound they made if she had tried; it was something like a cheer, something like a cruel, cold chuckle, and something like a screech. She sensed that they had actually been waiting, pressed against the Barrier that separated their Realm from the world, hoping she would give them that order. She understood that at some time in the past, Beltaire had done *something* to anger the Children of the Air. And she shivered as she felt their soulless hunger for revenge.

Air feeds Fire. Jason might have been waiting for just this moment for he acted instantly the moment the Sylphs appeared. He released all of the creatures of Fire he held in check, and the two sets of Elementals swirled around Beltaire, who shouted profanities in startlement and called up his own army of Salamanders to protect him.

Too late.

Air feeds Fire. The Sylphs created a vortex, a tornado around him, pulling in the Salamanders belonging to Jason and feeding their flames. Now Beltaire was surrounded by a miniature firestorm; although his Elementals sought to shield him, and although they were more numerous than Jason's, they were not as powerful. His own Mastery of Fire protected him for a while — but not forever. Not with the Sylphs feeding Cameron's few Salamanders and the Firemare, making them a hundred times more powerful than before. Beltaire's shouts became strangled cries as the air was sucked from his lungs.

Rose covered her ears, ducked her head, and closed her eyes, as Beltaire found just enough breath to scream.

Cameron lifted Rose to her feet; she collapsed limply against his chest, which told him all he needed to know about how recklessly she had spent herself. She would not have fallen into his arms if she'd had any energy left for herself.

He held out one hand, while with the other one he supported her, and his favorite Salamander, the one that had volunteered to serve as Firemare, dropped the lost spectacles into his hand. He put them carefully on for her; she finally raised her hand to guide them over her ears, and looked up at him, with a huge, livid bruise starting to form on the side of her face.

"Oh Jason — " She shook her head. "I — is he really — "

"He is," Cameron said gravely. She did not pull away from him. "And unfortunately, the manuscript went with him."

"I don't *care*," she replied fiercely, taking hold of him as if she never planned to let him go.

He took a deep breath, and in his turn sagged against the remains of a building beside them. "I am not apt with words of romance — " he began.

"Nor I," she answered awkwardly.

"Then I will reply for both of you," said a dry, impatient, ancient, and utterly exhausted voice. Master Pao limped slowly out of the smoke, with a younger Chinese man at his elbow — a man hideously disfigured by old burns. "You are in love with Rose; she with you. You are compatible, all will be well. However, the demise of the lamentable Beltaire has freed his Salamanders to rage where they will through the wreckage of the city, and there is very little any of us can do about it except to flee."

"You *charlatan!*" Cameron roared — or tried to. He discovered he lacked the strength for anything more than an indignant whisper. "Where the hell were you when we needed you?"

Then he took a closer look at Pao — and saw that the man was as exhausted and spent as they, too tired to reply.

"Master Pao was keeping the Dragons from shaking the earth until there were not two stones left standing from Los Angeles to Portland, Firemaster," said the unknown, and bowed. "Forgive me, Firemaster. I am Master Ho, Master of Eagles."

"Master of Air — " Rose breathed, and straightened. Cameron released her so that she could bow herself. "Are *you* the reason the Sylphs — that is, the Eagles — hated Beltaire so much?"

Master Ho simply bowed again, and gestured. "Please. All this can be explained in the Firemaster's home where it is safer. Look — " He pointed behind Cameron who turned, and saw the red glare of flames just beyond the building that they were sheltering near. He started; he had thought that the growing heat was entirely due to the fight among the Salamanders and Sylphs, not a growing conflagration!

"Dear God — " He started for the fire, intending to try to do something about it. "There are people still trapped in those buildings, alive!"

But he did not get more than a foot before falling to his knees.

"You have no strength left, nor she, nor I, nor Pao," Master Ho said, coming to his aid and helping him back to his feet. "I am sorry, Cameron. These poor victims must live or die without our aid, and we will not help them by perishing with them."

Jason bowed his head, momentarily choked by frustration, and looked up to see Rose gazing gravely and tenderly at him. "I do not want to admit it, but — my own Salamanders are spent, and I cannot hope to control a single Elemental that is spending out its rage. You are correct. Do you have transportation?"

Master Pao clucked, and a small cart clattered into the street, pulled by a pair of donkeys. "In!" he snapped, and Cameron found enough strength to lift Rose into the back before clambering in clumsily himself. Master Pao somehow dragged himself onto the driver's seat; Master Ho climbed up beside him, and the cart bounced away, at a much faster pace than Cameron would have expected given that it was being pulled by two such tiny beasts.

He held Rose against his shoulder, and she seemed perfectly content to be there. "Was Pao right?" he asked softly.

"When have you ever known him to be wrong?" she replied, and managed to dredge up a smile for him.

And that was all that he needed. Out of the ashes, out of the pain, out of the rubble, the most precious possession of all remained intact.

Epilogue

Rose Cameron bit the end of her pen, and finished her translation. Master Ho would be pleased, she thought. *She* was rather pleased with it, herself.

In the past year, San Francisco had arisen from the ashes of the fires that destroyed the greater part of the city much like the legendary Phoenix. Much to the surprise of some, and the dismay of others, China-town had been rebuilt as quickly as any other part of the city. That was due, in no small part, to heavy investment by Jason Cameron.

It had been impossible to contain Simon Beltaire's angry Salamanders until their rage ran out, and by that time, the city was in ruins. What the earthquake had not shattered, the fires had consumed. So many people had been burned in the wreckage of homes and lodging-houses that in all probability the real death toll would never be known. The irony was, many of the fires had begun with purely natural origins, but when the Salamanders got done with them, they rampaged with completely unnatural ferocity.

Master Pao and Master Ho had taken refuge with Jason, and Master Pao still lived here at Jason's request. Master Ho had completed Rose's Magickal education, steering her through her Ordeal — which after the events of April eighteenth had been child's play — before returning to the rebuilding of China-town. One other thing he had done before returning, since he was an ordained Presbyterian minister, was to formally wed Jason and Rose.

Jason would never be entirely human again — not outwardly. But inwardly, he was more human than he had ever been, except, perhaps, as a child. She teased him that all she had to do was take off her glasses and it wouldn't matter anyway — without her glasses, he was nothing more sinister than a man with an exceptional beard.

Master Pao had come through the ordeal the worst of all of them. He was much more frail than he had ever been; the Dragons had demanded much of him in exchange for sparing the countryside. Once the burst of energy was spent that had sustained him through the earthquake and its aftermath, he collapsed, and had to be tended for weeks after. But he was fit enough now to concoct his medicines, and it was his medicines that kept Jason free from pain and with his rage under control. The power of a Firemaster and of a Master of Dragons had kept the precious contents of his shop intact through all of the fury. His Apprentices, both in Earth Magick and in herbal medicine, had brought every box, cabinet, and chest to him here. Every so often, one of his Apprentices would roll up the driveway in a donkey cart with a troublesome patient. Master Pao would dispense wisdom and herbs, and the donkey cart would roll away, back to China-town.

Rose never had learned how and why Master Ho had clashed with Simon Beltaire, nor did she really want to. She knew enough of that dreadful man to know that she did not want to learn more.

She rose, stretched, and went to the window. Jason was exercising Sunset, the two of them going through some complicated dressage movements. In a moment, she would go down and join them for a ride, taking her own gentle little Arab mare, Sunset's mate Sunrise.

She wondered, as she watched them, how long he would remain content to stay at home. *Not much longer,* she guessed. Now that he was fit again, he would talk vaguely of travel-plans.

Well, why not? According to Master Pao, he could probably even move freely among the natives of many of the South Sea islands and in the Far East. They would think him not much different from any other "white devil."

Except, perhaps, a great deal kinder than most. The beast has a truly human heart.

And in the end, that was all that mattered.

MERCEDES LACKEY

The Hottest Fantasy Writer Today!

URBAN FANTASY

Knight of Ghosts and Shadows with Ellen Guon
Elves in L.A.? It would explain a lot, wouldn't it? Eric Banyon really needed a good cause to get his life in gear—now he's got one. With an elven prince he must raise an army to fight against the evil elf lord who seeks to conquer all of California.

Summoned to Tourney with Ellen Guon
Elves in San Francisco? Where else would an elf go when L.A. got too hot? All is well there with our elf-lord, his human companion and the mage who brought them all together—until it turns out that San Francisco is doomed to fall off the face of the continent.

Born to Run with Larry Dixon
There are elves out there. And more are coming. But even elves need money to survive in the "real" world. The good elves in South Carolina, intrigued by the thrills of stock car racing, are manufacturing new, light-weight engines (with, incidentally, very little "cold" iron); the bad elves run a kiddie-porn and snuff-film ring, with occasional forays into drugs. *Children in Peril—Elves to the Rescue.* (Book I of the SERRAted Edge series.)

Wheels of Fire with Mark Shepherd
Book II of the SERRAted Edge series.

When the Bough Breaks with Holly Lisle
Book III of the SERRAted Edge series.

HIGH FANTASY

Bardic Voices: The Lark & The Wren

Rune could be one of the greatest bards of her world, but the daughter of a tavern wench can't get much in the way of formal training. So one night she goes up to play for the Ghost of Skull Hill. She'll either fiddle till dawn to prove her skill as a bard—or die trying. . . .

The Robin and the Kestrel: Bardic Voices II

After the affairs recounted in *The Lark and The Wren*, Robin, a gypsy lass and bard, and Kestrel, semi-fugitive heir to a throne he does not want, have married their fortunes together and travel the open road, seeking their happiness where they may find it. This is their story. It is also the story of the Ghost of Skull Hill. Together, the Robin, the Kestrel, and the Ghost will foil a plot to drive all music forever from the land. . . .

Bardic Choices: A Cast of Corbies with Josepha Sherman

If I Pay Thee Not in Gold with Piers Anthony

A new hardcover quest fantasy, co-written by the creator of the "Xanth" series. A marvelous adult fantasy that examines the war between the sexes and the ethics of desire! Watch out for bad puns!

BARD'S TALE

Based on the bestselling computer game, *The Bard's Tale.*™

Castle of Deception with Josepha Sherman

Fortress of Frost and Fire with Ru Emerson

Prison of Souls with Mark Shepherd

Also by Mercedes Lackey:

Reap the Whirlwind with C.J. Cherryh

Part of the Sword of Knowledge series.

The Ship Who Searched with Anne McCaffrey

The Ship Who Sang is not alone!

Wing Commander: Freedom Flight with Ellen Guon
Based on the bestselling computer game, *Wing Commander.*®

Join the Mercedes Lackey national fan club! For information send an SASE (business-size) to Queen's Own, P.O. Box 43143, Upper Montclair, NJ 07043.

Paksenarrion, a simple sheepfarmer's daughter, yearns for a life of adventure and glory, such as the heroes in songs and story. At age seventeen she runs away from home to join a mercenary company, and begins her epic life . . .

ELIZABETH MOON

THE DEED OF PAKSENARRION

"This is the first work of high heroic fantasy I've seen, that has taken the work of Tolkien, assimilated it totally and deeply and absolutely, and produced something altogether new and yet incontestably based on the master. . . . This is the real thing. Worldbuilding in the grand tradition, background thought out to the last detail, by someone who knows absolutely whereof she speaks. . . . Her military knowledge is impressive, her picture of life in a mercenary company most convincing."**—Judith Tarr**

About the author: Elizabeth Moon joined the U.S. Marine Corps in 1968 and completed both Officers Candidate School and Basic School, reaching the rank of 1st Lieutenant during active duty. Her background in military training and discipline imbue The Deed of Paksenarrion *with a gritty realism that is all too rare in most current fantasy.*

"I thoroughly enjoyed *Deed of Paksenarrion*. A most engrossing highly readable work."
—**Anne McCaffrey**

"For once the promises are borne out. *Sheepfarmer's Daughter* is an advance in realism. . . . I can only say that I eagerly await whatever Elizabeth Moon chooses to write next."
—Taras Wolansky, *Lan's Lantern*

*   *   *   *   *

Volume One: Sheepfarmer's Daughter—Paks is trained as a mercenary, blooded, and introduced to the life of a soldier . . . and to the followers of Gird, the soldier's god.

Volume Two: Divided Allegiance—Paks leaves the Duke's company to follow the path of Gird alone—and on her lonely quests encounters the other sentient races of her world.

Volume Three: Oath of Gold—Paks the warrior must learn to live with Paks the human. She undertakes a holy quest for a lost elven prince that brings the gods' wrath down on her and tests her very limits.

*   *   *   *   *

These books are available at your local bookstore, or you can fill out the coupon and return it to Baen Books, at the address below.

THE SHIP WHO SANG IS NOT ALONE!

Anne McCaffrey, with Margaret Ball, Mercedes Lackey, S.M. Stirling, and Jody Lynn Nye, explores the universe she created with her ground-breaking novel, The Ship Who Sang.

PARTNERSHIP
by Anne McCaffrey & Margaret Ball

"[*PartnerShip*] captures the spirit of *The Ship Who Sang*...a single, solid plot full of creative nastiness and the sort of egocentric villains you love to hate."

—Carolyn Cushman, **Locus**

THE SHIP WHO SEARCHED
by Anne McCaffrey & Mercedes Lackey

Tia, a bright and spunky seven-year-old accompanying her exo-archaeologist parents on a dig, is afflicted by a paralyzing alien virus. Tia won't be satisfied to glide through life like a ghost in a machine. Like her predecessor Helva, *The Ship Who Sang*, she would rather strap on a spaceship!

THE CITY WHO FOUGHT
by Anne McCaffrey & S.M. Stirling

Simeon was the "brain" running a peaceful space station—but when the invaders arrived, his only hope of protecting his crew and himself was to become *The City Who Fought*.

THE SHIP WHO WON
by Anne McCaffrey & Jody Lynn Nye

"*Oodles of fun.*" —*Locus*
"*Fast, furious and fun.*" —*Chicago Sun-Times*